Tiny Pretty Things

Also by Sona Charaipotra and Dhonielle Clayton

Shiny Broken Pieces

Tiny Pretty Things

Sona Charaipotra and Dhonielle Clayton

HARPER TEEN
An Imprint of HarperCollinsPublishers

HarperTeen is an imprint of HarperCollins Publishers.

Tiny Pretty Things
Copyright © 2015 by Sona Charaipotra and Dhonielle Clayton
All rights reserved. Printed in the United States of America.
No part of this book may be used or reproduced in any manner what-
soever without written permission except in the case of brief quo-
tations embodied in critical articles and reviews. For information
address HarperCollins Children's Books, a division of HarperCollins
Publishers, 195 Broadway, New York, NY 10007.
www.epicreads.com

Library of Congress Control Number: 2014952540
ISBN 978-0-06-234240-9

Typography by Torborg Davern
16 17 18 19 20   CG/RRDH   10 9 8 7 6 5 4 3 2 1
❖
First paperback edition, 2016

To Navdeep, for all the things you did, and continue to do, to help make all our magic (and mayhem) possible

Cassie

IT ALWAYS FEELS LIKE DEATH. At least at first. Your muscles stretch and burn until they might rip. The bones in your hips threaten to rotate right out of their sockets. Your spine lengthens and twists into impossible shapes. The veins in your arms swell, blood pulsing through them. Your fingers tremble as you try to hold them taut but graceful, just so. Your toes jam into a pretty pink box, battering your feet with constellations of blisters and bruises.

But it all looks effortless and beautiful. I hope. Because that's all that really matters.

Studio B is a fishbowl today, and I wish the three glass walls were blacked out or covered up. I can feel Liz's glare hot and heavy, her face pressed up against the glass. I knew she wanted this—maybe even more than me—but that doesn't mean she deserved it. She'll claim that I got lucky, that it was nepotism, that being Mr. Lucas's niece has its perks. I mean, Bette told me she said as much in her drunken babblings last night. But I know better. I earned this.

Morkie barks orders at the corps girls, then turns to the pianist to nitpick a chord pace for the spring ballet, *La Sylphide*. I'm the only Level 6 girl cast as a soloist, and while the others pretend to be happy for me—well, most of them anyway—I know they're hoping to see me fail. But I won't give them the satisfaction. Even though it's hard being the youngest one in here. And earlier, when one of them asked me if I was fifteen, I wanted to lie and say I was seventeen or eighteen like them. As I watch the other dancers spin across the floor in a series of pirouettes, I keep my smile plastered across my face. I won't falter. I can't let them know how hard this is. My muscles ache and my stomach churns, empty from a morning spent reliving last night's revelries. I never should have let Bette talk me into drinking. I'm definitely paying the price now.

The music stops abruptly, and Morkie towers over Sarah Takahashi, making her do the turn over and over again, yelling corrections in Russian like Sarah understands her. Sarah bows, and it seems to infuriate Morkie even more. She's my understudy and a Level 8 girl. An 8 girl should've had the lead—an opportunity for the company masters to see her talent and offer her a spot.

I take every second of this break to review the variation in my head, to think through the music. Morkie does the steps one by one, stamping her little heeled ballet slippers. Even nearing seventy, she's still a strong portrait of grace—a true *danseuse russe*.

Bette slips through the door. And she lets it bang closed so I know she's here. I hate how she always finds a way to announce herself, but I could never tell her that. Everyone watches—her halo of blond hair pulled taut in its bun, her designer dance skirt floating around her like cotton candy, her pink lipstick expertly applied. She's told to find a spot in the back, and plops down right near the dance bags. There were rumors that a fat check from her mom secured her a seat in the studio to learn the role, too, but I didn't dare ask her. She's been so gracious and helpful. Defending me to Liz and the others when I first got here, showing me the ropes, threatening the other girls if they didn't stop messing with me.

Will enters a few moments after. His red hair is gelled up, and he's wearing a face full of makeup. He blows me a kiss and waves. It was announced this morning that he'd be my *pas* partner's understudy. He sits in the back with Bette.

Morkie calls me to the center. The music starts, light and fluttery and serene. Usually I let it take me, the notes lifting me away so I'm no longer myself, the movements of my arms and legs transforming, allowing me to become the forest fairy romancing the Scotsman. But today I'm very much anchored in my too tall, lumbering body. I can feel the pull in each muscle as I glide across the floor, trying to make sure I land every step in the right spot.

I catch myself looking down at the tape marking the stage placements, focusing on the counts in the music. I try not to think of each precise motion making up the variation. Old habits. Bad habits. I should know this by heart now. I tell myself I'm as light as air. But my feet are a second too slow, my arm movements too heavy.

"More! More!" Morkie yells, her voice bouncing off the mirrors. I feel my smile falter. I'm totally graceless in her presence. My confidence seeps out of me with my sweat. Scott waits for me stage left. I flitter over to him, presenting my hand. He pulls me into his chest.

Morkie yells over the music. "Smile. You're in love with him."

My grin looks pained in the mirror. My stomach muscles clench when his hands squeeze my waist as he prepares to lift me.

Morkie waves her hands in the air. We stop midlift.

"You're supposed to be in love. Where is it? Where is it?" she says, motioning me out of the center. "Did we make mistake in casting, Cassandra?" Her Russian accent makes the words sharp, tiny knives that tear at my insides. "Find it! Find the reason we picked you." She waves me away with one skinny arm.

Sarah takes my place with Scott to practice the flying shoulder lift I couldn't do. I tell myself that it's fine. Necessary. Both boys have to learn how to lift Sarah, then me. Just in case. Frustrated, I head to the back corner, toward Bette and Will. "You've got to," I hear her whisper, but he shushes her as he watches me approach.

"Hey." He grins, patting the floor next to him. "Rough start, huh?"

I catch my breath, wiping away the little beads of sweat on my top lip. As Bette's ice-blue gaze settles over me, I feel disgusting and heavy and off. Will gives me a sad frown, like I'm a puppy who's just been kicked. "Don't take it to heart," he whispers again. "Morkie's a beast."

"You okay?" Bette asks, offering a smile that's half grimace.

"I don't know where it all went," I say, closing my eyes. I stretch my limbs out every which way. "I was fine yesterday. You saw me."

"You looked scared of him," Will says, his eyes on Scott, tracing his every movement. "Have a little crush?"

"I have a boyfriend," I snap without meaning to. I wish I was partnering with Henri, but he's at the Paris Opera School. I trust his hands. "Sorry, I can't figure out what's wrong with me."

"Hmm," Bette says, noncommittal. "Too much alcohol is my guess." And it makes me remember how she kept filling my cup with the expensive wine she'd taken from her mother's collection, despite my protests.

I nod my head, eager for an excuse. "I should've gone straight to bed after we hung out."

"You didn't?" Her forehead crinkles with surprise.

"Sometimes I dance late at night, so it can all stick in my head when I finally sleep." I put a hand on my forehead, not sure why everything is coming out of me right now. But I can trust her. Alec told me so, even when I doubted Bette at first. And Will is Alec's best friend. "My legs are a mess." I scoot over a little, pressing my back against the glass wall that faces out onto the street. The warmth of sunbeams erases the cold that's settled in my stomach. Even though it's spring, I'm shivering. "What should I do?"

Bette and Will share glances. They know what Morkie wants. They've been here forever. They know how to please her.

"You need to get it together," Bette says, picking invisible lint off her impeccable sweater. "Morkie doesn't do drama or excuses." She leans into a stretch, warming up as if she'll be called to the center any second. As if she's here for a reason. "And you need to not drink so much."

"Ouch, Bette," Will says.

I try to keep the shock off my face. "I actually never drank before," I tell her in a whisper. If Bette is surprised, she doesn't let it show. But it's humiliating to say it. Before I came to New York and moved in with my cousin Alec and his family to go to the conservatory, my whole world was just dance class and school and sitting on the couch with my British host mother, waiting for a call or text from Henri. New York is totally different from London. "I didn't know it would hit me that hard." I want to call Bette out for pushing the wine on me, but I don't. She's pretty much the only real friend I've made since I've got to New York, and I'm not about to mess that up.

"Some days we're just off," Will says, and pets my leg like that will help.

I feel my eyes get watery. I lick the strawberry gloss off my lips, hearing my mom's scolding voice in my head as I do it. She says it's totally unladylike. I look over my shoulder and watch Sarah Takahashi nail the lift with Scott that I couldn't. Morkie beams at her.

"Don't worry, Cassie," Bette says. "Will can help you look good out there. He'll rescue you like he's always done for me." The word *rescue* lands hard. Will's eyes dart around the studio, like he's watching a fly.

Bette flashes me a smile that's so big I can see all her teeth. Perfect, just like the rest of her. I'm called back to the center, and now Will is too. I can feel Bette's gaze following Will as Morkie shows Will and me the next part of the *pas*. We mark the movements one at a time, with painful precision. It takes me almost an hour to perfect them the way Morkie wants them before she lets us try on our own. Then, finally, I stand in the center, ready to show her what I've learned.

I prepare to dance, waiting for the chord of music to start moving. My mind quiets: the worries, the criticisms, the faces in the glass all drift away. I see Will ahead waiting for me. I pretend that it's Henri. I step into my first movement, folding myself into the music, each arm motion embodying the cadence. I jump and turn and leap and glide. I flutter over to Will.

"Right on the melody," Morkie yells.

Will's hands find my waist. He lifts me up into a flying shoulder lift. His right shoulder presses into my butt, carrying my weight, effortless.

"She's not a box, William," Morkie says. "She's a jewel. Carry her like one. So pretty. So light."

His fingers press into my hipbones as he struggles to hold me there.

"Beautiful, beautiful," Morkie yells over the music. "Smile, Cassandra."

I smile as hard as I can. I keep my eyes on the mirror and focus on Morkie's instructions. Here comes the fish dive, slow, graceful, deliberate. Except it's not. Will's not supporting my weight anymore, and I wobble, trying to counterbalance, but it's too late. His fingers feel like they've disappeared. Not at all like we've practiced. With his support gone, my right leg drops.

I topple, like I've fallen off the edge of a cliff. The floor feels so far away until I hit it.

ACT I

Fall Season

1.

Bette

THEY SAY ANTICIPATION IS SOMETIMES sweeter than the actual event, so I'm going to enjoy every moment of the waiting. Mr. K certainly loves dragging it out. We swarm around him in the American Ballet Conservatory lobby, waiting for his annual speech on *The Nutcracker*. Then he'll reveal the student cast list. Twice a year, in the fall and the spring, students get to replace the company dancers for a night at Lincoln Center, a test of our mettle. A taste of our future.

That piece of paper basically sums up your worth in our school, the American Ballet Company feeder academy. And I'm worth a lot. Alec and I hold hands and I can't contain my smile. In just a few moments, my name is going to be on the wall next to the role of the Sugar Plum Fairy, and the rest of my life can finally begin.

I saw my older sister, Adele, dance the role six years ago, when I was cast in the part of a cherub and bouncing around in gold wings and my mother's lipstick. Back then, the anticipation *wasn't* the best part. Back then, the best part was the heat of the lights on my skin and the presence of the audience before us, and dancing in perfect time with my little ballet girlfriends. The best part was the scratchy tights and the sweet metallic smell of hair spray and the sparkling tiara pinned into my baby-fine hair. The glitter dusted onto my cheeks. The best part was the hole of nervousness in my stomach before getting onstage and the rush of joy after we pranced off. The best part was bouquets of flowers and kisses on both cheeks from my mother and my father lifting me in the air and calling me a princess.

Back then, it was *all* the best part.

The school's front doors are closed and locked. Mr. K's speech is that important. I glance over my shoulder through the big lobby windows and see a few people with red noses, bundled up to fight the October air. They're stuck on the stairs and in the Rose Abney Plaza, named after my grandmother. That door won't open again until he's finished. They'll just have to freeze.

Mr. K rubs his well-groomed beard, and I know he's ready to start. I know these little things about him, thanks to Adele, a company soloist. I straighten up a bit more and wrap my hand around Alec's neck, tickling the place where his buzzed blond hair meets his skin. He grins, too, both of us perfectly poised to finally take our places as the leads in the winter ballet.

"This is it," I whisper in his ear. He smiles back and kisses my forehead. He's flushed with excitement, too, and I just know that from here on out I will love everything about ballet again. Both of our auditions went well. I remember how ridiculously happy Adele looked when she was dancing the Sugar Plum Fairy, and how the role got her plucked straight out of the school and given a spot in the company, and I just dream of feeling that full. There's no one standing in my way. Even Liz is struggling a little bit this year. And no one else can do what I can.

I drop my hand down to his and squeeze Alec a little tighter. Alec's best friend—my ex-friend—Will glares at me. Jealous.

Parents and siblings grow quiet, standing behind the expanse of black leotards.

"Casting each of you in *The Nutcracker* isn't just an exercise in technique," Mr. K begins. Our ballet master speaks slowly, like he's just deciding on the words right now, even though he gives some version of this speech every year. Yet I cling to every word as if I've never heard it before. Mr. K is the single most deliberate human being I've ever met. He makes eye contact with me, and I know my fate is cemented in that quick connection. That look my way is purposeful. It has to be. I bow my head a bit with respect, but can't stop the edges of my mouth from doing their own little upward pull.

"Technique is the foundation of ballet, but personality is where the dance comes to life. In *The Nutcracker,* each character serves an important purpose to the ballet as a whole, and that is why we take such care in assigning each of you the perfect part. Who you are comes across in how you dance. I'm sure we all remember when Gerard Celling danced the Rat King last winter, or when Adele Abney danced the Sugar Plum Fairy. These were seminal performances that displayed unbelievable technique as well as exquisite joy and beauty. The students stopped being students and transformed into artists, like a caterpillar leaves its chrysalis and becomes what it was designed to be—a butterfly."

Mr. K calls us his butterflies. We're never his students, dancers, athletes, or ballerinas. When we graduate, he'll give the best dancer a diamond butterfly pendant—Adele still only takes hers off for performances.

"It is because of Adele's and Gerard's relationships to the roles of Sugar Plum Fairy and Rat King that they experienced such success," he adds. "It was the connection they forged with the part."

I bow my head even farther. Mr. K talking about my sister is another deliberate nod to me, I'm sure of it. Adele's performance as the Sugar Plum Fairy has been a topic of conversation since the first night she'd performed it six years ago. She was only in Level 6 ballet and hadn't even turned fifteen yet. It was unheard of for such a young dancer to be given such a role over the older Level 8 girls. And when I was that seven-year-old cherub hugging my sister with my fiercest pride and congratulations, Mr. K approached us both with a confident smile.

"Adele, you are luminous," he'd said. It's a word I have been itching for him to call me ever since. He still hasn't. Not yet. "And darling little Bette, I can tell from your lovely dancing tonight that, in no time at all, you will be following in your sister's footsteps. A Sugar Plum Fairy in the making." He'd winked, and Adele had beamed at me with agreement.

He is surely referring to that moment now. He is letting me remember his prediction and assuring me that he had been right all those years ago.

I shift onto my tiptoes, unable to suppress that bit of excitement. Alec squeezes my hand.

Mr. K's voice softens. "Young Clara, for instance, must be sweet and invoke the wonder of Christmas with every step and glance." His gaze drifts to a pretty *petit rat* in a pale blue leotard, her dark hair in a perfect bun. She blushes from the attention, and I'm happy for tiny Maura's moment of joy. I played Clara when I was eleven. I know the thrill, and she deserves to experience every second of it.

Years later, I still think of that performance as the most fun I've ever had. It was right after the Christmas season that my mother started showing me old videos of Adele and asking me to compare my technique to hers. It was that Christmas when everything between my mother, Adele, and me shifted beyond recognition, distorting into a bad TV drama. I get a little lightheaded just thinking about it. I can still hear the whir of the X-ray camera like it was yesterday. Looking too hard at those memories isn't a good idea, so I close my eyes for an instant to make the thoughts disappear, as I always do. I give Alec's hand another squeeze and try to focus. This is my big moment.

"Uncle Drosselmeyer must be mysterious and clouded—a man with a secret," Mr. K says. "The Nutcracker Prince should be regal and full of confidence. Untouchable and elegant, but still masculine." Mr. K looks then at Alec, who breaks out into a fully dimpled grin. He is describing Alec to a tee, and I lean against him a bit. He lets go of my hand and wraps his arm around my shoulders. As if this moment weren't wonderful enough, Alec's affection has me soaring even higher. Mr. K lists off a few more characters and the necessary qualities the dancers must bring to them. I smooth my hair to make sure I look perfect for my big moment.

"And the Sugar Plum Fairy," Mr. K continues, his eyes searching the crowd. "She must be not only beautiful but kind, joyful, mysterious, and playful." His eyes are still searching the crowd, which is strange, since he knows exactly where I am. I try to dismiss it as a bit of Mr. K playing around, as he's known to do.

The Sugar Plum Fairy's ideal qualities—they're not mine. They are not words anyone has ever used to describe me.

But the part is mine. I know it is because of the way Mr. K finishes his speech.

"Above all else," he says, "the Sugar Plum Fairy must be luminous."

I squeeze Alec's hand again.

That is me.

I am luminous, like Adele. It is me. It has always been me.

But still, Mr. K's eyes do not find their way to mine.

2.

Gigi

I NIBBLE AT MY BOTTOM lip until I taste blood. The spot is a tiny heart thumping harder than the one in my chest. My teeth sink into the cut despite the sting, and I can't stop. I won't go to the bathroom to see how bad it is. I can't miss all the excitement. I can't be anywhere else.

Shoulder to shoulder, we are a sea of paper-thin bodies. One large gust could push us around, like the fall leaves tumbling past the lobby's picture windows. We are that light, that vulnerable, that afraid. Nervous excitement flutters through me. Even the little ones, the *petit rats,* gnaw at their fingernails, and the boys hold their breaths. The gurgles of half-empty stomachs churning a ballet diet of grapefruit and energy tea invade small pockets of silence when Mr. K finally pauses, all showmanship.

We listen intently. The occasional whisper is a firework. The melody of his Russian accent makes the words feel heavier, more important. He paces before us, waving his hands in fiery motions, and leaving the scent of cigarettes and warm vodka wrapped around us. I fixate on every word coming out of Mr. K's mouth like I could catch each one in a mason jar.

Our other teachers are lined up behind him. Along with Mr. K, there are five of them that decide our fates. The piano accompanist, Viktor, the lowliest of the lot. His smile holds a cigarette, and he barely speaks but knows everything—all the things *they* think of us. Then Morkie and Pavlovich, our ballet madams. We call them the twins—though they're not related and look nothing alike. Their narrow eyes flit over us ever so briefly, as if we're ghosts they don't quite see.

Lastly, there's Mr. Lucas, the board president, Alec's father—and Doubrava, the other male teacher.

Mr. K concludes his speech by congratulating us on making it through the audition process like the budding professionals we are. They all retreat into the admissions office. Someone whispers that they've gone to get the cast list. The open space feels lighter without them in it. Everyone starts to talk softly. I hear the words *new* and *black* and *girl* whispered in various combinations. After one month here at school, the first major casting makes me feel my skin color like a fresh sunburn. I'm the only black ballerina aside from a little one named Maya. Most times, I try not to think about it because I'm just like everyone else: classically trained, here to learn the Russian style of ballet, with a shot at moving from the school to the company.

But my skin color matters more here than it ever did at my California studio. Back there, we held hands while waiting for the cast list and hugged each other with hearty congratulations.

Aurora in *Sleeping Beauty*, Kitri in *Don Quixote*, Odette in *Swan Lake* came in all colors. There were no questions about what looked best onstage. There were no questions about body type. There were no mentions of the Russians' love of the *ballet blanc*—an all-white cast onstage to create the perfect effect.

Here, we tug our hair into buns, we all wear colored leotards that signal our ballet level, we put on makeup for class, and we only learn the Vaganova style of ballet. We follow traditions and age-old routines. This is the Russian way. This is what I wanted. This is what I begged my parents to send me across the country for. My best friend, Ella, from back home, says I'm crazy to come this far just to dance. She doesn't understand when I tell her that ballet is everything. I can't imagine doing anything else.

Someone whispers, "Who will he choose to dance the Sugar Plum Fairy?" but she is quickly hushed. Besides, we all know that it will be Bette.

Everyone wants a soloist part. Everyone wants to be the prima ballerina of the American Ballet Conservatory. Everyone wants a spot in the company. Everyone wants to be Mr. K's favorite. Even me.

The moon stares in through the glass, even though it's barely past dusk. At home it's still the afternoon. Mama's just finishing up in her garden about now. I wonder if she's waiting for the cast list news, too, and if she's finally getting excited about me being here. She wanted me to keep dancing at my local studio. Keep ballet a fun after-school activity.

"You could permanently hurt yourself," she'd said before I auditioned for the conservatory, as if the rigor of ballet is like falling off a bicycle. "You could get sick. You could die." Death is her favorite threat.

I fight the nerves. I fight the feeling of homesickness that creeps up on me. I fight the weird knot forming in my throat as I look around and it sinks in that I am the only black ballerina in the upper ballet levels. I'm lonely here. Most of these kids have been at the school for years, like my roommate, June, and Bette and Alec, who'll likely be cast as the leads this year. I watch Bette lean her golden head against his, a matched set, and hear her sigh, content, knowing that her big moment is coming. I suppress a little pang. I just got here, I'm the new girl. I shouldn't want what she has—the role, or Alec. But I can't help it. I look away, trying to find somewhere else to put my thoughts.

I stare up at the hundreds of black-and-white portraits of the American Ballet Conservatory graduates who went on to be apprentices, soloists, and principals in the American Ballet Company. They cover all the walls in the halls here, looking down on us, showing us what we could become if we're simply good enough. In the almost fifty years of history on the wall, there are only two other black faces in a white sea. I will be the third. I will earn one of the few spots in the company saved for conservatory members. I will show my parents that every part of me can handle it: my hands, my feet, my mind, my legs, and my heart.

I scan the crowd for my aunt Leah, who is decked out in leggings and a hand-knitted sweater dress. I can hear her voice above the others, a little too loudly introducing herself to other parents and guardians as Mama's younger sister and an art curator at a Brooklyn gallery. She grins and waves at me. With her pink knit hat and freckly brown skin, she's as much an outsider as I am in this lobby, and she's been a New Yorker for decades.

I wave back. The girls around me tense up. My roommate, June, moves a small step away from my side. Even my waving is too loud, but I don't care.

The office door cracks open, its squeaky hinges hushing everyone. We all gasp. I put a hand to my chest. Clapping echoes through the room as he reenters. Mr. K's pretty secretary walks to the board with a sheet of paper, her arms outstretched to tack it up.

Mr. K looks around. "*Podozhdite!* Wait, wait." He raises his hand before she exposes the page.

He crisscrosses between us. He's dark—almost ominous—dressed in all black. Anton Kozlov, a *danseur russe.* Frantic energy bubbles through me. The other dancers squirm and part, giving him way. I drop my head, my body still jittery whenever he comes near. I haven't quite overcome it.

I will my hands to settle. I will my muscles to relax. I will my heart to slow. Beside me, I hear other girls' breathing accelerate. We are one sphere of nervous, nauseous focus. I try to use Mama's calming technique: listening to the noise inside our gigantic pink conch shell. I picture my dad finding it in Hawaii that summer. I attempt to listen for the gauzy melody, but the calm doesn't come.

I hear footsteps, then see my reflection in the toes of two black shoes. Two of Mr. K's long fingers lift my chin and I meet his mottled green eyes. Sweat dots along my hairline. I feel dried blood mar my mouth like a tiny streak of Mama's paint. All eyes turn to me. Our ballet madams watch. The parents go silent, including my aunt Leah. I lick my cut, hoping to stop the pulsating thrum.

Mr. K's face looms right above me. Heat gathers in my cheeks. I can't escape his gaze. He holds me there and everything slows.

3.

June

I DON'T MIND THAT MR. K'S interrupted his speech to lift Gigi's chin and force her to pay attention. It's terrible, but I like seeing her get in trouble for her California spaciness. Serves her right. He didn't say a word. But I know he's sending her a warning: tune in. Always.

I sip tea from my thermos to hide my smile. The bitter *omija* herbs warm my irritable belly, calming the bile that's constant company. I fight the urge to retreat to the bathroom and escape to the cold comfort of porcelain and an empty stomach. But I can't afford to miss this moment. I have to know where I am now.

Mr. K's secretary holds the page close to her chest, as if we'd attack her for it—and maybe she's right.

"Luminous," he says, then goes on to repeat it five more times, asking dancers close to him to define it, to describe what it means onstage or else he'll delay the casting announcement even further. They quake and stutter, unable to answer him. If he'd have asked me, I'd have known just what to say—to be luminous onstage means to glow, to shine, to own it. It's a quality few among us possess, but I know I'm among the very few. Still, they don't give me the roles I want, no matter how well I think my auditions have gone. But it's only a matter of time.

A tingle tickles its way up my spine. The worry, the anxiety, the nerves. I savor it. My classmates, they're all stupid and empty-headed, wrapped up in their emotions, unable to see things clearly. They don't pay attention. If they had, they'd already know whose name will be written in each spot. Mr. K never changes. Those who have been here forever know his habits, his choices, his patterns. Newbies don't stand a chance. Ballet is about routine, training the muscles to obey tiny commands. I've been here since I was six—shuttled back and forth from Queens until I got old enough to live in the dormitory above us. I know the drill.

It all comes down to this: the casting of *The Nutcracker*. The first ballet of the school year. This one starts the game. I can't wait to finally be in it.

By now, the American Ballet Conservatory is more like home than the two-bedroom apartment in Flushing that I shared with my mom. I know the studios, the academic classrooms, the café, the student lounge, my corner bedroom. I know that the elevator won't take you to floors thirteen to eighteen. I know every stair-case exit that lets you onto boys' dorm floors, all the dancers in the black-and-white photographs, quiet places to study or dark corners to hide from the RAs, the best places to stretch or make out. Not that I'm doing much making out. Or any, really.

The lobby crowd thickens with more adult bodies. Parents. Someone opened the door for them. They're here to pick up the *petit rats* or to nose around to find out who got what role. When Mr. K's ex-wife Galina, a retired Paris Opera ballerina, was here, she'd block the door and gather us—her *petit rats*—all around her, willing us to be silent as we watched the older girls get cast. Any serious dancer tells their parents to stay in the far hallway or, even better, just wait by the phone. Mr. K doesn't like when we act like children who need mommies. We may be young, he says, but we're supposed to be professionals.

My parents are not here, of course. My mom refuses to set foot in the atrium. When she does come, she just pulls up out front of the school and makes me take the rice cakes, the endless packs of seaweed and tea she's brought for me from the car. And I don't have a father.

Gigi's big-haired aunt keeps inching closer and closer to us students, and I can hear her talking. It's distracting me from hearing Mr. K explain how difficult it was for him to choose student roles this semester. I let my eyes burn into the back of Gigi's head. I want to tell her that she should've clued her aunt in and told her not to talk until after the cast list is revealed. I want to whisper under my breath, *joyonghae*—be quiet—just like my mom always does. I need to hear every word out of Mr. K's mouth. His announcement will show how far I've come, what he thinks of me now.

Mr. K pauses and the parents clap awkwardly. He nods, placing a finger to his mouth. Maybe he'll add something new.

Probably not. I could give the spiel myself. And I know his cast list before his little blond assistant tacks up the page.

Gigi shakes in front of me, trembles working their way down her back and legs. She's like one of the *petit rats* at the front of the pack. I feel her fear and excitement. Mr. K will cast her as Arabian Coffee, just like the other brown girl from two years ago. Gigi's exotic like her. Can't even remember her name, she gave up so quickly once it all got tough. She complained it was so lonely being the only black girl at school. Try being the only half-Asian ballerina. Not quite right anywhere. That's tough. And Mr. K's just predictable enough to put minorities in ethnic roles. He'll cast the pack of Korean girls as Chinese Tea. But my face isn't Asian enough to join them. And I wouldn't want to. I want to be as far away from them as possible.

Everyone knows Bette Abney will be the Sugar Plum Fairy. Ever since her sister landed it when we were kids, no one has stopped talking about her performance. And the mean girls always get what they want here. Bette isn't anywhere near as luminous as Adele, but that's what Mr. K will do. Her feet are good—quick and light—and she is undeniably elegant. Even though we aren't friends (and never have been, nor will be), I actually wouldn't mind seeing her as the Sugar Plum Fairy if I had to lose the role. Bette has a razor-sharp edge. It's a fascinating contrast to her sweet, doll-like face and stately pedigree.

Her lapdog roommate Eleanor will be her understudy and nothing else, of course. And Bette's clone, Liz Walsh, stands two bodies away from me, in consummate formation. Chest out, soft hands at her sides, and feet in first position. Her body ballet perfect. An icy brunette, she'll be just right for the Snow Queen.

But even though she looks relaxed, Liz's eyes are wild, darting about the room, and I'm glad I don't have to feel that desperation. No matter how many knits she piles on, it won't hide her underweight body. I sip my tea, happy it leaves me satisfied, without the pains of hunger. The white girls don't know much about diet teas from Asia. They fill themselves with calorie-packed American brands. We should tell them. But of course we don't.

"Mr. K, c'mon already," Alec shouts out. "Let us see the list."

Mr. K breaks out in a smile. Only blond and blue-eyed Alec can get away with that. His father stands beside the other male ballet teacher with a bright grin on his face. Alec is the son of the president of the board of trustees. He can do what he wants.

Alec heckles Mr. K once more. He will be the Nutcracker Prince and he will dance with Bette. It makes sense for the only couple in our grade to dance together. Of the sixteen girls and six boys in the junior class, only two of the boys are straight—the new superstar boy, Henri, and Alec.

Bette beams and touches the side of Alec's face like some doting wife, and Alec's best friend, Will, jostles his shoulder. Bette thumbs her silly locket, the one she's worn forever. It was probably a gift from Alec. I touch my bare neck. The only jewelry I ever want is Mr. K's butterfly pendant.

Redheaded Will, of course, will be relegated to playing old Drosselmeyer. Slack chested and delicate, Will could dance the female variations better than most of the girls in our class. If allowed on pointe, he would. His eyeliner is always expertly applied and he possesses a grace most of our class would kill for.

But Mr. K and Doubrava frown at him, and until he becomes supermasculine—a true male *danseur russe*—he'll keep getting stuck there.

Mr. K steps into our midst once again. He's winding us up for the big finale. He's finally ready to tell us. Dancers shuffle out of his way. Gigi keeps throwing glances back to that aunt of hers, and she almost does a jump with excitement. She'll learn soon enough not to do that here. Never show how you feel about a particular role. People are watching. Always. They'll take what you want.

Mr. K stops at Henri, glaring at the mess of hair around his shoulders. Even though the dance mags have called him the next great ballet star, a mini Mikhail Baryshnikov, we still treat him like he's nothing. He came for the last summer session. Henri says something in French and gathers his dark, shaggy hair into a ponytail. He used to date Cassie Lucas. I shudder, thinking of what the girls did to her last year, how we all have to suffer through those seminars on competition now. He doesn't talk to anyone, and no one wants to talk to him anyway. Guess they worry he knows the things that happened to his girlfriend. That he might tell someone who matters. Ballerinas have their secrets. He has a mean glint in his eyes.

I would cast him as the Rat King just because of that.

While Mr. K inspects a few others, the room simmers and bubbles into a rolling boil. I review all the major parts, counting them out on my fingers, and assigning each of my classmates their obvious role: Clara, the Nutcracker Prince, Snow Queen, Snow King, Uncle Drosselmeyer, Arabian Coffee, Chinese Tea, the Russian Dancers, the Mechanical Doll and Harlequin, the Spanish Dancers, Snowflakes, the Sugar Plum Fairy, Reed Flutes, Dew Drop Fairy, Mother Ginger.

It's not till the end of the list that I realize my mistake. I didn't cast myself.

WINTER PERFORMANCE: *THE NUTCRACKER*
Cast
Major Soloist Parts

Clara: Maura James
Older Clara: Edith Diaz
The Nutcracker Prince: Alec Lucas
Snow Queen: Bette Abney
Snow Queen Understudy: Eleanor Alexander
Snow King: Henri Dubois
Drosselmeyer: William O'Reilly
Arabian Coffee: Liz Walsh
Chinese Tea: Sei-Jin Kwon, Hye-Ji Yi
Sugar Plum Fairy: Giselle Stewart
Sugar Plum Understudy: E-Jun Kim
Rat King: Douglas Carter
Dew Drop Fairy: Michelle Dumont

4.

Gigi

IT'S MIDNIGHT. CASTING DAY IS officially over. The shock and the excitement of it all keeps me up. *I am the Sugar Plum Fairy. Me, Giselle Stewart! I am Mr. K's* korichnevaya babochka. His brown butterfly. I let the words flutter around in my head like my own little butterflies in my windowsill terrarium, all light and frantic and impossibly beautiful. They keep me company here.

I got a handful of congratulations that felt mostly strange and hollow and a few stiff hugs. Like it was all for Mr. K and the teachers who were watching.

I can't stop thinking, fidgeting. My muscles itch to move even this late—past curfew, past lights out. It's the only way I'll be able to clear my head, get some sleep, and be fresh for morning ballet class tomorrow. I slip out of bed and tiptoe from my side of the room, careful not to wake my roommate, June, on my way out. I listen for the nighttime RA patrolling in the girls' hall before sneaking out. I should rest. Mama would insist on it if I were home. It's the healthy thing to do. But I know what I really need is to dance. Especially now. I need space to think it through. I need space to get ready for it all.

The elevators have cameras, so I take the stairs down eleven flights to the first floor. I don't want anyone to know I'm out of bed. I'm a bit breathless as I tiptoe to my secret place, passing the administrative offices, through the lobby, and dashing from hall plant to hall plant, hoping not to be spotted by the front desk security guard. The whispers from earlier follow me, buzzing in my ears and my head as if the parents and other dancers were still standing there, mocking me.

The black girl. The new girl. She's no Sugar Plum Fairy. Her feet are bad. Her legs are too muscular. Her face won't look right onstage. It should've been Bette. Bette's sister was luminous, you heard Mr. K say it. Gigi could never be that.

The ghost words push me forward. I walk as quietly as possible down the hall. The ballet conservatory is at the back of the Lincoln Center complex, in one of the beautiful buildings that makes up the performing arts center. The first time I walked along the promenade, it seemed impossible that there was a place that housed it all: dance, theater, film, music, opera, and more. The studios on the first floor are glass boxes that let in light. I graze my fingers along the cool panels as I pass.

I hold my breath and duck past the nutritionist's office. Her charts and scales and cold metal examining table provoke hysteria, and the tiny woman wields the power to boot a dancer out of the conservatory for falling underweight. It's enough to keep me eating, that's for sure.

I jump when I catch sight of Alec slipping out of one of the studios. It's the middle of the night, practically. Our eyes meet. I open and shut my mouth like a fish, and start to mumble out some explanation for why I'm down here. He smiles like he's not going to tell anyone.

"What are you doing up?" Alec says, grabbing my hand and leading me to a dark spot in the hall away from a camera. The gesture means nothing, of course. He belongs to Bette, whose face is porcelain and smooth and whose words and expressions are so carefully chosen they are always dead perfect. My hair is frizzy and wild and I never say the right thing. I hope my hand isn't clammy.

"They're always watching," he whispers. "You've got to know where to hide." His body is close to mine. He smells good, especially for someone who's been dancing all evening, and I take an illicit breath of his woodsy deodorant and the sweetness of new sweat making his forearms glisten in the dark.

"I like to dance at night," I say, trying to remember how easy talking used to be back in California. "I go to the locked-up studio. The one in the basement." I don't know why I tell him this.

"Just came from a late-night workout myself," he says.

I try on a smile and force myself to hold on to Alec's eye contact. Secretly, I'm wondering about him: why he dances, what he dreams about, what kissing him might be like. I've never really been this curious about a boy before. Boys are distractions. Well, to ballerinas. Not to normal girls.

Bette's boyfriend, I say in my head, even as I take note of how wide his shoulders are, how I can make out the shapes of the muscles under his tights and hoodie. There's something so romantic about a ballerina couple. You can't help admiring their beauty and symmetry when they walk down the hall together. Long limbs and blond hair and a graceful ease that can't be denied. And onstage, I bet the audience can sense that they're together.

I mean, obviously.

"You won't tell on me, will you?" I try to flirt like girls in the movies.

"I won't tell if you don't, Sugar Plum Fairy," he mock whispers. There's nothing sinister in the words, no threat. If anything there's a laugh underneath it all. I smile back. I'm not sure anyone has really smiled at me for the entire month I've been here. Though he's always been so nice to me.

"Deal," I say, and reach out to touch his arm. I don't know why. The deal doesn't require a touch to lock it in, but letting my fingers rest on his strong forearm is a strange reflex. His muscles tense, but he doesn't pull away immediately.

"You're an interesting choice for a Sugar Plum Fairy," Alec says.

I don't know what to say to that.

"I mean, you'll bring a lot of energy to the role," he says, filling the space where I am not talking. His arm grazes mine—a breath between our skin, so close I can feel the heat of it, but neither of us moves away to get more space.

"Thank you," I say, letting myself believe, for just one second, that Alec is just as curious about me as I am about him. "Didn't Cassandra dance it last year? Wasn't she only a sophomore?" I don't know why I say it, and I wish I could erase the words after seeing his face twist into a pained expression.

He nods. "Yeah, she did. Cassie's my cousin."

A strange silence stretches between the two of us. No one really speaks about the girl who left last year, which makes me sad and curious. And I didn't know she was his cousin. I start to say I'm sorry.

"It's cool. Let's not talk about it. Let's talk about you dancing the role." It's not lost on me that Alec smiles when I smile right now, or the way his eyes light up when I say in way too small a voice that I'm excited to work with him. And he doesn't move away. I wonder if he needs to get back upstairs to his room, if he needs to get some sleep.

"I'm excited to work with you, too," he says, the blueness of his eyes glowing even brighter.

There's a noise at the opposite end of the hall. He moves away. "See you tomorrow, okay?" he asks.

"Yeah," I say.

"Don't stay up too late," he says, and walks in the opposite direction, leaving me to think over the words and the light touch while I walk farther down the hall, farther into the dark.

The corridor dead-ends at a staircase that leads down into the basement level. I've noticed people never walk this far down the hall. I race down. This area is separate from the student rec lounge and the physical therapy room, like it has been purposefully blocked off. There's a studio here that's locked up. A small studio window gives a view inside: the shadowy outline of stored objects. The first week of school I'd asked June about the unused studio, and she'd said it'd always been under construction, and that the teachers hated it because it had no windows, and ballet needs light. The Russians call it *plokhaya energiya:* a room brimming with bad luck and darkness, and so it isn't used.

But I don't believe in superstitions. I don't exit the dressing room with my left foot first or sew a lucky charm into my tutu or kiss the ground in the stage wings before going on for a performance or need other dancers to say *merde* to me on opening night. At home, my parents have their silly broom to sweep out evil and often burn sage to keep the house energy clean. But I only believe in my feet and what they can do in pointe shoes.

I pull a bobby pin out from my bun and push it into the old lock, waiting for the tiny bolt to ease downward and click out of place. I like to be in places where I'm not supposed to be—in my old high school's attic or in the empty house in my San Fran neighborhood. There's a tiny thrill in picking a lock and exploring a space that others want closed up.

The lock gives without much effort. I look to the left, then look to the right, and disappear into the dark space. Dirt and debris crunch under my sandals, and I run my hand along the wall, and click a switch.

The one working light sputters, and then buzzes on. The bare lightbulb flickers an erratic pulse. Its half-light illuminates covered objects, a partially gutted dance floor, and mirrors draped with black sheets. Broken and decayed barre poles lean at odd angles, coated in a constellation of cobwebs and dust. The air is thick and inviting.

I head to my little corner, plop down my dance bag, and

inspect myself in the only uncovered mirror. Descending from the upper corner of the glass, a tiny fracture stretches across my reflection like a lightning bolt. Mama says looking into a broken mirror is bad luck, but I don't care. My lip has a hilly scab. I can't believe I bit it so badly. That my nerves made me do that. The ugly aberration replaces whatever is pretty about my face. I won't let myself get nervous like that again.

My phone buzzes in my bag. My parents. They know I'm still up. I click them to voice mail. I know what they want. They'll ask if the nurse checked me after the cast list excitement. They'll gloss over my accomplishment, only wanting to know how I'm feeling physically. Since I came out here, they treat me like I'm sick, some patient who shouldn't be out or who should be in a wheelchair, or better yet, a bubble. I was officially cleared to dance at the conservatory months ago. I try not to think about it. I don't want anyone to know. Ever.

I turn on the music on my cell phone. *The Nutcracker* score sounds tinny and distant, but it will have to do. I need to dance. I dig my pointe shoes out of my messy bag and put them on. My legs start first, extending out of my hips so far I feel like I'm on stilts. Long and tall, I stretch from the top of my head down to my tiptoes, trying to become one straight line. As I dance my mind quiets and my body takes over. I follow the current of music, each chord a wave, each note a splash. My feet move to match the rhythm, drawing crazy, invisible patterns on the floor.

My heart's racing. I tell myself it's just from the dance and the excitement of landing the role. But a voice in my head whispers that it's because I'm thinking of Alec, too. *Bette's Alec.* My chest tightens. *Control your breathing.* I haven't had one episode, not in ballet class, not in Pilates, not in character dance, not even once all last year at my old regular school. I'm fine. I will my heart to slow. I'm in control of my body.

I come down off pointe, wipe the sweat from my forehead, and put my hands on my head until I can catch my breath. If I stretch a bit, maybe I'll relax even more. If I focus on the deep pulls in my muscles, I can get it together. I push my leg across the barre to feel the stretch and the calm that usually comes afterward. My muscles tremble, my feet spasm, my hands shake. My fingernails are purple. The light flickers off for a long moment. Sad darkness surrounds me until the light comes on again. *Maybe I'm not good enough to dance the Sugar Plum Fairy. Maybe I'm not cut out for the role. Maybe I'll disappoint Mr. K and Alec and prove everyone right. Maybe Mama was right—I'm not well enough to dance.*

"Shut up," I say to the mirror. "Chill out." I fight the negativity. "I got the role!"

My heart's not slowing down. This hasn't happened in a whole year. My body usually obeys. I sit on the floor and press the soles of my feet together so that my legs form butterfly wings. I press on my knees. I try to breathe like a yogi—deep, slow breaths. Nothing will take this away from me. Nothing.

5.

Bette

NO ONE HAS SPOKEN TO me since the cast list went up, not even Eleanor, who is breathing heavily in the bed next to mine, so comfortable with mediocrity as an understudy that she can sleep right through her failure. I do all the tricks: counting sheep, picturing myself afloat on the ocean, pretending my body is filling with grains of sand and getting heavier and heavier.

It does nothing for me. On endless loop is one impossible thought: *I am not the Sugar Plum Fairy. I am not the Sugar Plum Fairy.* I assume I have text messages on my phone from Alec, checking to make sure I'm okay after I ran off and hid in my room, but nothing can interrupt the flow of those words and their hold on my mind. Which is why it takes me a few moments to register the loud knocking at our door at one o'clock in the morning, when the dorm should be all silence except for roommate whispers or secret hookups.

"Bette?" Eleanor says, and it's her voice, sleepy and soft, that breaks through the loop. Then the harsh knocking and our RA calling out my name, louder and louder.

"Jesus, what's going on?" I say, and get myself out of bed and to the door. Eleanor moves more slowly, rubbing her eyes and grumbling about the time and the noise. Our sour-faced RA is at the door when I open it, and she rubs her knuckles as if the incessant knocking has caused her an injury.

She does not look pleased.

Then again, neither do I.

"Your mother," she says.

"You can't send her away?" I say.

Eleanor is awake enough to scoff behind me.

"So not my job," our RA says, and she stomps off, slamming the door to her room behind her and probably waking up the students who didn't already stir from all the knocking. A few people have opened their doors, and others are shuffling behind them. The gutsier ones take the elevator right after me and come down to the parents' lounge on the first floor, though Eleanor tries to motion them away and Liz threatens them with bodily harm. It's useless: my mother always puts on a show, and they know it. Besides, these girls have been waiting a decade for my downfall. They wouldn't miss it for the world.

She's right outside the elevator when the doors open, moments away from heading up without permission: steely, skinny, mouth in a line so straight I could use it as a ruler. My mother. She smells like red wine and rare steak and the angry kind of sweat.

"Bette," my mother says, her lips tight and too pink from Chanel lipstick, which has been hurriedly drawn on over red wine–stained lips. The *T*s in my name land hard. She pulls me past the front desk and toward studio C. The three other elevators open with a ping. More students pour out. She doesn't seem to notice, or care. Someone laughs, but the cowards mostly hide near the elevator bank or chat up the front-desk guard, waiting to hear whatever she's come to say to me. They are too far away to smell the booze on her breath or to see the unfortunate pit stains that have ruined her couture gown. But they'll be able to hear every slurred word. "Next time, please tell me the truth about how your audition has gone."

My mother doesn't raise her voice. Not ever. It's more powerful all low and practiced anyway, and she knows it. Even when the vowels are long and loose and the words slip on top of each other, she stays in control of the volume. We're WASPs; we don't shout.

"It's not like I'm some understudy, Mother," I say. I do not let my voice break, but my eyes are filling with tears. During the last winter ballet, I was the only Level 6 girl, besides Cassie, to dance a soloist part. I was the Harlequin Doll, cast with the Level 7 and 8 girls. I try to remember that feeling, but my mother erases every inch of it.

"I'd already called some very important people to come see you perform, Bette," she says. "You said your audition went *well*. I took that to mean you were ready to be *seen*. When your sister—"

"You want to take it up with Mr. K?" I say. "I killed it. He smiled. He ever smile at Adele? At anyone? He was practically beaming."

"Maybe it was because he was laughing at you. Did you ever consider that?" she says. I tell myself that she would never say this if she hadn't been drinking, but I know that's not true. She keeps that pink Chanel smile on her face and her eyes don't leave mine. She's not that drunk. There is not a pinch of sadness or regret in the words coming out of her mouth.

Eleanor and Liz slink out of the late-night shadows. Our unspoken rule is that neither of them will leave me alone with my mother if things get out of control, and I guess this qualifies. Eleanor, Liz, and I give one another a look, and both of them take a few steps closer to me.

"Hi, Mrs. Abney!" Eleanor's voice chimes out, a welcome interruption, but too light and pretty for this time of night and this kind of conversation.

"Hey, Mrs. Abney!" Liz adds, her tone thick with exhaustion. My mother ignores them both. She's not done tearing me to pieces, not yet.

"You don't think. You just act," she says. "Just like your father. That's your problem."

I decide not to cry at the mention of my father, but promise myself that I can feel upset about it later, alone in my room, maybe when Eleanor is in the shower or something.

"Who got it?" my mother says then. I can practically see her little ears prick up like a dog's, hunting for the next target. She's come straight from her charity event to find out the answer to this very important question. Her eyes settle on Eleanor, then comb over Liz—my only obvious competition.

"Doesn't matter. Not me," I say. I didn't want to say Gigi's name. I don't want to hear the things my mother will say about her or the accusations she will make. I don't want Gigi, if she's listening somewhere with the rest of them, to think she matters to me. Or my mother.

"Who, Bette?" She leans in a little closer, so that instead of just seeing the Chanel on her lips I can practically taste the shit, that pitch-perfect perfume and the acidic way it mixes with her boozy breath. The combination hits my taste buds hard.

"New girl," I mumble.

"Oh Christ," my mother yells, breaking her vow to stay silent and calm in spite of everything. Liz steps away; even she can't handle it. Eleanor grabs my elbow, like I might topple over from the cruelty without her help.

"Her name's Gigi," Eleanor breaks in. "She's really a totally different type from Bette, so I don't think it was even really about the dancing—" She tries hard to protect me from the unstoppable gale wind that is my mother.

"Gigi . . ." My mother puts it all together. The woman spent the summer reading up on the newest recruits to the conservatory. If anyone can put a face with a name, it's her. "Gi— no." She stops. Her eyes widen as she stares at Eleanor's red face.

I should feel relief. The pressure is off me so fast I almost lose my balance, all that weight just sliding away. Eleanor's grip on my elbow tightens.

"Well," she says. "We can certainly fix that."

I grab for her arm, knowing she's going to head right for Mr. K. She knows he sometimes stays very late in his office. But my hand is too shaky and sweaty from the third-degree interrogation that's just gone down. And so she escapes, her gown sweeping behind her as she makes her way to the office with the kind of singular determination only ever rivaled by my sister, Adele. If I'm lucky, he's not there, and she'll just leave an angry, drunken voice mail that I hope his secretary will erase in the morning. She already has her cell phone in her hand, armed with everything she needs to make a fuss and to make a joke of our family.

"It's okay," Eleanor whispers in my ear, which means it definitely isn't. Eleanor only ever says that when things are really bad. Liz doesn't say a word. Just lets her forehead frown and her mouth purse, acknowledging the complete mortification of this moment. She knows it's bad. She doesn't lie to me. Not even to make me feel better.

Other students punch at the elevator button, no longer trying to stay quiet. There are guttural laughs and a few imitations of the great, drunk Mrs. Abney.

I look over at one of the elevators. Will stands there holding it open for everyone, red hair gelled up with the color-enhancing treatment he puts in every night, his cell phone in his hand, no doubt sending out mass texts (and hopefully not video) about what just happened. And I know he's the reason half the school is down here watching in the first place. He loves seeing me fall.

Eleanor tries to hold me in place, so that I don't run after the vultures, but I practically throw her off me. Maybe I got drunk on my mother's breath. I don't know. But I'm getting really tired of keeping it together, especially when it doesn't make a difference. I fly after the students, fueled with the desire to hit one of them. I almost do, too. June's just a hand's length in front of me, and I could push her too-skinny ass straight into the elevator doors if I wanted. And I do want to. Just to hurt someone. Just to feel a release.

Hitting her will only get me into more trouble, though, and she's not the person I hate most of all right now.

"Watch out, ladies! Bette's a real animal," Will calls out with a smug grin on his face. I want to slap the look off his face, but I shove past him, past June, past all of them, making sure to elbow as many girls as possible on my way to the last elevator. I don't let anyone get in with me. It zips up to the eleventh floor. I throw open the door to my bedroom. And then the door to my bathroom. And there she is, the girl I hate. The one I really want to punch. I draw my hand back, make my first real fist, and punch the mirror. Hard. So hard it shatters around my hand. So hard that sad pieces of glass clatter in the sink. So hard my knuckles start to bleed. It hurts, but not as much as the rest of the day.

6.

June

AT 7:30 EVERY MORNING AND 8:30 every night, on the dot, my mom calls. Like clockwork. She wants to ensure that her good little girl remains exactly that, which means I have to be tucked away in my room, safe and sound, a half hour before curfew. To confirm that I'm actually in the dormitory and not just pretending to be, she doesn't call my cell phone but rather the pay phone in the girls' hallway—a relic from the old days. What she doesn't realize is that I am always here—in the studios, the dorm, a classroom, or the student lounge. I do nothing but study and dance. I am her good little girl.

I watch the hall and wait to see if Gigi's back. That nut got up at six a.m. to go to Central Park to feed the ducks. Last time she brought me a flower for my desk, which is kind of nice or whatever. She's really into nature, but she should be stretching or seeing how Bette's looking this morning, since she slept through all of last night's theatrics. She's the Sugar Plum Fairy, after all, and that means she is probably Bette's next victim. Or everyone's victim for that matter. We don't handle change to our hierarchy very well. I'm still shocked by Mr. K's decision. And I'm still on the fence about Gigi. Some days I like her, some days I don't. It's been so long since I've had a friend, I don't know what to do, how to behave.

This morning I'm worn out from staying up late to watch Bette's mom cut her down to size. I didn't relish it the way the other girls did, but I like to know what I'm up against. I like to know everything about everyone because it all matters at this school—what you eat, what you wear, where you came from, how much you weigh, your ballet training, who your friends are, how much money you have, if you have good feet, if you've won any competitions, what kind of connections you have, if your parents have season ballet tickets, if your mother or father was a dancer, if you know the history of ballet. And I plan to know it all. About every single dancer here. That's the only way to be on top.

I thumb the pay phone's receiver at 7:26 a.m., my stomach griping as I wait for it to ring. I feel like I ate too much for breakfast. My mom is always exactly on time, so, knowing I have exactly four minutes, I run into the hallway bathroom. I throw up a mix of water, tea, and grapefruit. Two fingers bring it out smooth and soundless. The third grade was the first time I ever did it. I caught my mom vomiting after a dinner party at the neighbor's house. She'd swept me from the bathroom, her face clammy and hands shaky, telling me that American food can poison you, and you must always get rid of it. I asked her why she'd eaten it in the first place, and she said that one has to eat to be polite. Never be a bad guest or you won't be invited again. And that would be shameful.

Now, I get rid of most things I eat. Even Korean food.

I bury those thoughts, though. It's all for ballet, for my love of the dance. My head feels clearer now. My stomach is calm. Back in place, I glare at the phone, hoping to catch it on the first ring. I check my watch. One minute until half-past. Restless, I run through basic positions—first, second, *plié, tendu,* and *pas de bourrée*—when she finally calls. 7:30. On the dot.

I grab it before the second full ring. She doesn't waste time with greetings. Doesn't waste time confirming that she's actually talking to me, and not one of the other girls on the hall. Her voice fills my ear. "I got an e-mail from Mr. Stanitowsky. You have a D in math. A *D,* a sixty-two percent. I don't understand what the problem is. You have it so easy. Kids in Korea are at school *after* school. They work hard. You dance all day, and still you get poor grade."

I try to respond, but her tirade continues. "You know, *E-Jun,* colleges look at everything. You will not get into good school. You will not be successful."

She'll never call me June. Always my Korean name. She buzzes on and I move the phone a little away from my ear. Even now, after I've been at the conservatory for nearly a decade, it still doesn't occur to her that this is my dream. That this is my reality. That I will be a dancer. That I won't go to college. To her, it's some silly, short-lived phase that I'll eventually grow out of. It's a résumé builder, perhaps, something to put on my college applications, but nothing more.

I attempt not to listen or to care and to discount her mis-pronounced words, but each one finds its way into my ear. My cheeks are hot and sweat clumps up my foundation. I work desperately to look perfect. To have that doll-like ballerina face. Delicate and soft. The feel of the makeup on my skin and the scent of the powder remind me I've transformed into a ballerina, something better than being just a regular girl.

If I add another layer of powder I feel like I can erase this stress altogether. My mom yells and I dig through my dance bag—half listening, half worrying, half obsessing—hoping my missing compact is floating around in the mess of shoes and bandages and leg warmers jumbled inside. I order my little compacts special, and I'm useless without them. My newest one has been missing since yesterday. I had to use an old one earlier, and there'd barely been any makeup left in it.

"It's time to give up dancing, E-Jun," my mom says.

"No," I say. It just slips out.

"What did you say?"

There's silence. Korean kids aren't supposed to talk back to their parents. Only white kids do that—and being half-white still doesn't afford me that privilege. I hear her breathing accelerate. Whether she's willing to admit it or not—and usually she's not—dancing is in my blood. I may not have the white-blond hair or crystal blue eyes, but I belong here just as much as Bette or Eleanor or even Alec.

"You danced," I whisper, slightly afraid she might reach through the phone and slap me.

She clears her throat and I know she's smoothing the front

of her ironed skirt and trying to remain composed. Sometimes I wish she'd tell me what it was like when she danced here, or share those tips only veteran ballerinas know. I wish she'd put on one of the old leotards she hides under her bed and dance with me in a studio.

I listen to her breathe for three more beats. She finally speaks: "What did you have for dinner last night? Stay away from that fatty American food. I'll drop off *jap-chae* and *baechu gook*." And there she goes, burying her secret, the thing my mother will deny until the day she dies. "Maybe Hye-Ji can tutor you in math again. I was speaking to her mother. Mrs. Yi says that Sei-Jin and the other girls always ask you to their parties, but you never go. Sei-Jin and Hye-Ji are nice, pretty girls."

Sei-Jin is *not* a nice girl. Deep down, neither am I. Our moms think we're sweet and obedient kids, behaving just how we would if we'd been born and raised in Korea. Sei-Jin and I used to be roommates and best friends. My heart squeezes a little, even though I don't want it to. I glance at Sei-Jin's room door, our old room door, and remember how close we used to be. I haven't had a real friend since her.

I tell my mom a lie. "I went to one tea that Sei-Jin had. And they all spoke Korean the whole time. And really fast. I couldn't keep up."

"That's your own fault," she interrupts, not taking any of the blame for the way she raised me. I know little Korean phrases, all the foods, and just enough to eavesdrop during her Korean social events, but not enough for a full conversation, which is depressing when I think too long about it. "I raise your allowance, you take a language class. Will help on college applications. Oh, also, you sign up for the SAT? The academic counselor says one is in late October and . . ."

"I have rehearsals for three hours every night for the next two months," I say, quietly seething. "I told you, I'm the understudy for the Sugar Plum Fairy."

"Understudy," she says with disdain. I want to give her the understudy speech Morkie gives after every casting: that I could be thrown in last minute, that I was picked because I'm a fast learner, that I can handle the pressure of dancing the role for the first time live, that it's an enormous responsibility.

"E-Jun, that's all you'll ever be. They'll never cast an Asian in the lead. You accept that. The Russians never did, even when I was there. . . ." She pauses, tucking those secrets back in. "Better start working on getting into good college now."

"They cast a black girl as the Sugar Plum Fairy. My roommate, Gigi," I say, not really sure if that made things worse or better. Point is I didn't get the role.

Silence follows again. She says the word *understudy* again. I can hear her disappointment turn to anger. "I'm serious now, E-Jun," she says. "No more nonsense. Time to focus. This will be your last year if you can't be any better than understudy. No more dancing. You'll be going to the public school in our neighborhood." Then she simply hangs up, not even waiting for me to argue or to say good-bye. Listening to her talk about dance, you'd never know she'd walked through these very halls, lived in one of these tiny dorm rooms, danced in the studios, was part of the company. But something happened, something bad, and she never told me why she'd stopped.

She's since become a successful businesswoman, importing high-quality dancewear from Korea, and she wants me to follow in her footsteps and eventually take over. That is the Korean way. What little of it that I know. She raised me all alone—her parents disowned her for staying here and having me. I'm all she's got. So part of me knows I should obey her. Be a good daughter. Go home on weekends, and shop with her at the Korean markets on Saturdays, attend church with her on Sundays, and return to the time when I used to curl up in her bed like a little spoon in front of her.

But the thought of going to a public school unnerves me, making me want to throw up again. Now, the bathroom is full of girls getting ready for ballet class, and my stomach is basically empty. So I head to the Light instead. It's a little storage closet at the end of the eleventh-floor girls' hall that's become a confessional booth of sorts. No one knows who started it. But it's been here forever. Wallpapered with a collage of pictures, kind of like a living, breathing picture feed—from famous ballerinas to gorgeous costumes to the perfect arched foot to anonymously posted inspirational quotes and messages. Even things from the '80s. There's a tiny TV and DVD player, and a cabinet filled with discs of the greatest ballets ever performed, if one needs some inspiration. And I could definitely use some.

I slip inside, still reeling from the conversation with my mom.

If I can just have one chance, I know I can do this. I am a prima ballerina. I just have to make them see. I have to make my mom see. I can't leave the conservatory. I won't. The Sugar

Plum Fairy is my shot. Maybe my only one. The understudy is just one little step away from the lead. I've got to make it happen. No matter what. I fight off my thoughts about Gigi, how we sometimes stay up late watching old sitcoms and online videos of classic ballets, how she's always leaving me little notes and flowers. This is too important. This is my career.

I riffle through my duffle bag for my compact, and my old jewelry box distracts me. A gift from a father I've never met. It fits perfectly in my palm. I carry it with me everywhere I go, a promise that I will someday find him. I run my fingers along the back, winding the tiny key and opening the lid to watch the little ballerina twirl. *Muyongga,* dancer. The sweet melody reminds me of all the things I love about ballet: the control, the beauty, the music. In ballet, I can work on things over and over and over again until I achieve them, training my muscles until my body submits to what I want. It doesn't matter who my family is or if I have friends or if guys like me—only what my body can do.

A copy of the cast list is up on the wall, alongside ones from previous years. I see Gigi's name above mine. I stare until the typed letters blur, until I can see my name above hers. I can't be invisible anymore. No matter how nice Gigi might be to me.

The staring contest with the wall helps me calm down, the conversation I just had with my mom drifting away. I won't give up. I'll push someone out of the way to get it. I pick up a marker from the floor. My hand shakes. Guilt creeps into me, but on the wall, in bold black ink, I write: *Gigi should watch her back.*

7.

Gigi

A WEEK AND A HALF after the cast list went up, we've settled into our rehearsal schedule. We pile into the second-floor studio E, where I won't be able to see the rest of the sunset. I've been trying to follow Mama's advice and watch it every day in order to stay positive. "Don't carry worries around," she always says. "They're heavy." It's hard to hold on to her words here. Nerves erase them easily. But I have to, and it helps that I haven't felt sick since the list was posted. So they have nothing to worry about.

Eleanor walks into the studio beside me and I make a joke about our ballet madam's new haircut, just to get her to talk to me. It's hard to have real connections or even conversations with the girls here. She laughs, and so do I.

The room is a mess of leg warmers, pointe shoes, and chatter as we stretch our bodies so they'll fold like putty. June rests her head against the wall, her legs two arrows shot in opposite directions. She always warms up, even though she doesn't get to dance in the center with the rest of us. She only sits and marks variation movements and timing in the understudy book off to the side. I imagined that we'd rehearse together, laughing, teaching each other little things, moving in sync, like we used to do back home. But she won't. No matter how many times I ask her if she wants to.

Bette finishes tying on a translucent dance skirt as if she has all the time in the world, and she's watching me from her peripheral vision, like I've angered her even more by coming to rehearsal with Eleanor. Like I've broken some rule. There has never been a knife sharper than those blue eyes of hers. And where her eyes go, everyone else's follow. It takes only a few moments until the eyes of the whole cast are on me. Enjoying my audience, I make a fart sound with my mouth. Some of them laugh, some of them frown, and Bette rolls her eyes.

I plop down next to June and smile, and she gives the worst imitation of one in return. I've learned it's just her. Not to take it personally. I peel off my warm-ups: cutoff sweatpants that used to be Mama's and one of my old T-shirts cropped at the top and bottom. I sew new ribbons onto my pointe shoes, my fingers fumbling with the needle and dental floss and slippery satin. I try to shake out the nerves in my hands. Today I have to mark my solo for timing and progress in front of everyone. I've only had a week and a half of character instruction with Morkie and Pavlovich. And I should've broken these shoes in yesterday so they'd be perfect. I pull the dental floss through the shoe and it snaps.

Get it together, I tell myself, resewing. I stand and push my heel on the front of each shoe, feeling the glued fibers in the toe box break under my weight. With quick fingers, I work with the inside of the shoe, peeling back the fabric to expose the leather shank, like it's a banana, and use my pliers to pull out the tiny nail. I remember crying when I had to break in my first pair of pointe shoes. I thought it would make them ugly instead of able to support all the new movements I would make. I cut away part of the shank under my heel right where the curve in my arches begins. I secure it with quick-dry glue and tape, then test my weight. I pad my toes with a swath of lamb's wool, slip the shoes on, and tie the ribbons in a square knot.

Eleanor warms up next to me, and her shoes make a weird crunchy noise. We look at each other and burst into laughter.

A bag clobbers my head. "Oww!"

I glance up.

"Oh! I'm so sorry! I didn't see you there," Bette says, standing above me, no longer hovering in the background. Bette plops down in the small space between Eleanor and me, and pulls aside a bit of the fabric covering the mirror. All of them are draped with curtains because Mr. K insists that reflections distance dancers from becoming their characters, that they make dancers lazy.

Bette stares at herself. Her lips, when they are pursed together and painted with that hot-pink lipstick, are an impossible heart shape. With a mouthful of clips and pins, Bette slicks her blond hair into the perfect bun. Each strand obeys her touch, unlike my own hair. She adds hair spray to seal it in place.

I feel my curls fighting against the bun, transforming into a frizzy nest. I should've gone to all the trouble to straighten it or asked Aunt Leah to take me to the hair salon. I search the mirror for Bette's gaze. Casually, artfully, she applies fake eyelashes, dark and feathery, like the wings of my butterflies in their terrarium upstairs. I touch my cheek. My face is naked—no makeup, no lipstick, no eye shadow. Since the first day of school, June's warned me that I should make up my face, that it is part of being a serious ballerina, that the teachers favor it. But I can't. I don't like the feel of it on my face, clumpy and goopy. The lipstick Bette wears would make me feel like a clown. I only wear it for performances, and even then I can't wait to wash it off in the green room room afterward.

She must notice my fingers tiptoeing over my bare cheek, because she stops her expert application to look at me. "I love how you don't do anything with your face," she says, but I can't tell if the word *love* might actually mean hate. I am not fluent in the language these ballerinas speak to one another. The girls at my old dance studio were never like this. "Don't you just love it, Eleanor?"

"Mmmm," Eleanor says.

"Oh. Yeah. Mama's always saying she thinks makeup is dishonest, so . . ." Of course, as soon as the words leave my mouth I want to catch them and press them back in. "I mean, not that she's right, I just never really got into it." I give her the biggest, most sincere smile I can muster. "You always look beautiful, though," I add. "Seriously." I feel like an idiot.

"I really admire your confidence and everything," Bette says, so smooth she erases how awkward I was. "But you really should put on a little something. Playing the part and looking the part are sometimes the same thing, don't you think?"

I don't really agree, but she was so graceful in forgiving my faux pas that I nod a little. She hands me a compact and a blush brush. "Just try a little. You'll love it," she says, matching the largeness of my earlier smile. "And boys like it."

I sweep on a tiny bit of the powder, and maybe's she's right. The blush complements my skin tone. I have an extra glow. I'm just about to keep the conversation going and bask a little more in the attention Bette's suddenly lavishing on me. But before I can say anything, she's on her feet and hooking her foot on the barre. The moment is over. Liz tramples over. She whispers something in Bette's ear, and looks down at me, crinkling her thin white nose like she's smelling garbage left out on the curb.

The boys shuffle in—Alec in the lead and Henri last, as always. Alec winks at me, then swoops in and gives Bette a hug. I feel an unexpected twist of jealousy.

"You coming over tonight?" she purrs in his ear, just loud enough for us all to hear.

"Let's see how tired we are after rehearsal," Alec says. I could swear he shifts his eyes for a half second over her shoulder and looks right at me. Smiles, even. But it's too quick to tell.

"You promised," Bette says. It's not a whine, which would be below her. It's a statement of fact, and she crosses her arms over her chest, straightens her back, taking the stance of a lawyer questioning a witness.

"Can you continue your soap opera later, please?" Will says, interrupting the long look between the two of them. "I'm sure you'll get your way."

Bette bristles, even though it's a compliment, I think. A confirmation of Bette's beauty, her seductive powers, and most of all how much Alec must love her. Alec gives her a kiss on the cheek, and my heart twists a little more when Bette takes his face and moves it so his mouth reaches hers. The whole room looks away from them, as if on cue. As if they've been doing this their whole lives. Which, I guess, they probably have.

But I haven't, so I don't know the rule about giving Bette and Alec their little private moment, and my eyes alone stay on them. So it is only me who sees Alec slide Bette off his mouth. Her whole forehead creases, and he tries to kiss her cheek again, but she turns her face away from him and takes a step back, so full of hurt I can practically smell it.

She catches me looking straight at them, as ill advised as staring straight at the sun. Bette makes an audible, animal noise, but covers her mouth before it's all the way out. Whatever niceties we just exchanged while making ourselves up in the mirror have disappeared. I was not supposed to see what I just saw.

I look away what feels like hours too late. I lift on pointe in a series of *relevés*, bounce on the balls of my feet to loosen the shank further, and make sure my toes feel comfortable in the toe box.

Mr. K storms into the room with the other dance teachers on his heels. They take seats along the front of the studio. We all scramble forward.

Mr. K claps his hands and nods. "We will mark the last part of *The Nutcracker* this evening. I want to see the progress. Snow Queen, you're up first. Snowflakes, gather around her, and others dart in and out of the center like windblown flurries. We'll just do the first two minutes, since your *pas* with Henri hasn't been practiced yet. I want to see your entrance, Bette. Henri, stand off to the side as if you're getting ready to join her."

This is Bette's first run-through, and when she moves she is a snowflake skittering across the floor: the very definition of grace. Her turns are effortless, her flourishes melodic, her hands and feet and face perfect. The other girls twirl around her, trying to keep up, but they are mere beginners in her presence. She holds her arms and hands in just the right way—the way our teacher Morkie holds hers. Her face is soft and she knows just the right way to turn it, a moth looking for the light. Everyone watches her in awe. A twist of pain stabs at me. Does everyone feel like Mr. K's made the wrong decision? Do they think Bette should be the Sugar Plum Fairy? I fight away those feelings.

Mr. K yells above the music, "More charisma, you are the snow. Lighter. Lighter!"

Bette's cheeks turn red. Morkie says something in Russian and Bette adjusts her leg. She does one pirouette and the music ends. We all clap. Bette curtsies and exits stage left. She puts her hands on her head and I notice that they're shaking.

Mr. K turns to Morkie. "The turns are sloppy. They're not spotting properly."

Morkie answers in Russian. Mr. K throws his hands up. "The basics should be sharp, so ingrained, that they're automatic. Second nature. They look like amateurs in here."

Mr. K motions for Bette to return to center stage. She stands before him.

"Your whole combination was pretty. Your *piqué* turns, pirouettes all fine. Nice extension and perfect body alignment." He strokes his goatee. "The difference between the kind of performance that gets you in the corps and the one that lands you Aurora, Kitri, and Odette is character, feeling, and transformation, butterfly. I need to forget who you are, Bette Abney, and see only the Snow Queen before me." He dismisses her, and she curtsies and hurries from the center. She leans into the barre with her back to everyone.

Mr. K plops down where Bette left, on the actual floor, to make sure the male dancers fly over him for their leaps and jumps. All the boys look nervous, except Henri. He does so well that even Alec hovers a little too close, watching how high Henri soars. I've seen his high jumps photographed in dance mags, which called him and Cassie an up-and-coming dance duo.

Finally, Mr. K extends his arm to me. My turn. I gulp and shuffle to the front, ready to dance. Viktor starts my music. I present my arms in little flutters, then wait for the third beat, inhale, and step into my first *piqué*. Mr. K waves his hand in the air before I can start. He paces about the room with his hand on his mouth. "Sorry to interrupt, *moya korichnevya*. One thought before we proceed tonight . . ." He scratches his head.

My stomach sinks. I fidget in my pointe shoes and wipe sweat from the back of my neck. I pretend to push some of my bobby pins farther into my bun, but it's an empty gesture. Not a curl is out of place.

Mr. K and Morkie fuss back and forth in Russian. He puts his hands up, and she stops talking.

"Can we use the mirror, maybe?" Will says, like he's translated their squabbles. "Just for today? I know it's a safety blanket, but maybe it would help. I know it would help me."

My chest collapses in relief at Will's suggestion. I have never practiced this early on without a mirror. He gives me a wink when I glance at him gratefully. I mouth the words *thank you*.

"Fine, fine. Boys, push back all the curtains." Mr. K shakes his head and frowns at us. Disappointed. He tells them all to split up. The boys scramble about to different areas of the room and pull back the black drapes.

My music starts again. I concentrate on my footwork and the variation. I start to dance, tiptoeing across the floor. It flows, my mind letting go and my body taking over. My feet find every chime and melody. I feel ready to smile, to stop thinking about the steps, and let the music guide me. But I hear whispers rise above my music.

They grow louder and louder until I'm pulled out of the dance, my focus shattered.

"Do you see that? Look!"

"It's written back there. Kind of random, right?"

"Creepy. It's about Gigi."

Viktor's hands bang the piano keys in frustration, and he stops playing. Voices explode through the studio. I wobble from the sudden drop in energy. I put my arms out to catch my balance. I don't have to worry that someone's seen the awkward move: they're all looking at the mirrors. Every last one of them, crowded into a pack. One of the girls points.

The teachers burst into a flurry of Russian, and I move to the edge of the crowd.

"What's going on?" I say, all out of breath and too quiet for anyone to really hear me. The bodies block my vision. My heart races and my hands begin to shake as people turn to stare at me. Mr. K motions for Doubrava to come. They shout at each other in Russian. He hollers for everyone to get back.

Bette watches my face. The boys grip the curtains they've just pulled aside, seemingly frozen in place. People shuffle away from me and whisper. I can't see anything over the crowd, all the bodies blocking me, fluttering around like butterflies. All I hear is my heartbeat. I push through the bodies.

Mr. K peers at the glass, shaking his head. I hear him say, "Who did this?" He turns to glare at us all. He repeats his question three more times, and lunges at us. "I will not tolerate this type of behavior in my school! Not again! Ballet is supposed to be beautiful. You're making it ugly."

I want to ask, "What happened?" But I swallow hard. I feel shaky.

Mr. K stalks through our now silent group. My head feels light from my racing heart and all the voices and the confusion. I get a clear look at the mirror. A message is scrawled across it in pink lipstick:

The Sugar Plum Fairy has farthest to fall.

8.

Bette

FRIDAY NIGHT REHEARSAL ENDS EARLY after the message is discovered. I'm on a high with a rare chunk of free time, so I'm going to use it wisely. I took a pill after seeing the way Alec rushed to Gigi's side after the message was revealed, and another after hearing snippets of Gigi's conversation with Mr. K about the bullying incident and her delicate feelings.

Eleanor's in the café, so I use our private bathroom to smooth a deep red 1940s Dior shade on my lips. But that won't save me from the teachers' suspicions about who did it. There will be the ones who recognized my loopy handwriting or the Chanel lipstick that is my signature color, and my sister's signature, and originally my mother's signature. A saturated pink that was way too obvious and will probably get me into serious trouble. But I couldn't resist putting the message up there. It was sloppy. I didn't even want her to see it yet. Will did that on purpose. He knows me too well. I used to be much more discreet. Undetectable.

I remember the secret pranks Liz, Eleanor, and I played on Cassie last year: putting purple hair dye in her conditioner so her blond curls got all stained, shredding up her leotards and tights just to see her get in trouble with the Russians for not having the right thing to wear for class, slashing all her shoes or soaking them in vinegar, trashing her room. But nothing compared to the look on Gigi's face today. She's such an easy mark. And the message was so much more clever, and the thrill of it made me feel powerful, but I can't make the same mistakes I made last year.

I check my cell phone for a message from Alec. Nothing, but three missed calls from my mother, and no plans to call her back. I am certain Gigi's mother bakes cookies and sends care packages and tells her she's perfect as she is. Gigi has the glow of someone who has lucked out. She'll probably get a special delivery after she tells them about the message and her hurt little feelings.

Leaning hard on the edges of the bathroom sink, I imagine Alec's hands around Gigi's waist, lifting her in a tutu and spinning her around during their *pas*. I imagine her liking the feel of his touch. I imagine him kissing her. I imagine him liking how different she is, her curly black hair and light brown skin and cute freckles and California mellowness. Two pills aren't enough to erase those images and feelings. I swallow the third one dry and can taste the bitterness as it goes down. I'll have to get more soon if I keep up this pace. The same energy that had me raring to go now gives me a new, singular focus. Find Alec.

The hum of the Adderall in my bones and buzzing in my head obliterates any sort of potential pity party. My entire body and mind want only Alec, now. After the pills, there's only ever room for one desire at a time.

My phone buzzes, and I bristle, thinking it's my mother harassing me still, but it's Liz. She's at the coffee shop on Sixty-fifth street, and, she reports, so are Alec and Will. It's not an invitation exactly, but rather a warning. I don't want Alec and Will alone together.

I slip off my ballet slippers and step into flats, but don't bother actually getting dressed. Alec likes me in my leotard and dance skirt and leg warmers and slicked-back hair. He likes to pull the blond mass out of its perfect little bun and snap the leotard off my shoulders. I shiver at the thought. I should not have had that last pill. I'm practically rabid thinking about him, and that's no way to get his attention. Alec likes me icy and unreachable.

And Will hates when I get Alec's attention.

The evening guard has his boot heels on the front desk, his hands folded over his belly, and is in a deep sleep. I sign myself out. I slip out of the building and use the short walk to get myself under control. It's chilly for late October. Usually New York City holds on to the summer heat a little longer. I'm shivering when I get to the coffee shop, fingernails blue. Snow Queen it is.

Alec's at a table by the window, wrapped up in a striped scarf and a cashmere sweater. Freshmen and sophomore ballet girls watch him over calorie-filled cups. Even a study group of girls from the nearby Catholic school snatches glances at him. I hate being just one of the many girls drinking in Alec's good looks. But here I am, standing just inside the little coffee shop and letting my gaze linger before I approach. I like seeing him when he can't see me. No games. No pressure to look pouty and together. Just the pleasure of seeing someone beautiful and sure.

It doesn't last.

From her corner, Liz smiles, flashing me a knowing look, as Alec waves me over. I'll owe her one. I don't go over to Liz's table, not wanting Alec to know she texted me. That I have eyes everywhere. Will is behind him, partially hidden by a wooden beam. Too close to Alec. I grimace at how pathetic it makes Will look. I can never decide if I'm pissed at him or just feel bad for him.

"Here to see me?" Alec says, lighting up. I love that I have that effect on him, still.

"Of course she is," Will says. His eyebrows reach toward each other. He used to be so fun. He used to be normal. He used to keep his feelings to himself.

"Aren't you going to offer me a seat?" I say. I keep my lips pursed and let Alec look me over.

"I like you standing," Alec says, trying to be edgier because I told him I liked it. Another girl could get shy in a moment like this. But I've been ass naked in front of costume designers and teachers and classmates. I've had them pinch my sides and weigh me in public and measure every last inch of me to see how far away from perfection I am. So I'm not shy. I put a hand on one of my hips. I let him take me in. He's probably right. They're probably all looking at me. I'm a prima ballerina, no matter what Mr. K has to say about it, and the rest of them can see it all over me.

"You look great," Alec says at last. Which means I've won this round.

Will sighs loudly. I sit down hard on the chair, drowning

it out. Finally, I wrap one of my feet around Alec's ankle. He responds by pulling me into him and kissing me on the mouth, hard. He smells like coffee and hard work: he got his extra practice in. Smelling his sweat, I feel a pinch of guilt at being in here snaking my foot up Alec's calf instead of throwing myself into practice, doing pirouette after pirouette, and using the early rehearsal end to keep working on my variation. I kiss him again to make me forget.

"Okay, enough, you two," Will says. His voice is tense now, too. Just like his face. He's saying the same words he always has, but they sound so, so different.

"Can't you give us some alone time?" I snap. I can't take any of his little jabs tonight. I press myself even harder against Alec, shrinking that centimeter of space between our bodies. Will looks like he's about to say something else, but something in him must melt a little, because he nods and gathers up his stuff. The tiny surrender is enough to make me smile his way, but he misses the look and he'd probably misinterpret it anyway. The secret smiles and eyebrow raises we used to share don't work anymore. He stopped being my surrogate little brother this summer, and now I just don't know what we are.

"Alec, call me later?" he says. He lands hard on Alec's name, and even pauses to accommodate the space where my name would have been. Just one more person who hates me. I know it won't help matters, but I lean my head on Alec's shoulder and put a territorial hand over his. Will leaves, taking long dancer strides across the coffee shop. I still like watching the way his limbs move, still admire his impenetrable grace. I'd love even half of his passion. I'd tell him so, if we were speaking in anything but clipped, one-syllable words.

"Get your own boyfriend!" I call out, when he is already half out the door. Will's shoulders slump and everyone in the shop has heard me. He turns bright red, like his hair. He's not quite out beyond the conservatory walls. Boys from Kentucky aren't supposed to like other boys. His eyes look sad when they meet mine. I hadn't meant to hurt him. Not really.

"Harsh, B," Alec says. "Can't you guys get over your little spat?" He smirks and puts a huge hand on my thigh. The warmth of his hand travels through my thin tights.

"Not yet." His hand feels good on me, so I don't move it away. "So stay out of it," I say back, so he knows I'm not some weak, delicate flower scared to tell him what to do, like the other ballerinas who would love a chance to be with him. He loves me because I'm fiery, feisty, stronger than anyone else.

Neither Will nor I have told Alec the details about our fight. Because the fight is about Alec. Sometimes the words tickle my lips, and I want to tell Alec the secret Will told me, but the bigness of it keeps me quiet.

"You're all wound up today. And I'm guessing that's why you put that message up about Gigi," Alec says. I put several inches of space between us, losing the warmth of his hand on my legs. I hate that he said her name. That he ever has to say it. Sounds too pretty coming from his mouth.

I think about lying to him. Saying I didn't write the message. But he keeps talking.

"Look, just because Mr. K didn't cast you as the Sugar Plum

Fairy doesn't mean what you think it does. Don't be like those other girls who get all catty and start messing with each other. You're better than that."

I'm not better. I am that girl. I've just been good at hiding it from him.

"The Snow Queen is an opportunity to show Mr. K—"

"I'm fine," I say, louder than I'd intended. "Stop looking at me like everyone else is. You know I'm fine. I'm great. Can't I just come visit you?" I hear the edge in my voice and try to soften it into something sexy, kissing his neck and letting the last few words land on the stubble just below his chin. "We haven't been able to hang out much."

"Always happy to see you," Alec says, but it takes him a moment to reach for my body again. He sounds sad, disappointed in me. It's a familiar cadence to his voice these days. He grabs the menu from under his coffee mug. He starts making creases and folds in the paper. "You need your congratulatory flower then, if we're celebrating," he says. He's been making me paper flowers since we were little kids. His Japanese nanny taught him origami and it's a strange hobby that girls tease him about but clearly think is secretly sexy. Which it is. I love watching his hands manipulate the paper. Every crease is careful, gentle. Like him.

He finishes, and it's a perfect rose, made even more beautiful by the menu's text on the petals.

"For you," he says. "And if you want to talk about it . . ." But his voice fades out because we both know that's not going to happen. "Well, I'm sure you'll enjoy working with Henri," he finishes, the smirk firmly back on his face, like it never left.

"He's been asking about you. Tips for partnering you." Henri and Alec are roommates. "Dancing with him might get you in one of those magazines." For the first time ever, I hear a small pinch in his voice, and I know he doesn't like Henri.

"Maybe it will." I shrug, putting the paper flower behind my ear, where I secure it with a bobby pin. We've never danced with other people before. Alec and Bette are always paired. Our names have been listed beside each other so often that it's burned into my memory. I don't want his name next to Gigi's. I don't want to dance with Henri.

"I guess at some point we'd have to get used to partnering with others. It'll be weird at first. Gigi's got a different—" I kiss him to erase her name. It feels good to let go and to have him here with me. Just us. For at least this moment, Giselle Stewart can't take anything else from me.

I take Alec back to my room. Sneaking him in is as finely choreographed a dance as any we do onstage. We shuffle past the sleeping guard and into the elevator together. We push the fourth-floor button first, to check that the RAs are all still there. Their office spans the entire floor. They continue to answer the phones and dole out meds to several puffy-faced freshman girls who've no doubt cried themselves headaches. Not one looks up at us as the doors ping open. Then Alec goes to his floor on the tenth, because the RAs watch the elevator video feed. I go to mine on the eleventh, and let him onto the floor through the staircase exit.

"Out," I say to Eleanor, but smile to soften it after I open my room door. She's stretched across the bed, I'm sure doing her "visualizations," but if she were a real threat, she'd know she'd be better off actually still in the studio dancing instead of lying there thinking about dancing. One of Adele's performance videos—the ballet *La Bayadère* from three years ago—is on my flat screen. I click it off and don't comment. She's been watching old films of my sister a lot lately. And I wonder what's next. Will she show up at Adele's apartment like a fan girl? Will she ask my sister for technique tips?

"We're roommates, Bette," she says, in a voice I've never heard come out of her before. "I'm not your little slave. And hi, Alec. Congratulations on your role."

"I let you be my roommate," I say. I don't even have to lie. Eleanor couldn't afford this room—Adele's old room—the only one on the hall with a private bath. "Don't make me remind you, okay? That's embarrassing."

"Bette," Alec says. He never used to scold me like that. He liked that I said what was on my mind. Plus, Will used to be my snarky sidekick, and the two of us would make Alec laugh with our snide little comments.

Eleanor's face falls. I guess it was my intention, but I'm not some robot, and she's supposed to be my best friend. I take a deep breath. We've been getting into fights like this a lot lately, and I promised myself I would try harder to get back to the way we used to be. But some days I can't even remember how it used to be, who I was, who she was, and what made us friends. Since I didn't get the Sugar Plum Fairy role, nothing feels right. And she's been watching these videos and disappearing for blocks of time and not telling me where she's going. She's keeping secrets from me. She's making things weird lately.

"Alec's just gonna hang out for, like, an hour. Could you work in the lounge maybe? You're looking hot lately. We all know you'll be bringing a guy over sometime soon, right?"

I even wink. And pout.

Her cell phone rings. She jumps to silence it, then caves. "Holding you to that," she says on her way out the door.

"Cross my heart, hope to die," I say and grin. It does feel good, remembering that we actually kind of love each other. I miss her a little, the second she's out the door.

"Just an hour?" Alec says into my neck.

"We can make it a good hour," I say.

And we do. But the whole time feels like another big audition, and this time the challenge is to be the sexiest, the most desirable, the wildest. I wrap my legs around him so tight I'm surprised he can still breathe. I can be the girl he fell in love with years ago. The girl he still loves now. The only girl he wants to partner with.

We don't have sex, though. Alec says he's tired and needs to conserve his energy for tomorrow's rehearsal. I'm naked by the time he throws that one out, and I can feel my face shift from sexy to pissed.

"We always have rehearsal—" I say.

"I have a huge role. And a *pas* to practice."

"With Gigi," I grumble, then explode. "You shouldn't have come up here then. Where the hell is my shirt?" I scramble out of bed to find something, anything, to cover up what he's rejected.

"I thought we still had fun," Alec purrs in my ear. He kisses the lobe, and then down my neck.

"Just seems weird that you don't want—"

"I want you. I always want you. Just freaked out about impressing Mr. K tomorrow. I swear. This weekend I'll be back to my normal self, okay?" He's blushing, like we've both failed at our sexy, romantic relationship tonight.

When he leaves, he kisses me on the head and for just that one moment when his lips hit the space where my hair meets my forehead, I've won. It isn't about Gigi.

"Tell Eleanor to come back in, okay?" I can still make him do things for me. He nods.

"Can't wait to tell her all about me?" He likes to tease me, and even reaches down to tickle me. I squirm and hold back laughs. I could do this forever with him.

"Eleanor and I don't sit around talking about our boyfriends all night," I tease back. "Don't get the wrong idea." I let out a flirtatious laugh and touch his shoulder. He's surprisingly tense. He even blushes a little. "Even if I love you," I tack on, like maybe that's what's bothering him.

He doesn't say it back, just kisses my forehead again. I almost repeat *I love you*, like maybe he just didn't hear, but I can't take the risk.

It's a long, lonely five minutes before Eleanor reappears. I don't want us to have another awkward spat right now. I just want my old friend back.

Eleanor throws the door open. "Done?" Her face is still rosy, like the first day I ever met her. Six-year-old would-be ballerinas auditioning for the conservatory, standing in tiny leotards, hands and feet ready to be examined.

"Can we watch *Breakfast at Tiffany's*?" I say. My voice is quiet and I just want her next to me, sharing a blanket, watching the TV like it's a portal to a world outside this stupid dorm. Eleanor sighs. I'm sure she thinks she's supposed to stay mad, but I know she just can't do it. Not strong enough.

We lie on the futon-couch thing we have set up and get to the part when Audrey tears up her apartment in grief. Eleanor's breathing has slowed. She always falls asleep first. Her head flops on my shoulder. I wish I could sleep as soundly as she does. But I know I won't be able to for a long time, until the spring ballet and my second chance to snag the lead.

"What do you think of Gigi?" I whisper into the dark, knowing she won't hear, except in her dreams.

"Mmmm," she says, which I decide means Gigi's no big deal. Nothing special.

"She can't take everything from me, right?" I say, and listen again for Eleanor's nondescript sigh. It comes, and I try to let it comfort me as much as it would if we could actually talk about this.

A few tears come before I finally fall asleep. Quiet ones. Just between me and the dark.

9.

June

I WALK TO MORNING BALLET class alone, super early, so I can have studio C all to myself and get my head together before it starts. I've piled on the layers—it's late October and the chill has already started seeping into every pore. Plus, layers give me just enough invisible padding. I blend right in with the rest of them. But I know, really, that I need to make Morkie *see* me. That's how you become a star. Catch your teacher's eye.

Right outside the studio, I almost drop my thermos. Sei-Jin's boyfriend, Jayhe, sits on a booth seat in front of the glass, where everyone gawks in at us. He's slouched, in unlaced Converses and slim black pants. His red hoodie is up and he's looking at his phone.

I haven't seen him since Sei-Jin and I stopped being room-mates and friends. Almost two years ago. When did he start wanting to watch her dance? He looks sort of the same. But cuter. Less awkward. I've known him longer than Sei-Jin. We went to the same Sunday school as kids, he lived three blocks from me, and before I moved to the conservatory his *halmeoni* used to watch us both after school. She'd call me her little grand-daughter, and I would swim in his blow-up pool. I even know he has a blue-bottom birthmark on his butt. But now, Sei-Jin and Jayhe are like a version of Bette and Alec: made for each other, perfect, royalty in our Korean community.

He leans forward and looks up at me.

I feel my face get hot. I'm afraid my makeup will run. He doesn't say anything, just stares.

"Hi," I say, not sure why I'm even talking to him. In the ninth grade, I lost all my friends when Sei-Jin turned on me. Everyone disappeared. Even him. Especially him.

"Hi," he mumbles back, rubbing his sleepy eyes.

"What are you doing here?" I say, taking another sip of tea to fill in the space between his delayed responses. I wonder if he's skipping school. I wonder if he's changed.

"Sei-Jin," he says. "Supposed to watch now, I guess."

I try to make more small talk and realize that this is the first time I've actually spoken to a boy from outside the conservatory in a long time.

"Are you going to finally join ballet class with us? Remember when you used to try to do pirouettes in your basement?" I laugh, surprised at myself. For a second, I feel like I'm back in my old life. The one with friends and people who wanted to be around me. The one where I had inside jokes and memories and traditions. The one where I made room alongside ballet for hanging out, marathon chats, and adventures outside of school.

He kind of smiles. His cheeks are fuller, and there's a touch of stubble that wasn't there before. It makes my breath catch, with regret or maybe something else.

A throat clears behind me. Jayhe squirms and looks away from me, like I'm not there anymore, like he wasn't talking to me at all. The tiny connection is lost. The feeling of my old life disappears in an instant like a popped bubble.

"Not so pretty this morning, are we, June?" Sei-Jin says, pursing her perfect pink lips.

She startles me. She sounds the way a snake might, if it could speak. The other girls twitter behind her, too scared to say anything themselves, but happy to look me over, laugh in my face, whisper in fast Korean, and point at my body like it's a dartboard for their own insecurities. The new Chinese girl is on the edge of the pack, arms crossed, lost in translation, but still finding a way to nonverbally participate.

"Oh, you don't look that bad," I say in response, proud for a half second that I came up with a comeback. Sei-Jin steps closer. I can smell her breakfast and make out the scent of that same soft pink lipstick she's worn since middle school. Trying to be like Bette.

When we first moved to the high school dorm floor, Sei-Jin and I were inseparable, *jeol chin*. Best friends. She was the sister I never had. But at the start of tenth grade it all changed. That was when she started a rumor about me, forced the RAs to move me out of our shared room, and never spoke to me again. It was really early on a morning like this one, a cold fall day, and we'd been sitting at the twin vanities her mom had bought for our room—just like the ones in the American Ballet Company dressing room. Sei-Jin's mom was nice enough to get me one even though my mom couldn't afford it. The bulbs cast a warm glow on our faces.

Sei-Jin opened her makeup case. "You should start wearing more makeup," she'd said, removing a blush, lipstick, and powder. "Especially to ballet class."

"I'll just sweat it all off," I said. I was so clueless then.

"Real ballerinas dance with it on, without a drop of sweat on their faces." Leaning in close, she took my chin and pulled me into the light, like she was one of the makeup artists that made us up before our tiny girl parts in the company ballets. "You ever notice that?"

I didn't answer.

"Close your eyes," she said. I obeyed. I always obeyed.

She brushed the powder across my face, the strokes like butterfly wings fluttering against my skin. Then she used her soft fingertips to add blush to my cheeks, and rubbed a waxy stick of lipstick on my mouth. "These colors will hide your yellowy undertones. My mother always says you don't want your skin to be the color of a dead chicken wing." Her voice was full of wisdom. "This type of palette is best for us." And I was in awe of the way she used words like *undertones* and *palette,* words I'd never heard before.

She wiped a smaller brush across my eyelids. "This will create a shadow. Like you have a crease along your lid. It'll make your eyes appear less slanted. The Russians don't like our eyes." She set the brush down.

"I don't care if they don't like it," I said, hating that so many

Asian girls go through surgeries to change their eyelids' shapes. That Sei-Jin wanted to be one of them.

"Oh, yes you do. Everyone cares what they think. Even though it's disgusting. Too hard not to care. You won't get the things you want if you don't," she said, rubbing her fingertip near the corners of my eyes. "Look," she instructed.

I opened my eyes, unsure about what I was going to see. A different, softer girl gazed back at me. Sei-Jin leaned her face close to mine, her eyes big and doelike.

"See? You look different," she said.

I felt different. Special. I felt like a soloist or principal in the company. Not like myself, who couldn't seem to do anything effortlessly. I tried to say thank you, but I couldn't find the words.

She lifted my chin again.

"You look very pretty," she said, her voice just a whisper. She stared at me, and a weird energy stretched between us. She leaned in close. I saw the two tiny freckles on her nose and felt her breath on my face. I couldn't move. I couldn't pull back. Then she kissed me. Her pink lips pressed into mine. Soft, warm, and strange. I'd never been kissed before.

Her eyes closed. I kept mine open. Not sure what to do. I watched her eyebrows lift.

She tried to part my lips with her tongue.

I pulled away. "What are you doing?" I said. My heart lodged in my throat. The noise of it thumped in my ears.

Her nose crinkled, and a deep blush climbed from her chest up her neck and to her face. "Uh, sorry."

She turned her head to her mirror and took a lipstick from

her bag. Her shaky hand applied more to her lips. I wiped the gooey paste from my mouth on a tissue, some of it mine and some of it hers. I watched sweat appear on the back of her neck. I wanted to say something. That it was okay. That she was my best friend. That I didn't know why she kissed me, but I would be here to help her figure it out. I looked at the clock. It was almost time for class. I got up to leave. Sei-Jin didn't move to follow me. She sat, transfixed by her own image in the mirror. I didn't know what to say.

I tried to wait for her to come. She didn't. I rushed to the door.

"E-Jun," she called out.

I turned around. She just looked at me.

"Tell them I'm sick, okay?" she said, her eyes brimming with tears.

"Okay," I said.

"I don't—I'm not—" Her voice broke. "I was just—"

"Of course not," I said. Korean girls don't kiss other Korean girls. They kiss boys. They marry boys. I wanted to ask more, wanted to know why she kissed me and what was really going on. To let her know that she'd be okay, no matter what. That I'd be there for her.

"It's all right. All of it—" I started to say, but she put her hand up, and I had to go.

Before the end of that day, Sei-Jin asked the RAs to move me out of our room, and a week later a rumor surfaced. That I was a lesbian and she didn't want to live with me anymore. My mother was called, and the guidance counselor lectured me about making other students feel uncomfortable.

Sei-Jin's wearing that same shade of lipstick now, and I bet her mouth tastes like it did all those years ago. A mix of lipstick and grapefruit and tea. Probably a lot like mine does, actually.

"You're always second favorite, aren't you?" Sei-Jin says, taking a step closer to me.

Sei-Jin's sweet perfume wraps around me. She bats her big eyes. "Understudy for Gigi. No one's first choice. You think you're so great, but no one else does, huh?" Her eyes narrow.

That hits. My momentary quick wit vanishes, and I fidget, trying to squirm out from under her gaze. It only hurts when it's true, I guess. I feel the jewelry box shift in my duffle bag and hear the tinkle of its insides. I don't know if she's thinking of my father, too, but I can't help myself. The only thing my mom ever said about him was that he started a new family, one he prefers more than us. What Sei-Jin says is true in more ways than one.

Of all the things she's called me—a bitch, a poser, a wannabe-white girl—this is the worst. Understudy. I remember my mom's words on the phone. And her threat. If I can't do better, I'm getting pulled out.

"Nobody wants you," Sei-Jin says.

I want to say that *she* wanted me. I want to bring up the kiss. Which I never have. Not in all these years. But I don't. I've kept her little secret.

Jayhe says something to her in Korean. She stops.

"You already won," I say at last. Sei-Jin doesn't know what to do with that. I want Jayhe to see her as the bad one. The other girls throw a few Korean insults my way, and even though I can translate some of it and know how rude they're being, they can't come close to hurting me the way Sei-Jin just did. Sei-Jin hushes them, waving her hand in their direction the way I've seen Bette do to Eleanor and Liz. She really is trying to model herself after Queen Bette, and she's pulling it off. The girls quiet instantly.

I turn to retreat into the studio.

"I found this," Sei-Jin says, and reaches into her own bag. Something glints in her hand, and I know immediately what it is. My missing compact. She knows how important it is to me. It's always in my bag or on my desk. I imagine her riffling through my room. I grab for it, like a child, and am surprised when she lets me have it. Her mouth twitches, holding back a smile. I open the compact, but inside the mirror is broken, and the glass has cut the perfect little powder cake. It's destroyed.

"Oops," Sei-Jin says.

The hall is now full of dancers and they all must be watching, because the space is silent and I feel the heat of a dozen pairs of eyes on my face.

Jayhe says something else. Sei-Jin and he spar back and forth. I wonder if it's about me. I click the compact closed, wondering if I can glue the tiny mirror back together again.

Morkie sweeps everyone into the studio for class. We warm up, complete our barre exercises, then Morkie makes us do *fouetté* turns in the center. I go to the front of the class, squeezing between some of the other girls. I spread out my arms to get them to move. Some grumble. Others mutter under their breath. I don't care. I want her to see me turn.

The music starts. The other girls around me finish their four turns. Just what Morkie asked for. But I can't stop. I spin and spin and spin, stamping out the conversation I had with Sei-Jin. I do one revolution for every insult and mean word.

I feel eyes on me for the first time. Morkie walks in front of me. The other girls move away from me. I know they want me to stop. I know they're thinking that I should've just done the four turns Morkie asked for. I am alone in the center. A spinning top.

I've lost count of how many I've done. I finally come down off my leg.

"Bravo!" Morkie says. She calls me dedicated in front of everyone. She says my *fouettés* are perfect. Usually, I'm a ghost to her and all the teachers. Not worth noticing. But not today. I took the risk. I pushed myself to show off a little.

Everyone claps for me, except for Sei-Jin. Some rub my back and give me compliments that don't feel fake or ridiculously transparent. Gigi squeezes me so tight I feel like I can't breathe. She grins like she's proud she gets to live with me. I fight the warm feelings it gives me. I even see Mr. Lucas, Alec's dad, watching from behind the glass wall—which he almost never does. He gives me a strange little smile and nod.

When I curtsy and return to the barre, I catch Jayhe's eyes on me through the glass. He's standing instead of sitting now. I hold his stare for what feels like an eternity, then turn my back, trying to fight off a smirk, the weight of his gaze heavy on my slim shoulders. Not so invisible anymore.

I know what I'm going to do to Sei-Jin.

10.

Gigi

I'VE BEEN VISITING THE MIRROR in studio E every night, looking for the edges of the message Bette left me. The girls told me it was her, and probably Liz, and maybe Eleanor, too. It was cleaned off days ago. Everyone else seems to have forgotten the way it looked, but I hear the threat in my head like my performance music. Each time it repeats, I get more determined to be the best Sugar Plum Fairy, more determined not to give into the ugliness and pettiness of it all.

I take the elevator to the first floor. Then I take the stairs to my basement room.

It's empty, aside from dust bunnies in the corners and the creaks and clacks of the old radiator and the buzzing of nearly dead lightbulbs. But I get lost in the mirror in this room, too. I can't move, can't close my eyes to meditate, just keep looking at my reflection. Mama always says it's unnatural to spend a lot of time in front of the mirror, that it calls out the worst of us. But for a dancer, the mirror is home.

I try to focus and imagine myself filling with light, the way I did in yoga class with Ella back home. I want the beams to erase the message and all my worries about it. Then I lift one of my legs, first to the barre, and then toward my ear. I want to become one straight, impossible line, from my left toe on the ground all the way to my right toe in the air. But my body isn't responding as it usually does. There's a little ache in my heart. I can't decide if I'd prefer it to be over Alec or something medical. I'm not sure which is more dangerous.

"I can help you with that," a male voice cuts through the silence.

I pivot with my leg in the air, assuming it's Alec. He's the only one who knows I dance down here. I beam, and turn to face him with a look far too eager to be truly innocent.

"Happy to see you, too." It's Henri Dubois, the other new kid, and he's staring me down. He has eyes like the people in Mama's artwork, dark and dreamy and haunted. He runs his hand through his dark, shaggy hair. He's still in his dance belt and tights, and I can't help looking between his legs. Those dance belts make everything look enormous. He catches my gaze and steps back, so I look at the floor.

"I've got it. I think," I say, and sink even farther into a stretch.

He approaches me.

We haven't said more than three sentences to each other. The only things I know about him come from articles I read in dance magazines. He was one of the rising stars at the Paris Opera School. *Was* being the operative word, at least according to the gossip. Rumor has it that he was kicked out.

"Oh, come on," he says. "Ballet is a team sport." He walks the rest of the way into the room, dodging broken barre poles.

"How'd you find me?" I say, bringing my leg down on my own. I'm not ready for his hands to be crawling up to support the place where my thigh meets my hipbone. I should be upset he's found my hiding spot. I want only Alec to know about it.

I lower myself down to the floor, which seems safer for about one second.

"I was not looking for you." He sits in front of me. His accent is attractive and flowing, and I can't help liking the way his words blend together. For sixteen years I haven't had a single spark of interest in ballet boys, in any boys, really, but suddenly I'm all butterflies and unexpected sweat. I don't feel like myself. My head fills with new thoughts and feelings and ideas. Henri has probably always been cute in class and rehearsals, but I've never really *noticed*. In the strange, broken light of the notorious basement studio, though, he makes my throat go dry.

"You hide in here, don't you?" he says. "When I don't see you in the rec room with everybody else, you're in here."

I don't answer. A half smile creeps across his mouth, and I'm not sure what's so funny, but he has the most perfect dimples. I'm tempted to rest my thumbs in them. See how deep they are.

"Shouldn't you be cooling down from rehearsal?" I say, for lack of anything better.

"Shouldn't you?" he spits back, then grins. "You ballerinas take things so seriously." He mutters something in French, and I like the way it sounds and how his mouth curves as he speaks it. "Let's stretch, Giselle." He doesn't call me Gigi, but says my name the way it's supposed to be said—all long *l*s and soft *e*s. I want to tell him my parents met as twentysomething ex-pats in Paris. That they'd named me Giselle after the famous ballet.

"We need a little music," he says. He pulls out his phone and the button clicks echo until tiny chords ping from the device. Suddenly, *The Nutcracker* pours out. He opens his legs in a *V* and reaches for me. With strong hands, he pulls my hips toward his and adjusts my leg placement, like a doll's. Not once does he ask, just curls his fingers around my legs and spreads them. Part of me doesn't mind the feel of his touch. Part of me doesn't feel like myself. He touches me like we've been friends for a while. And strangely, I welcome it.

He removes his moccasins, and we touch our feet together, letting the soles kiss. The balls of his feet are calloused and his toe joints are thick and raised—he's got the feet of a dancer. Our legs make a diamond shape until he pulls me forward. I elongate my legs into a straight line. I haven't stretched with a boy like this before. I never join in with the other students when they do it. There were no boys at my California studio, so the girls would stretch each other. Here, there don't seem to be any boundaries. I'm not used to all this touching, but I move even closer though my mind says no, don't stretch with him like this.

"Don't hyperextend," he warns.

I scoff and show off my flexibility. The space between my thighs inches closer to his dance belt. As he leans forward, I spot a tiny mole beneath his right eye. He's so close he could kiss me if he wanted, and I wouldn't be able to stop him. I've never been kissed before. A few close calls, a brush against my lips, a stage peck, but nothing real. Not a kiss with heat.

He rolls a white mint in his mouth. The tiny orb oscillates above and below his tongue—a white boat in a red ocean. Sweat dampens my brow and my hands get clammy. He doesn't seem to notice, and just interlaces his fingers with mine. My heart jumps a little. I tell it to stop. I should get up and go to the dorms and get ready for bed. But I can't. I feel glued in place.

"Come this way." We change the stretch. He tugs me forward, lifting me off the floor, and I lie just above him, two inches from his chest, a deep tug in my hamstrings, pulling out the soreness caused by new rehearsal jumps. We hold the position and then switch. When he falls forward, I can feel his breath on my stomach. The hair on my body lifts and a faint pulse thrums between my legs, like a tiny drum.

I snap upright, knocking into him. "I'm all loose," I babble, and close my legs, waiting for the new sensation to disappear.

The room feels too quiet. I hear the light buzz. It reverberates under my skin, half pleasant, half terrible. I hear his breathing. I hear the acceleration of my heartbeat. *Control your breathing.* He holds me in place, and his eyes study my expression. A chill rushes over me, like there are a thousand pairs of eyes on my face. Before I can dodge him, Henri leans forward and his lips brush my cheek and the side of my lips. Too close for comfort.

I snap backward. His face falls. "Giselle, I'm so sorry. I don't . . . know . . . why I did that."

I don't know how to react.

"You just remind me of my ex, Cassie," he says, dropping his head. "You're both just really good. . . . I miss her."

I open my mouth, but nothing comes out again. I tell myself to get up and leave, but my body is heavy and awkward. I don't know how to go without making things weird. We're both the new kids at school. He got here just a few months before me, in the summer. We're supposed to have a connection because of that.

I fill the silence. "So. France. I've been there. Well, Paris. And Toulouse. And . . . and Bou . . ." I stumble over the pronunciation. "Boulo . . ."

"Boulogne." His voice is so low and husky compared to mine that I blush. He presses his thumbs into my leg muscles. "When you speak French, let your lips go soft and move your mouth slower."

I nod. He makes me say the city name again, but I fumble with the long French syllables.

"So you've been many places in my country," he says.

I nod again. My parents have an apartment in the nineteenth *arrondissement* near Sacre Coeur and we go most summers so Mama can paint, but I don't say any of that.

"I was born in Charenton-le-Pont, just outside of Paris. My *maman* and I moved into the city when I was eight."

"Is that when you started dancing?" I ask.

"*Oui* . . . eh," Henri says, "I think I was almost ten."

"Ten," I say with a shock that embarrasses me. Most dancers start when they're five, or even younger.

"I am a quick study. Ballet became my obsession. I have

many," he says. "Are you from New York?"

"Me? Oh, no," I say. "California."

"I have never been. Just seen it on American TV. Beaches, sunshine, surfing, little dogs in big purses, car chases." He teases. "All smiles."

I slap his leg playfully. "There's much more than that." He rubs my hand and I pull it back. I quickly ask another question. "Do you miss home? Do you like it here?"

"Do you?" he asks.

"Yeah, I guess. It's growing on me."

"You should be careful," he says. "Cassie wasn't." He touches my arm. My stomach flutters and I wonder if I'll ever get used to all these boys around me—Alec, and now Henri.

"What happened to her?"

He grimaces, and though I want to know, I don't press any further. I know the discomfort of talking about something you don't want to.

"Just watch out," he says. "Especially after that mirror thing." He shakes his head and mutters a word in French that feels like a curse.

"The girls told me it was Bette, most likely," I say, not quite sure I should accuse her to other people.

"Be careful with that one," he says, fingers grazing my cheek, almost as if he doesn't realize he's doing it. I try not to flinch. "I don't want you getting hurt."

The overhead bulbs dim, threatening to go out. The shifts in light make a mess of his face. In the new shadows, he's a different person. Heavier brow, hidden eyes, frowning mouth. I feel like we shouldn't be in here alone in the dark anymore. The last few notes of *The Nutcracker* ping out of his phone and then it's just me and Henri and the silence. He reaches for me again as the lights stamp out, and he kisses my cheek.

11.

Bette

IT'S LATE—ALMOST NINE P.M. CURFEW—but I head to the first-floor studios. I take the most public route I can think of, making sure to pass by a few open dorm rooms and even take the elevator to the basement past the student lounge. I want them all to see me exactly as I am: hardworking and dedicated and not willing to be thrown off course by something ridiculous, like Gigi Stewart, who probably got the Sugar Plum Fairy part by letting Mr. K touch her for a few beats longer than was actually necessary. Maybe she let her lips graze his neck. Or worse. It wouldn't be the first time girls had thrown themselves at Mr. K for a role. And it wouldn't be the first time he gave in to it, either.

Just a little something I learned from in-depth conversations with Adele. She slipped up and told me about those too-close moments brought on by hard work and late-night rehearsals. How working so intensely on something brings out feelings.

How things might cross the line. And about how girls can get caught up in it all. But Mr. K's never tried anything with me.

I know the history of this place backward and forward, and when an unknown, awkward nobody gets cast in an important role, there's usually a good reason for it. My assessment makes me feel better.

I walk by the rest of the dancers with pride and a new leotard. Even during class I am the perfect ballerina. Even in a room by myself with all the doors locked, just me and the mirrors and the music, I am everything Mr. K and my mother and Adele and the school have ever asked me to be.

I am perfect.

I go back upstairs to the main floor, through the lobby, which is now being wiped clean of an earlier reception for the *petit rats'* parents. I take another long route, fluttering past Mr. K's dark office and the cast list. I peek into each studio, just so I know who's dancing and who's slacking off or prioritizing an English paper or a new boyfriend. Eleanor is in one of them, but she's just doing barre work and checking herself out in the mirror.

We used to always rehearse side by side, pushing each other to do better and complimenting each other's footwork. Somewhere along the way, though, she said I was too intense during practice and it wasn't fun anymore. I guess she's not wrong. And she does look happy now, inching away from the mirror, mesmerized by her own body. I would never want to take that away from anyone—especially not her.

I run into Liz. She's drenched and clearly has been in the basement weight room. Not that she needs it. Her eyes are all hollowed out lately, and her arms and legs so thin and wiry that I worry about her strength. But we don't call each other out on things like that.

"Pilates?" I say to her.

"Elliptical," she breathes out, panting, wiping sweat from her face. It's very unbecoming. "I burned six hundred calories."

I frown at her. She doesn't need all the extra workouts. In the past year, she's shrunk down from a respectable size two to an I don't know what. Negative two, if there's such a size. How does she even find anything to fit her anymore?

"God, Bette, stare much?" she says as she pats the last few drops of wetness away, smoothing down her hair. "Hey, so, I've been meaning to ask—what's it like practicing with Henri?" There's a wink in her voice, but I don't like the implication. Alec and I have had our ups and downs, but at the moment, we're very much on again.

"Yeah, he's hot," I say, already heading in the other direction, my tone colder than it should be. "But you know I have a boyfriend."

"Uh-huh," Liz says, pulling her long dark hair into a high ponytail, and I can't help but stare at her too-lean legs, not sure whether I should worry about her or be jealous, as she peers into the other studio, where a few of the boys practice jumps. She's looking for Henri, no doubt.

Things between Liz and me have been good lately, but there was a time when we competed for everything—including Alec. But he made his choice pretty early on, and after a few petty incidents, Liz realized there was no changing that. It was just making her look desperate. Plus, we finally figured, we're more powerful together than working against each other. It just makes sense.

She heads up to shower, and I'm about to enter studio C when I remember a little something Eleanor mentioned earlier—that Gigi practices in the old basement studio. I'd stored the information, and now I want to test it out. I want her to know she can't do anything in this school without me knowing about it. I don't miss much around here. She'll learn.

I pass the nutritionist's office. I pause at the top of the staircase. I remember being little and sneaking to the edge of these steps with Eleanor and Alec and Will. We'd dare each other to go stand in front of the locked door. Whoever did it the longest always got candy from a secret stash and, most important, glory.

Voices drift up to me. I can see the door is open a hair and I'm nothing if not graceful, so I tiptoe down, dip under the window, and peek in through the slightly open door without being heard or sensed. There she is. Gigi. The Sugar Plum Fairy. Except she's not dancing. She's on her back, legs splayed, Henri pressing on her thigh as he stretches her out in semidarkness.

I don't know why, but I shiver as I watch. Almost like I'm outside in the crisp fall air. I remember that Cassie used to come here, too. The insomniac girl who got in trouble for dancing all night. The girl with the perfect 180-degree *grand jeté*. The only Level 6 girl to land a major soloist role last year, even above me. I don't like thinking about her. I want to forget that I even knew her and how good she was. And especially that she's Alec's cousin.

Henri lets his hair drop around his face and says things I can't hear. I don't like the way he touches Gigi and makes her laugh. I don't like how his fingers graze a loose curl near her neck. Her voice is light and delicate—it's too pretty. Henri is eating it up. And if Henri's eating it up, I worry that Alec will fall for it, too, when they start rehearsing.

My stomach twists. I can't remember a time when Alec and I weren't together. My first memories have him in them, from family dinners when my dad was still around to dance classes and kissing him in the school's dark corners. It was always just us.

I take out my cell phone and zoom in on Gigi and Henri with the camera. I click the picture button. The flash is too bright, so I duck and slink away quickly, quietly. I don't get caught when I do things like this, and I don't need that to change. I run back to the upstairs to studio C and throw myself into the Snow Queen variation. I do five, ten, twenty pirouettes, but the image of Gigi and Henri races through my head alongside my music.

I drop down off pointe and pace the room. I scream at my reflection and hope no one hears me. Or sees me breaking down in this glass box of a space.

I cover my ears and let my head bob on my shoulders, falling into a deep stretch. I try to revel in the pink message and its cryptic cleverness. The powerful way it made me feel writing it and waiting for someone to discover it. How Gigi's face had fallen, how lucky I was that everyone saw it at the same time. I was probably the only one who spotted the tears in her eyes. I hope she's cried every night since. That's not quite true. I hope she goes back to California. She'll be happier there anyway, so it's not even that terrible that I want her to leave. It would be better for everyone. The girl is too fragile and sweet and mellow to succeed here. In some ways, I'm just looking out for her. She'll realize it soon enough. That ballet is too much for her. That it makes you do things. Makes you do whatever is necessary.

I remember Adele's advice before my first casting audition. She yanked me out of the pack of *petit rats*. "You don't get many shots, peach." Her hands were in my hair, redoing my bun the proper way with a hairnet. "So when the opportunity comes"— she leaned into my ear—"you've got to claw your way to the top."

My body relaxes at the memory. Adele would approve. Maybe not of these methods. But of my motivation for sure. I grab my warm-ups and head upstairs to my room. When I open the door, Eleanor jumps from the futon and turns off the TV. I see those old videos of Adele out on the floor.

"Again?" I say.

"She has perfect feet, Bette," Eleanor says. "Arched like bananas." I can't even fight the compliment she gives my sister.

"Can I use your printer?" I ask, wishing I didn't have to, but I've been avoiding my mother, so I couldn't possibly ask her to send me new ink. I don't have time to go get more.

"What for?" she asks, clicking the TV back on.

"Just a little surprise for Gigi." My voice lifts an octave with excitement. "Got pics of her and Henri in some compromising positions."

Eleanor frowns. "We're not doing that again, are we?"

Her words bite and I almost drop my phone. "We are," I snap, waiting for her to look away from me and apologize for her weakness. To join in on the little fun I have planned, like she's done a thousand other times before.

"Uh-huh. Sounds great," she says, easing slowly back into watching my sister perform a perfect rendition of Kitri's solo from *Don Q.* "Let me know how it goes."

I don't let her hesitation stop me. I plug my phone into Eleanor's computer and wait for the picture to load. I try to block the screen, so she can't see, but she doesn't even look up. Eleanor can turn into sort of a saint at times. But I know how to get her to do things. I print the picture, delete it from Eleanor's downloads folder, and slip out the door while Eleanor's still in an Adele trance.

The eleventh-floor hall is empty. Everyone's mostly in their rooms listening to music, in the upstairs student lounges watching TV, on other floors, or sewing shoes and stretching. I go to the Light, and tap three times on the door. No one is in there. I lock the door behind me.

I exhale, surrounded by pictures of primas and beautiful thin bodies and perfect feet. The day after I turned twelve, my mother shipped me off across Central Park to the school dorms. Finally old enough to live on my own here. Back then, I used to visit this closet every night. I used to fall asleep on the floor sometimes, and the RAs would have to wake me to go back to my room. I run my fingers over the collaged walls and find a spot for the picture in my hands. Before I tack it up, I see a message that makes me smile: *Gigi should watch her back.* I rub my finger over it. Someone else hates her as much as I do. I'm not alone.

I grab one of the glue sticks that sit on top of the TV. I wipe it all over the back of the picture. I slam the page on the wall and smack it hard, like I'm hitting Gigi's face a thousand times.

I step back to admire the picture among the others. At first glance you can't tell it's one unlike the others. I wish I could see the look on people's faces when they spot it, and the look on Gigi's face especially.

12.

June

I'M LUCKY MY WEIGH-IN TIME is at 5:10 p.m., after academic classes. Gigi is off somewhere by herself, probably smelling the flowers she keeps plucking from God knows where, and I have the room to myself. She's been at it for the past few days, claiming that her mama says a flower's scent helps boost happy brain chemicals. I don't care about being happy. Only about being the best.

I think through what I've eaten today: three cups of clear tea; half a grapefruit sprinkled with a pinch of sugar; one rice cake; a half-pint of soup; a mixed green salad, no dressing; and a half scoop of tuna. Although I must admit, I didn't touch the tuna. But I count it because it was on the salad. If there were any day I could eat, it would be today. Weigh-in Wednesday is on every calendar in these halls. For some of the girls, like Bette, it isn't ever a problem. They're carrying a few extra pounds here and there, just what they need to keep Nurse Connie's confidence.

But I need more. Nurse Connie has rules. For my height, I should be 110 pounds, a hippo in tights. Instead, I make sure I'm a model of grace, with perfect posture; a lithe, lean frame; a prizewinner all around. I do what I have to do. It's all a concerted effort. Because I take my work and myself seriously. Unlike some of the other girls.

When I weighed myself this morning, the scale read 99 pounds. A number that the other girls would kill for. A number that means I'm light and liftable. But here, anything less than 100 pounds at my age and height gets you sent packing. And I can't let that happen. I won't let that happen.

I pour myself a tall glass of water from my electric teapot. It's my fourth in half an hour. Today, I need the water weight, as slight as it is. But it won't be enough. So I sit at my desk and pull a needle and some thread out of my dance bag. From the desk drawer, I take four pieces of the Korean won my grandmother gave me the one time I met her. They are ideal: heavier than American coins. I pick up my clean Wednesday leotard from its labeled bureau drawer and flip it inside out. We're required to wear them for weigh-in. A little mesh pocket lifts from the crotch area—the perfect don't-go-there space. I set four won on my digital food scale. The numbers blink: 612 grams, 1.34 pounds. Just right.

The won fit perfectly in the leotard's little pocket, and I sew the tissue paper–wrapped coins into the flap. Unnoticeable to anyone but me. I pull the leotard on over my pink tights and smooth out the edges, so nothing protrudes. The coin-filled pouch pushes between my legs like the maxipads I don't have to wear anymore, since I stopped getting my period. I pull on a chiffon dance skirt over my ensemble. No one will ever know.

I step on my floor scale. The numbers calibrate and settle on 101 pounds. A warm flush rushes through me. Just to be sure, I drink two more glasses of water.

I take the elevator to the basement before going to the nutritionist's office on the first floor. I stop in the computer lab, printing out a hastily written English paper, since I have some time to kill and can't stand the nerves when I'm just standing around waiting for my appointment.

The computer lab has been officially taken over by the Korean contingency. They do everything in a big group: eat, watch Korean soap operas on their laptops, and spend weekends at Sei-Jin's aunt's brownstone on the Upper East Side. Right now they are all video chatting with faraway relatives and it's an assault of fast-paced Korean, so speedy I can't even make out the occasional noun. I fight the pinch in my stomach, burying the nagging desire to be part of their group. I've seen exactly how cruel they can be. So why do I still want that?

Sei-Jin sees me, and as usual, throws out some insults in Korean, commanding the whole room to laugh. I'm sure she's calling me a banana or whatever the Korean word is for a halfie.

I recognize Sei-Jin's mother on her computer screen, and a part of me wants to wave hello. Just so Sei-Jin is forced to talk about me and make up some lie about why we aren't friends anymore. Just to make her feel that pinch of discomfort in catering to Korean social graces. Sei-Jin's mother used to visit the conservatory when we were smaller, and she always reminded me of my own mom. When we lived together, Sei-Jin and I would compare notes on them, complaining about their constant stress and their ugly haircuts and disdain for American music and food. I taught Sei-Jin how to say curse words in English, and we'd whisper them under our breath when our moms made us angry. She'd delighted in the sounds, and taught me a few key phrases in Korean that I once let fly at my mom during a particularly heated argument. It was worth facing my mom's wrath when I got to tell Sei-Jin about my triumph.

That feels like a long, long time ago. I don't even remember myself in that friendship. And I definitely don't remember her.

She takes off the headphones and microphone. "When my mother saw you walk in, she asked who the ugly new American girl was," Sei-Jin says, just as I'm about to exit with my English paper in hand. Her accent emphasizes the harshness of her words. "I told her it was E-Jun Kim, and she said she couldn't believe it. She said whoever your father is, he must be one ugly American pig."

She emphasizes the insult *pig,* like it's a current thing normal American teens use. I want to laugh at her. I want to push her out of the way, and explain to her mom how our friendship changed.

"Oh, right, you don't have any idea who he is. Yes, must've been a pig to make you."

I try to stop my body and face from reacting, but the parts don't listen. I inhale sharply, stumble over one of my own feet, and wish away the sweat gathering behind my ears. I try to remember my plan to hurt her.

"Oh, I'm sorry," Sei-Jin says, watching my face. "Maybe I translated wrong?"

She smiles, but even then her perfect creamy skin doesn't crack. Not a single dimple or smile line or flaw. She hasn't translated wrong, of course. Her English is perfect, but she always blames her cruelty on the language barrier anyway. And I can't even defend my mystery dad. I have no idea who he is. Only that he's white and practically a ghost. The other girls pause their own individual conversations to watch Sei-Jin and me.

Most of them came from Seoul when they were six, right when I enrolled. At first we were all friends. They stayed with nearby Korean relatives, and my mom would invite them to do things in the city with us. We'd have dinners and sleepovers. But after Sei-Jin spread the rumor, they all took her side. That's when they stopped speaking in English around me, or coming to my room at night to talk about the stupid American girls. I went from being part of their group, part of something that felt so comfortable, to being a total outsider.

Now Sei-Jin likes the others to believe that I don't fit because I'm half-white, because I can't speak much Korean, because I'll try to make out with them all. It's enough to offend their prudish ways and keep me away, for sure. But really, Sei-Jin is scared of the secret only I know about. How would they treat her? What would Jayhe think? She'd be the one all alone, left out.

"My mother said your mother slept with a lot of people to get ahead," Sei-Jin says. "She said your father was probably one of the teachers or someone with a bunch of money." She cocks her head. Unable to defend my mom—for all I know, it's true—I walk out without another word. But I know her mom said none of these things. Those were my theories I used to go through with her when I was upset with my mom for not telling me about my dad. Sei-Jin's mom is always nice to me when she sees me. Always pats my head and tells me how pretty I am.

Heat crawls up my neck, and I try my hardest not to look back, even though I can feel Sei-Jin's heavy gaze on me, her mean words still ringing in my head, taunting me. I walk slow and straight and composed, as if she's not affecting me at all.

After my run-in with Sei-Jin and her followers, the nutritionist's office is almost a sterile, metallic relief. Almost. At least I can sit on the cool metal table and savor the quiet until Nurse Connie shows up to ruin everything. The white tissue paper crinkles under my butt as I fidget with anxiety. Her office is sandwiched between the studios on the first floor, a constant reminder that she's in here lurking and ready to make sure we're all following the rules about our weight.

The tools of Nurse Connie's trade are on display in the office: two gleaming, mean-spirited scales, one digital and one traditional. And there, on the wall, are tape measures, strung like snakes that nip at your wrists, your waist, your thighs, threatening to expose your darkest secrets. When these come down, you know you've gone too far, that home beckons, that your skin and bones aren't enough to sustain you any longer.

I've only had to face the snakes once, in eighth grade, when I hit ninety-six pounds, and the school called my mom, who nearly hauled me home. I ate and ate and ate that weekend, gorging myself like a fat pink pig, until I hit one hundred and they let me come back to school.

I feel the weight of the coins, comforting, and that's what I think about when Nurse Connie breezes in, not saying a word before taking my blood pressure—it's low again—and checking my heart rate.

"Remove your dance skirt, please," she says.

"I didn't mean to—" I stutter.

She waves her hand in the air. Today, she doesn't want to hear it.

"When was your last menstrual cycle?" she says.

"Two weeks ago." The lie comes out effortlessly, because I track when my period would come if I still had it. Just to be prepared.

"Are you sexually active?"

"No," I say, and wonder if one day that answer will change. She gives me safe sex reminders. I remember last year how crazy sex rumors went around about Cassie cheating on her Paris Opera school star boyfriend, Henri—futile attempts to break them up and pollute their budding fame as ballet's new It couple. But I wonder if they were having sex. If that helped them dance so passionately together. If Nurse Connie had to give her more than just gentle reminders.

"Stand," Nurse Connie says, and I do, stepping onto the wobbly pad of the traditional scale, old-school and as mean as any of our teachers. Meaner, maybe. I close my eyes and hold my breath, wondering if the air might make me heavier. She shifts the weights from one end to the other and back, dark and calculating, determining my fate, as she does every week.

"Hmmm," she says. The concerned tone seeps into my pores. A cold sweat drips quietly down my back and dots my hairline, taking my makeup with it. And that's when she says it. "About a hundred and one. Not good. Get on the other one."

I do as she instructs, stepping automatically on the digital scale, as I've done once a week for a decade now. I clasp my hands together in almost prayer formation. I gather my breath, again. Liquid churns in my stomach. She doesn't look happy. She holds a chart that records my height and weight and soul, deciding whether or not I deserve a place in these halls.

"One hundred and one," she repeats, and I exhale with relief, though it is peppered with fear and doubt and, yes, satisfaction. "Not good at all, E-Jun."

"I know." I can't tell her that I just needed to get above one hundred. That was my goal.

I step down, like a good girl, and take a seat, praying, praying, praying that those snakes don't slither my way today. They'll give me away for sure. She touches my leg muscles. I wince and imagine she's about to say my legs are too skinny, my arms too frail to support the ballet movements. That at some point I'll collapse, unable to support my own weight. And I can't have that now, not when I'm so close. Not when I can nearly taste it. Not when my mother is threatening to pull me out of the conservatory.

"I know I don't have to remind you of this," she says with a patronizing tone, "but you need to eat more. Tell me, what did you have for breakfast and lunch?"

I don't tell her the real items. Instead, I repeat my memorized lines: "Half a grapefruit, a cup of nonfat yogurt with fresh cherries, two bananas, a salad with tuna, coffee and cream." As I give her that embellished list, I can almost feel the bite of the imaginary caffeine and calories swooshing in my stomach.

She looks intently at the chart, seeing right through my lies. "You weren't in the cafeteria last night. I don't have your signature on the list." Her evil sign-in sheets stare up at me—her prison-inspired way of making sure we are present for all meals. "What did you eat for dinner?"

"My mother brought me some *baechu gook*." I smile sweetly, knowing that the foreign words will fluster her. "Because I've been working so hard, you know, as understudy for the Sugar Plum Fairy."

She smiles back, but I know she doesn't quite buy it. She needs to focus on girls like Liz. She's the one who's severely underweight. I kind of want to say that, but I know it'll only make me look guilty. She rests her hands on the tape measures. I hear my heartbeat echo in my ears. *They're coming down.*

"Well," she says, "I'd like to see you back up to a hundred and four in two weeks, with a goal to get as close to a hundred and ten as possible. And I want to see you at the cafeteria each evening. I will look for you myself, and the resident advisers will be informed, too, and make sure you're eating a proper, balanced meal." Suddenly her voice is ice. "Because, E-Jun, you know this is very serious. You're sixteen now. And you know the rules. From now on it's one strike and you're out. There are no more second chances."

I do my best to maintain that sweet smile, but I can feel it slipping. My heart threatens to leap from my chest. She's not on my side. Not any of ours. She'll report us, and start the paperwork to send us home. She'll get the guidance counselor involved and then Mr. K. She doesn't care what it means to be a dancer. What sacrifices it takes. And she knows that Mr. K will easily let me go. That I'm nothing. I can be replaced. Girls are a dime a dozen in ballet—not like the boys who are treated like princes. Another girl will be plucked from some audition somewhere.

"Sure." I move to grab my bag. "I know. One hundred and three. Next week."

"One hundred and four," she reminds me sternly. "And if you can't, we'll have to just schedule a bone density scan."

"I don't need one of those," I say, the smile disappearing from my face.

"It'll tell us exactly what you need, actually. And find all the things my scales miss."

I chew the inside of my mouth and don't know what to do. Say something else. Turn around and walk out. Lunge at her. Cry. Last year, one of the Level 6 girls got a bone scan, and it showed all her little secrets: how little food she ate, how she didn't get her period anymore, how many stress fractures she'd danced through just to keep her roles. They sent her back home after that. To Texas.

"I'll ask my mother if I need one," I manage to get out.

"No need. I have her medical waiver. That's enough for us to order one if we need to. I am here to take care of all the dancers, to do what's best for them, so they can be strong and healthy onstage."

I try not to breathe too hard. I want to call her a liar.

"Oh, and Gigi's your roommate, right?" she asks, like she hasn't just said something that could potentially ruin my entire life.

"Yes," I say, a little harsher than I meant to. I don't want to be *Gigi's* roommate. I was here before her. She should be *June's* roommate. *June,* the girl who's been at the school for ten years.

"You headed up to your room now?" she says.

"Yes," I say, cautious, unsure of what she wants.

"Tell Gigi to come down and see me, please. If she's up there. I have something for her." She taps the top of a messy pile of sealed envelopes. One has Gigi's name printed on it.

"Okay," I say. She goes into the interior office without saying good-bye. I know she's done with me. I pluck the envelope from the stack. There are so many envelopes here, she won't miss this one. She'll think she's misplaced it, and print out another copy of whatever it is. I thumb it between my fingers, wondering what's inside. Even if it's nothing, it's still good to know everything. Or maybe it's something that'll keep her from dancing. After all, injuries are the reasons for understudies. I rearrange the rest of the envelopes and slip out the door, my prize in hand.

I leave the office, hiding a smile, excited to return to my room for some light reading. I'll just take a peek. No one will ever know.

13.

Gigi

"WE NEED TO PRACTICE OUR grand *pas*," Alec says after rehearsal is officially over tonight. "I need to get our lifts just right."

He takes my hand and leads me out of the rehearsal space to studio F across the hall. I feel Bette's gaze on my back, but ignore it. I'm not doing anything wrong. We do have to practice. He closes the door behind us. Not that it could hide us in here behind all this glass. Right away he goes to the barre and takes hold of it. I stand behind him, admiring the muscles in his legs and how broad his shoulders are. I've never wondered about what a boy might look like undressed. I've never considered what little details I might be missing, given all I already see of their bodies.

"Let's warm up again," he says. "Then practice the lift. You up for it?"

I nod, and drop my bag against the wall, ignoring the mess that spills out of it. I don't bother putting on pointe shoes, instead just slide off the squishy mukluk slippers Mama sent me from her trip to New Mexico, and walk barefoot to him. We stretch our legs onto the barre. My limbs feel twitchy being so close to him. When my parents and aunt moved me into the dorms, Alec was the first one to introduce himself. Marched right up with a smile and welcomed me to the conservatory. And every day after that he'd check on me, asking me how my day was and how I was adjusting, always ready to give me little tips here and there. He's the one who told me that June's frowning isn't about her not liking me, that it's just the way her face is. I chuckle at the memory. Alec gives me a what's-so-funny look.

"Nothing," I say, pushing deeper into the stretch.

"Did you always dance?" he asks.

"Yeah, pretty much," I say, leaning to the right, feeling the stretch up my side. "You?"

He follows my pattern. "My whole life. My dad danced here. The great Dom Lucas." He mimics Mr. K's thick Russian accent.

"Oh, right," I say, feeling a little stupid for not remembering that. "I always forget Mr. Lucas is your dad. That must be . . . amazing."

"My sister and I like to forget," he says with a sad smile. "He doesn't act like much of a dad."

I don't know what to say, so I just let my hand find his back, and stroke the spine in a few long, careful brushes.

"I'm sorry," I say at last. "I didn't know."

He smiles back at me, and then guides my body to switch sides with his. I gaze around the room. We're alone, but it makes me feel strange. Seasick. I try to snap out of it. This is what I wanted, right? And I'm getting it.

"Can you help me stretch my leg?" I ask, not really needing him to, but wanting him to touch me.

"Yeah." He moves closer. I place my leg on the barre, then he lifts it gently off until it's above my head. I look up at my foot. My hip loosens and I feel a satisfying pull.

"That feel okay?" he asks.

I nod, feeling each one of his words land on my cheek. I want him to kiss me. I shouldn't have a crush on him. Even saying the word in my head makes me blush. He's with Bette. We're only dancing together. It'll be all over after *The Nutcracker* performance. He lowers my leg, then I lift the other one for him. And he repeats the movement, pushing into me, his chest against my leg. He taps a beat along my thigh and I try not to laugh.

"Hey!" I say with a big smile.

He flashes his signature grin at me and puts my leg down. "Here, let me try a few of those lifts. Do you mind? I'm struggling with them."

I almost ask him if I'm too heavy. But I bite my tongue. He's used to dancing with Bette, who is smaller, wispier than me. I shake off the thought. I shouldn't worry about something so foolish when my body is so strong and reliable. I need to focus on getting these lifts right, finding the right partner rhythm with him. *The Nutcracker*'s grand *pas de deux* is one of the most intricate and difficult partnering variations. The audience anticipates the dance between the Sugar Plum Fairy and her prince the entire ballet. I won't let it be a disappointment.

We don't do the lifts in the staged, practiced way we're

supposed to. We don't mark our movements, the way our teachers showed us, then slowly slide into the dangerous positions. Instead, Alec just grabs me by the waist, presses his thumbs into my back, and raises me sloppily into the air for a shoulder lift. It isn't a sanctioned ballet move. It isn't part of our choreography or anything we would ever rehearse in the pressure cooker of the ballet class. But I soar and he is strong beneath me. I throw my head back and let myself get lost in the cracks of the ceiling. My arms stretch behind me, my heart thumps, and Alec's arm muscles twitch below me.

The way down is slippery and hot. He lowers me so that my body meets his, our torsos kissing. I am all tingles in my spine, my stomach, my heart. The beat pulses all over me, and I'm embarrassed. If he touches my skin, he'd feel it, and know how excited he makes me. We do the lift a few more times until his thumbprints are permanently indented in my back, and little raw blisters have started to form. I don't let him see the pain as he slides me down for the last time.

I stand below him, my head still back so that I am lost in his eyes. And while I'm distracted by the way blue meets green meets black at the very edge of his pupils, he surprises me by touching my face. Letting his fingers linger along my cheek and down my neck, like he's drawing shapes on my skin, leaving a burning a trail behind.

I want him to kiss me. I want to know what his mouth tastes like. I want to know how his tongue would feel. I inch back because standing there, framed by the glass panels, peering in, breath fogging the glass, is Eleanor.

I pull away from him.

"What's wrong?" he says.

Eleanor disappears down the hall. I don't say anything about her. "What about Bette?"

He scratches his head and shrugs.

I chew my bottom lip, and have to stop myself before I split the skin there again. "Aren't you together?"

"We were always on and off. Hot and cold. Like in a cycle, sort of. One that's off. But now"—he touches my cheek again—"I want something different. Like you."

I hold his gaze as excitement flushes through me. I feel the cheek he's touching grow warm, and I hope his use of the word *different* isn't related to the color of my skin, and just that Bette and I have opposite personalities.

He cups the back of my neck, and wraps a loose curl around his finger. I try not to flinch, and fight the urge to not want him to touch my hair. What if it's all sticky from the product I put in it? What if the curls feel rough to the touch, and not smooth and silky like Bette's perfectly straight blond hair?

"I'm going to talk to her. Tell her it's over. It kind of has been, these past few weeks."

I fight away a smile. "How are we different, besides the obvious?" I rub a finger over my forearm to highlight the color.

"When I saw you helping one of the little girls with her first pair of pointe shoes, I knew," he says. "I watched you outside of studio A."

"Oh, Celine," I say, remembering catching the little one, struggling to break in her first pair of pointe shoes.

"You were late for class, and didn't care." His comment causes my cheeks to redden again. "Let me show you something." He pulls me forward and out of the studio. We climb all ten flights up to the eleventh floor, and he won't tell me why we were taking the stairs instead of the elevator. I work hard to keep my breathing calm and even. I'm nervous about him being so close to my room or, worse, Bette's. We duck through the hallway exit door. There isn't an RA doing hall rounds yet. We slip past slightly open doors and the bathroom. He tugs me forward. I try not to laugh. I try not to get us caught. I hear only a few girls. Mostly everyone is getting a postrehearsal snack in the café. We go to the very end of the hall.

"Have you been to the Light yet?" he asks.

"The what?" I say.

"You haven't then." We step into a dark closet at the tail end of the hall. I always thought it was just a storage room. He pretends to fumble for the light switch, and rubs his hands along my neck and over my bun.

"Alec," I say, not really wanting him to stop. He clicks on the light. The small space is collaged with pictures: Anna Pavlova, Mikhail Baryshnikov, Margot Fonteyn, Rudolf Nureyev, and others. Quotes about ballet. Quotes about dance. Perfect bodies, perfect feet, perfect costumes. Conservatory graduates. Company members. Dancewear ads featuring up-and-coming primas. All white faces, startling as first snow. I try to suppress a sudden pang of homesickness, of wanting to belong somewhere.

"What is this?" I say.

"June didn't tell you about this? It's been here as long as the school's been open. No one knows who started it."

Of course she didn't. She hasn't been talking to me much at all lately. No matter how much I've been trying to connect with her. He tells me more as I run my fingers over the walls, trying to soak up each quote, studying each image.

I see my name and lift up on my tiptoes, but can't reach. "Alec," I say.

He comes up behind me. I feel his hips press against mine and it flushes me with warmth. There's barely an inch between us. I can feel the warmth of his body through my leotard.

He reaches over me, takes down the note, and scans it before crumpling it up. He's about to toss it on the floor, but I take it. "I shouldn't have brought you in here," he says. "I should have known they'd be at it again."

I scramble to read it. It says *Gigi should watch her back*. I trace my fingers over the words. Suddenly, I'm angry. "See anything else?"

He points to a picture to the left. It's of me and Henri stretching that night in the basement studio. I rip it off.

"I can't believe it," is all I can say. "We were just stretching. He kind of crashed my alone time." I'm fuming, and trying to keep it from showing on my face.

"Do you like him?" he says.

"Who, Henri?"

"Yeah."

"No," I say, wanting to add that I like him. But I don't.

Alec doesn't say anything, but I can see a small smile in the corner of his mouth. He takes the picture down, crushing it in his hand.

"I'm sorry I brought you here. All that stuff has ruined it."

"No, I'm glad you did," I say. "I should know what I'm in for, right? The enemy you know, and all that?"

"They did the same stupid stuff to Cassie," he says, finally. "It started just like this. Notes left in her room or bag. Even stuffed in her shoes."

"Who's they? What exactly happened to her?" I ask, while still combing over the walls for anything else, my stomach churning with anxiety. His warning echoes Henri's.

"It's hard to be on top here. It's even harder to be great and still have friends. Especially for the girls. The boys like the competition. We thrive on it. Makes us work harder. The girls make it dark, full of drama. The competition brings it out. They let it get to them and act crazy." He tucks one of my curls behind my ear, and I try not to cringe, hating that he touched my hair when it's all sweaty and has a ton of product in it. "Cassie had to take a rest. Well, she's still resting."

"A rest?" I say.

"Yes. While she was here she got hurt, and it affected her badly. So my aunt put her in an institution. My dad calls it a rehab center," he whispers. "Please don't tell anyone that. No one at all."

"Of course not. What did they do to her?" I ask, the words careful and soft.

"All sorts of pranks," he says without elaborating. "Then it all got to be too much."

"Who did it?" I ask, unsure if I should bring up the fact that

Bette left that message on the mirror.

"I don't really know. A lot of different people. Making it hard for teachers and Mr. K to figure it out. Bette and her were close, and even she couldn't find out."

I try my best not to frown. Or think that Bette must've had something to do with it. She seems like she's at the heart of everything in this school. He tells me about how they all used to hang out.

I nod, and turn away from him. A white page sticks out on the wall of colorful cutouts, folded over, inviting. I missed it before. Curiosity pushes me to look at the page while Alec looks at the opposite wall and talks about growing up with Cassie.

I gulp. It's my medical report from late September. My latest EKG. The line's spikes and dips go up and down like a kindergartner's artwork, exposing my weird heartbeats. I rip it down and crumple it into an angry ball.

"What's wrong?" Alec says, making his way to me.

"Just shocked about what happened to Cassie." I feel horrible for lying, but he can't know. No one can know. How did this get in here? Who would be able to find something like this? I tell myself to calm down, to breathe easy. I can't get my heart to slow down, though. The stress. Or maybe it's Alec.

His arm brushes mine. I let my hand slide into his. He leans forward, and I know we shouldn't be in here, we shouldn't be standing this close to each other, I shouldn't like him. He surprises me with a kiss. A real one. Warm and wetter than I had expected and so deep I'm scared he will find out all my body's terrible secrets just from the exploration of our mouths.

We kiss for so long my lips go numb. So long I forget to wonder whether he is Bette's or mine or just his own person. So long I forget to protect myself, forget to control my breathing, forget to be afraid of anything at all. So long I don't care about what things were put up on the walls around me.

And just when all the fear has drained from my body through the opening and closing and exploring of our mouths, it floods me again. I push him away a little. My heart is thumping hard, and I can't catch my breath. This is wrong. I want him so much, but he's not mine. Not yet.

"Bette," I whisper as light as I can, not wanting the weight of her name to fill up the small room.

He tells me that they're done. He tells me that he'll tell her. He tells me how much he wants me. I press myself against him, kiss him first this time, letting the feeling of his lips and the taste of his mouth erase all the secrets and lies that are swirling around me.

14.

Bette

WHEN I GET BACK TO my room after rehearsal, Eleanor's there in her flannel pajamas with her eyes closed, deep in one of her visualizations. I hear her chanting each movement of the Snow Queen variation. I slam the door hard to snap her out of it. It's Friday night, and I'm itching for some fun, but she's already in pajamas. As usual. I try not to be furious.

"Alec came by," she says, without any hint of irritation. She thinks we can talk about Alec like he's a movie star or my prom date, but what I have with him is so much bigger, so much more serious, than any of that. "Looked sad you weren't here. He said he texted you, and waited an hour in the stairwell for the RA to leave the hall."

A smile starts inside me and turns itself outside. My heart squeezes and I hope she's not just adding that "looking sad" bit to make me feel better. Alec and I haven't been *right* since the last time he was over here. It feels like it's been months. I squeeze my phone. Sometimes I don't answer his texts right away because I want him to know that I'm busy. I want him to wait a little. I want him to know that I am a serious ballerina and life doesn't stop for him. Even though it kind of does.

Eleanor's phone starts to ring. She clicks it to silent. It starts up again. She tries to talk over the annoying pings.

"Who's that?" No one ever calls her. Unless it's me. Her mother's even too busy to call her with all her starving siblings.

"No one." Her face turns redder by the second, and her voice buzzes when she's nervous, and it's going crazy now, shaking and speeding up. "Did you like Morkie's new additions to the solo? She's moving away from—"

"I don't care about rehearsal," I say, eyeing her. I push again about the phone call and she won't tell me, so I change the subject. "You tell Alec where I was?"

"I didn't know where you were. Where were you?"

"Who was calling you?" I snap back.

Eleanor sighs. "My older brother." She's lying. She doesn't make eye contact and her bottom lip does a little quiver. I know her too well. When did we start keeping secrets from each other? I can't let her know it bothers me, though. She'll need me soon. That's for sure. It's always that way.

"Anyway, Alec left you a note," she says.

I am a crush-struck twelve-year-old when she hands me the ripped sheet of notebook paper with Alec's familiar handwriting on it. My heart surges, the way it used to when we were thirteen and just learning how to kiss each other.

B, Koch Theater? I'll be on the steps. —A

I tell Eleanor not to wait up and to cover for me if anyone checks, which they won't. As long as we're at rehearsal, at classes, and making weight, the teachers and RAs and nurse don't actually care what happens to us.

Once or twice a semester, we take what Alec calls a "field trip" to the Koch Theater, late enough at night that the curtain has already fallen on whatever show is happening there, and the janitors will gladly take a few hundred bucks to ignore us. Alec's got access, his parents are on the board of everything, and he has a way of learning security codes and passwords. It's just one more thing I like about him. Good guy, but still interesting.

When I get to the theater entrance, he's there, in his red-striped scarf and gray wool peacoat. His eyes flutter across my face like he's really not looking at me.

"Hey, stranger," I say, resting my hand on his forearm, familiar and safe, trying to warm things up. I'm thinking about Thanksgiving break looming and being alone in his room at home and making up for lost time. That big, plush king bed and his freshly washed sheets that always smell like lavender.

"Come on, it's cold," he says, not pulling me in for a hug or kiss. He taps in the right security code and we enter the backstage area. It's pitch-black, so we search for lights by running our hands all over the walls. They startle on, or at least a few bulbs do. The stage is half-lit, the auditorium is all dark, and Alec and I are alone at last. The wings are empty and the curtains hold the familiar smell of velvet, of dust, of something I can't describe.

Alec climbs onto the stage, does a few quick but precise jumps and turns, and then sits on the polished floor with a distinct lack of reverence. I approach the stage more carefully. It's my church. Even when I forget what it felt like to be a tiny dancer, the expansive and imposing stage makes me feel small and light and alive again.

I lie on the floor and stare at the high ceiling and imagine myself in costume, perfecting the most complicated and intricate choreography Morkie or Mr. K could possibly conjure. I want to sleep onstage, and always feel the warmth under rows and rows of lights, twinkling like faraway stars. Usually, Alec and I would roll around a little, his hands in my hair, mine in his, the wood creaking under us and the lights warming us up even more. But today all he does is frown down at me.

I sit up. "I've kind of missed rehearsing with you," I say, widening my eyes. I try to lean my head on his shoulder, but he scoots away. "I love you, you know."

He doesn't say it back, so I just let the words sit in the almost dark. They echo. We are too small and too uncertain for such a majestic space.

"Bette?" My name sounds good in his mouth. Sweet. He barely hits the *t* at the end.

"Mmm-hmm?" I make the sound as sleepy and sexy as I can. The hum vibrates and my lips are stirred from the sensation. I want to kiss him desperately.

"Look, I brought you here," Alec says after a brief pause, "to tell you face-to-face that it's over."

I don't think I heard him right. But then he starts again.

"We can't be together anymore. We've always done this

on-off thing. We just can't anymore."

Each word punches my chest. I shudder away from him, wondering if I'll ever take a full breath again. My eyes, my lungs, my heart all sting.

"Over?" I start, knowing if I yell the sound will be magnified and echoed back to me with terrible accuracy. "You think that's it?"

I want to control my voice so badly, but my insides are pounding with emotion and even my bones seem to be throbbing from the hurt.

"You're still one of my oldest friends—"

"Friends?" I say. The word is way too little to fit the bigness of Alec and me inside it. I am so small on this huge stage. I want to be wrapped in a blanket and curled into a cozy space, not lost in the magnitude of the history here. It doesn't feel safe. And his words hit like bullets.

"It's just time. We've kind of been off for a while."

"Off?"

"It's just been weird this year. It's time. Even Will noticed—"

A white-hot hate for Will explodes in my chest. "Will's in love with you."

The words come out bitter and spiteful and obviously I have lost focus, because as much as I hate Will, I never wanted Alec to know that. The reason Will and I aren't friends, the betrayal of your best friend saying he's in love with your boyfriend and expecting you to sympathize, to be kind about it. He asked me to stop being so affectionate with Alec, because it hurt him. It still makes my heart pound with anger. And now he's told Alec to break up with me. What else has he told him? What else will he tell Alec?

"What about Will?" Alec says with shock, as if he didn't hear the words. The truth.

I don't repeat the words that changed everything between Will and me this summer. "You heard me."

We sit in silence.

"I shouldn't have even brought him up," Alec says. "Please don't say stuff like that about Will, though, okay? He's my best friend. Aside from you. Let's just . . . Let's forget this part of the conversation." His eyes look watery, like he might cry. *Alec is too soft*, Adele has always said. But it's part of what I love about him: the secret soft space that isn't too far below the surface.

"I need us to be okay even though we're not the same *us* anymore," he says. "It's just time, I think."

But it will never be okay. It's broken, whatever we had. And things will never be the same.

I don't let him walk me back to school. Instead, I go to Adele's. One avenue west of school. The cold freezes any tears welling up inside me, and I take two pills. I'll have to text my dealer for more after my mother gives me my weekly allowance. I'm running low. Adele's place is a decent doorman building with marble floors in the foyer and pretty fake plants. A lot of the dancers live here, usually together. It's nothing like the town house we grew up in, but Adele calls it cute. The doorman lets me in. He's seen enough of me, and probably way too much of my mother.

I take the elevator up to the seventh floor. I knock light at first, then harder. She doesn't like unplanned visits. If we could schedule our phone calls and rehearse our chats, she'd be even happier. The door opens only a slit. Adele's sleepy blue eyes stare back at me. Her thick blond hair falls around her shoulders perfectly, like she hasn't just gotten out of bed. Willowy white legs stand in flawless formation. Even just standing in the hallway in the middle of the night, she's a model of grace and the perfect ballerina.

"Bette, what is it?" She doesn't move to the side to let me in. "It's late. Everyone's sleeping." She lives with three other American Ballet Company members.

"Can I come in?" I ask. "It's only eleven."

"And tomorrow's opening night for our *Nutcracker* season. Or did you forget?" Her eyebrow lifts, and she leans forward just like our mother to inspect me.

The fog of Alec's breakup and losing the Sugar Plum Fairy is distracting me from things I'm supposed to know. I should have the company's opening nights and closing nights memorized if I want to be part of them one day. I should've remembered that she does eight ballets a season as a soloist, so she's perpetually tired and distracted.

"Your pupils are all dilated." She reaches a hand for my locket before I can step back. "Chill with these, okay?"

I pull away. I thought my pills were a secret. "With what?"

"You know what I'm talking about. I can tell."

I've never been quite good at lying to my sister. "I've just . . . it's just—I just—"

"Go back to the dorms. Take a hot shower. Until you're pink. Until you've gotten it together. Then call me. Tomorrow." She closes the door before I can say anything else, and there I am, alone again.

The next day, Mr. K cuts rehearsal short, and if I was the kind of girl that sent thank-you notes, I'd send him one. Being around Alec after the news he dropped on me is too much. So I choose to not deal with it. Instead, I focus on the glitter. It's all about the glitter. Red lips, eyes lined in purple, glitter on my cheeks, my shoulders, my collarbone, any part of me I want them to look at.

"Whoa," Eleanor says when she opens the door to our room. I haven't chosen a dress yet, so I'm mostly naked, except for heels and layers of makeup and my locket.

"Get your ass in gear." I'm dragging her out tonight for a little fun and distraction. It's Saturday, after all, and normal sixteen-year-olds in New York City would be out.

"Rehearsal sucked, huh?" Eleanor says, stripping off her leotard and tights. Her hair's still in a bun and I reach over to undo it myself. "Alec joining us?"

I flinch, signaling to her that I don't want to talk about it. I haven't told her or Liz anything. I don't even want to picture his face: his smile full of pity while watching me dance the Snow Queen variation and not the Sugar Plum Fairy, the sound of his whistle after Gigi danced. It's probably for the best he won't hook up with me right now. I don't want someone looking at me like that when we're kissing, touching, having sex. I'll just wait until he wants me again. Until he sees I'm still better than everyone else. I think he's just confused about his feelings right now. Has to be. He's never danced a *pas* with anyone but me. I'll forgive him for not knowing what to do. And for us not having our usual amount of time together.

"Just me, you, and Liz tonight," I say, clipping the words.

"Alec was being too nice to Gigi," Eleanor starts. "I even saw—"

"We're not talking rehearsal anymore tonight. Or Alec. And most of all Gigi," I order. "Get your hair down and your boobs out."

I'm a little giddy from coffee and pills and all the adrenaline of dancing for the last five hours. Eleanor pulls away from my hands in her hair. It's a mess of congealed hair spray and sweaty strands, and a shower of bobby pins rains from her scalp to the hardwood floor. We've been playing with each other's hair and helping each other in and out of costumes since we were little girls. There's really no distinction between her body and my own. Backstage, she'll help me pull my costumes on and off for quick changes, and I've always helped her perfect her makeup.

"You're cleaning those up." She gestures to the spilled bobby pins. Already she's pushing her hair back into a less structured but still painfully tight ponytail. As she pulls it back, her eyebrows rise. Her face is too chubby; the whole thing makes her look fat. "I'll clean them up while you get ready," I say.

"I'm tired, and so many parts of my body hurt. Do we have to go out?" Eleanor says, but even as she whines she grabs her towel and turns toward our private bathroom, because she knows I'm not taking no for an answer. "And is our laundry back?" she asks, like it's her housekeeper who washes, folds, and delivers our laundry to the front desk every three days. "This is my last towel."

"Yeah, it came today. Your bag is in your closet." I riffle in the bright pink laundry bag on my bed. "Found these, too." I dangle a pair of frilly black panties that are straight out of a lingerie store. "They aren't mine. Are you hiding something from me, El?"

Her mouth drops open. She grabs at them and starts to stutter out a million reasons why she has something other than her usual cotton underwear. How it's nothing. How they were a gift.

"You want someone to see those, don't you?" I say.

She tries to change the subject. "I should just go to bed. So tired."

"It's Saturday night. No Pilates tomorrow. We're going out! You can wear the silver dress." I take out the shiny minidress I bought over the summer, the one she fell in love with, hanging it on the closet door for maximum effect. Eleanor walks up to the dress with religious reverence and touches the fabric.

An hour later, it's hugging her body and she doesn't even look like a ballerina anymore. Eleanor has always been like my own personal Barbie doll. Her mother never taught her all the little tricks of being a girl that my mother taught me, so she lets me take over in that department. When we were twelve, the costume mistress Madame Matvienko pulled her aside and told her to get her act together, that she looked like a slob. She came to me, snotty and crying, asking for my help, and I've always been there for her since day one at the conservatory. Tonight she lets me tease her ponytail and line her eyes in the darkest kohl. I purple her lips and drape four long, beaded necklaces over her neck. She's so tiny under all that makeup and shine and sparkling beads that she practically disappears.

As my mother would say, the dress is wearing her.

My dress is the color of my skin: ivory-white and off the shoulder. Green high heels. Nothing to hide.

I knock on Liz's door and give it a little push. "Ready?"

It's dark and smells like a mix of sweaty feet and leotards and vomit. Eleanor says she can't take it and stays in the hall. Liz is all wrapped up in blankets and not in the dress I told her to wear for tonight. Her roommate, Frankie, isn't in the bunk bed above her.

"Why aren't you ready?" I say. "And it smells terrible in here."

"It's too cold to go out," she says, looking up at me with hollowed eyes, wrapping herself tighter, and clicking on her heating pad.

"You sick?" I ask, not wanting to deal with the fact that this is all something else. The sudden weight loss. Well, not so sudden when you think about it. But I don't want to think about it. At all. And she's been bragging to me about it. Sending me little texts when she meets her goals.

"Yeah," she says. "I'm so tired." I tell her that I'll bring her some tea. "Stay in bed, okay? You need the night off."

After delivering Liz's tea, Eleanor and I take the long route out of the building—down the elevator for a basement visit first. I avoid any talk about Liz. I can't add another bad thing to think about to the growing pile in my head.

"Can't we just go straight outside?" Eleanor complains, already limping in my expensive heels. She tugs at my five-hundred-dollar dress. "We do this every time."

"This is the best part," I say. "And I need it, okay?"

The coed student lounge is full—some watch TV, Henri and a few boys play pool, others play air hockey, and Alec strums his guitar in the corner.

Will spots me and sighs loudly, which gets Alec's attention. I blow Will a kiss. He used to go with me when I went out. It used to be all five of us—Alec, Liz, Will, El, and me—out in a little pack. Now I can't stand the thought of him going anywhere with me. He frowns, looking the same as he did the first day I met him. New kid sobbing outside of the boys' ballet class after being caught by Mr. K in pointe shoes. I'd consoled him. That reality is so far away.

I bump Henri's pool cue on purpose when I pass by.

"Pardon," he says, then steps so close to me I can smell the chocolate he must've just eaten.

"Move," I say. "You're in my way."

"No." His eyes scan me from top to bottom. "You stepped in my way. Made me miss my shot."

Eleanor grabs my hand. "Let's go," she says, trying to pull me away.

I glance back at her, only to see if Alec is watching. And he is, his hand frozen on his guitar, which makes me happy. He still cares. I turn back to Henri. I put a hand on his chest, and push a little. "Are you going to make me stand here all night?" Instead of irritation, I decide to flirt and add a smile, enjoying the whole thing.

"Would that be such a bad thing?" he says, his lilt teasing. "Or maybe you're going to invite me to go with you? Isn't that what girls like you do?" He takes my hand from his chest and holds it, squeezing it a little, until I snatch it away. I step forward, planning to walk through him. He's nothing. He's nobody here. Dancing a *pas* with me will make him something.

"You don't know anything about me or this place," I say, loud enough for everyone to hear.

"I've seen your type before. Plenty of you at Paris Opera," he says. "Yes, you're nothing special. In fact, I know all about you." He leans close to my ear. "Especially what you did to Cassandra. Pretending to be her friend."

I snap back and feel my cheeks redden. I give him a look that screams *You don't know anything.* I hope my face doesn't betray me, doesn't reveal that I know what he's talking about.

Alec walks past us without even stopping, without even checking if I'm okay. I follow his back with my eyes, not understanding why he didn't stop to help. Even Eleanor shifts away from us, leaving me cornered by Henri.

"I know a lot, Bette Abney. I know lots of things you probably wouldn't want me to know. And I plan to prove it. Show everyone who you are." He lets his fingers graze my collarbone.

"Don't touch me," I say.

Does he really know the things I did?

I can't seem to move.

He laughs. "Your secrets are safe with me," he says. Then he adds, "Well, maybe not."

Eleanor bucks up. Finally. She grabs my shaky hand and pulls me away from Henri. In a daze, I let her drag me all the way to the school's side door entrance. I don't even put my coat on before we step out into the cold November air.

"What's wrong?" Eleanor says, but I ignore her, my thoughts haunted by Henri's accusation, by Cassie and what I did. I sink down to the stoop, my legs weak and wobbly. All I know is, if I'm going down for this, I won't be alone. We were all in on it together.

Last year, I thought it would be a brilliant idea to get close to Cassie. After all, she's Alec's cousin from the Royal Ballet School, here to take on New York, she'd always said with her fake British accent, thinking it was cute. Not just a normal new girl who'd be easy to get rid of. But she was too good, and it got so hard to watch her come in and dance the parts I wanted, the parts I'd been training for at this school since I was five.

In April, I sat along the edges of studio B, watching Cassie's *pas* run-through for the spring ballet *La Sylphide* with Scott Betancourt, a senior boy likely to be offered an apprenticeship with the company. My mother made sure I got to be there, probably after accusing Mr. Lucas and Mr. K of preferential treatment. She always knew how to throw her weight around in just the right ways.

Scott labored when lifting Cassie over his head that day because she was all clenched up, stomach muscles braced and flinching at his touch.

"Let him hold you," Morkie had yelled. Cassie tried to adapt. She wasn't as pretty when she was worried. I tried not to smirk, fought with my lips to stay relaxed. I tried not to enjoy that she wasn't as good as the teachers always said. That I could've been cast. Should've been cast. I liked seeing Cassandra's eyes get all big and watery with confusion and worry.

Morkie clapped her hands in an angry beat along to the music. "Ballet is woman," she'd hollered, and continued to scold Cassie about letting Scott support her in the flying shoulder lift and hold her low in the hips because she was so tall. "He's trying to make you look beautiful. But you don't trust him."

Will slipped into the studio while Cassie and Scott resumed their battle to dance like soul mates. He'd sat down next to me with a huge smile on his face, and I knew he wanted me to ask. I'd thought about not giving in, but I needed to know what he was doing here. "Why are you in here?"

"Mr. K says I get to understudy this *pas*." The words tumbled out so fast he was almost screaming them.

"When did that happen? You didn't tell me." He was supposed to be one of my best friends. I would expect a text, at least, right after he found out.

"Two days ago," he said. "I didn't want to mess it up. Make sure it was for real first."

"I'm so happy for you," I said, feeling a knot of jealousy tangle in my stomach. I glanced at the glass wall where Liz stood in the hall, glaring at Cassie, and thought through all of our midnight chats, where Liz, Eleanor, and I plotted to mess with her a little. "Is it all official? The casting?"

"Yup," he said, pushing down into a deeper stretch.

"Can't be taken away? Not a 'let's see how rehearsal goes' thing in case you mess up?" I whispered, an idea storming through me.

"Why?" He sat up, and I pulled him closer. We'd spent so much time curled up like this with our secrets and gossip and machinations. I smoothed down a hair sticking up on his head. And I remembered what I loved about him the most: he was solid and thoughtful, and certain. He would always help me.

"Favor?" I said, in just the right way, the way that always got him to do whatever I needed him to. "You owe me for getting you out of that fiasco with your mom catching you with Ben, and that other time when you needed Vicodin and—"

He frowned, and pushed a hand over my mouth, annoyed. "Okay, okay. What?" he said, a little pissed now. I bit his palm.

"Drop her," I'd whispered quickly, before I could lose my nerve. "Just once. And not too hard. Just enough."

His nose crinkled a little, so that I knew he was judging me.

"Injuries change cast lists," I'd said, sort of not believing what I actually was saying. Like I'd stepped into some alternate version of my life, where I could just do whatever I wanted. "You owe me. Your mom even thinks we're dating. I still text with her, you know?" The silence stretched between us so long I thought he'd never say anything again. That I'd finally done it. Ruined us. But somehow, I kept that icy calm, that sheer force that the women in my family have, even though I was seething inside. He shouldn't have even hesitated. I patted his leg in just the right way. My way. "Please."

My hands were all shaky, and I gazed around for Morkie and Viktor. They hovered right beside the piano.

Will started to speak. I railroaded through his response. "C'mon, you have to." I managed a smile to soften it. Alec always said I'm beautiful when I smile. Cassie rushed over and plopped down beside us before he could answer me. Will and I swallowed the entire conversation, and I felt lost, afloat, unsure of my footing. Cassie whined for a while about drinking and being "off." I pretended to sympathize, but come on! She was the only sophomore Level B girl to get a solo. I didn't feel bad for her at all.

Then Morkie called them to the center. Will looked back at me, and for a minute I wanted to tell him not to do it, and tell him I was sorry for bringing up his homophobic mother. But my mouth just hung open. I had to dance her part. I had to be like Adele, a ballet prodigy. And this could make it happen, make all my dreams come true.

The moment Cassie fell out of Will's arms, I'd flashed her a smile that was so goddamn pretty she wouldn't ever forget who was on top, who she should thank, who she should've been afraid of.

The memory sends shivers down my spine.

I'd had nightmares that evening. The kind that came with screams and flung blankets and a desperation so deep I woke Eleanor up. She'd brought me water and a cool washcloth, like I was her kid and not her friend. Even when I was hurt or sick or panicked, my mother never did that for me. Just having Eleanor in the room with me wasn't enough, though. I needed someone to share the responsibility. I needed to take off a tiny bit of the weight of what I'd done. I couldn't very well tell Alec. He was so good, so right all the time, and not to mention related to Cassie. He'd hate me. He'd never speak to me again. I couldn't bring it up with Will. He made it clear that our conversation never happened. That it'd been an accident.

So I told Eleanor. Begged her to tell me it was okay. Made

her promise, on her life, on her reputation at the school, that she wouldn't tell anyone else, ever. I had never been so honest with someone, but it seemed like the only way out of the guilt and panic. She hugged me and said she understood. I cried into Eleanor's pillow. Slept much more soundly in Eleanor's bed with her spooning me. We never spoke of it again. I waited every day for a month to get pulled into the office for what I did. But it never happened.

The memory won't go away. Eleanor squeezes my hand and whispers, "Henri doesn't know anything, Bette." And even if she's lying, it makes me feel a little better, like no one will ever find out.

I let Eleanor take me back upstairs to our room where I curl up with that memory and a white pill to try to erase it all.

15.

June

AFTER REHEARSAL, WE'RE ALL HERDED into the assembly room, which is an offshoot of the lobby. The room is full of skylight windows and reminds me of a solarium my mom took me to once. The whole night sky spreads above us and I could find it pretty if I wasn't too busy fixating on Nurse Connie, Morkie, and Mr. K. They whisper in front of us, exchanging glances that mean we are about to have a serious conversation. Around me, everyone rehashes rehearsal, but I can't. I want to know what they're about to say. It must be big, since they didn't let us go straight to the café for a snack, then homework, and then bed. They hate to disrupt our evening routine. Maybe a casting change?

I don't like surprises.

Gigi plops down next to me. She's twitchy and agitated, and I wonder if she's discovered her medical report in the Light yet. If she knows I took it, and just isn't saying anything. That was sloppy of me. The last time I checked the closet, it wasn't there anymore. Someone took it down. I gaze at her chest and wonder how her heart could be so messed up and it not show. I didn't really understand the terms, but looking at the EKG, it was pretty obvious that something's really wrong with her. And I sort of feel a little bad for a second. Just one.

"Why are we meeting?" she asks, pulling her wild hair from its bun, and surrounding me with the scent of the greasy crap she puts in it. Coconut oil, I think. It makes my empty stomach heave.

I shrug in reply, not actually wanting to talk to her. I turn my attention back to the front, back to Mr. K.

The Korean girls sidle past us. Sei-Jin pauses right above me. "Oh, don't play coy, June. Don't ignore your roomie." She winks at Gigi like they're old friends. "You know exactly why we're meeting."

"Go away, Sei-Jin," I say, not acknowledging her presence with eye contact.

"It's ballerinas like you that make them waste all of our time," she adds before plopping down not too far off. I squirm at her taunt.

Mr. K claps. Three hard ones, his signature. "Please heed the seriousness of what we're going to say tonight. It is of the utmost importance. You are dancers. Your bodies are your instruments. They are sacred, and must be cared for as such. And I will not hesitate in making the necessary changes if you fail to do so. And I have. Liz is gone."

Everyone looks around for her, like he's lying. I watch Bette put a hand over her mouth, like even she didn't know.

"She will not be returning, and we will be selecting someone to dance her role, Arabian Coffee. We want to see who can rise to the occasion. And we're considering shuffling some people around, and adding the Harlequin Doll to the cast list just as we did last year. So don't get too comfortable in your part."

Gripes and mumbles explode through the room. He waves his hand in the air to silence everyone. "The moment you think you're on top is the moment you've lost your passion. Might as well retire."

Then he puts his arm out to Nurse Connie, who steps forward.

My stomach gripes. I bite my lips and scratch at my tights. This can't be good.

"We would like to make a few announcements regarding health before opening night of *The Nutcracker*," Nurse Connie says. Her voice doesn't have the lovely depth of Mr. K's, so the sound is anemic in comparison. Forty ballerinas groan and lose interest. "We all know this, of course, but I'd like to reiterate that the rule still stands. If you fall underweight you will be sent home. No questions asked. No excuses made. Underweight dancers will not be tolerated. Even very talented ballerinas. As I'm sure you can all see."

I prefer Mr. K's straightforward address to Nurse Connie's pointedly vague one. Still, what she is going for works. My stomach drops a little. I start to sweat behind my ears. Liz is gone. And it could've been me. I was close again, last week, to falling under. I can feel Nurse Connie's eyes fixed only on me.

"I've brought along my trusty food pyramid poster," she continues, and I can't help it—I sigh. Even with her eyes right on me, gauging my response, I can't muster up the appropriate, thoughtful, curious expression. Not again.

Nurse Connie and Morkie exchange another pained look, and Nurse Connie goes on to talk us through the food pyramid herself. She also has posters for BMI and height-to-weight ratio and the evils of laxatives and diet teas. She describes what happens to girls who starve themselves: the loss of hair and bone density, peach fuzz on cheeks, kidney failure, tooth decay. The consequences crash around in my head like train wrecks and car accidents. I focus on my hands, blocking it all out.

Morkie just stands there with her arms crossed over her chest, neither endorsing nor disagreeing. I always get the feeling Morkie and Nurse Connie are in a silent battle with each other over our bodies. Over my body. And every time, Morkie wins. Ballet is most important. What the Russians want—beautiful dancers— trumps everything. Unless you go too far like Liz. Unless you get out of control.

I tune it out. Gigi does not. She is scratching away at a pad of paper taking notes. Notes! A little bit of pink tongue peeks out of her mouth as she scribbles, and I decide that I don't just find her annoying, I actually hate her. All the nice moments we've had, the times where I thought we might be able to be friends, are gone. Each one of her pen strokes echoes, making me flinch.

It must be half an hour before Nurse Connie packs up her posters and finishes handing out pamphlets. She looks each of

us in the eye when she gives us the little packet of insane bro-
chures she's brought for us. I do not imagine it when she lingers
next to me.

"Please look these over, June," she says in a fake whisper. If
she were a real nurse, she wouldn't accuse me in public like that.
There has to be some law against that. "You still have some work
to do." She pats me on the shoulder.

I count to twenty. She waits for me to look up. Like she won't
move unless I do. My makeup runs a little, and I give in and look
up, so she can see my eyes and move on.

I fly out of there, ignoring Gigi's questions about whether I'm
headed back to the room or not. I dash into the closest studio to
get my head together. I can't let anyone see me like this. They
might think Nurse Connie's speech had something to do with
me. I have to keep it together. I have to make them see that if
they're going to give out a role or shift things around then they
should move me.

I rest my leg on the barre, stretching deep as I breathe in and
out until the tinges in my muscles disappear. I think about Liz
standing on those scales, about the number that flashed. It had
to be super small. And I fight the urge to want to be as small.
I wonder how long it took her to pack her things. If she goes to
another dance school, she'll have to tell them what happened,
they'll call Mr. K, and she might never get to dance again. This
kind of thing haunts you. I shudder. I hear Sei-Jin and the other
girls giggle as they shift past the studio's glass walls and open
door. Their conversation drifts in.

"I need to hurry up and shower. Jayhe's almost here. He's

gonna kill me for being late," Sei-Jin says loud enough for everyone to hear. Typical.

I hear the other girls fawning over her and her big plans. On a weeknight, no less. This impresses them. They follow her mindlessly, like little ducks in a row, gasping about his hair, and his perfect teeth, and how strong he is, despite not being a dancer. Idiots. I used to be jealous of her after she started dating Jayhe. And I'm sure she knew it. She paraded him through the school. But really, I knew she was putting on a show. I knew I had the power to blow her perfect little life to smithereens. I just chose not to. Because of the friendship we had once. Because of what we used to be. *Jeol chin.* Best friends.

Once they're gone, I take the elevator down to the basement and to the place where Sei-Jin always meets Jayhe to sneak him into the building. Past the rec room is a weight room that has a side door that leads out to the school Dumpsters. A service staircase and an emergency exit with a broken alarm. That's where he'll be waiting. All of eighth grade, it used to be just she and I waiting for him, peeping out into the dark for his head to appear. She used to tell me how she didn't really like him at first and how she was just dating him because her mother wanted her to. She also used to date one of the white boys. Shane, who graduated last year. Jayhe never knew about that.

I guess she loves him now. Maybe.

I perch near the window, waiting to see him. I don't know exactly what I'm going to say, and this whole sabotage plan is starting to feel half-baked. I should've plotted it out. I'm too shaky. But this opportunity couldn't be better. Before I can rehearse the conversation in my head, I see a shadow in the dark and then his face. His hair is shaggy and black and the black-rimmed glasses he always wears drift down his nose. A rush of heat hits me. I remember how it felt to *like* him.

He spots me in the window and scrunches his nose up, like he's confused. I open the door for him.

"Hey," I say.

"Hey," he says, sliding past me, careful so we don't touch. "What are you doing down here? Where's Sei-Jin?"

"She's still upstairs," I say. "We had a late meeting after rehearsal."

"Oh" is all he says, shifting back and forth from one foot to the other.

"I was down here lifting weights," I lie.

He laughs. "Seriously? What can you bench?" he jokes, his voice husky and teasing. It sends an unexpected shiver up my spine. He's being weirdly nice. "I bet you can't even lift fifty pounds," he says, a grin spreading across his face. "I bet you only weigh fifty pounds."

His words hit, and for some reason I can't control the tears that pour down my cheeks and the sob that escapes my mouth. I can't remember the last time I cried, and the thought of that makes me cry even more. This is not part of the plan.

"I'm sorry, June. I didn't— I was just—" He pulls me into a hug, his body warm and strong. For some reason, this catches me off guard. I bury my face in his hoodie, let the spicy scent of his cologne mellow the shakiness out of me.

He keeps apologizing and trying to get me to calm down,

but I stay there. He asks me if he should go get someone or call my mom. I don't answer. So then he just stops talking, strokes my hair, and squeezes his arms tight around me, as if he's done it a thousand times before. So tight I think I could disappear. He somehow takes the sharpness out of me.

I look up at him, even though I know my makeup's a mess and I'm a mess. I want to ask him, "Why did you disappear? Why did you choose her over me? Weren't we friends? Did you believe the things she told you about me?"

"My *halmeoni* asks about you all the time," he says, mimicking her soft accent: "'Where's that little girl with the too-light hair?'"

She would always say my hair was unusually light for a Korean. A pale, ashy brown. I didn't have the heart to tell her that my dad was white. He doesn't answer any of the questions swirling through my head, but he makes me smile.

We laugh, and I hiccup. He wipes a tear from my cheek. And I feel like I'm that little girl in his basement again.

"Ballet makes you all so sad. You never used to be like this."

"How was I?" I ask. "How did I used to be?"

"Bright," he says, which is a strange word. But it feels right. Before he can clarify, I lean up and kiss him. My first kiss with a boy. Quick and urgent, like he might disappear altogether, like he might fall out of my grasp again. But he doesn't. His mouth is warm and tastes like a cinnamon stick. He doesn't push me away or pull me close, but I feel his mouth press into mine a little, and I know he's just kissed me back.

16.

Gigi

SATURDAY MORNING LIGHT FLICKERS THROUGH the window and, in response, my butterflies flap their wings, their tiny shadows flitting across the windowsill. I remember when my dad brought home my very first terrarium.

"They're for good luck," he said, placing the glass box in my bedroom window with his big brown hands. I was eight and on bed rest for exhaustion, spending days and nights in my nightgown gazing at the trolleys chugging past my window on the tracks.

"Why do I need luck?" I'd pressed my nose close to the terrarium, wondering if I could train them to perch in my hair using my curls as twigs.

"Everybody needs a little." He adjusted the container while I watched the monarchs flutter around inside. "Some people believe butterflies are the souls of the dead. Those who have come back to us."

I gawked at those tiny creatures and their round eyes, wondering if one was Granny or my third-grade teacher, Mrs. Charlotte. I wondered if that's what people became after death.

Even now, I'm thinking of Cassie, who of course I never knew, and who isn't dead, but maybe in a place that's worse—being unable to dance. I thump the glass and greet the twelve little ones who came across the country with me. I pull two flowers from the congratulatory bouquet Mama and Dad sent me after I finally told them about landing the Sugar Plum Fairy role, and place them inside the cage. The monarchs tickle my arm and land on the petals, ready to sip their nectar.

"Okay, little ones," I say to them, then realize June's still in bed. Across the room, I hear her gentle breathing. I'm shocked she's still asleep. Not like June at all. She's usually up and in the studio before me. She doesn't believe in sleeping on weekends. And I've gotten used to having weekend mornings to myself in the room.

I check my phone. A tiny hope floats up when I tap on the screen. Maybe there'll be a text from Alec. I sigh. He's broken up with Bette, but I don't know what that means for us. We've texted a lot, and practiced our *pas*, but nothing else really.

There's only one message from Aunt Leah: *Doctor's Appt @ 9:30. Your mom scheduled it. Sorry! Coming @ 8:30.*

I set the phone back, disappointed. On my desk there's a baggie of tiny origami turkeys with funny facial expressions. I look up at the calendar on my wall. You can lose track of the days here, your focus singular and intense. Thanksgiving is next week.

Who left this? I quietly rummage some more, searching for a note or message.

"It's from Alec," June whispers.

I flinch and don't turn around. She hates being woken up.

"Sorry," I whisper quickly, but she rolls over without a response. I clamp my hand over my mouth to hold back my smile. I touch the tiny turkeys, running my fingers along each crease and fold. I wish I could share this with her. When I first got here, I wanted to be her friend so bad, but she didn't say more than two words to me. She opens and closes like a morning glory. And lately, she's been closed up tight, not wanting to grab meals together or rehearse.

I leave the room. I shower, unable to stop thinking about Alec. I run my fingers over my lips, remembering our kiss in the Light closet. The thought of his kisses gets my heart pounding, but it feels good. I don't try to calm it down. I don't try to control my breathing. I close my eyes as water hits my shoulder blades and wonder what it would be like for his lips to find that same spot.

I have never wanted any boy before, not really, and definitely not someone as dangerous to want as Alec. The feeling is so strong this morning, I worry that I won't be able to keep zipping it in. It has breath and life of its own. Besides, I don't know that I want to stop it. At home, guys tried to hang out with me— redheaded Robert, who came to all my birthday parties despite being the only boy there; skater-boy Noah, who asked me to the eighth-grade dance; and Jamal, who left love notes in my locker all through tenth grade. But I never paid any attention to them, running off to my dance classes and private lessons. But Alec makes me pay attention to him. Even though I know I should worry about Bette's reaction.

I go to the RA office on the fourth floor, where I'll wait for Aunt Leah, though I'm sure she'll be late, like always. Will is sprawled out on the far couch with an icepack on his knee.

"What happened to you?" I ask.

He doesn't open his eyes at first. So I repeat my question. Then he turns his head and says, "Prevention." He adjusts the ice. "I ice every day regardless of injury to keep inflammation down." His voice is sharp and moody.

"Oh," is all I can manage to say. No wonder he is such a flawless dancer.

"I'm surprised you're up," I say to fill the quiet.

"Why? I'm always up early," Will mumbles. He's Alec's best friend, and that's all I know about him. And despite the fact that he's amazing in rehearsal, Mr. K never looks pleased with him. "Where you going, anyway?" he adds, sizing up my jeans, sweater, and coat.

I flush, and for a second ponder telling him the truth. But that would be stupid. "Brunch. With my aunt." It's not a lie, really. We actually will probably get brunch after my doctor's appointment. "Do all the boys get up this early on a Saturday?" I try, in the hopes that he'll mention something about Alec, and if he's up, too. He smiles in that preparatory way that will surely lead to a juicy story or some information.

"You like him, don't you?" he asks.

"Like who?" I say, knowing full well he means Alec. But Will is not exactly my friend, and I'm not exactly sure it's safe to say anything at all to anyone.

"Don't pretend now," he says. "He tells me everything."

I blush and look away.

"So, do you like him?"

"Maybe," I finally say.

"You're not like Bette, so I like you. I could get to like you and him together." He shifts the icepack around on his knee, and plays with his hair. June calls him "Carrot Top" in private. "Yeah. Maybe the two of you won't be so bad."

"Okay," I say, not sure how to respond to that.

"Bette's a bitch, you know. She's, like, empty. Seriously empty. And you know she's the one who wrote that message on the mirror. I'd recognize that too-pink Chanel lipstick anywhere. She can't get enough of it. She thinks it's so cute."

"Really?" I say, even though I know it was her.

"Be honest . . . come on. You can tell me. You know you think it was her. We all know." Will is trying to look concerned, but he isn't hiding his eager smile. "It's her signature. Trust me. Any and all pranks lead back to her."

The confirmation makes sense. And it gets me wondering: if she wrote the message on the mirror, then she must've left the picture of Henri and me, and my stolen medical report in the Light closet. I ponder confronting her. "Why does she act like that?"

"I can't even say that it's 'cause Bette's so damaged. Or blame it on her messed-up family. The one thing about this place"—he looks all around, ready to share his secret—"is that it brings out the worst shit. The worst shit in all of us. Even I've done stuff I'm not proud of." He moves the icepack to his other knee. "Maybe it's ballet. I don't know. There's only room for one star. And everybody else doesn't matter. They blend into the background, like stage ornaments. Bette has always been that star here. Set up by her sister. A legacy, a done deal. Well, until you came around. I like it. You're different."

There's that word again. "Because I'm black?" I straight out ask, hating that being *different* can be a code word for being black, for something that isn't white.

"No"—he shakes his head and adds a laugh—"because you're not the type to take someone down just to be on top. Your dancing is, like, that good. You don't need to. Not desperate. Not Bette."

"Then why does everybody love her?" I ask. "Even Alec."

He releases the longest sigh I've ever heard. "They've been together forever. Since we came here. I've been stuck with them as a *couple* since I was six."

I imagine Bette and Alec as six-year-olds, blond and little and perfect for each other, and my stomach twists. I don't want to compete with her in another arena; it's already too much in the studio and onstage. I'm being so stupid. He and I don't match. I should stop this crush. Stay focused.

Will talks more about them as kids. I picture Mama's wall of photos of me: fuzzy curls, brown skin, sun-kissed cheeks, little hippie dresses caked with mud and sand, and Mama's paint all over my hands. I'm not the girl who's supposed to be with him. I don't look like I fit perfectly by his side, like Bette. Alec and I are mismatched puzzle pieces.

"I know he . . . thinks the world of you, Gigi." He's working his face into gentle kindness, but he's bitter and pleased right under the surface. His eyes are bright and the edges of his mouth keep twitching up. "What's it all like?" he asks.

"What's what like?" I look at him again, confused.

"Having him like you?" he says.

I don't have an answer. I don't understand the look on his face. I try to say something. Nothing but a weird mutter comes out.

The phone at the desk rings. An RA comes down the hall and grabs it from the desk. "Gigi, your aunt is coming up," she says.

"Just be careful here. Careful with Alec. Careful with everybody," he says, then leaves me sitting there, head buzzing with all his revelations and the echo of a warning, along with the trail of his too-flowery cologne. A chill settles in to my stomach.

Aunt Leah appears in an elevator. "You ready, kid?"

She hugs me, squeezing my arms, rocking back and forth—like always. Her hair smells like Mama's curls, full of shea butter and citrus. In this moment, I miss home and Sunday morning breakfasts, the smell of my dad's coffee, and listening to him read the paper to my mother while she sketches.

Aunt Leah signs me out and we walk to the subway. She holds my hand, just the way she did when I was a little girl, and I let her. Her hand looks just like Mama's—thin brown fingers and two freckles in one of her smooth, round nail beds.

I can smell the park and wish we could go there instead of to Mama's doctor friend, who agreed to examine me on a Saturday.

Mothers push strollers. The smell of roasted chestnuts wafts from the vendors as we near the subway entrance. We enter the station. Aunt Leah squeezes my hand to get my attention. "Lost in a daydream? You're quiet today. Too quiet. How's school? Ballet? Boys?" She swipes me through the turnstile and we wait on the platform for the next train. "Are there even any straight boys?"

I laugh. "Of course," I say. "That's a stereotype." I think of Alec and Henri, how they're pushed by Mr. K to exude that extreme Russian masculinity. And I think about Will, and the flack he gets for being gay. The fact that he might never dance the lead role, not at the conservatory. No matter how good he is. I worry that maybe some people would say the same about me.

"And how are you feeling these days? You know, in class, after intense exercise?"

"Fine. Normal." I keep my answers short. I hear the worry in her question. My parents call me enough with their anxieties. "I'm fine," I say as the subway train approaches. The noise drowns out her follow-up questions.

We travel down to Times Square. People zoom by and fill the streets and sidewalks. I get bumped from the left and right, trying to stay in step with Aunt Leah. Billboards blaze with thousands of lights. I gawk at the Broadway theater signs. I still haven't seen a show. I haven't seen much of the city, in fact—just the area surrounding school and Aunt Leah's Brooklyn apartment. She keeps asking me to do things with her, to explore, but class and rehearsals keep me busy. And Alec, too, of course. But she doesn't know that.

I follow her through the throng of people. Men and women

hold out goods for me to buy and others ask for change. The crowd has a frenetic pulse and the tide pushes us both into the heart of Times Square. We turn off Broadway. When we approach the doctor's office, I can already see the machines, feel the cold chest goop, the iodine making its way through my veins.

My palms start to sweat and my heart races. This is my first doctor's appointment since I left California in August. And that was just a checkup before leaving for the conservatory.

"It'll be over before you know it," Aunt Leah says, patting my back. "I promise."

Once we're inside, I block out everything.

"Your aunt will wait outside the door while you change into the paper gown," the nurse says. "Then Dr. Khanna will be right in to see you." She pulls the crinkly paper garment out of a drawer, laying it on the examination table. I cringe at the sight of it. It doesn't cover a thing.

"Make sure the open part faces front," she reminds me, then closes the door.

After I've undressed, the doctor comes in, and then Aunt Leah. "You want me in here, love?" she asks.

I nod. She takes a seat along the perimeter of the room.

"Hello, Giselle. I'm Dr. Khanna," the man in the white coat says. He rubs his thick black beard.

I bunch my top closed before shaking his hand.

"Nice to meet you," he says, while warming up his stethoscope. "So you're a ballerina?"

"Yeah," I answer.

He motions for me to uncross my arms so he can listen to my heart. "May I?"

I clamp them to my sides so the paper top doesn't open. He places the cold stethoscope against my skin.

"Your heartbeat is accelerating. Are you nervous?"

I nod.

"There is no need to be. You must've had these exams a million times." He pats my shoulder. I've had one every six months since I was born.

"Please relax." He grabs the tube of goop from the counter. I smell the latex as he nears. He squeezes out a dollop. "You're going to have to open your gown a bit more."

My cheeks flame. I look at the ceiling and let my arms drop. The gown top opens and I feel the cool air on my breasts. He spreads the goop on the top of my chest. Whenever he comes too close to my breasts, my stomach clenches. Then he places electrodes—they look like mini suction cups—on my chest. He pushes buttons on the machine beside the examination table.

The screen lights up like a computer and I see my heartbeats flash in peaks and valleys. Numbers flash, and the machine makes a squishy sound, a whooshing that reminds me of a San Francisco breeze, only electrified. The doctor makes small talk about ballet and the last show he's seen—*Swan Lake*—but I hear nothing but the machine's whooshes. I try to stay calm, so I don't get in trouble. If my heartbeat is too irregular, he'll say I can't dance. That my heart is having trouble. That it's too much of a risk. That it's too dangerous.

I hear my dad's deep voice: "Bean, you have to be careful.

You're not like everyone else. And that can be good and bad."

I was diagnosed as a baby, had surgery, but didn't really understand it all until I was four years old and trying out dance for the first time. My parents enrolled me in all the classes: jazz, tap, and ballet, but in a particularly jubilant tap class where we ran around clicking and stomping our metal-clad feet on the ground, I turned red and fell to the ground. The teachers didn't think anything of it, just gave me a glass of water and told me to sit the next one out, but they let my parents know I was all worn out when they came to pick me up. I remember Mama scooping me right up and taking me straight to the hospital, not even waiting for my dad to follow or get in the car. He had to take a taxi to meet us there. I read *Highlights* magazine for hours and wailed when the doctors put cool metal tools against my skin.

It seems like a long time ago, but I'm the same little girl right now.

Dr. Khanna clicks a button. I can't hear my heart anymore. "Okay, all done. Good job, Giselle. You can get dressed and come to my office where I'll print out your EKG results." He lets me get dressed alone, and when I go to his office, he's all business and I'm myself again: covered up and calm.

"Well, Giselle, I don't think I need to remind you that your ventricular septal defect is quite serious if not watched," the doctor begins.

I don't know why he doesn't just call it what it is. *The hole in my heart is bad.*

"Today your heart shows a bit of distress, so I recommend you lessen your stress levels and decrease strenuous activities—"

"I have to dance," I say.

"Approximately how many hours a day do you dance?"

I run through all the hours in my head: morning ballet, character and repertoire, and rehearsal. "About six hours." After my answer comes out and I see the look on their faces, I know I should've lied.

"Well . . ." He pauses. "It's quite unusual for someone with your condition to be as athletic as you are. It's almost dangerous, Miss Stewart. You should be checking in with the nurse after each block of dancing." He shakes his head. "Six hours . . ." He hands me the EKG report, telling me to give it to the nurse at school for my file. I fold it and put it in my pocket, planning to do just the opposite. Someone is nosing around in her office. Someone has looked in my file. Nothing is safe.

"But I'm not leaping and jumping the whole time—sometimes we're just at the barre or stretching," I say.

"Still, that being said, you need to make sure you are being careful. With you doing so much exercise on a daily basis, even when you're not, you could still have a palpitation. It's risky behavior for someone with your condition." He gets up and walks to his shelf. "I'd like you to wear a heart monitor." He flashes a small device that reminds me of my dad's stopwatch.

"I . . . I don't want to wear it," I blurt out.

"Gigi . . . ," Aunt Leah starts, her face full of shock and disappointment at my outburst. "If the doctor says you have to, then you do." She addresses Dr. Khanna. "I know her parents will fully be behind this."

"I'm afraid she really needs to," Dr. Khanna says, setting the monitor. "Just to be safe." He pushes buttons and I hear a chirp. He explains how to turn it on and off and he attaches it to my wrist.

My attention wavers in and out as I think of wearing this around my wrist, having to explain it to Morkie, having to make sure it doesn't beep during class.

I fight angry tears as we leave the office. My new monitor firmly in place around my wrist. Aunt Leah and I don't speak the whole trip home, and when we get to the dorms, I give her the smallest pinch of a kiss on the cheek and then practically sprint to my room. I face-plant on the bed, feeling the monitor press into my wrist, and stare at my little butterflies for a while, glad June's out for the moment. I can't trust anyone with this.

I won't be different from the others. I won't let it be the next thing that makes me stick out. Black girl. Black girl with a heart monitor. Black girl who has to be careful. Black girl who shouldn't be a dancer. I get up, take off the monitor, and tuck it into my desk drawer, where no one will ever find it. Where I can forget it even exists.

17.

Bette

I CAN'T STOP LOOKING AT the snow falling outside the windows. There's a kind of perfect symmetry to the first snowfall coming in the first week of December, on the first night of dress rehearsal. I had a pill just an hour ago, so my focus is intensely directed wherever I decide to put it, which right now is on the tiny white glimmers of hope whirling outside the massive picture windows in the Koch Theater lobby. Guests drift by, and I feel their curious eyes on me, wondering what one of the dancers is doing out here, instead of getting ready.

Everyone else is backstage, but they're not missing me. Besides, Mr. K isn't even here yet, so there's no rush, no need to give in to the anxious flutters flooding my system, no need to fan the fire by forcing myself to stay in the totally cramped dressing rooms.

I used to love dancing at Lincoln Center, but Alec has kind of ruined it for me. Usually, he'd be out here with me, or we'd be holed up in a dark corner exchanging backrubs and ballet gossip. Alec can gossip with the best of them, and always has the juiciest news from the trustees and teachers. When Mr. K's divorce went viral a few years ago, he was the first to know. Which meant I, of course, was second.

No sign of Alec today. He really hit the off switch this time. Avoids my texts, calls, nudges on social media. I faked sick and avoided the Lucas family's annual Thanksgiving Day dinner at his Hamptons house, even though my drunk and pissy mother almost had a heart attack about it because we had to have dinner at home for once. Will was all too happy to blast pictures of himself waiting for the jitney to head out there.

I try not to think about it as I use the windowsill as a makeshift barre, extending my leg, pressing my nose to my knee. Passersby wrapped in scarves and puffy coats and knee-high boots barely glance in, uninterested. I can't compete with the magic of the flurry of a first snow, even in my full Snow Queen regalia.

I check my cell for the millionth time. Thinking maybe Alec will text something other than "Good luck tonight." Something more like, "I miss you. I made a mistake. I should've never broken up with you."

I toss my cell phone into my bag, not caring if the screen breaks. There's nothing from Adele either. She's on a plane headed to Berlin for a dance gala exhibition. My mother hasn't even called to wish me good luck. She said, over Thanksgiving dinner, there's no point in getting all excited about something that doesn't really matter. Then she asked Adele to pass the sweet potatoes. Adele had a pained look on her face the whole time, and kept apologizing for my mother, which only made it feel worse.

Not to mention, I can still feel those sweet potatoes on my hips. I ask my mother not to make them every year, but every year she still does because Alec's little sister, Sophie, loves them, and I have no control over the deliciousness of maple syrup and marshmallows masking the actual taste of vegetables. I have so little sugar otherwise. Just the look of the casserole beckons me: that autumn-orange color, the sweet swirls of mush drooping from the barely there burned clouds of marshmallows. I shiver, running my hands over my hips, my thighs, imagining the sugar attaching itself to me just because I dared to delight in the memory of that airy, sweet succulence. I want to take another pill, will away the thoughts. But I took the last of them earlier.

Digging in my bag, I pull out my phone again. Still nothing from Alec. I text my dealer. Really, he's not mine, but rather this guy who lives in the neighborhood and makes a killing off desperate ballerinas. I know I should stop. I've seen it all before. Too much time hanging around the company dancers' apartments with Adele, watching them balance all the stress and pressure with a mix of cigarettes, pills, diets, pain meds, and tiny salads. But I need this right now. I ask him for more Adderall and to surprise me with something a little stronger. He likes the flirty subtext of my message, and I know he'll give me a few things for free.

After the dealer distraction, I can't help but give in and text Alec. *I miss you.*

Then, of course, I can't take my eyes from my cell phone.

I do halfhearted *pliés* and can just make out my reflection in the window: wrapped in white and silver. He'd still think I was beautiful, I think. Maybe.

My phone dings in response. *You'll do great, B*, he texts.

Not enough to give me hope, exactly, but more than enough to make me want him immediately.

Can we talk? I type in quickly, before I have a chance to worry about it sounding needy.

There's no response. My heart turns into a brick and drops to the floor. Every other December dress rehearsal since we were little, Alec has shown up with a bouquet of paper roses and a kiss. Even when he was too little to know how good it made me feel, he'd put a hand on each of my cheeks, and hold my face before going in for that first dress-rehearsal kiss. Even at twelve, the guy knew what he was doing.

The little snow flurries have escalated, and the wind has picked up, so there's nothing outside now but a wash of white. It's time to go backstage. It's time to care about the performance. It's time to prepare myself to dance with Henri.

The calm of the lobby is in complete contrast with the chaos of backstage. Stick-figure girls move at fast-forward speed, twisting their hair into buns, layering on stage makeup, doing contained versions of their choreography, marking the steps with little hops and hand flutters and complicated feet movements that take up only a few square inches of space. The smell of rosin and hair spray and stage makeup wafts through the air—the scent of ballet.

I swallow and walk to one of the mirrors. I don't ask for

permission, don't say *excuse me*, or even put a hand on any of the other dancers, asking them to move aside. I just keep my head high and my gaze focused on the spot at the mirror that I have deemed my own, and take slow steps with the confidence that they will all part and make room for me.

Which they do. It's all I have left: the ability to make them move for me, the illusion of power.

Shaking hands apply lipstick, silver shadow, silver eyeliner, midnight black mascara. They are so out of my control, they can't possibly be mine. I practically blind myself with the liner, an impossible feat, since I've been putting on my own eyeliner before dress rehearsals and performances since I was eight, when Adele taught me to keep my lips parted and my eyes pointed skyward.

"You look amazing," one of the corps members says in a small voice, like she's been planning out that sorry sentence for hours.

"We all need to look amazing," I say. "Mr. K expects nothing less."

I used to do this a lot last year: talk about Mr. K with authority, report back on little things he'd said or done. It was easy last year: Mr. K and I spent so much time together that I could always pull out some saying of his or remind the girls of his vision for the ballet. I knew about their costumes before they did. I had insider information and would pull back the curtain to show them just an edge of each little secret. Enough to keep them on their toes. Enough to keep them in awe.

I'm trying to do it again today, but the most personal

interaction I've had with Mr. K lately was him telling me I needed to work harder.

Still, these girls don't know the difference. They all nod their heads as if I'm the Messiah, delivering a message from the ballet god. Like I really am the Snow Queen, emerging from the miniblizzard outside to deliver messages of their fates. I take a huge breath and my hand stills so I can get mascara all the way from the base of my lashes to the white-blond tips without a hitch. The shakiness is slipping away, finally.

Until I hear the music-box sound of Gigi's giggles.

"Alec!" Her voice pokes out from the cloud of laughter. An airy sigh floats behind it, the hard edges of his name all smoothed out.

And I can't stop myself from whipping around to find the source of the sound. Or from making a strained, animal noise when I finally do see them. Gigi's leaning against the wall directly outside the mirrored dressing room, and Alec is holding her foot like it's something that could break. Something that's fragile. Something that could give way to blood and weakness and pain at any minute. One hand cups that tiny, ready-to-break foot, and the other is on her thigh, pushing her whole leg so that it's parallel with the rest of her body. His body comes in close to hers, and he's got his patented Alec smile on his face. Doesn't break eye contact, even as her eyes dart all over, even as her giggles come out in eager little bursts. He stays steady and strong. I know this side of him well.

My anxiety deepens. Gigi is in the costume that should have been mine: plum and gold and intricately beaded. The guy that should be mine is breathing on her neck, the prerehearsal moments that should have been mine, stolen and on display in front of me. In front of everyone. His Nutcracker Prince jacket is open and I see his bare chest. She touches it playfully, like she's done it a thousand times before.

My muscles feel cold, my feet feel like they're falling asleep, and I can feel the extra Thanksgiving weight on me as surely as I could feel the weight of soaking wet jeans. The only cure, the only thing I can think of to help me calm down and get back into my body enough to dance the Snow Queen and make them all fall in love with me again, is to have Alec hold me and whisper to me and treat me the way he used to. And it will happen. As far as I'm concerned, we're getting back together.

One last look in the mirror reveals at least my costume is beautiful and my skin shimmering with pixie dust. I look regal, even if I don't feel that way.

I can do this.

I walk away from the mirror and over to Alec. I stand close, making sure my bare skin is against his, our arms touching. He moves away, so there's a breath of air between us, and I shift my weight immediately so that there isn't.

"Hey there," I say, trying to give some of that soft, Gigi-like air in my voice, too, but it comes out flat and hoarse. I should stick to what I know.

"Hey," he says, smiling enough so that his dimples show, but not so much that I believe him. He's still holding her leg, even though I'm there. Like he doesn't care that I'm standing here.

"Can we go for a quick walk?" I say. I mean: Can we go to

the lobby, can we steal a kiss, can you watch the snow fall with me and tell me I'll be magical on that stage? "Would that be okay with you, Gigi? If I steal your . . . partner? It's just that we have a ritual we've been doing forever."

Gigi blushes and makes about a thousand different little gestures: a shrug, a hand wave, a tremble. It's infuriatingly adorable.

"I can't right now, okay?" Alec says, placing Gigi's foot back on the floor. His hand lingers too long on her calf, and he doesn't straighten up as quickly as I know he could. She gets all quiet.

"After?" I say. There are girls who would give up now. He just said he couldn't, meaning he doesn't want to be with me after all. He's broken up with me and he's drooling over the new girl, making sure some part of his body is in constant contact with some part of hers. I don't care. She's nothing. A silly virgin. A passing fancy. I'm not letting us evaporate like some puddle, some accident.

We're getting back together.

"Sure, maybe," he mumbles. It is the first time I have ever heard Alec mumble. His mouth is practically closing in on the word, that's how small the noise is. "I need to go focus," he continues, a little louder, but still not his true voice. "Focus before we start. Okay?" I don't know whose permission he's asking, but I doubt it's mine.

Gigi blushes. Anger stirs itself into my anxiety, and my whole body's buzzing with way too many feelings. I will not be able to dance if I can't get myself back under control. The Snow Queen would never have trembling legs or boiling blood. And when Alec slips away without another word, I feel the urge to cry moving from my rib cage to my throat and into my sinuses, like a foreign thing, attacking me

"Stage fright?" Gigi says, like she's had it, too, which I cannot imagine. She is not the kind of girl who scares easily, if this semester at school is any indication. It doesn't seem like anything that happened to her has had any effect.

"Not usually," I say.

"Well, you look beautiful."

That shuts me up. Not because no one has called me beautiful before, and not because I don't feel beautiful. There are white feathers in my hair and white tulle haloing my waist, and so much makeup around my eyes that they have nearly doubled in size. But the way Gigi says it, so simple and bare . . . I have never heard anyone say something and know how much they believe it to be true. Gigi hasn't put on her makeup yet, so her light brown face is still naked, too, like her voice, and for a horrible instant I think: *Yes, I can see why Alec is choosing her.*

But he can't. Not ever. Please, no. I can't let him go. I won't.

"They did a wonderful job with your costume, too," I say. It is as close to a compliment as she's going to get from me.

"Thank you!" she says, beaming. Her eyes are expectant, like our conversation could continue, when I want nothing more than for it to end. I don't get her. Why doesn't she bring up the lipstick on the mirror or the photo I left in the Light closet? She has to know it was me. Other girls have been whispering about it. If I were her, I'd bring it up. And I kind of want her to, just so I can be mean and make her look crazy and accusatory. But no one dares mess with me.

"Just so you know, Alec and I aren't really over," I say. If I'd thought it through more, I would have said something smaller, scarier, more threatening but less clear. Something like what my mother would've said. I scold myself in my head for being an amateur all of a sudden. "This is, like, our pattern, so don't get too excited about being with him."

Her pretty mouth curves into an O. She starts to say something, but I try making a cool, clean escape. Except when I step backward, I run right into another bony body.

Eleanor. But not just Eleanor. Not Eleanor outfitted as my understudy or going invisible in her corps costume. No. This is Eleanor with a small, elegant gold headdress and a taut, golden bare belly. Long, sheer harem pants. Small gold top. Eleanor has transformed into Arabian Coffee.

And she's grinning. Girls and boys peek out of the dressing rooms and look up from their warm-ups. All eyes on Eleanor and her exposed rib cage and the prettiness none of us ever knew she possessed. They shout out congratulations. "Why are you in that costume?" I say.

"I'm taking over," Eleanor says through her smile, so full of joy I think she is just as close to breaking as I am, just on the opposite side of things.

"They gave it to you?" I say, not meaning to sound so harsh. My words hang in the air for a moment over all of us, and there's shock all around.

Her forehead wrinkles with hurt.

"Congrats," Gigi says. "You so deserve this. I hope Liz gets better, though." On her brown face is the perfect balance of concern for Liz and support for Eleanor. It's impossible, how good she is. Too good.

She goes in to hug Eleanor, and I beat her to it, pulling Eleanor close and away from her. I am proud to feel a surge of actual happiness for Eleanor. I squeeze her arms tight. "Look at you," I say into her ear, and I can feel her heart beating at a rapid pace through her skimpy costume. I hold on tight, the one person who loves me no matter what.

"When did this happen?" I whisper.

"A private audition with Mr. K." She whispers so fast I can barely register it, and she doesn't hug me back as tightly, quickly slipping from my arms and into Gigi's arms. They jump and giggle and whisper something I can't quite hear. It's clear that this isn't the first time they've laughed together like that. Like friends. And just like that, I've lost everything.

18.

June

THE NEWS DOESN'T FEEL REAL. Just like the kiss with Jayhe didn't feel real.

I have to ask Morkie to repeat herself, which is embarrassing. It's nine a.m. and we're in studio C. Most people are sleeping in, trying to get every last minute of rest before opening night.

"Do you want to dance?" she says. "Then show me you know it."

Viktor plays the music for the Harlequin Doll. My feet whisper along the floor as I take my place in the center of the room. I keep my head bowed. Eight hours before opening night and I'm at school in the studio with Morkie, Doubrava, and Mr. K. They're standing along the mirrors, waiting for me to show them if I know the choreography. There are three other girls here. Two other Level 7 girls, and one Level 8.

I step into the dance. I will show them that I know all the steps. I spend hours studying every role in every major classical ballet. I've seen *The Nutcracker* performed live every Christmas since I was little enough to remember it. I've memorized every girl's role, and could probably dance the boys', too.

I try to be delicate and light, an embodiment of all that's great in *The Nutcracker*'s Land of Sweets. I try to picture my mom right in front of me, watching and seeing me nail it. I try to hear the applause in my head. I try to remember how it felt when Morkie praised me weeks ago for my pirouettes.

I finish. I don't dare move out of the bow.

Mr. K nods. "Well done, butterfly. I've never seen you move like that before. You've been working hard."

"Yes," I acknowledge.

"You dance like you really want it. Like you know," he says, doing a circle around me. "In Russia, being a dancer gives you a place in history. A life more intense and special than the others. It sets you apart from the rest of the world. I feel that in you."

A bright blush creeps up my neck.

He says something in Russian to Morkie, who nods at me, too. They're starting to see me, really *see* how hard I work, how much I want this.

He doesn't let any of the other girls dance. The Harlequin Doll is mine. A soloist role. He trusts me enough to get it ready and perfected in just eight hours. I wonder if this has ever happened before. I wonder if I'm finally special to him.

The news spreads. The cast timing and music are all adjusted. After spending hours in the studio—and skipping lunch—I have my new *Nutcracker* costume fitting. I go to the third floor and wait outside Madame Matvienko's costume room with the other girls in our black leotards and white practice tutus.

I sip my *omija* tea to keep my stomach calm. I will be fitted for three costumes—the Sugar Plum Fairy one, just in case Gigi doesn't dance for some reason that'll never happen, my plain pink corps one for the Waltz of the Flowers ensemble dance, and the bodysuit for the Harlequin Doll. Across from me, Gigi hums and I glance up from my place on the floor to shoot her an evil look, implying that she should be quiet.

She stretches flat along the floor like a pancake. Alec's loud voice escapes the costume room, and each time it rings out, Gigi gazes at the door like a puppy. She doesn't even hide it. Pathetic. I guess they're really together now, even though she's been babbling to me about how he hasn't "asked" her. So she can't be sure. What she should be sure of is that if Bette didn't hate her before, she definitely does now.

Bette marches into the area. "They're not done yet?" she asks, waiting for someone to answer her. One of the younger girls chimes in, saying the boys are running late, her eagerness to please Bette written all over her face. Bette pops a piece of fruit in her mouth. "How's everything, Gigi?" she asks. "You feeling okay?"

"I'm fine," Gigi replies curtly. "I'm not sick." Her voice lands hard on the word *sick,* like it's the last word on earth she'd ever want to use. Her eyes narrow, and she eyes Bette suspiciously. "Why are you asking?"

"Well, Mr. K wanted me to check in on you. I am one of the girls that's been here the longest. I just wanted to follow up with you about things. I probably should've checked on you a while ago. Been busy and all. We really don't tolerate bullying here. There haven't been any other incidents, right?"

Gigi doesn't look up from the floor, like she's trying really hard to focus on her stretching. I squirm a little, thinking about how I added to it. I wonder if Bette's seen that medical report. I wonder if Gigi has, too. I feel a pinch of regret, but only for a minute. I try not to think of Cassie either. Things were at their worst with her.

"I'm fine, Bette," she says, as gracious as ever. "Thanks though."

Bette bats her eyelashes over her blue eyes and adds a little giggle, then continues. "Let me know if anything else happens, okay? I'm here for you."

Before Gigi can respond, we're called into the costume room. It's full of light and perfume and the smell of makeup. We only get to be here twice a year, and the costumes we need are brought over from the company's storage. I savor every moment. Tiaras line one table, while costume ornaments and handmade pointe shoes and ballet slippers sit primly on another—little pink layers piled one on top of the other like miniature cakes. Once we all settle in, the mood is airy. Here, we're just girls playing dress up—the best part of ballet.

The volunteer mothers bring around our costumes. During dress rehearsal, some costumes needed readjusting and one final check. Gigi and I stand together as ours is presented. A rich plum costume drapes down from a wooden hanger, jewels stitched along the bodice. My fingers graze the fabric just as Gigi's do, too, and we admire it, both wanting to wear it forever.

"You'll be gorgeous in this," the mother says to Gigi. She doesn't even look at me. Like I don't even have a chance of wearing this costume. She knows all too well how the ballet world works. I don't let it pinch. The woman helps Gigi change into the tiny costume, and it squeezes her rib cage snugly, clearly needing to be let out a little. I hide my smile, knowing it'd never need to be let out for me.

I put on my corps costume—a pink, frilly, knee-length outfit worn by all the girls who will play flowers in the group dance. It itches.

"Put this hairnet on." One of the mothers hands it to me. I pull it over my bun and head, then go to the wig area. They fit me in a white wig that smells like baby powder and mothballs and looks like it should be atop the head of some seventeenth-century judge. I see other corps members reflected in the room of mirrors. We are all the same girl.

I change out of that costume and into the checkered body-suit costume for the Harlequin Doll. Black and white diamonds cover my whole body and a white neckpiece that reminds me of a coffee filter is fanned around my throat. There's a gold keyhole in the back where I'll be wound up onstage like the tiny dancer in my music box.

"E-Jun Kim!" Madame Matvienko shouts my name from the front of the room. And I realize by her frown that she's called my name more than once. I approach, head down, and curtsy to her. She's just as important as the other Russian teachers here, even though she's only the costume mistress.

"Turn," she says without emotion—her face cold and wrinkled, her hair cropped close around her head, her lips frowned up and pursing like she's an angry fish. She leans forward in her chair and slides a measuring tape around my waist. I fight the urge to look down and see the number. Instead, I focus on holding my breath. I feel big, as if the tape measure has to stretch. She places pins in my waist and stands to adjust the old wig on my head.

"Hmm. Wig too big," she says, removing it and placing another one on top. "But costume fit just right." She pats my side and I release. "You look so much like your mother, but your body remind me of your father," she says. "So narrow, so tall, such a tiny head on top of it all. Just like him."

"I'm . . . sorry?" I say, barely able to get the word out. It must be a mistake. She must be confusing me with Sei-Jin or one of the other Korean girls. I know they think we all look alike.

"Tiny head. All of his children. Very funny. Such a tiny head for such a powerful man, no?" Madame Matvienko finally looks at my face and notices, midlaugh, that my jaw has dropped, that my cold, clammy skin is as pale as I've always wanted to be. My legs shake so badly I have to sit down.

"Who are you talking about?" I manage to say, in a voice so much higher than my own that I swear it didn't come out of me at all. Madame Matvienko is the one turning white now, then red, then almost green with what I assume is the nausea of saying something dangerous and wrong.

"I'm confused. I thought you were . . . one of the others. But of course not. You're E-Jun, E-Jun Kim. You look so much like the other Asian girls. All of your tiny waists and pretty hair. All the same. Excuse me."

She tries to smile and pass it off as an honest, ignorant, racist mistake. But I get the distinct and terrifying feeling that there was no error. Madame Matvienko knows who my father is. Maybe they all do. I get so dizzy, I have to sit down on one of the crappy metal folding chairs. Every part of me is instantly drenched in sweat, and I can't muster up a single word. The thing I've wanted to know all my life—the answers might be right here.

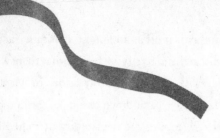

19.

Gigi

MY BOBBY PIN SLIDES RIGHT into the lock, easing the bolt left with the slightest click. I should be at the dorm packing my dance bag with everything I'll need for opening night. I should be stretching my feet or soaking them in an ice bath in the physical therapy room. I should be mentally preparing myself for tonight, and my heart for the long program. All the American Ballet Company ballet masters will be in the audience, hunting for new corps talent. All the company dancers, off for the night, will be watching us dance their roles. Judging us. And Mama and Dad will be in the front row with Aunt Leah, all taking deep, worried breaths when I step onstage.

But there are a few hours before I have to officially worry about those things, so I push my way into the American Ballet Company shoe room on the third floor of our building. It's closed now for the night. We've all gotten what we needed for the show. The hallway is desolate and the lights are out. I slip inside, falling into the heavy scent of satin and rosin. It's my second time sneaking in here after hours. I never get enough time in this space. I am never allowed to explore. I have to take the chance while I can. The shoes will be housed in our school building for only another month or so, then moved to the new company building next door.

Posters on the wall advertise different brands of pointe shoes. A counter window is a portal into the back storage room, where cubbies hold piles of stock pointe shoes and leather slippers, and, in labeled boxes, custom-made ones for company dancers. They entice, like delicate pink candies sealed in pastel wrappings.

I lift myself over the counter and sneak into the back. I run my fingers over the different shoes and admire the names written under their sections. Shoes for each corps girl, shoes for each soloist, shoes for each principal.

It was a pair of pointe shoes that first made me want to be a ballerina. They were the first I'd ever seen, stuffed in a garbage can in downtown San Francisco—pretty pink satin stained brown by coffee grounds and trash. I'd reached in before Mama caught me, getting ahold of one shoe. I wanted to take it home, clean it, and keep it forever, but she wouldn't let me. After that she bathed me in sanitizer and signed me up for a ballet class. She thought it would be light and easy. Something a girl born with a heart defect could do without much threat of injury. But when I got serious, and the teacher said I was good, she wanted to pull me out.

"It's too much stress," she'd said over the dinner table after I received my acceptance letter to the conservatory.

"I love it," was my constant response. I sewed elastic on my pointe shoes, determined to have at least a dozen pairs ready before I left.

"You could be hospitalized. One wrong move. One intense practice or performance. I'm not willing to lose you," she'd said, like she wanted to scoop me up in one of her summer canning jars, only to be stored in the pantry until winter.

She'd cried when I told her I'd rather have one year dancing than a lifetime without it. She'd cried when my suitcases were packed and Dad drove me to the airport. She'd cried when I told her I didn't want her to come to New York to help me settle in.

I pull out several principal dancers' shoes and slide my feet into them, even though I know they won't fit and that I shouldn't ruin someone else's brand-new shoes. I don't stand on pointe. Just let myself feel what it might be like to wear these shoes, be like these women. And any worries I had about being at the conservatory and pushing through disappear.

Half an hour before curtain, backstage is a frenzy of half-dressed girls and a frazzled crew, trying to finalize everyone and everything. The nerves are zinging in my stomach, like my butterflies when they're startled. I can't believe it's finally here, the moment I've dreamed of all my life. I try to remember how calm I'd felt earlier. Tonight I'll finally see my parents in the audience, show them why I had to go so far from them, show them that it was worth it.

I slip to the edge of the stage, right where the thick, velvet curtains will part in just minutes. I peer through a crack as the audience pours in, and that's when it hits me, the stage fright. My heart is racing, the adrenaline surging through me. I do the breathing exercises Mama taught me, but it's not working. I place two fingers on my wrist, trying to quiet my thoughts long enough to track my pulse. If I had been wearing that monitor, it would surely be shrieking now, drawing everyone's attention my way. I try to focus on counting: 68, 73, 84, 96, my heart rate climbing up and up and up. Faster and faster, out of my control.

I know that I'm pushing it. But how can I give up this moment? How can I march over to Morkie before she takes her place in the audience, and tell her I can't do it? That I'm feeling the warning signs? I can't not dance. Not now. Not when my feet have carried me this far. *Breathe, Gigi, breathe!*

I count again, slowing down this time, really listening to the heartbeats. 57, 62, 78, 85. Breathing in and out, in and out, I feel my muscles relax. And then I startle, as arms circle my waist, and hot breath hovers on my neck, sending goose bumps up my arms and my heart racing once again.

"Alec," I say, turning so I'm fully embraced by his arms. I lean into him, breathing in his soapy scent. He's wearing his gold-and-red brocade Nutcracker tunic and tights, the headpiece mask left in the wings. The heavy stage lights hit the gold of his hair, setting it ablaze, and there's something different in his eyes tonight. Something that makes my heart race even faster.

"Showtime," he says, his voice clear and warm in my ears, even through the din of the crowd backstage. "I'm honored to be your partner."

Leaning back onto one knee, he does a little bow, and I grin at him. "I'm glad to be your partner, too," I say, extending my hand to lift him up. He kisses it as he rises, pulling me back into his arms.

"And I'm hoping," he says, whispering now, even though we're so close, even though everyone else has fallen away, "that you might think I can be something more than just, you know, your *pas* partner."

Is he asking what I think he's asking? The heat flushes through my cheeks and neck and chest, warming me from head to toe. "I'm hoping," he says, his mouth hot on my ear, "that you might be my girlfriend." He's nervous, which I've never seen before.

And I look up into the ocean of his eyes and nod. He pulls a small box from inside his jacket. Red and tiny, with a golden ribbon embracing it. Like the presents under the Christmas tree on the far corner of the stage.

I can't help but laugh as we both plop down on the floor in our resplendent costumes and I tear into the box. Backstage hands call for the ten-minute curtain warning for the second act. But we don't stop. Inside, nestled in white tissue paper, is a tiny rose charm, just the size of my pinky nail, made of gold, complete with a little stem and even thorns.

"For you," he says. "For luck." And that's when he finally kisses me again.

Minutes later, like in a dream, the music is playing and I'm waiting in the wings. Backstage is charged with tension. The other dancers tiptoe behind me, coming on- and offstage in preparation for my entrance. My palms shake and tiny beads of sweat seep into my costume. I feel their eyes and their worries: *Will I mess up?*

My muscles quiver. Thousands of other ballerinas from all over the world have worn this costume and danced this role. I hope I can dance the part as well as them. I fluff out the skirt, just as the costume mistress Madame Matvienko did. Alec's rose sits in the folds of plum-colored tulle. I sewed it into the lining of my costume. I haven't stopped twirling it between my thumb and forefinger. I dust my shoes in rosin one last time to make sure I don't fall.

June passes by, ready to enter with the rest of the corps. I feel her eyes skate over me on her way onstage. She looks beautiful and willowy, and I wish we were closer. I wish we were close enough to hug each other. She gazes over at me. I nod at her, and she nods back. "Break a leg," I mouth.

"You mean, *merde.*" She flashes me a slight smile.

I give her one back and turn away. I try to focus on nothing else but my performance. We've all worked for weeks on these roles, all day long, and just for six minutes onstage. Six minutes to show the ballet masters what you've learned. Ballet must be picture-perfect, because when you make a mistake, a trained eye can spot it.

After ballet school, there are so few professional jobs. Famous companies already have their principals and soloists, and may only have room for you in the corps, where you have to work through the ranks. You have to love it, and dance your way up. For me, dance was just always about the flow, the movement, the passion. But now, I want to zip through the ranks. Being onstage makes it all worth it.

I don't know what to do with my hands. I smooth the edges of my perfect bun, my curls blown-out into sleek perfection. The jeweled tiara digs into my scalp. I try not to lick off my lipstick. I hear Morkie in my head: "If you are nervous in the wings, then you will have a great performance."

The first time I was ever onstage, I was six and dancing a peasant child in *Sleeping Beauty*. I remember sleeping in my costume for days leading up to the show and obsessing over each little step. My old ballet teacher had said the difference between a good dancer and a true ballerina is that a ballerina must be perfect—like a doll come to life, made just for the stage.

I will be a doll.

I will be a fairy.

I peek out from behind a curtain, but can't see anything beyond the stage. The audience is bathed in darkness, but I feel their eyes watching. I've never danced for this many people before. It feels strange to be dancing for more than two thousand people. I shake out my arms and legs. The audience's applause hits me in waves. I hear a girl whisper my name, as if I don't know that this is it, the moment I finally take center stage.

It's a party and the Nutcracker Prince is introducing little Clara to all the wonders in the Land of Sweets. And I am one of them. I will present myself to the audience and the other dancers. Large jewel-like lights bathe the stage.

My music starts—little droplets of sound fill the space. I listen to the chiming melody and feel the musical phrases. I want to dance on top of those notes. I smooth my costume and tip-toe onstage. The lights warm my skin, erasing my nerves. The tension disappears and I've stepped onto a different plane—one where I am no longer Gigi but the Sugar Plum Fairy.

I jump onto my toes. My feet sync with the music, and my body glides. As I throw myself into the motions, I don't see the others anymore. I blend with the music and the movements. My arms are elegant lines of muscle over my head. I keep my head up, only watching my shadow to ensure I look perfect. I smile at the audience even though it's hard to breathe and sweat drips down my back.

My solo ends. I curtsy and hear the roar of applause. I recognize Mama's whistle. I hold a grin and move to the side, while Alec comes center stage. My chest heaves and I try to catch my breath without being seen. My heart is flailing, thumping in my chest like a bird caught in a cage, wanting to be wild again. We're supposed to be ethereal beings onstage, even through the most tiring variations. But now I'm spent. I double over, trying to find more oxygen. The tightness is cutting into my euphoria, the lack of air causes my muscles to twitch and spasm. I will my heart to slow, to calm. I want to enjoy this moment, not fight my own body. I breathe and count, breathe and count, and finally the rhythm finds itself and slows. I'm still overwhelmed with emotion and fatigue and bliss. But I only have a few minutes until Alec presents his hand to me.

We perform our *pas*, his hands holding me at every turn, supporting me during every lift. I feel the heat in his hands on my waist when he lifts me, experiencing his touch everywhere—my legs, my arms, my fingers, my toes—like the way the warmth of a shower hits you all at once. When he lifts me, his long fingers move beneath my tutu. I try not to shiver. I bat my eyelashes at him and throw coy looks his way as we nail each gesture, making it look like we've been dancing together our whole lives. His clever hands anticipate my every move and I fold easily into his arms without hesitation.

And then it's over. The ballet ends and the curtain goes up for bows, each group of dancers taking their turn before the audience. Alec and I wait in the wings holding hands. My fingers knit into his. Shaky from fatigue and excitement. "You ready for this?" he whispers.

"Yes," I say again. I place my other hand on my chest, willing my heart to slow. My head feels light, and I try to hold on to everything going on around me.

"You were perfect," he says, before pulling me back on the stage for our final bows.

We shuffle across and everyone makes room for us. We are last to go to the front and present ourselves to the audience. We curtsy and bow, then turn to our ballet masters and do the same. They nod and clap and shout bravo.

A tiny *petit rat* tiptoes out with a bouquet of flowers for me. I hug her and she squeezes my waist tight. The crowd thunders, their roars vibrating the stage. Everything blurs around me like I'm caught up in the currents of a tornado. Suddenly, Alec twirls me, making the audience clap even louder. I blush and smile with embarrassment. Then he pulls me into a kiss. The crowd erupts.

I lose my grasp on the flowers, letting them fall onto the stage. His mouth is soft and wet, his tongue tastes like a chocolate mint. It's like the kiss we shared before, except this one isn't private. This is for the world to see, and I no longer have the spasm of worry about whether he might still be in love with Bette instead of me. I don't hear the crowd anymore. I don't hear the dancers around us. I hear my heart and his and I feel that pulse race between my legs again. I fold into him, and lose myself in that one perfect moment, knowing how very, very rare this kind of joy is.

ACT II

Spring Season

SPRING PERFORMANCE: *GISELLE*
Cast
Major Soloist Parts

Giselle: Giselle Stewart
Giselle Understudy: E-Jun Kim
Bathilde: Bette Abney
Count Albrecht: Alec Lucas
Queen Myrta: Eleanor Alexander

Willis: *Sophomore corps de ballet*
Willis Soloists: E-Jun Kim, Sei-Jin Kwon
Hilarion: Henri Dubois
Prince of Courland: William O'Reilly

20.

Bette

THE SPRING CAST LIST WENT up twenty-four hours ago and I have taken exactly five pills since then, blowing through the last of the new ones I just got. I ignore the pills' side effects: my pounding heartbeat, the shakes in my hands, the dry mouth. I can deal, because I need them, their odd mix of peace and razor-sharp focus. Mr. K put the cast up super early this year—the last week of January instead of mid-February, like usual. He says it's so we have more time, but the whole thing is a mistake. And now, there's nothing to think about during rehearsal but the slow ruination of my life.

But the pills did make me dance like the floor was fire and I was the flame. Not that anyone is watching, of course. The Russians have stopped paying particular attention to me. *Poof!* Just like that after all these years. And Alec rubbed Gigi's shoulders the entire time, which I guess means they're officially together.

Eleanor's no help. She just stretched and watched her body

in the mirror, as if she'd never seen it before. Which maybe she hasn't, in its new glory. She must have lost five pounds over winter break, and muscles have popped up in her legs that I don't think were there before. Winter break was a blur of disappointment for me, filled with endless hours of TV stupor and avoiding the calorie-laden crap my mother always fills the kitchen with. I worked out with Adele during the break at the gym with her trainer. And my mother paid one of my former ballet madams, pushed out of teaching at the conservatory by Mr. K, to come over every day.

I'm shaking by the time ballet class is over, from the pills or anger or exhaustion, I can't tell which. I wave to Morkie on the way out the door, but before she has a chance to acknowledge me or comment on my precision or the two pounds I managed to drop during break, Gigi stops her and starts blathering away and waving her hands around, like she's the one hopped up on some super-speed elixir. Alec dashes out before I can talk to him. He doesn't wait like he used to.

No one waits for me. Eleanor is off to a practice room probably, but I can't stand the sight of myself in the mirror for one more second. I get paralyzed somewhere between studio A and the elevators, and I lean against a wall to gather myself. I used to go to Alec's room after a long rehearsal. Or watch movies with Eleanor. Or research dance competitions and summer intensives. Or imagine myself dancing the roles that I thought had been promised to me years ago.

Now, none of that is an option. I unwind the ribbons on my pointe shoes, and slide my feet out. I unwrap the tape and give each toe a little rub. They all ache from the pressure, the hours of work I've been putting in.

My hands fumble with my empty locket, my thoughts tumbling down into a place filled with my worst nightmare. Being average, one of the corps, a nobody. The chaos of the classes letting out can't compete with the trauma in my head, so I don't even notice Henri approach.

"We're going to rehearse together," Henri says. He grabs my wrist, which hurts a little, and gives one quick tug. It yanks me right back to reality.

"Uh, no we aren't." I pull back and the result is a hiccup of pain in my wrist.

"I could teach you a few things," he says, and goes for my wrist again, like he's been given permission to touch me. "You should just get over it."

"Get over what?" My black leotard sticks to my back and my stomach, my tights itch, my muscles burning underneath. I can't forget what he said to me. What he claims to know about the things I did to Cassie.

"Not being cast in the role you wanted," he says, like we're friends and he's sad for me. When Adele heard I got shafted again, she told me to just keep my head down, to keep working, keep looking for opportunities, that cast lists are whirlwinds that constantly change. My mother threatened to pull me out and send me to a rival ballet school, to get Mr. K fired, to take back the Abney endowment to the conservatory. But this time I'm trying to just listen to Adele, the one who actually has exactly what I want.

"Come on, let's have a little fun. That's what's missing from your dancing," Henri says, crossing his arms in front of his chest and smiling. His dimples are deep dents in his face, and his biceps bulge when his arms cross, so for a minute I let myself explore what Cassie found so attractive about him. He really looks like he does in all the dance magazines. Now that I've made room to see him. Now that Alec has disappeared.

"The last thing I'd ever want to do is go anywhere with you," I spit back, wondering if he's suddenly forgotten how I didn't speak a word to him during our *pas* rehearsals, passing messages through our sophomore understudies, like some messed-up version of the telephone game. I have to remind myself that I don't care how many magazine spreads or dancewear endorsements he's got. He's nothing. Even if he does know the one thing that could really ruin me.

"You shouldn't be so mean all the time," he says with that signature smirk, leaning closer. "It isn't good for your looks. And you'll make even more enemies."

I look through him like he's invisible, pretending that the words coming out of his mouth are just white noise, and walk ahead.

"Your attitude might inspire me to start telling people things about you," he says, his French accent thick with irritation.

"You don't know anything about me," I snap back.

"Oh, but I do." He points a finger at the hallway ceiling. "Did you know there are cameras here? And, of course, in the studios? Even Studio B?"

A flush overwhelms my entire body, right down to my toes, a

knot hardening in my stomach.

"Did you know that they record everything, and can even pick up conversations?" he says.

I can feel the tears, hot and angry, ready to spill. I pivot carefully back around to face him, my face stone, not betraying a thing. "What did you say?"

"I seem to have finally gotten your attention," he says.

"You don't know anything," I say. I sound exactly the same as my mother did during arguments with my father. "There are no cameras. I've been here, like, forever. Don't you think I'd know something like that?" I say, though I'm not quite sure.

"There's a French place," Henri says. "In the East Village. They let me have wine if I stay in the back. Owner knows my dad. It's nice."

"I'm not going anywhere with you."

"Oh, but you are. Because I'm someone who knows your little secrets. The types of things that could get you thrown out of school. Or better yet, sent away. The kinds of things that will follow you, and your family. Might even lead to a lawsuit. You don't know exactly what I'll do with the things I know, so I'm confident you'll meet me out front."

He leaves me standing there in a blend of misery and aggression and confusion. "Fine," I call out. "But let me at least change."

"I like you like this," Henri says, "but okay."

I hate that last comment. I push away all the reasons why I get dressed and skip history class and lie to Eleanor about going to Adele's in order to leave with him. He's waiting in the school lobby, all dressed up with a smug look on his face, like he knew

I'd show up. Like he knows exactly how to make me do what he wants.

"French food's too heavy," I say, carrying my coat, still unable to commit to leaving the building with him. What I really mean is that *all* food is too heavy lately. Celery, carrots, broth—all my standbys are making me ill. Catching sight of my reflection now in the foyer mirror, I'm sick to see my hips pushing out past my waistline, my cheeks fuller than usual. The lines of my body are all wrong in these regular clothes. I can't balloon to the size of a regular girl. The two-pound loss didn't do enough. My little pills don't seem to be speeding me up, helping me focus, *or* keeping my weight down. Meanwhile, all I dream about or see when I close my eyes for longer than a blink is Gigi's lithe, lean body, twirling and leaping and finding its way into Alec's strong arms.

Thirty minutes later we're in the back booth of the smallest French bistro in all Manhattan. Everything is red: the booths, the fringe on the lamps, the carpet, the wine, its stain on Henri's lips. His foot has found mine under the table, and while he downs steak, he keeps paying aggressive footsie with me.

"It's not happening," I say again. "I don't why you've dragged me here, or what you think is going to happen."

"Play along, at least," he says.

I don't, and at first this makes him smirk and tease me and try grabbing my hand, but about halfway through the bottle of wine the waiters have been feeding him, it starts to piss him off. I just want to know whatever it is that he's figured out and be done with it. I'll find a way to discredit it all. Cassie is a crazy person now. Her injury pushed her over the edge. That's what I've heard.

And no one believes those types.

"What," he says, a slur marring his accent, "you don't like the restaurant? Cozy, no?"

"Not my style," I say, sipping the wine even though it will stain my teeth. "When you get a cute little freshman girlfriend, you can bring her here to seduce her." This finally shuts him up, and he finishes his steak pretty quickly. I don't touch the food on my plate. Just stab it around with my fork, volleying the image of Gigi's face and Henri's eyes in my head. "I don't have any more time to waste on you. If you really knew anything, you'd bring it up by now."

The owner comes to the table and they fire back and forth in French. With my meager childhood lessons, I can barely keep up. Henri turns in his chair, jumping deeper into the conversation. He doesn't bother introducing me. Which is fine. I turn my attention to the couple sitting nearby, who fuss about their middle school son's math grades, when Henri's phone, faceup on the table, starts to light up.

I crane to peek. It's Will. He calls twice, then a series of texts flood the screen. Lots of desperate *Where are you?* and *Do you want to play pool?* or *Watch TV later?* They remind me of texts a lovesick girl sends to a crush. I try not to smile, and wonder if Henri is into both girls and boys. That wouldn't be a totally off-the-wall thing in the ballet world. But even better yet, Will has a new crush, and it's not Alec anymore.

Henri ends his conversation too soon, and snatches his phone from the table and my gaze.

"I'm going to the bathroom, then leaving," I announce,

pulling on my coat. "I don't actually care anymore. Say what you want. No one will believe you." I get up before he can respond.

The bathrooms are in a nook in the back of the bistro, where they store aprons and high chairs and a sad, lonely-looking old pay phone. I smooth the bun I kept my hair in and put on a fresh coat of my *Dior* red lipstick. He won't say anything and no one will believe a word. After telling myself that a few times, I text my pill dealer and tell him to meet me at the school building when he can.

I'm not surprised to see Henri leaning against the wall when I come out of the ladies' room. He wraps an arm around my waist, his fingers stroking my side. I push at him. He grips me tighter, like he's going to lift me above his head, like we're in the studio practicing a *pas*. It tickles, and I wince away but end up pushed farther into the corner, farther into the dark.

"Don't think about trying your shit with me," I say, giving him a little shove. He pushes me back. "Get off me!"

"How does it feel?" he says.

"How does what feel?" I look around for waiters or other customers who need to use the bathroom. It's like they've been told to stay out of the little dark nook.

"To be backed into a corner. Like what you did with Cassie."

"I didn't do anything to your precious girlfriend. We were friends." The lie is delivered perfectly. Conversation over. I try to step away again, with some amount of grace, but he just holds tighter. Blocking me.

"*HEY,*" I say, louder, more meanly. "Back off."

"Oh, come *on*, Bette," he says instead, the whisper of his voice hitting my throat, feeling too much like someone's fingers strangling me. "Don't be a bitch. Obviously, I know what you did to her—" I cut him off with a shove. Not with my hands, which I can't access because of the way he's holding me, but using my whole body, slamming into his.

The force of it must have been impressive, because he finally moves a little.

"Just shut up. I didn't do anything," I say. I mirror his ugly whisper, my own voice making me shiver. "You're making shit up. You're desperate." I'm practically spitting on him now. For an instant he made me feel small and powerless and scared in this corner, and now I want to make him pay. The way he pawed at my skin, stepped in my way, manipulated me into coming down here in the first place gets my heart pounding. But I'm Bette, and I won't let him make me forget that. "You're not Cassie's hero, so stop trying to be." I'm talking fast now. Too fast. I'm on fire.

I think about what it would be like to tell Mr. K about Henri grabbing at me, forcing me into a dark corner, and not letting go. No one would believe him then. For a delusional moment I picture Mr. K pulling me to his chest and letting me cry on his perfectly pressed shirt, but then I remember that's not who I am to him anymore.

I probably couldn't even get a moment alone with him if I begged.

"I'm lying?" he says, stretching out the word with his accent, until it almost sounds funny.

"Get a life," I say, sliding past him.

"You had something to do with Will dropping her last

spring," he says before I'm two steps away from him. "She fractured her hip, and is still recovering from that injury. But I bet that's what you were hoping for."

I freeze, trying to keep my face calm and expressionless. Did Will tell him? Would he do that? I pivot back around.

"And I bet you did all those other little stupid things to her, too." His words have my heart plummeting into my empty stomach, a boulder in an empty well. *Thud.*

"I also have a theory, after being around you these past few months. Seeing how you look at Gigi, how you operate." He grabs me again, so close I can smell the wine on his breath. "You *made* Will drop Cassie. She said the lift was perfect. And I plan to get pro—"

I erase the word *proof* with a hard, disgusting, sloppy kiss. I shove my tongue into his mouth and let his into mine. I let it erase his accusations and whatever else he knows. I have to do what I can to protect myself. Maybe if I give him just a little bit of me, he'll forget all about Cassie. I've come this far. I can't lose now.

21.

June

I'M WITH MY MOM AT her favorite restaurant, Cho Dang Kol in Koreatown. I didn't even get to shower or change after rehearsal or have a few minutes to think through how I need to find a way to get a soloist part again. Morkie praised me for how well I danced the Harlequin Doll in *The Nutcracker,* but the spring cast list doesn't show any progress. My mom just popped up outside and an RA came and plucked me right from the studio. She clearly has something on her mind, since she won't stop pursing her lips. But I'm distracted by the cacophony of noise outside. We're too close to the big Macy's store for comfort, and confused tourists keep wandering inside and asking for pad thai and curry.

I sip kimchee tofu broth and water, and push the rest of the food around on my plate. I remember loving the food at this place when I was younger, when I liked food. But my mom is on high alert, so every few minutes she'll raise her eyebrows, point to my plate, and watch as I pick up a few bites and swallow them. My throat's killing me. Every bite that goes down feels like metal scraping the raw, hidden parts of me, and I wonder how anyone could actually enjoy eating. Chewing disgusts me. I blame my body for why I didn't land Giselle. I can fix it. I can make it work.

"You're too skinny," my mom says at last. It takes almost the whole meal, eaten in silence, just to get to that thought. I know she worries, I know she loves me, but she's never been quite sure of how to show it. "Need to eat more." She pushes a plate of mandu across the table, juicy and meaty dumplings that are nearly bursting. They make me want to throw up.

"No," I say. I find it's best to say as little as possible to her. The more words I give her, the more ability she has to shift them around and get them to fit her own purposes.

"No point in being so skinny if you're not going to be a ballerina," she says, folding her hands in her lap and again raising her eyebrows, commanding me to take another bite.

I eat, knowing it won't stay in me for long anyway. It chafes all the way down, and the pain brings tears to my eyes.

"I am a ballerina," I say.

"We had a deal."

It's not like I thought she'd forgotten the things we'd talked about at the beginning of the school year. She is not a woman who throws threats around without purpose. But I guess I had pushed the ultimatum she gave me into some dark, cobwebbed part of my brain, hoping I'd never have to actually look at it.

"Hmm?" is all I can muster. I can't really play dumb. I know she notices me avoiding eye contact, twisting my napkin in my hands, but I can't think of anything else to say. The waiter drops off the spring flavors of sorbet in the middle of our table. Even though it's barely even a few days into February.

"Our agreement. If you couldn't move from being an understudy to something more substantial, you would finally return to a good academic school and be a good student and become something worthwhile. You remember?" She spoons a pink glob into her mouth. I imagine it melting on her tongue, the sugar finding its way into her face and body.

She doesn't even blink. She clicks her spoon against the glass bowl, her gaze on me, and even the waiters know to stop rushing around us so that she can make me sit in my own shame. Why doesn't she want me to dance? Why did she even enroll me in the school in the first place?

She takes a folder from her purse and presents it to me. "School papers." She taps the forms.

"I need to use the bathroom," I say.

"Principal says you can go during the summer to make sure you are on grade level for math and science," she adds, like I've said nothing at all. "You can take summer class, too. Ballet school doesn't give you a good education, this I know."

I don't say anything, but keep shaking my head. No, no, no! I will be at a summer intensive just like every other summer. I will dance all day. I will eliminate all my flaws so that when the fall semester starts, I am perfect.

I glare at the pages my mother has laid down in front of me. Her scrawled handwriting fills in the details. The only line that is blank is the one reserved for information about my father.

"Who is my father?" I ask. "I know he was a dancer."

She jumps back in her seat like I've slapped her. "E-Jun—"

"Maybe he wouldn't want me going to a public school," I say, because it sounds like something kids say on TV. "I have a right to know. You don't get to make all the decisions for me." I say that just to watch her face shift and fight that familiar, uncomfortable expression as she tries to hold her gaze on me. My mom continues to stare me down. She believes if she glares at me long enough, I'll stop.

"I could get emancipated from you," I say, thinking of the one girl at school who bragged about doing this. "I could even make you tell me who he is by calling the police," I say, knowing this little bit extra will be enough to unhinge her. And it does.

She makes a loud harrumph and clears her throat. She asks the waiters for the check and shakes her head, as I was just doing. Her shakes are more forceful, and she doesn't stop. She just keeps shaking and shaking, like if she does it for long enough, the right words will come out.

"Your father . . . ," she says, trying to imitate my softer, less shrill voice.

"Also," I continue, gaining momentum, "I'm not just an understudy. I'm one of the willis with a solo. They're important to the ballet."

"We both know that's nothing," she says.

But her head's still shaking and she's still mentally chewing on the idea of me finding out who my dad is. The thoughts spill out all over her face. I haven't exactly won this round. But then, neither has she.

I can't match her stare for much longer, so I stand.

"E-Jun," she shouts after me as I run toward the bathroom. It's dingy, the floor wet with footprints and who knows what else. But I can't help myself. The porcelain toilet beckons me. My eyes fill with tears, and my mouth with saliva. I kneel on the floor. My body is trained to want to purge, so it's not hard to get what's inside out. I don't even have to use my finger, just let my tongue swipe the back of my throat. Then I retch.

Everything leaves me. Liquid, anger, food, pressure. Each time my stomach heaves, I feel more of it lift off me—little balloons of sorrow set to float away. Even if it's just for a minute, I feel free. The tile under my knees cools my hot limbs and my head buoys above the toilet. I prepare for one last purge, the empty one that tells me I have nothing left. I can't stop vomiting. The liquid keeps coming.

All I hear are my tears, my heartbeat, the buzz of the *Giselle* performance music in my head. I let myself empty one last time, then drag myself off the floor. I open the stall door and freeze. My mom's standing right outside like a guard. I'm so surprised, I stumble backward. I should've known it was too risky to do this here. I should've waited until I got back to the dorms.

"Oh, June," my mom says, looking a little devastated. "Maybe no public school. Maybe you need hospital."

Two hours later, I'm back at the dorm. My mom and I didn't say a word to each other the entire ride back. It's eleven o'clock. I should be in my bed, resting, or rehearsing if I'm going to stay up this late. But I can't. Too much has happened, and I'm so exhausted, I can't sleep. I head back downstairs to the front hall.

It's mostly dark and quiet, although a studio or two has lights on, meaning someone's rehearsing still, striving for perfection, and hasn't gotten booted to bed by an RA. Usually, that person would be me. But tonight I'm feeling defeated. I need to do something to defuse this situation with my mom, something that won't let her snatch my dream away from me—not when I'm this close. So I'm going to find my dad.

If what Madame Matvienko said is true, maybe my dad walked these very halls. Maybe my mom met him here, and dancing really is in my blood. Maybe I'm a legacy, too. The thought thrills and infuriates me. I stand in the lobby, the snow swirling outside the picture windows, coating the Upper West Side in a pure, powdery white that will turn dingy and dark tomorrow. But tonight, it's beautiful. It flutters down in swirls of white, and I have half a mind to go out there, let it envelop me, let the cold seep into my bones. Instead, I stare up at the portraits of all the ABC dancers who've come before me through these very halls, marking the school's history and success. My mother's right. There are no Asian dancers featured here on the wall, although the school will happily take their money, importing dozens at a time for the golden opportunity of making it to the stage. But what does she know? Things are different now, right? They have to be.

Anyway, it's not her I'm looking for here. It's my other half—my father, a reflection of myself. Where does my forehead come from, or my caramel-flecked eyes? My too-light hair? I look for myself in the bone structure of the white male dancers that grace the walls, mimicking their smiles, trying on their faces, trying to find myself. But it's no use. In the shadowed hall, I'm invisible once more, even to myself.

When I get back upstairs, the room light is on. Despite my best efforts, my face is still splotchy from crying, but at first, Gigi doesn't say anything. She knows I like my space. She putters around the room in silence, hovering over her butterflies, pausing to sniff the roses that sit on her desk. She sits briefly, tapping her pencil on the table as she does her math homework, then shuffles through her closet. She's got this random excitement she keeps trying to contain, but it's not really working. She sniffs one of the roses again. Probably an early Valentine's Day gift from Alec. They make me think of Jayhe, and our kiss. But even those thoughts don't erase what happened tonight with my mom.

I know Gigi's dying to speak, so I sigh loudly, a cue that she can talk if she wants to. She always wants to.

"It's snowing." She's peering out the window; tiny little flakes are still coming down. The sprinkle of white has turned the city-scape into a candy confection.

"I know," I snap. My stomach grumbles. I used to love the snow when I was little. My mother and I would pile on our heavy winter coats and head out to the park in Queens, which was empty then, a blanket of white covering the former fields of green. Even how the snowflakes seemed to be fatter outside of Manhattan. We'd have snowball fights and make snow angels, and she'd tell me stories about Korea. She never talked about her time at the conservatory, or why she left, but she loved telling stories about her life with her three sisters and how they'd help their mom with the cooking and the sewing. How simple things were then, and how she'd make little *hanbok* dresses to wear in the plays the girls would put on. I loved the stories about her sisters—the tall one, the cranky one, the baby. She was right in the middle. It made me want a sibling, too, someone to make memories with. Still, back then, I was happy with just the two of us, my mom and me. But as I got more serious about dance, she got more and more quiet, till we hardly talked at all.

"We should go outside," Gigi says, her eyes twinkling with glee. But then she looks at me again, and ducks her head. "Or maybe not. Lots to do. And it's late." She sits back down at her desk, and starts dismantling a math problem.

"Do you miss your family?" I ask her, folding down my covers, crawling into bed. I don't know where the question comes from, or how it escaped my mouth, except that I can't stop thinking about my mother. All this time, I thought I was a fatherless child, but I'm finally realizing I lost my mom a long time ago. I'm an orphan. "It must be hard."

She looks up at me, the twinkle fading, a sadness seeping in. "Yeah. There's so many things here I'd love to share with them," she says, tapping her pencil again. Always restless. "It's cool having my aunt here, though. We went to see the *Chocolate Nutcracker* in Harlem over break. The all-black cast. And we have this list of must-hit restaurants around town—we've been trying to cross one off each week." She looks down at the flat expanse of her stomach. "Although I've been trying not to overindulge."

"I'll take you out for Korean food one day," I find myself saying, like my mouth has a mind of its own. "There are a few really awesome places in Midtown." And I never go for fun anymore, not since Sei-Jin and I imploded. I do miss wandering with friends around Herald Square and the street nicknamed Korea Way, like it's been snatched straight from Seoul. "Do you talk to your dad a lot?"

"At least once a week," Gigi says, looking at the photo on her desk. It's Gigi and her parents on the beach, wind-tousled hair, glistening skin. They look happy. "I think me leaving was harder on him than on my mama. Even though he doesn't say it."

I look across the room at my own desk, bare, no mementos, no photos. "I never knew my father," I say, sitting up in bed. I haven't talked to anyone—except my mom—about this in ages. If ever. Sei-Jin was the last one I told about it. "I think he was a dancer, too. But I don't know. My mom never talks about him."

Gigi is silent, unsure of what to say. So I speak again. "But I want to know about him. I'm going to find out. Even if it kills me." Or my mom.

"You should," she says, grinning. "It's such a big part of you, I'm sure. That's why you're such a natural, a born dancer. It runs in your blood." She smiles to herself, then at me again. "You know, I'll help if you want. If I can."

I don't know why this surprises me. If Gigi's anything, it's helpful. Even to someone like me, who's been less than welcoming. Maybe I should try more. But I shake it off. "Thanks, but I think I'll be okay."

I turn around in my bed, my face toward the wall. I will not cry. I will not cry. Especially not in front of her. I don't know how to let anyone get close to me like that.

22.

Gigi

TIME GOES BY IN A blur here, much faster than it does in California. With rehearsals and classes and homework—and Alec—my days are a whir of activity. I usually sneak away to the park in the mornings to find a quiet moment or two—it's just a few blocks away, looming and majestic, but some of the girls don't even realize it exists. June never comes when I ask her to go with me.

These days, she says, it's too cold. I kind of love it—the way the air puffs white when you breathe out, the fresh snow on the ground. But she's always reminding me that it will be black in a day or two. And then she retreats back into herself. So it's right about this time of night that the homesickness starts.

Dusk settles in, and it's dinnertime here, but hardly anyone eats. It's midafternoon in San Francisco, right around the time when I'd get home from school and my mama would make me a snack—her homemade blueberry granola and yogurt, or hard-boiled eggs and whole wheat toast—before I headed to rehearsal. She'd paint in the studio next to the kitchen, and my dad would come in from his office, ink-stained hands from reading at least ten different newspapers, a big grin on his face. He'd fire off a gazillion questions about my day, about the ballet we were rehearsing, about school, how I was feeling and if I had had any heart palpitations.

And the worst was when he'd ask about boys.

I never had anything to tell him about boys back then. Before here, before Alec, there was no one. Much to my dad's relief. That's all different now. Alec makes me feel good, feel like I belong, like this whole thing isn't just a fluke. He makes me miss home less. He makes me happy.

I move my butterfly terrarium to my desk, and I crack the window open. Snow collects on the sill, and some of it flutters inside. I watch it accumulate into little mounds and can't focus on my math homework. I love how the little flakes pause on the window before melting into drops. Back home, the mist over San Francisco never transformed into anything this pretty. This is what February should look like. This is what Valentine's Day should be like.

My phone buzzes. I can feel June simmering as I comb through my pile of blankets in search of it. Every little thing I do seems to bug her this week. She's been all weird and moody, more so than usual June behavior. Makes me wonder if there's a boy. Or if she'd even tell me if there was one. And any moment of temporary friendship we had seems long gone. It's almost like the last conversation we had about her dad didn't happen. When

I complained to my friend Ella from back home about it over text, she said June's attitude was probably about the cast list. She reminded me that I don't know what it feels like to be an understudy, that I don't know what it's like not to be picked first.

"Do you want to rehearse together tomorrow after Pilates?" I ask June.

She doesn't answer for such a long time that I almost forget that I asked the question in the first place.

"No," she finally says.

"Want to go down to Times Square after Pilates instead?" Before I moved into the dorms and to this school, I thought I'd have a close friend to do everything with, like many of the other girls have. No such luck here.

"Why would I ever want to go there?" she asks, a sour look marring her face. "Too dirty. Too loud. And tourists."

I stop trying, and take out my phone. Alec's name appears in the text box two seconds after I push in my passcode. My heart accelerates too fast. I get a little dizzy with excitement. While I was at home in California, he was in Switzerland with his family for most of winter break, and we messaged back and forth. But I don't know exactly what it means to be someone's girlfriend. We also haven't kissed since that night onstage, swept up in classes and rehearsals since we got back from winter break.

The text reads: *Meet me outside of the building* :)

I let out a little squeal as I text him back yes.

"Now what?" June complains. "What're you so excited about?"

I can't hold it in. "Alec asked me to meet him."

I wait for her excitement, but she sighs.

"For Valentine's Day!" I gush.

"Oh, wow," she says in a monotone pitch. "Sounds thrilling." She tries hard not to roll her eyes.

I put on the new dress my parents gave me for Christmas: a vintage 1940s tea dress my mom found at the thrift store a few blocks from our house. I pull on tights, and wet my hair a little, working a cream into it. I pull at the curls so that they billow around my face like a halo. I put on cute, dangly earrings and an armful of bangles. And then, for a minute, I ponder wearing my monitor. I open the drawer where it's hidden and peer down at it. I can hear Dr. Khanna's words again: *Even when you're not exercising, you could still have a palpitation.*

June pretends to have her nose in her history book, but I catch her watching me. So I leave it there, even though I know I should put it on. Even if it's to prove to Mama, Daddy, Aunt Leah, and Nurse Connie that I don't need it.

I put on my winter coat and hat, and head for the door. "See you later. Cover for me, will ya?"

I tiptoe into the hall. Bette's door is wide open and music drifts out. As I ease past and toward the elevator, I hear a whistle.

"Well, don't you look beautiful," Bette says, appearing in the doorway in little pajama shorts and mukluk slippers. Her legs are two long, pale beams of light: smooth and stark and flawless.

I don't know what to say. Each time I see her, I think about calling her out about the mean things she did to me last semester, but it doesn't seem worth it. After all, I did get the lead role. Again. And her boyfriend. Bette's used to winning. If I can just keep the peace—but that's seeming more and more unlikely as she stares me down, her eyes like ice and her mouth still impossibly red from that lipstick she's always wearing now, even in pajamas.

"Uh, hi" is all I can manage, suddenly feeling frumpy and inadequate, even though I'm the one all dressed up. I wonder what she used to wear for special nights with Alec. I wonder what they used to do, if tonight feels different to him. A good different, I hope.

She plays with a lock of her silky blond hair. "Heading out for Valentine's Day?"

"Yeah . . ."

Bette eyes me—the perfect skin on her forehead scrunches. A pang of guilt hits me, knowing that she probably misses Alec, and this time last year she would have been the one going out with him.

"Did you guys get a room?" she asks, pointed, and all my guilt falls away, like an anchor dropping. "We used to do that. The Waldorf. It's Alec's favorite—"

I know she's going to keep at it, so I turn away from her. "Bye. See you later."

I wait for the elevator, feeling her eyes burn into my back.

"Hey, Solomon," I greet the front desk guy, and he beams. I'm the only dancer who actually uses his name. I sign myself out, leaving the time blank, and he lets me go outside. I keep thinking about what Bette said, but I'm determined not to let her ruin this night, to ruin Alec for me. Snowflakes flutter down from a dark sky, their tiny shadows making perfect pictures on the sidewalk. I let them rest on my nose and melt into my skin. I think I'll grow to love East Coast winters. As a California girl, I know I shouldn't like the snow, but there's something clean and fresh about it. I love how the ice crystals have the power to quiet the streets and force people inside.

The *petit rats* race out of the building from late classes, headed home. They giggle and point at me. Some ask me for my autograph, but I promise to give it to them tomorrow before morning ballet. I turn away from school and into the bustle of the city. I blow air from my mouth just to see it change into little clouds. I hear a whistle and turn to my right. Alec's standing there.

He leans into a lamppost. He looks like he belongs in college, not in high school. He's wearing a winter coat, a red knit hat, and nice pants. I try to walk slowly so I don't fall. I see his big white smile and I can't help myself. I speed up, fighting the urge to run.

"Hey," he says, when I'm close.

"Hi," I say, surrendering to my feelings, jumping up into his arms. He kisses all over my face. I kiss him right back, all over his face. I like the little stubble he's left on his cheeks.

"Someone's just as excited to see me as I am to see her," he says, and we just stand there for a minute, the snow dotting our jackets and hats. I let him kiss me again, on the mouth this time, and the warmth erases the cold. I let him push the peppermint candy from his mouth into mine. I let him rest his hand on the small of my back. I let him lean into me so he can feel my body.

I can't resist a smile while his lips press mine, causing him to grin. If this is what it means to be his girlfriend, I could be it forever. He releases me, leaving me to suck on the mint. He pulls me forward into the snowy night. "Let's go! We're going to be late."

"For what?" I say.

"Our reservation."

I love the way he says *our* and *we* and *us*—those words only ever referred to my parents or my friends from home. The new meaning wraps around me and I remember watching couples kiss on the trolley, wondering how they got "there," to that place where touching and kissing is like talking. I remember never believing I could ever have anything like that. I remember never really wanting it. And now, all I want is to do those things with Alec.

He leads me.

"Where are we going?" I ask, eagerly following.

"You'll see."

We walk past an entrance to Central Park, where the path is quiet, and we walk through it from west to east. I love how each time I go to the park I see something new. We step into a fancy Italian restaurant called Maria's on the Upper East Side, and Alec opens the door for me. The restaurant is warm, aglow with votive candles. We brush off, and Alec dusts snowflakes out of my curls. A waiter leads us to our table and I fight the permanent grin on my face. My cheeks hurt from all the smiling and cold air.

"Can we sit near the window?" I ask. "I want to watch the snow."

The waiter looks at me like I'm ten years old, but obliges, leading us to one of the side tables. I look around at all the couples sharing wine and dipping their bread in oil. Is this what grown-ups do on Valentine's Day? I mean, this and fancy hotel rooms, maybe? I feel like such a kid compared to Bette, compared to Alec. I remember making cards with my mama's paints and special paper and handing them out at school, and my dad bringing home two bouquets, one for her and one for me. That was the extent of my Valentine's Days for the past fifteen years, and now this year it's different. I still feel like a kid playing dress-up in my mama's heels.

Earlier my dad called, leaving his sweet message, and he even sent a dozen roses. I laugh out loud remembering his card.

"What's so funny?" Alec asks, pulling me out of my memory.

"My dad," I say, "and the Valentine's Day card he sent me."

I laugh again. "He said that he was my only valentine, despite the boy I kissed onstage. I think he's still trying to figure out . . . like . . . what we're doing. I haven't really said anything to them."

"Oh, yeah?" he says with a tease.

"I mean . . . like, yeah," I admit. "They were on me about being on my phone all break texting you."

"My dad, too. I ran the phone bill up while we were in Switzerland." He takes my hand. "Well, I'd never want to compete with Mr. Stewart. But you know I like you."

"Is that so?" I try to flirt, then feel my cheeks redden. The words are brand-new and sweet as anything.

"Uh, well, I guess." He rubs his head. "I sound like an idiot right now. I'm usually better with words. And you never really answered my question, when I asked you to be my girlfriend."

My mind replays the night of the *Nutcracker* performance

and us backstage. I remember him asking, and me being so surprised. I start to laugh. "I guess I didn't officially say yes." I quickly practice saying yes in my head like a whisper, so I don't scream it in the restaurant. A deep heat rises in me from the pit of my stomach all the way to my cheeks.

"I guess I should ask again," he says.

"That you should," I say back.

He puts his hands to his chest, like he's playing Romeo from the ballet. "Giselle Elizabeth Stewart, will you be my girlfriend?" He reaches for my hand to make it even more exaggerated and cheesy. "Wait! Wait, before you answer." He riffles through his pockets, pulling out a tissue-wrapped wad. He slides it across the table.

My legs shake under the table. I feel like I'm going to burst with emotion. I unwrap the bundle, and it's a tiny bouquet of origami roses made of red paper. His signature.

I finger one and notice each has a different shape. "Alec . . ."

His mouth curls into his crooked smile. "So . . . ?"

"I already thought I was your girlfriend!"

He grins at me like he's the happiest guy in the world. And I can't help but grin back. When I thought of what this first year here in New York would be like, I never expected to earn top soloist roles so quickly. I never expected to love being in the city. And I never expected this. I never expected Alec.

Still blushing, I stumble with my pasta order when the waiter comes, because my mind is all over the place. What do people in relationships do? Every movie romance races through my head.

"So, girlfriend?" he says.

"Yes, boyfriend?" I answer, then feel silly, like we really are in some romantic comedy.

"Will Mr. Stewart be happy with the confirmation of this development in our relationship?" he jokes.

I think of my dad just shaking his head back and forth like he does when he's trying to hide a laugh. Mama will frown, as she thinks boys are a distraction in youth, especially to an artist— she didn't meet my dad until she was in her late thirties, which is why they only had me.

I parrot him. "Will Mrs. Lucas be excited about me?"

His face drops and all the excited energy between us swirls away, like water down a drain. His smile goes away and he leans back in his chair. I freak and fidget with the napkin in my lap. "Did I say something wrong?"

"No," he says, looking down. "I just don't really talk about her, is all."

I open my mouth to ask why, but he keeps talking. "She left when I was little," he says.

"Who was the lady with your dad at opening night?" I whisper, feeling nosy and ridiculous, but overwhelmed with the need to know.

"My stepmother," he says, dipping his bread in the olive oil.

"Oh," I say for lack of anything better. I'd assumed it was his mother because they all share the same perfect white-blond hair and bright blue eyes.

"She's a real bitch," he mutters. "My mother left because my dad had a problem with staying away from other women."

My face must look puzzled, because he explains.

"He cheated on her a bunch, so she took off," Alec says. "But didn't take me with her. Or my little sister, Sophie. Haven't seen my mother in almost six years."

My heart sinks. How could someone not want Alec and leave him behind? I reach for his hand under the small table. He lets me hold it and I trace words like *sorry* and *like* and *love* and *amazing* into his palm.

"I've never really talked to anyone about this," he whispers. "Not like seriously."

I don't say anything, and I fight away questions about if Bette knows—just let the silence settle between us and let my hands tell him everything I want to say. He lets go and rubs his warm palms along my leg, lightly pinching the softness of my inner thigh. It sends a shiver through me, and I wonder if his hands will wander farther under my dress. I wonder if he booked us a room tonight. I wonder if I'm ready for that. My heart starts to thump heavily and a little wave of light-headedness hits me from all the dancing earlier and the excitement of the date. It's a reminder of what's wrong with me. Should I tell him about my condition? A familiar emotion crops up. I don't want anyone to know. I don't want him to look at me differently.

Alec changes the subject away from his mother, and brightens, talking about dancing the part of Count Albrecht in our upcoming performance and how it could launch his career early, how dancing the role of Giselle could do the same for me. He explains how all the company ballet masters and madames will be there, and some from rival schools and companies, hoping to steal us away. I try to listen but somehow can't seem to quiet my questions and newfound insecurities about being afraid to tell him something so personal, even though he just shared with me.

"You want to start rehearsing for our *pas* early? Before Doubrava and Mr. K want to work with us? So we're ready?"

"Huh?" I say, completely tuned out.

"Did you hear anything I just said?" he says. "What's wrong?"

"Nothing," I say.

"What just happened?" He stares at me like he's trying to find the answer on my face. "Just tell me. I can tell something's up."

"I can't," I whisper. "It's nothing."

"C'mon . . ."

"I can't," I say sharper than I intended. "I'm sorry. I just . . ."

He starts running his hands over his buzzed head and taking sips of water. Sip. Glass down. Glass up. Sip. Glass down. Over and over. I don't think he's actually thirsty at all. And now I've ruined it.

"This has been so nice." I try to smile and reach for his hand. He lets me rub his palm, but he doesn't stroke my fingers, doesn't try to hold my hand in his own.

I pick at the rest of my food while he pays.

"Thank you," I say, "for dinner."

"You're welcome." He stands and we get our coats. He still holds my hand on the way home, but it doesn't feel the same as when we walked to dinner. He doesn't squeeze it or hold me tight like he wants me close. My feet are heavy boulders as we tread back to school. The lights are out and it's almost eleven. He stops me before we go inside.

"I really wish you wouldn't keep things from me. That's something Bette used to do."

Her name hits me in my chest.

I open my mouth to protest and say *it's complicated*, but he pulls me close abruptly, and kisses me hard. It's not the same kind of kiss he gave me at the beginning of the night. It's rough and pushy and aggressive—all the things Alec is onstage. When he releases me, I look around to see if anyone's watching. Then he takes the elevator up to his floor without another word.

Restless, I decide not to go to my room. Instead, I head to the basement studio. I race through the lobby, the empty office corridor, disappear down the staircase, go inside the room. *Plokhaya energiya.* Bad luck. The Russians are right, and tonight I feel it wrap all around me like long fingers as I step into the darkness. I don't turn on the light. My feet know the path, and my body curves around every heap. I barely make it to my place in front of the mirror before the tears begin to fall.

Alec's scent is trapped in my clothes and the night replays in my head. I hear myself refuse to tell him about my condition. I hear the insecurity in my voice. I hear the disappointment in his. I imagine him in bed, thinking he doesn't really love me at all. How could he, when he doesn't even really know me? When I won't let him really know me?

I push the button on my cell phone, hoping and wishing that he texted me something, like *It's okay that you didn't tell me whatever it was* or *I understand, I'm not mad* or *You can tell me in your own time.* But the screen is empty.

I finger the little roses he gave me.

I flash the phone's light on the cracked mirror, letting the beam reflect and illuminate a path to the corner. The beam breaks into thousands of tiny suns from the splintered reflection. But something's different. Parts of the mirror are covered. I lift the cell phone screen and more tears come before I even really register what I'm seeing.

It's pictures. Pictures of Bette and Alec. Naked Bette and partially naked Alec. Taped all over the mirror. Arranged in a big, terrible heart shape. I wipe the frantic tears from my eyes and see the final touches: a huge, fully-blossomed black rose taped to the mirror, in the middle of the heart. The rose terrifies me. The pictures are a reminder of my inadequacies. But the rose is a threat. There's a tiny slip of paper attached to its thorny stem, and I prick myself prying it off.

It's just messy handwriting and a message so simple it turns my insides cold. My heart's beating at a strange pace, reminding me again I should be wearing my monitor.

Happy Valentine's Day, Gigi! Be careful with your heart, and with Bette.

23.

Bette

I'M STANDING ON THE SCHOOL'S front staircase, waiting for Eleanor and our cab. She's late. She's always late these days. It's almost ten, and we've got rehearsal tomorrow, but I'm determined to not let Valentine's Day be a total wash. I shiver and pull on my coat. It's not very heavy, but the fur collar warms my cheeks. A vintage rabbit fur bolero stolen from my mother's closet. A classic. I push away thoughts of what Alec and I used to do on Valentine's Day. Our tradition of making snowmen in the park or going dancing, all dolled up, like we were tiny versions of our parents.

I stare at the door and think about going back inside to wait when I hear my name. It's Adele. She's wearing one of those Russian trooper hats, ice-white, like her hair and skin. Her eyes almost glow blue in the darkness. Her coat hugs her body, and even though she has on layers, you can't tell. Those kinds of fabrics would make me look huge. Of course, Adele escaped the family curse of curves without any help, according to my mother and everyone else I've ever talked to. But we can't all be as shiny and spindly and delicate as Adele.

The day before winter break was over, my mother asked if I was wearing a padded bra. When I said no, her eyebrows shot up to the sky and she gave me her pouty-lipped pity smile. "Well. At least the boys will love you," she'd said. Adele, so kind it hurts, told my mother to stop harassing me. I think Adele being nice about it made it even worse.

"Did you get my texts?" she says, so annoyed that her face starts to resemble our mother's.

"No." I buried my phone at the bottom of my purse to avoid looking for texts from Alec that will never come.

Her cheeks are pink from the cold, and it makes me think back to when we were little, running around on the winter beach in Montauk. Before our father left and took the beach house with him. "What are you doing out here?" she asks, frowning at my thin jacket, my gloveless hands. "Mom told you I was coming over today, didn't she?"

She looks up at the school emblem over the door lovingly. And for a moment I just want to sit next to her on my bed, her old one, let her sew ribbons on some of my new pointe shoes, bitch about our mother, hear all the company hookup gossip, and rehash what went wrong during my audition for the lead role in *Giselle*. But that would mean being me. Tonight, I want to be someone else. I want to be somewhere else, I want to forget all the things going on between these walls. Especially with Henri.

"Yeah, guess I forgot. Now I'm headed out. It's Valentine's

Day," I say. "You don't have plans?"

"I'm trying to be promoted to principal, Bette. There's no time for plans outside of ballet," she says. Her words are pointed: if I were more like Adele and less like myself, I'd be the elegant and ethereal Giselle. But I'm not like Adele. And being around her tonight would keep slapping that reality in my face.

Adele used to say, "So many ballets are about love, so we have to know a little about it, right?" Maybe Adele was in love at some point, but we aren't the kind of sisters who share those sorts of details.

"Well, we should talk. I feel like you're flailing. Mom said you never gave her the details about what happened at the *Giselle* audition."

"Maybe because I don't want to talk about it." My eyes find an ice-covered railing to fixate on.

"How can I help? I'll show you whatever little details of the variation you missed. At this point, you've got to be cast in better roles. You have only one level left at school." She touches my arm, concerned, and I can feel my temper simmering.

Eleanor flounces out at last, and saves me from further conversations with Adele. "Where are we going?" Eleanor says before seeing Adele. Then her mouth drops open and she gets this stupid, starstruck look on her face. "Oh, hi, Adele," she says in a weird, pitchy voice. "You coming with us? Please say you are."

"Well, Bette didn't say where you were going," she says, showing all her teeth, like she's onstage.

"Let's go," I say, examining the bottom part of Eleanor's dress that peeks out from under her coat, trying to get her away from

Adele as quickly as possible. I won't lose another person who is in *my* life. Not even to my sister. "Red on Valentine's Day? Cliché much?"

"I got this out of the lost and found last year," she whines, and I know I shouldn't have said that. She's trying hard to work on her looks.

"And you probably brought bedbugs with it to our room," I say, not knowing why I can't stop my mouth from saying hurtful things tonight. Maybe it's the fact that it's Valentine's Day, and I've never been dateless before.

"Bette." Adele starts to scold me.

"We have reservations," I say.

"We do?" Eleanor says.

"Yes." I grab her arm, and pull her forward to reinforce the lie. "I'll call you tomorrow, Adele."

We leave her on the staircase and head down the block. I crane to look for the Town Car I called for, but can't stop looking at her dress. It's so familiar: a deep scarlet and fringed on the bottom. The kind of dress you don't forget. I can't place it.

"I think it was Cassie's," Eleanor says, her words slow and deliberate, like I might have trouble comprehending. She looks at me and I avoid her eyes. Avoid memories of Cassie. Avoid memories of what I did or didn't do to her. Forget what I did with Henri to secure his silence. But of course that's why I recognize the dress. Cassie wore it a year ago, last fall, to the back-to-school party I always throw in September. It's in a hundred pictures. She spun around and around in it all night, saying she loved the way the fringe felt hitting her thighs. I swallow hard: the promise of a great night fading fast.

Our driver pulls over to the curb. I yank El into the car, still reeling from her ridiculous audacity to wear something of Cassie's and then tell me about it. She stumbles out a thousand apologies as we climb in the car.

"First stop. Seventy-fifth and Fifth," I tell the driver.

"Liz's house?" Eleanor says.

"Yeah, she's coming with."

"Is that a good idea?"

"Does it matter?" I glare at her like she's speaking Chinese.

"Have you spoken to her since she left?" Eleanor's eyes get all big with sympathy.

"Only online. But she's fine. In school and everything." Liz's new school's the kind of place where you wear expensive blazers and have fake IDs. A lot of celeb kids go there. "Why haven't you talked to her?"

"She's not answering my texts. Is she still dancing?" It's so weird for them not to be talking. It feels like everything is changing way too fast.

"She's taking a break from ballet until the summer intensives." The car pulls up in front of her luxe Upper East Side building. The doorman opens my side with a gloved hand. I tell him to call up for her. Moments later she comes slinking down in a too-tight bubble-gum-pink dress and checkered heels and big gold earrings, like she's fallen out of some terrible music video. Her legs are sticks and the hideous dress rides up because there's barely anything to hold on to. She throws her coat on the seat before sliding into the car.

I open my mouth to comment.

"Don't say shit to me about this dress," she says. "I'm finally small enough to wear it."

I feel Eleanor's eyes on me. They silently say, *She looks and sounds a little crazy.*

I can't exactly disagree, but we're this far along, and I still need a good night. I have no idea what to expect, but we head on our way downtown to a club I know will take our fake IDs. Well, according to Liz. Eleanor and Liz talk about her new school while I fight to stay part of the conversation, fight to keep my thoughts anchored in place and not drifting back to Cassie, Alec, and what happened with Henri.

We pull up in front of the club, and I'm ready for something fabulous and new and intoxicating. We step into line and take out our IDs. It's a thrill. This is what New York City teenagers do, according to my mother and TV and the occasional trashy magazine that ends up in the student lounge.

But when we get inside, it's nothing like what I had in my head.

The smell of liquor hangs heavy in the air, and though the club's decor has all the glitz I could want—fifty-foot ceilings, vintage mirrors, expensive art, chandeliers—the bar is just a bunch of plastic bottles of the cheap stuff and buckets of ice with a few beers nestled in. We could not be more overdressed in our tight-fitting cocktail numbers and over-the-top makeup. Everyone else is rocking leggings and ripped T-shirts and clunky boots and fake fur vests. We're the youngest by a few years. Everyone else looks college age and bored.

Eleanor's face falls on cue. "Um, gross," she says. "Can we not? We have Pilates in the morning."

"Just an hour?" I say, tugging her forward. Liz disappears into the crowd, like she belongs there.

"Where you going?" I call out.

"Be back," she says.

"I'll get us some drinks," I tell Eleanor, who's still frowning. "It's an adventure."

"You're drinking?" Eleanor's lips curl in disgust, as if I've said I'm going to urinate in the middle of the crowd or tattoo Mr. K's face on my stomach.

"Just one drink. Vodka?" I say. "Whatever."

Eleanor looks like she's about to tell me not to, so I cross my arms, getting ready to defend myself. "What's up with you the last few days? I can tell something's going on with you," she says, shaking her head at me the way a mother might. Not my mother. But someone's mother.

"I'm having a shitty week," I say. "You're going to make me talk about it now?" Eleanor's toes are peeking out of her sandals and I want to step on them. With a stiletto. I want to crush them, an impulse so violent and unexpected I take a noticeable step back and close my eyes for an extra-long second to get back control.

"I guess not," she says. "Just get me a water."

I make my way to the bar. And she follows. Henri's got my head all messed up. Every blond girl I see reminds me of Cassie. Like there're photographs of her all over the place. I watch one of the blondes dance, and it's like it's her. The grace of her movements, her ridiculous talent, resonates. I try to shake it off.

"I'll get you wine. It's fine," I say to Eleanor, who is busy staring at every person who passes her by.

Truth be told, I don't drink much. I have a glass of champagne on opening nights or gala events, or throw a few back when I need to get someone else to have some so I can get information, but that's it. I'm not an idiot. I haven't worked this hard and this long to throw it away on some foul-tasting carb-heavy crap, like I'm a suburban teenager with a sad dye job and a football-playing boyfriend and nothing to live for but the next party.

I'm special. Allegedly.

But just this once I want the taste of something normal and frivolous and poorly planned. I want to drink until Henri's threats lose their weight, until the *Giselle* music leaves my head, until I can forget all about Gigi Stewart and the fact that Alec has really left me. I watch a husky guy with a stained concert T-shirt order a drink by punching it into a touchpad screen at the bar, and I copy his technique, and the bartender brings me over a cocktail that is an appealing, watery pink.

I try to see where Liz has gone, but the lights flash on and off and I can't see much of anything. I feel a surge of panic the instant before I put the tiny red straw to my lips to taste the mixture. Adele once told me that the key to success is not letting it out of your sight for even one minute. My mother says the key to success is being better than everyone else. She says it with that look in her eyes, like some people (Adele) have it, and some people don't, and she hasn't decided which one I am yet.

I take my first swallow and I'm wishing I didn't cough, didn't let my eyes water, at that first burning taste.

"That good?" Eleanor says, raising her eyebrows and looking around like a captive squirrel. "See? This is what we are *not* missing out on." She takes her time looking over each and every guest. "Right?"

I don't agree, even though I'm supposed to. I like the loud, cranky music and the oversized plastic jewelry the girls all wear, the bored way they hunch over their drinks and lean against the walls.

Liz returns, downs one drink and then another, but basically ignores us.

"What's up with you?" My question an almost perfect repeat of Eleanor's to me.

"Nothing. I'm fine," she says, the syllables of her words falling sloppily over one another. "I just want to dance. I am a ballerina." She leaves us and sashays into the crowd, shaking and moving her hips like she was never a classically trained ballerina at all, like she's something else altogether.

I follow, determined to enjoy my night. I try to drop one hip and roll my shoulders forward. I move my feet so they are parallel instead of turned out. Like her. It feels all wrong, holding my body this way. I take another sip of the terrible drink and hold it in my mouth before I swallow it down. Then another. Then another. Eleanor starts gossiping about the conservatory's gay boys and who's hooking up with who, and before long, the drink—as disgusting as it was—is gone. My head is all fuzzy.

"I like this place," I say. I guess the vodka-filled version of me does. I like how dark it is, and the constantly shifting stream of scents: thick and musky perfumes, wine, tequila, beer, and body odor. I like the heavy, eye-covering bangs on all the girls and the strangers finding each other, meeting each other, going in for first kisses. I like the stream of banter, from which I occasionally can catch a few snippets about who's found an awesome spot in the West Village or which subway line is the crappiest.

At school it's all endless mirrors and the lemony smell of disinfectant in the mornings, followed by the smell of sweat in the evenings after we've all danced our asses off. It's all expected, routine, exactly the same as the day before and the days to come.

This ridiculous club is an assault on all my senses. A welcome assault. A relief. Not what I had in mind, but maybe even better.

I'd forgotten Eleanor was next to me, but there she is, shaking her head in disbelief at all the chaos around her: bodies grabbing and rubbing one another, a man shoving his tongue down a woman's throat and lifting up her skirt. I try to get Eleanor to talk about the music playing, but she says nothing. She usually never shuts up, always has an opinion on everything and everyone, always has something she's just dying to talk about. But here, in the real world, or at least this version of it, she's mute now that she's tuned into her surroundings. Shaking a little, even. Playing with her necklace nervously. Rubbing her red cheeks. She's a wreck.

I stumble forward a little.

"Are you okay?" Eleanor says, but I feel fine. Better than fine. Kind of good. Calm, like with my mother's Xanax, but excited, too. Ready.

"Are *you* okay?" I ask. "We should find Liz. I should tell her about Henri. I want to tell her how much I hate him," I say when the glass is empty. "I want her to know how he's messing with me. She'll know how to fix it." I haven't told her about what happened with him at the restaurant. I haven't told her much of anything lately.

"What's happening with Henri?" Eleanor asks, her eyes full of hurt that I know is from me keeping a secret from her.

"Who's been calling you? Where have you been running off to lately?"

Her mouth opens and shuts, but only strangled sounds come out, like the words are choking her. "It's nothing."

"Then nothing is happening with Henri," I say, walking off into the crowd to find Liz again. Of course Eleanor follows. We've been near the bar the whole time, like we never really committed to staying, but now we move through the crowd and the noise. As always, everyone's watching us. Sometimes with concern, sometimes with envy, sometimes with lust. We are legs and bones and pointy shoulders and necks that never end. We stand out.

"It's nothing," she calls out again, like she's trying to convince both herself and me.

"Whatever you say." I'm looking for Liz, but get distracted watching a pretty girl throw her hair over her shoulder and flirt with some guy whose hands are deep in his own pockets and hunched over. Maybe I don't need to find her. Maybe I just want to see what it would be like to be Not-a-Ballerina. I put a hand on my hip and tousle my own hair, the way she does hers. Sip at the ice in my cup. Even the ice has the metallic taste of alcohol on it. I saunter closer to the dance floor, Eleanor trailing me like a little lost puppy. Midstep I run straight into Liz. She's leaning in, talking to a sultry, foreign-looking older guy—Brazilian, Argentinian? She's hanging on his every word.

"Hey!" I say, too loud and too close to her face. Liz pulls away from me, and tries to look over her shoulder at the man like she doesn't have the slightest idea about who I am.

"Henri's been messing with me. Threatening me about what we did to Cassie. All that old stuff." The alcohol is like truth serum—the words tumble out despite the consequence. This finally gets her attention.

"Better be careful then," she shouts, sounding not at all like my old partner in crime. She moves away from the older man to face me. "You can't trust anyone—I learned that the hard way." I must look shocked, because she continues, her voice low and measured, like she's been waiting to say this. Like she's been practicing. "For example, I thought we trusted each other, but I bet you're the one who told on me to Nurse Connie. Got them to weigh me two times a week. Watch me like I was some criminal. You knew I was going to beat you soon." But her darting eyes give her away. She's scared. I can tell by the way she licks all the lipstick off her mouth.

I play with the too-short hem of my dress. I am the nakedest in the room. Looking for comfort, I turn my feet out again, throw my shoulders back, let my elbows find their tiny bend. Ballerina Bette can deal with the moment. "Who do you think you are?" I sound like my mother when she's mistreated by people who should know she's an *Abney*. She's important. She's rich. She knows people. "I didn't say anything to anyone about you. I was worried. But I still didn't say a word. You're one of my best friends."

"You're the only one I told my weight to. How else would they know to check on me?" The answer is obvious to anyone who looks at her—she's nearly a skeleton. But she insists someone outed her.

"I swear I didn't say anything," I say, trying to touch her wrist. I can't lose her, too. But maybe I already have.

The older man smirks at us before slipping away into the crowd of other girls who might be desperate enough to hook up with him.

She cocks her head and takes me in. "You're ridiculous."

My face turns an even brighter shade of red. I'm caught in a tornado of her anger and sadness. I don't know what happened. I miss her being at school even though I haven't gotten to text or talk to her as much as I've wanted. She's fuming now.

"This has you written all over it. I was getting too good."

Eleanor looks back and forth between Liz and me. "What's going on?"

"Bette turned me in. Made them watch me. Made them weigh me." She just sounds plain crazy now.

A man passes me two sickly sweet shots, like magic. I take them both. And when I hand the empty cups to him, I smile up at him in that wicked way I know Alec always responds to. But then, bolstered by vodka, I turn back to the matter at hand.

"How could Bette even do that?" Eleanor asks.

"I didn't do that, Liz. You're one of my best friends. Have

been forever." I'm slurring. "I've protected you. If anyone ever said anything about you, I'd tell them to shut up. I'd threaten them. I made girls afraid." I'm dizzy, I'm pissed, and Liz's accusations have swirled into the mess I'm becoming. I want to remind her how many girls I'd yelled at in the past for calling her Ana, a code name for anorexic, or claiming that she only ate a strawberry for dinner. My eyes are closed and the world spins and I can't find my center, my balance, the very core of me that I've been working on since I was a toddler. It's like, for that one minute, I am a different person entirely.

"You've done so many messed-up things to so many people, how can you remember? What's one last thing? Couldn't get rid of Gigi, so you got rid of me," Liz shouts. "Watch out, Eleanor. I bet you're next. The girls at school are so afraid of you. They don't even report half the stuff you do. But mark my words, Bette, karma's coming."

Before I can even begin to wrap my head around what she means, Eleanor takes my hand into her own soft, little one, her pudgy fingers wrapping safely around mine. The sensation is so familiar, so comforting, that for the first time in years, maybe in my whole life, I let myself be led. She drags me away, shouting at Liz that she's messed up and should go home.

We leave her there, and take a cab home to the conservatory. In the silence of our twenty-minute ride, Eleanor's unwound the necklaces from her neck and dropped them in her purse. She's unpinned her hair, letting all the frizz back in. She's even managed to get some of her makeup off.

"What were you thinking?" she finally says. I don't know

what she's talking about: the booze, the bar, the fight with Liz. All three, probably.

"Just wanted to have a little fun," I say. I sound faraway, muted, even to myself.

"Ballet is fun," Eleanor replies in a tight little voice. All her bravado is gone. All that's left is plain old Eleanor, even though she seems older and wiser. "She's really sick, Bette."

"Yep."

"Should we tell her mom? She needs help."

"Yep," I say again.

"We can never let it all get to us like that, right?" Eleanor says, her voice climbing to that familiar whine. I'm sick of hearing it. "Maybe we shouldn't try to deal with it alone. Maybe we should tell Mr. K, instead of taking matters—"

I grab her arm, forcing her to look at me, forcing myself back to steady. "I always take matters into my own hands. That's what you do. Because you have to fight. And you need to step up and take what you want, too." I don't know if these words are mine or belong to all the alcohol I drank. "You need to take control. Just like you did when you got that part in *The Nutcracker*."

Eleanor sighs, like she isn't hearing me. "Bette, what if Liz gets worse? Or comes back to school for the summer session?" she asks, all her bravado gone. "What are we going to do?" Eleanor blinks away tears.

"I don't know," I say.

Because I really, really don't.

24.

June

VALENTINE'S DAY HAS COME AND gone, but everywhere I turn it's still all pink and red and hearts and flowers. It's enough to make a girl want to throw up. Not that I haven't been on the edge of that already. The RAs haven't even changed the hall bulletin boards to the spring kites and windy clouds they always put up in March. And it's already the fourth.

Lately, I can't stop thinking about my father, about who he could be, about how I might find him. But I refuse to ask my mother again, and I won't go home. Which leaves me at a dead end, my brain on an endless loop, rehashing what little information I do have over and over again. I tried to ask Madame Matvienko again, but she closed the costume room door in my face, muttering in Russian like she didn't understand my question.

So I've been throwing myself into dance, rehearsing every spare moment of the day, and late into the night, when the others have abandoned the studios for studying or greasy midnight

Chinese food deliveries that they'll wear on their hips for months. Or hooking up. Like Gigi.

I stretch my leg across the barre in studio G, and can't keep myself from smiling in the mirror. Valentine's night, she came home all forlorn, like something went wrong on her oh-so-perfect date with Alec. She was all sweaty and worked up, so she'd either been dancing or something else entirely. But she had a paper towel wrapped around something she was trying to hide, something she tucked into the drawer, hoping I wouldn't notice, before she went off to shower. Of course, as soon as she was gone, I peeked. Photos of Bette and Alec. Pretty much naked. Bette is confident. And a true bitch to leave those for her.

I turn sideways in the mirror, and run my fingers over my stomach and hips. I've never been naked in front of a boy. Not counting summers in Jayhe's paddling pool when we were little. I could see why Gigi was upset. But she never said anything about it—not to me, anyway—and the next day, she and Alec seemed fine. He came and got her in the morning, and they went on a walk or something. Now, it seems like they're tighter than ever. She spends every waking minute with him, dancing, rehearsing, studying. And who knows what else. Maybe she has something to prove. To him. To herself. It can't be easy following Bette. Onstage or in life. I know I wouldn't want to be in her place.

As I finish my cooldown, the studio's empty—except for my mirror image staring back at me from every corner of the room. In an instant, I hate the way I look. My eyes are shallow, my cheeks splotchy. I wish they'd keep the mirrors covered. I'm sick of looking at myself. I danced well, but when I'm not on my toes, a weariness settles in, the exhaustion visible. It doesn't suit me. I have to shake it off. I bury the voice inside that whispers *You need to eat more if you want energy and strength.* I stretch out into a deep V, laying my chest down on the floor, spreading my arms out to reach for my extended toes. I can feel the pain in my muscles as they tighten and spasm, then release, a calm washing over me. I rise, and realize I'm not alone. Someone's watching me.

Jayhe.

He's standing in the doorway, and he ducks his head a little, suddenly bashful, when he catches me catching him. I can't help it, it makes me grin. The kiss we shared seems like ages ago. Now, I can taste it on my lips.

"Hey," he says. "You did good."

I nod, still smiling, and he takes that as an invitation. Which it was. Maybe. He walks in and plops down across from me. I'm so shocked I don't know what to do. "You've been working hard, huh? Sei-Jin said you got a solo."

I nod again and stand, taking a sip of water from my bottle. I wonder what else she says about me. Why would she share that I got a solo?

I start to gather my stuff. I quickly realize I smell like stale sweat and probably the same ginseng soap his mom uses, and want to put some distance between us. But he stands, too, as if to follow.

"Where are you headed now?" he asks, standing not a foot away. There's a smirk playing on his lips—which are so pink and so pale—as if he knows he's up to no good.

"Where's Sei-Jin?" I ask.

"Studying." He shrugs. "She's got a pre-calc test tomorrow, and she's been really cranky lately. I told her I'd see her later. And I . . . don't know . . . was thinking about . . . uh . . ." He shrugs again, suddenly unsure of himself. "You hungry?"

I look at him, shocked at his request. Then, I gaze down at my dance clothes, feeling a bit naked. I'm a mess. I'm exhausted. But this is too good a chance to pass up. And I should eat something.

"Let me go change."

I've been so distracted obsessing about finding my father that I've neglected my plans for Sei-Jin. But Jayhe's walking right into my trap. Or maybe, just maybe, he actually likes me?

Half an hour later, after a quick shower—for which I stole some of Gigi's strawberry-scented body wash—we're at the diner down the block. None of the ABC dancers ever come here. It's all burgers and grilled cheese and other stuff they'd never touch. Me neither, usually. But today I'm starving. I order a chili cheeseburger and a Coke. Not diet. I've never eaten anything like this. Jayhe grins at me.

"You sure?" he says, sipping his coffee. "I thought you dancers didn't eat." He pauses. "Sei-Jin hardly eats."

The waitress brings a bread basket by and I reach right into it, like I'm a normal girl, buttering the bread and taking a big bite. I haven't had butter in, literally, years. It's rough going down, like I can feel the fat coating my insides. But I make myself swallow. I'm going to be a different June today. A regular girl. The one Jayhe knew all those years ago.

"You never come down to the old neighborhood anymore,"

he says, taking a piece of bread himself. No butter. "To church on Sundays or to the festivals."

"I don't really know anyone there anymore," I say, taking another bite. "Except my mom. And she's too busy for things like that."

"Yeah, I heard that her company is doing great."

I nod. The table groans under the weight of all the food the waitress lays down in front of us. Jayhe immediately reaches for one of my fries, then dips it into the meat sauce on his spaghetti. The sight of it makes my stomach turn. My chili burger sits in front of me, expectant. Taunting. I've ordered it. But I don't know if I can actually bring myself to eat it.

"Does your mom want you to join her company? Or, like, go to college?"

"I want to dance," I tell him, hoisting up the burger and holding it in front of my face. Half the chili slips out the other side, plopping down on the plate like a dead animal. Which pretty much is what it is. I can taste the bile in my throat. "I'm going to dance."

"Sei-Jin is applying to Harvard and Princeton," Jayhe says, reaching for another fry. "She's going to study orthopedics." He dips it in his meat sauce. "You know, be a bone doctor. She thinks the dancing will make her stand out."

He won't stop talking about Sei-Jin. If I want my plan to work, I have to take control of this situation. I have to get him to stop thinking (and talking) about Sei-Jin. And I can't believe she doesn't want to go into a company. To at least try to audition for a company. To be a professional dancer. Will she throw it all away? What's the point of it all if she doesn't want to be a ballerina?

I make myself take a bite. The meat is still a bit bloody and salty in my mouth. The chili is hot and pungent, savory. The whole combination is delicious, unlike anything I've tasted. I swallow, and take another bite. Then another.

Jayhe grins at me. "Good, huh?" he says, twirling his spaghetti and slurping it up. He lifts his fork to me. "Wanna try it?"

I lean forward, just enough so that the V-neck of my sweater slinks low, and take the hand holding the fork, bringing it to my mouth. I slurp the spaghetti, just like he did, and grin. "Delicious."

I eat a fry, and then another, and another. Then look back up at him. He has a glint in his eye. I look down at my plate, sure I'm blushing, as the heat creeps down my neck. I look back up at him.

"So what will happen with you and Sei-Jin once she's off to Princeton or Harvard?" I ask. Jayhe's a smart kid, but he's hardly Ivy material.

He shrugs. "I'm sure I'll see her around," he says. "My parents want me to go to Queensborough, then help with the restaurants. Even marry her, maybe, 'cause her dad's so influential in Seoul."

"Is that what you want?" I ask, leaning forward again, looking right into his eyes. They're dark chocolate and sleepy.

He shrugs again, then takes another few bites. "I still want to draw."

Ever since we were little, Jayhe scribbled all over everything. He'd draw the old animes we watched at his *halmeoni*'s house, and he made endless portraits of me. I didn't know he still did it. But I'm glad.

"I'd love to see some of your art sometime," I say, picking at my fries. My stomach is screaming in protest, but I make myself take another bite. A normal girl. "If you'll show me."

It's almost dark as we head back to the dorm, walking through the leftover February snow in March, and I'm grateful, for once, that Gigi's obsessed with Alec. She's been holed up in his room for days, and I know she won't be back till bedtime. Or later.

Jayhe sits on my bed, completely comfortable, as if he's been here a gazillion times, as if we're just the same as we were once, long ago. I don't know why he's being so nice. I don't know why he's hanging out, pretending nothing's changed, after so many years of ignoring me. I don't ask him. I try not to care. It was thrilling sneaking him upstairs without being spotted by Sei-Jin or the other Korean girls.

I sit next to him, and we pore over his draft book, which he had stashed in his bag. He points out this drawing or that. His drawings are so good, so familiar, a grown-up version of his classic bold strokes, still with that wild touch of whimsy. As we reach the end, he tries to close the book, pulling it out of my hands.

"Wait," I say, pulling it back. "I'm not done yet." In the back, there are drawings of a dancer, long and lithe, all sharp angles and soft curves. They're beautiful.

It takes me a minute to realize they're not of Sei-Jin. "She's me," I say.

He looks at me then, for a long time. Like he's making up for all the moments we lost. My heart leaps, and my stomach lurches, but this time it's not the bile that's with me all the time. "I drew them the other day, when I was watching you. I don't really know why."

His fingers graze my arm, the heat of them penetrating through my sweater. He touches my cheekbones, my jawline, studying me, memorizing me.

"You're beautiful," he says. And then he leans in, kissing me.

My heart is hammering and my brain churning with thoughts of chili and onion breath and how it's finally happening for real and how I should have brushed or maybe thrown up or a gazillion other things. But he just leans close, his breath on my ear, and says "Sssshhh," as if he can hear my thoughts going a mile a minute, as if he's known what I've been thinking all along.

"It doesn't matter," he says. "It's okay."

It's dark when Gigi finally comes in. Jayhe left hours ago and since then, I've been lying on the bed, emptied and brushed and scrubbed clean, but I can still feel all the places where his lips have been, like he's marked me. Like I really am a different June.

After Jayhe left, I showered, and I looked at myself, naked, in the mirror, for a long time. I saw the way my ribs jutted and the way my backbone arched, visible, when I turned. And I thought, Maybe if he could find me beautiful, I could be. And I was so excited, and I couldn't wait to see him again and kiss him again and I almost didn't even care about how it will affect Sei-Jin. Almost.

But then I threw up. I had to. I couldn't hold it all in, not anymore. I weighed myself on the small scale I've got hidden in the closet—102. My first thought was to head back to the bathroom, or to the studio to dance it off. But, exhausted, I dressed in my oldest flannel pajamas and climbed into bed. It's been three hours now, and the shadows have fallen, and they're preying, like the old beasts Jayhe's grandma used to tell us about, feasting on my mind.

I have to tell someone. And since I can't tell anyone else, it'll have to be Gigi. She startles me when she comes in, flips on the light, and finds me sitting straight up in bed. "Oh, I thought I was alone," she says with an awkward giggle. "Were you sleeping?"

"I kissed someone today."

She grins. "Fun!" She shuffles around the room, taking off her snow boots, tossing her ski cap in the corner, shaking out her curls. "Anyone I know?"

"I can't say. But I had to tell someone."

I look up at her, and she has that glow, the light flush of first love, like a light's been switched on inside her. Maybe I have that glow, too? "He thinks I'm beautiful."

"Of course he does, June," she says, her smile genuine. "You are beautiful."

I smile back at her, and for the first time in a long time, I let myself think it's true. I lie back down on the bed, tired but happy, as she shuffles about, getting ready for bed. Then I realize what I've done.

"Gigi," I whisper, just as she opens the door to head to the showers. "Gigi, you can't tell anyone, though." She looks surprised, conflicted, as if she's tired of keeping my secrets. "No one can know."

She nods, quiet, and shuts the door behind her.

25.

Gigi

"SOMEONE TELL ME THE STORY of *Giselle*," Mr. K says at the start of rehearsal.

"She came here from California," Will calls out, winking at me. There's a twitter of giggles from some younger Level 5 and 6 girls who still think he might be straight, but the rest of us maintain serious faces. Mr. K doesn't really have a sense of humor.

"Someone tell me the story of the ballet *Giselle*, please," Mr. K says. His face is stern. "I didn't think I had to specify that. I didn't know you all wanted to behave like idiots tonight."

Hands go up and he scans them, settling on Eleanor to answer.

"Yes, Miss Alexander, please tell us what this ballet is about."

She bites her fingernail before starting. Bette cringes. "*Giselle* is about a young peasant woman who falls in love with a nobleman."

"Is that all?" he asks.

Her face turns pink as she opens her mouth to continue, but Bette interjects, "And because she's not allowed to love him, she dies of a broken heart." Her tone is cold and matter-of-fact as she glances back at me, flashing her big, feathery eyes in my direction.

Mr. K rubs his beard. "Must be the ides of March. You all aren't thinking." He paces before the mirror. "The ballet *Giselle* is about much, much more. You all have simplified the story. Taken out the most important part. The heart of it all. It's about nature and fate and love and desire." He points to the ceiling. "It's about the gods." He shakes his head, then continues: "Giselle loves someone she isn't supposed to. And he loves her."

Alec pulls me into his chest and wraps his arm around my waist. I feel his heart thumping, his thumb pressing into my hip-bone. We're back to normal after our fight on Valentine's Day. He swung by my room the next morning, and I took him to my little corner of Central Park, which was totally deserted. It looked like one of those I ♥ NY ads, the untouched snow, the trees weighed down in white, the morning quiet. And there, I told him. Not about my heart. But about my run-in with Bette. About what she said about the hotel, and that I couldn't compete with that. That I'm a virgin, and even though I really like him a lot—and if I'm being honest with myself, even though I may love him—I'm not ready for that. Not yet. And he took my hand and was so sweet when he told me that he liked me so much, too much. He said he'd wait, that we could go as fast or as slow as I wanted. That we're on my timeline. That we don't ever have to. That made me feel better; it did. For a minute. But then: those pictures.

I watch Bette, sighing and rolling her eyes and being dramatic as Mr. K continues his lecture. I can hardly look at her after seeing those naked photos of her on Valentine's Day. I haven't told anyone, not even Alec. I want to trust what he says, but I'm waiting for him to be honest with me—about what he had with Bette. They've known each other forever. They come from the same kind of family; they both belong in this world. He and I, we're all wrong together. Could his feelings for me ever be that strong?

"But the forces of nature did not commend this union. It was not sanctioned. This must be a hard thing for you all to make sense of. It is an Old World idea of fate," Mr. K goes on, certainly enjoying the sound of his own voice and the adoring looks he gets from the ballerinas. "Today, if you want something, you go after it. But people did not always believe this. And, as is still true today, when you go against fate, the result can be dangerous." He mutters something in Russian to the teachers, and I wish I knew what it was.

I catch Bette's eye. She is staring me down. Her pink lips turn up at the corners, the hint of her one dimple barely indenting the surface of her perfect face.

I try to focus and soak in Mr. K's words. The first time I ever saw *Giselle* was when my mother took me to the San Francisco Ballet. I practically held my breath the entire time as that ballerina glided across the stage, shimmering as if her delicate arms and legs were made of stars. I loved that we shared a name and I felt an immediate kinship with the role, even though I was certain I'd never be in love quite like that. Now I lean a little more heavily against Alec, wondering if maybe I'm finally tasting the kind of romance that drives the ballet.

"In life there are many things beyond your control. And in ballet, even more so." Mr. K's voice fills the room. "Some are born to dance, some are born with afflictions—things that stand in the way. And some are born in second place, always in the shadows of others, and no matter how hard they try or how hard they work, they'll never surpass them. That is what this ballet is about," he says. "The forces of nature. What is written in the sky. What you are born with. Butterflies, I need to feel love and danger in your variations. I need to experience the joy and sorrow of destiny." He finishes and waves us off. "Alec, Gigi, show me what you've got so far."

The teachers turn their backs and walk to their chairs at the front of the studio. Alec sneaks and kisses me on the mouth, like Mr. K's speech was a direct order to us. His hands cup my face, and I have never been steadier, held like that. After a few moments, he pushes his hands back so that his fingers find the back of my neck. I gasp at the spark of desire.

We move to the center. It's supposed to be midnight in the peasant village cemetery, and I'm in a world of female spirits who have died before their wedding nights. I inch forward in tiny half steps on pointe as the light gradually illuminates my path. I am dead, my skin and hair powdered white, transforming me into *Giselle*. My body blending with the stark whiteness of my long white practice tutu.

I move beneath imaginary drooping branches of cemetery trees with flowers in my hands. The dead spirits, the willis, swirl around me. The corps girls flood the middle. We dance together, and I am in sync with them all until Alec arrives at my grave. I hide and watch him as he places flowers there. I try not to smile at him, try to stay in character, despite how handsome he looks. We skirt around each other, and then dance our *pas*. He lifts me like he's been doing it for years.

"Yes, yes," Mr. K says.

"Push through," the other male teacher, Doubrava, says. "The minute you pose, the movement is over."

The Russian teachers clap when we're finished.

"We're getting better and better," I whisper to Alec.

"Yeah, it's so weird. We've only done one other *pas* together, but I feel like I've been dancing with you forever." He kisses my forehead, and prepares to cool down and stretch while other dancers perform in front of the teachers.

Everyone disperses, some off to dinner, others to studios to continue practice, most up to the dorms for showers. We are left alone, which I like. Even Bette doesn't linger to glare at me or try to get Alec to talk to her. Every time I see her, I think of those pictures. Seeing their bodies entangled like that, one endless puzzle, so that I don't know where Alec's ends and Bette's begins. I could never be that girl. A girl like Bette. One who would take off her clothes and let someone take pictures. A girl who could be so, so naked in front of a boy. A girl who would let a boy touch her like that. Insecurities have been piling up in my head. Is that the kind of girl Alec wants? I wonder if it was Bette's idea. Or Alec's?

I don't have the courage to ask him about it. To find out

whose idea it was. Would Alec want me to do something like that? Alec leans on top of me, pushing my back against the wall, and helping to stretch my leg. The *Giselle* score still trickles through the speakers. I start to hum, trying to regain my focus. I told myself I'd ignore it. I won't involve Alec. I can deal with it.

He opens his mouth to speak, but I put a finger to his lips, so he doesn't make a sound. This is my favorite part of the score. He licks my finger, then moves it to kiss me. His hands find their way to the small of my back, where he bunches my dance skirt. We are sweaty and sticky and almost naked in our dancewear. Tiny goose bumps cover me.

My heart starts to race. The dangerous kind. Where my head gets light and spots erase my eyesight and my hands get shaky. I push him away, and then I can't help but think of Bette. She would never push Alec away. The girl in those pictures would strip down right here.

"What's wrong?" Alec whispers.

I don't answer. He moves my leg to the side and hoists himself up a little. I'm trapped beneath his weight, but don't want him to move. He traces his fingers along my collarbone. "You even feel sad," he says. "We did awesome today. What just happened? You were happy a few minutes ago. This is the same thing that happened on Valentine's Day."

It all slams me again: the pictures still etched in my memory and the worries about someone being out to get me right behind them. The message on the mirror, the medical report, the black rose. What else will they do? Are they trying to get me to leave? Because that won't be happening.

"You've got to start talking to me." He pulls me close, so that I fold into his side, like a crease in a paper. I let my hand wander across his chest and I kiss him hard to forget about it all. We kiss for such a long time I fear I'm losing my breath. I can feel my erratic heartbeat drum in my ears.

I blush and move my arm awkwardly away. My fingers tremble and I rub my temples. I wiggle out from under him, and roll over onto my side. I don't know what to say or how to form the words to tell him about my condition. I riffle through my bag, and put on the monitor Dr. Khanna gave me. I thought carrying it in my bag would make me more responsible. My heart's so unsteady lately, I can't not wear it. I can't not worry.

"What are you doing?" He grabs my arm before I can clasp the band of the monitor. I surrender and let him examine it. "What is it? Tell me," he whispers, running his fingers over my monitor. "I've never seen you wear this watch before. It's like one of my sports watches," he says. "Doesn't seem like your style." He chuckles.

"It's . . . it's . . . not a watch," I say, clicking it on, so it can tell me how high my heart rate is and send a thousand little warning vibrations. I stare at a little hole in his tank top while I wait for him or the monitor, really, to say something. To fill the quiet. I poke my finger into the tiny opening, wanting to do everything and anything but tell him about my condition. I stare at his beautiful eyes and beautiful mouth. What will he say? How will he treat me? Will he still like me? My heart skips as the worries whizz around in my head. The stupid monitor buzzes. I'm all sweaty from his body heat and rehearsal and stress.

I sit up. I feel his eyes on me—full of confusion. I feel guilty that I don't 100 percent trust him with my secret. That I don't trust anyone here with it.

Alec leans up beside me and plays with a loose curl that's escaped my bun, twisting it around his finger.

"Something's wrong." His thumb draws shapes from my temple to my cheekbone. Then he leans in close and I feel his breath on my neck. "Don't you trust me?"

I gulp, then lie. "Yes, I trust you."

"Then what is it?" he whispers in my ear, each word tickling my skin, causing that thump-thump between my legs.

"I'm different," I say.

He continues to kiss my neck. "I know that. It's why I like you."

"No, like really different," I say. "Like . . . I . . . have a thing."

"A thing?" he says, his mouth now finding its way to the back of my neck. "You have lots of beautiful things. Like your neck."

The sensation flickers over me like a warm rain, and I can't concentrate to get the words out. He nibbles and kisses the back of my neck and my heart couldn't slow down if it wanted to. I want him to kiss me all over, in places I've never let anyone see, places he's not supposed to touch.

The monitor buzzes again, yanking me out of the moment. I squirm away a little, needing the distance to help me speak the truth.

"There it is again," he says. "Your watch."

"I need to tell you something," I say, my insides now kneading and twisting with fear. "It's not a watch." I practice the words in my head a couple of times as we sit in silence. Everything stops as his blue gaze fixes on me. "It's a heart monitor," I whisper, each word barely even a real breath.

"A what?" he says.

"Heart monitor," I repeat, making the words heavier. I'm trying not to look in his eyes, trying not to cry.

"Why do you need it?" He reaches for my wrist and I pull it away.

"I have . . . a condition," I start.

"A what?" he interrupts, but I clamp my hand over his mouth before he can finish. I need the quiet Alec right now, the one that would wander through Central Park in the snow just listening to me tell him about home, the Alec who sits to the side while I practice my solos and doesn't give any advice on how to make them better.

"Let me get this out, okay?" Tears creep toward the corners of my eyes and I fight them off. I remember all the times I've had to tell someone about my heart condition—how their faces have arrested in shock, how afterward they've treated me like I'm fragile, how beneath all their words and actions has always drifted a current of pity.

I don't want Alec to look at me like that. To treat me like I'm broken. I gulp, then spit it out. "I was born with a hole in my heart. It's called a ventricular septal defect."

Alec's eyes widen as I repeat the scary scientific words. "What does that mean?" he asks.

"My heart's messed up," I say. "And I have to be aware of it." I hold up my wrist to flash the monitor. "Always."

"Oh," is all he says, then strokes my hand.

"I'm fine," I say, and feel like I'm saying it one of the thousand times I've said it to my mama and dad on the phone.

"So . . . ," he says.

Before he can finish his sentence, I blurt, "I should be wearing it all the time, but I don't. I hate it. When I get too excited, it beeps or buzzes to alert me that my heartbeat has changed. It's like an alarm."

"It sounds serious. Is it?" His eyes flood with worry. "And you should be wearing it, if you're supposed to."

"It can be serious . . . but I'm fine," I say again. "You sound like my mama."

"Can it be fixed?"

I shake my head no. "They operated when I was a baby. But it'll never be perfect. So I've always just dealt with it."

I search his face for a reaction, but I can't read it. I feel like he's inched away from me. He must think I'm a freak. My hands start to quiver while he asks me more questions. He's going to break up with me now. I know it.

I prepare myself for the words. Sweat collects behind my knees. My head feels a little light. And my monitor buzzes again.

Alec stops staring at me. "Why did it do that again?" He reaches for me. "And you're shaking. Why?"

"I thought . . . thought you'd . . . ," I start.

"Thought I'd what?" he says, and then he looks at me, like really looks at me, all hard and deep, and my tears finally come pouring out. He pulls me down next to him and I rest my wet cheek on his chest. He wraps me up tight in his arms and I feel like I'll never fall. I let the tears rush out until there aren't any more. He is that quiet Alec again. The one who strokes my back, hums in my ear, and squeezes his arms tight around me.

I hear him whisper, "Gigi, I like you. And nothing you can say can change that."

The words wrap around me.

"Gigi?" I hear from the studio door. Both Alec and I turn around. One of the *petit rats* shuffles up to us. Her little brown bun looks like a chocolate cupcake atop her head. She curtsies. She's holding a small pastry box.

"This is for you," she says.

"Thanks," I say. "But you didn't have to give me anything. What's your name?"

"Margaret," she whispers. "It's not from me. One of the RAs told me to give it to you."

"Okay," I say, taking the box from her tiny hands. I wonder who it's from.

She scampers out of the studio while I untie the ribbon. Alec starts to nibble on my shoulder. "What's this?" I say, then smile at Alec. "Is this a surprise from you?" Just what I needed after telling him my secret.

"No," he says, craning to look in the box. "I didn't send it to you."

My insides get all squishy and weird as I pull off the note attached to the bottom. I flip it over. It reads:

For your heart—a little start. Hope it doesn't fall apart.

A small warning here: what crawls beneath, dark
and devious, it will be crushed. As for your little
secret: for now, at least, we'll hush.

I throw the card and rip open the box. Inside there's a moldy
heart-shaped cookie stuck on a sticky pad, surrounded by dead
cockroaches. Startled, I drop it.

I shriek in fear that quickly swells to anger, and jump up.

I run to the hallway. Alec follows, frazzled, furious. I can't
hear what he's saying to me. Girls whizz by in and out of other
practice studios.

"Who left this?" I shout, shaking the empty box. "Who's
messing with me?"

They stop and stare at me like I've lost it. And maybe I have. I
hear the blood whooshing through me and feel my heart pounding. Alec tries to pull me back into the studio with him. I can't
stop yelling. "Who? Who?"

They whisper to one another. Say I'm crazy. Paranoid. They
leave me there to scream and scream and scream until my shirt is
all wet and my knees are so wobbly I sink to the floor.

"Gigi," Alec says, his arms cradling me, pulling me up. "It's
just mind games. This is exactly what happened to Cassie."

I am shaking, and he tries to hold me up. But I feel like I'm
going to fall. "Alec, I just—"

"They're trying to rattle you." He pulls me back into the
studio, away from all the whispering and stares. "It's okay," he
repeats over and over again. "You've got to be strong here, Gigi.
We all want to be the best here, and you are. I know you have it

in you. But you can't let them shake you. You can't let them win."

"I don't understand why they're doing this!" I wipe messy tears from my face, and instantly want to bring up the pictures of Bette and him. But I can't. He pulls me close and strokes my back.

"It's Bette," I whisper. "I know it is."

"What?" He pulls back.

"It's Bette. It has to be."

"She gets desperate sometimes, but she wouldn't do that," he says. "Plus, she's deathly afraid of cockroaches."

"You don't believe me," I say, more tears pouring out.

"It's not that. I just know her, and that's really not her style. Is all. Not saying you're wrong."

"She wrote that message on the mirror. She did other things, too." I pull back. "You're defending her." My eyes are so full of tears, I can hardly see him. Everything's a blur. Maybe he still loves her. Maybe they aren't quite done yet. Why else would he take her side?

"She doesn't do that stuff," he says. She's got him fooled. He mumbles a bunch of things, but I can't hear him anymore. My ears fill with sounds of my own fear and tears.

He pulls me close even though I fight his embrace. "Everything's going to be fine." His words land in my hair, and his arms close in around me.

He says it over and over again, but I don't know if I can believe it.

At dinner in the café, people whisper all around me. My cheeks still feel hot, but I'm pouring myself into the book for English class and trying to find flavor in the bland piece of chicken on my plate as a distraction. This is the time when I miss the ballerina versions of Mama's food the most: steamed cabbage sprinkled with red chili flakes, black-eyed peas with a tiny portion of bacon (turkey, of course), chicken dusted with a mix of flour and breadcrumbs before it's fried in olive oil, all kinds of stewed greens.

Not even a comforting text from Alec can erase the homesickness today. I want to tell my parents. Talk to them about what's happening. But I don't dare. Mama already wants me back home. If she knew about this she'd demand I leave the school.

One of the Level 6 girls laughs in my direction, and I hear them whispering about my meltdown in the hall. I want to shout and scream again. Instead, I just shove away from the table and walk away, trying to stay calm and poised. They're not who I'm really mad at. I know who I should be mad at. And it's about time I faced her.

I take the elevator down to the second floor, and then the first, and I don't stop until I've looked through every studio, and find her in studio D, at the center, practicing pirouettes.

"Bette?" I say with an edge, pushing the door open. There's no pretense here, no reason to pretend that this is going to be a civil conversation. We both know she's been doing things to me. And it needs to stop. "We need to talk," I say, feeling a little like someone else. Someone not at all afraid of her.

"About what?" She doesn't move a muscle, staying in fifth position, and her nose crinkles like she's smelled something foul. Like that something is me. I straighten my back even more. I let my shoulders sink down and back, like they've grown the heaviest and most incredible set of wings.

"You did something terrible," I say, gaining confidence. "Actually, several terrible things."

"I did something terrible?" she says, finally turning to look at me. Her eyes narrow, but her face is steady, not backing down.

"The message on the mirror. The picture of me and Henri in the Light closet, the naked pictures on Valentine's Day, and that disgusting cookie," I say. "And I shouldn't forget the medical report. You went through Nurse Connie's medical files and stole private information."

"Pictures? A medical file? Cookie?" The tone in her voice makes me feel like we're talking about unicorns and leprechauns. Like I've made up a whole bunch of things. "What are you talking about?" she sputters out again, and seems so stunned by how angry I am.

"Come on," I say. "It's not like I don't know you hate me."

I inch toward her.

"Well, that's news to me," she says, "because I don't hate you."

"Then why did you do all those things? It's been you from the beginning. You're messing with me," I say. Her nonchalance stokes my anger.

"I'm messing with you," she repeats, mocking me, like we're in kindergarten and she's broken all the crayons in my box. "I don't know anything about a medical report or pictures. I heard about that cookie thing. That wasn't me. I don't do roaches. But fine. Yeah. The other stuff—the message on the mirror, the shot of you and Henri. Yeah. Sure. I wanted to remind you that Alec was mine. That this school was mine. And whatever. But you got Sugar Plum Fairy. And you got Giselle. So there's nothing to be jealous of here. You won." There's a finality in her voice, an exhaustion. "So you don't have to be worried about me anymore."

"What, and that makes it okay?" I say, trying to keep my voice from wavering and my hands from shaking. "You can do whatever you want because you're having a bad year? You can mess with me because you don't like me? Because Alec likes me? You can't do all this shit to me!" I didn't even know I was capable of swearing, let alone swearing right at someone. "And even now, you're not owning up to it all."

She sighs, like I'm some pestering child, checks herself in the mirror again, and says, "What are you going to do? Go all ghetto on me or something? Beat me up to get the answers?"

My eyes are tornadoes now, and though I've never hit anyone in my life, or been hit, I want to slap her. Throw my entire palm into her face so it leaves a mark. The word *ghetto* drums inside me. I want to shout that I've never been to the ghetto. My heart feels like it might just stop—the beats pulsing like a hummingbird's wings, the muscle threatening to give up.

"Stop being crazy," she says.

I take a few deep breaths, allowing my center to lengthen, so I feel twenty feet tall. I am a ballerina. I am in control.

She smirks, like she knows she's won. I take the pictures I've been carrying around out of my dance bag. I throw several of them on the floor. Images of her litter the polished hardwood: her breasts, the tops of her thighs, Alec's hands around her, touching her, her smug face looking right up at me. She moves forward with instant recognition—and maybe revulsion.

"Where did you get those? Have you been in my room?" she says. "Those are private."

"Stop being *crazy*, Bette," I mock her. She leans down to gather them as I kick them away. "Try denying those. And there are more." I leave her scrambling to pick them up.

26.

Bette

I SPEND THE NEXT TWO weekends at home to avoid any accusations about messing with Gigi. The RAs overheard her breakdown. It only took a little pressure from them before she spilled about the pranks, and that's all everyone has been talking about for the past week and a half. I still don't know who gave her those naked pictures of Alec and me that I kept in my keepsake box. Eleanor was out with me that night. The only other person who knew about them was Will. I know he hates me now, but we were close once—like brother and sister. Would he really do that to me? We've had to have individual meetings with the school counselor and the RAs about bullying. I'd rather deal with the biggest bully in my life—my mother—than all of them. And she's at her worst during family holidays. It's the Easter weekend.

We have a practice room at home that my mother had installed when I was twelve. An offshoot of the basement, complete with a wall of mirrors, a full barre, a professional sprung floor, and a series of ceiling fans. So weekends away from school aren't like a break at all. They never are. And there are no fun adventures with Alec to look forward to. No stolen moments in my bedroom or kisses pressed against the mirrored wall. Those moments with Alec had almost helped me erase all the terrible memories of my time trapped down in the basement practice room, but without him here they're rushing back at me.

"You showering soon?" Adele calls down, and I assume the sun is setting, but there are no windows down here, no hint of the real world. Not even a clock. Adele is allowed to take the morning off from dancing. My mother lets her help with the Easter holiday cooking and holiday happiness, but I'm expected to stay down here and "make sure I don't lose my pitiful role, the way I lost Giselle."

"Soon!" I call back up, but I'd rather break my ankles dancing late into the night than do what we have on the agenda for this evening. Easter dinner with Nana and Grandpa, and my horrible cousins from New Jersey and Connecticut, and, of course, the Lucas clan. I begged my mother not to invite them, since Alec broke up with me and is apparently in love with someone else.

"Whose fault is that?" she'd said.

"Whose fault is it that Dad left?" I asked in return. Adele squeaked like a crushed mouse the second the words left my mouth, and I gasped at the way the thoughts in my head sometimes get spoken out loud without my actually deciding to say them. I've gotten so used to casual cruelty at school that I'd forgotten what kind of impact it has at home.

My mother didn't slap me, but I know she wanted to. Instead she marched out of the kitchen and into the small breakfast nook connected to the kitchen, which, given the fact that no one eats around here, my mother has turned into a drinking nook. She knows the worst thing she can do is imply that I'm the one making her want to get trashed.

"Nice, Bette," Adele said. "Chill on the pills, okay? We don't need you high *and* Mom drunk."

I disappeared downstairs after that. Mom would have forced me eventually anyway, but it is easier to just to work my muscles until they spasm than to interact with my drunk, angry mother.

My phone buzzes for the eighth time this morning, and I ignore it. Henri's been texting nonstop, looking for a hookup. But I won't make that mistake again. I'd rather die from exhaustion here. Plus, I don't think he'll actually tell. Just a little taste was enough for me to get him on Team Bette. I hope.

I decide to work on pointe before I have to face my closet full of clothes that aren't pretty enough to make Alec love me again.

Against Adele's better judgment, I down a little pill before wrapping the ribbons of my pointe shoes around my ankles, pulling leg warmers up over my tender knee. I iced it late last night, but it's still throbbing from hours in the basement yesterday. Usually, I can fight through the soreness, the aches, the little pulls and twists that inevitably happen. But an old injury flares up, and either the physical pain or the memory is distracting me so much that I'm not able to get in the zone.

No one knows about my knee, except Mr. K, who noticed me favoring it once when he was doing a one-on-one session with me last year. He'd touched my kneecap with a finger he'd kissed.

I'd told him it was all better.

But today I can practically feel it swell with pain. It feels like it could burst through my tights, like it could grow so heavy with the weight of the pain it could pull me to the ground. It could be psychosomatic, I think. I look into my reflection for signs of insanity.

I look scared and pained, but not insane. Which means, I suppose, the pain might actually be real.

Pain has weight. Adele's the one who told me that.

She'd visited me in the hospital, that Christmas after our father left, and showed me the scar I'd never noticed near her hairline, from when she'd hit her head when she was a tiny ballerina child.

I don't want to think about any of this, but by the time my slippers are on and I have lifted myself to my toes, my old injury is screaming and throbbing, and I can't possibly dance. So I sit on the floor, trying to stretch, but I remember instead.

My father left without warning, and my mother, who had always loved the ballet and the fact that Adele and I were doing so well at the conservatory, suddenly took her interest to a whole new level. She pushed us *hard*. Adele was ready for it: she was in perfect shape and had been dancing long enough to be able to handle the extra time my mother insisted we put in over the holiday.

I was twelve and just making the transition from girl to woman, from little cherub in *The Nutcracker* to Clara, at long last. At school, my meals and rehearsals and time were monitored carefully. Every stretch, every leap, every newly acquired skill was accounted for by Morkie and the other teachers. My mother didn't know the rules. She didn't care about the structure or the care with which a girl transitions through her adolescence.

She spent her evenings crying over my father in the master bedroom while I tried to drown her out by watching old musicals on the computer in my room. She spent her days drinking white wine and torturing me.

Now I lie on my back, bringing my leg toward my face. I coax it gently, and the pull is delicious, satisfying. But I'm holding back a breakdown, thinking through these memories. My fingers shake a little. I did not give my mind permission to go here.

That Christmas, my mother starved me. Emptied the refrigerator of all food except apples and celery. In the mornings she'd allow me an egg and half an English muffin, but the rest of the day she kept me on coffee and celery and sometimes an energy bar for dinner, if she couldn't get up the energy to sauté a chicken breast.

She starved me, and she made me work. Hard. Harder than I did at school, and with fewer calories to help me along. Like she's done this Easter holiday, she practically shut me in the makeshift basement studio all day. Sometimes she'd have Adele coach me, sometimes a retired teacher from the conservatory.

Even back then, I knew my body the way I do now. I knew when I needed to stretch more, when I needed a break, when I could push harder. But she didn't believe me. And I got too scared to speak up. I was so, so little. So I let her push me and push me until my knee ballooned from the stress and I was so weak that a cold turned to pneumonia. I spent the second half of Christmas break that year in bed, with an overnight stay in the hospital.

I remember being grateful for the needle in my arm, the IV filled with glucose pumping into me. I could feel it going through me: a cold, ghostlike strumming in my veins. At last.

I line my legs up next to each other, stretching them out straight in front of me so I can compare the shape of one kneecap to the other. Now the inflammation is small but terrifying. The doctor had heavy warnings about the chronic stress condition, and every few months I notice a new kind of pain taking shape under the skin.

This is the worst it's been in years. Like muscle memory, my knee knows to swell up the second it enters this home, this studio, and especially on any holiday.

I recognize Adele's light steps coming down the stairs. My mother's are unfocused, faltering, hard. Adele's are soft ballerina steps. She walks on her toes at all times, like she forgets how to be human and only remembers how to be a dancer. It's one of the things I'm most afraid of. That I will be exactly like Adele, or that I won't be enough like Adele. Both thoughts are chilling.

"You've gotta get ready, Bette," she says. But her eyebrows jump when she sees me cradling my leg. "Oh sweetheart, your knee?" She rushes to me, joins me on the floor, and lifts my leg out of my hands like it's a newborn baby. Adele isn't kind about my personal life or my mother or my broken heart or my struggles at school. But she cares about my body. When I'm hurt, she's there, doing everything in her power to make it better. It's how I know she loves me.

"It's not a big deal," I say. But the pain is making me a little dizzy. Either the pain, or the fact that I have to spend the evening with my mother and with Alec.

"Can you walk?"

"Of course I can walk."

"I didn't know it still acted up," Adele says. She runs her fingers over the swollen parts. "I'm so sorry. I'm just so, so sorry I let that happen—" Adele has one tiny line on her face, near the top of her forehead. And I know it's from her guilt over that Christmas. That she didn't put a stop to it. That she didn't understand how bad it had gotten.

She lifts me to my feet. "You need help showering?"

"It's really fine. It'll go down, I promise," I say with a smile. I don't know why I'm acting like I'm fine. I wonder, if I milked this, if I could get out of facing dinner and just stay in my room. But it's too late. Adele's already seen me walking without much of a limp, and working my way up the stairs with only a little help from the bannister. As soon as we're back on the main floor she's distracted by my bumbling mother, who is struggling to open a bottle of wine, but who is at least dressed in her Chanel best and looks appropriately maternal and holiday ready.

"Wear that black dress of yours, Bette," my mother says, not even noticing my swollen knee, my limp, the way Adele keeps rubbing my back. "And please do your hair. Big curls, I think. I'm tired of seeing it all stringy around your face. It's not attractive. Needs volume."

Adele makes me an ice pack, and my mother scrunches her nose at that, like it's a distraction rather than a necessity, and she doesn't bother asking what I need ice for.

The Lucas family declines my mother's invitation for Easter dinner at the last minute, and my mother spends the entire time bitching about Mr. Lucas's new wife. Even though she's not really that new.

I'm back at the conservatory before seven p.m. Seeing my sister has given me a newfound mission. I change into a leotard and a dance skirt and don't go to the studios, but to Mr. K's office, which is nestled between the studios on the first floor, just like the nurse's office. I don't know why I'm feeling so reckless. But the thrill of it all makes me feel like I'm my old self again. And I have to risk it.

I knock, even though he can see me in the doorway. "Mr. K, do you have a minute?" I say in a half voice that makes me sound like one of the *petit rats*.

He waves me in, and I squish down in his high-backed chair. His office is just how I remembered it: wooden bookshelf holding Russian literature, ballet portraits, trophies from his students' competitions, a photo of himself on the Maryinsky Theater stage, shaded lamps and their low glow, the scent of hand-rolled cigarettes and alcohol. I know where he hides his little office bar, and the vodka. (Another secret Adele shared.)

Nestled into the old, familiar space, I fuss with my hands in my lap.

"Bette, why are you here?" Mr. K says finally, a hint of irritation marring his smooth baritone. So I look up, making my eyes go wet and shiny and alluring, like they get on the stage. For one glorious moment I lock eyes with his, and my adrenaline surges. It's a reflex, after all the dangerous attention he unloaded on me over the last two years. Not that his lips a little too close to my neck or his hand on my body during that *pas* rehearsal felt *good,* exactly. But there is nothing quite like Mr. K really seeing you. Even Adele agrees, and she got more attention than she bargained for. I remember snooping through her cell phone and seeing texts from him, little missives calling her his tiny, pretty thing, asking her to meet him at odd hours. Her texts back were very businesslike, but I know that she didn't mind his attentions. Underneath the scruff and bluster, he's quite handsome, Mr. K. He must be in his early forties, and he's maintained himself well, his dark hair neatly cropped, and full lips framed by his trim beard. In the old photos on the wall, you can see that he oozes charm and charisma on the stage, a commanding presence that no doubt leaves his patrons wondering how he expends all that energy offstage. But whenever I'd ask her, Adele would blush and change the subject, except to offer PG insights, like "Mr. K likes women who look demure but are secretly powerful—especially onstage." Still, I remember all those nights in the dorm that I'd knock on her door late at night, awoken by a nightmare or growing pains, and her roommate would tell me Adele was off to a "private rehearsal."

I want to make him remember those times with my sister. I want him to know that I know, and that others can know, too. Even though that's not something he'd want to get out. That's not something that would sit well with the board or others in the ballet world or even the cops. I want him to remember how good

I am and give me the parts that belong to me.

"I think I am having a hyperextension problem. *Adele* told me you're good at spotting these things. Better than the nurse," I lie. "Would you take a look? I'm scared it's what's holding me back. Why things have changed so drastically this year."

He cocks an eyebrow up, and waves me over. "Fifth position."

I almost like being alone with him in his office, letting him inspect my leg muscles. I obey, and lift up my dance skirt.

Kneeling, he moves my feet, turning them out, then his fingers graze over my thighs and knees, firm, businesslike, strong. I look down, and his face is emotionless, expressionless, like he barely sees me. So I bow down, into a deep *plié*, catching him off guard as his hand shoots up my thigh and under my skirt.

"Bette," he says, surprised, pulling his hands back. "Careful."

But I deepen the *plié* farther, until I'm on my knees, eye to eye with him, face-to-face. "I'm feeling a bit of a sprain, a pulled muscle, maybe," I say, taking his hand and moving it to my upper thigh. "Right here."

His breathing is shallow, shaky. He knows what I'm asking. "Adele said you knew exactly what to do when it happened to her." I pause. "To work out the kinks."

"Bette"—he stands abruptly, and steps away, creating space between us—"I don't know what you're implying, but—"

I stand, too, and step forward, closing the distance. "It's all right, Mr. K," I say, my voice a whisper. "I know you like to look at beautiful things." I untie the ribbons on my skirt, letting it fall, letting him see the shape of me. I stretch in a way so that one of my leotard straps falls off my shoulder. I push my arms together a bit to show a little of the cleavage that I never actually wanted. "I won't tell if you touch."

He sits down at his desk, busying himself with a stack of papers and then the computer screen. "Bette," he says, his voice stern, unyielding, "I thought you were getting back on the right track, but clearly things have escalated. Are you doing all right at home? Are things okay with Alec? Maybe it's time we set up an appointment with the school psychologist. Of course," he says, looking up at me pointedly, "that's something I'll have to discuss with your mother for approval. But"—he grimaces—"it seems like the next logical step."

I hear the threat in his voice, and realize slowly that despite the fact that he's known me since I was six, the man doesn't know me at all. I don't take well to threats. "That's unfortunate, Mr. K," I say, my voice soft and feathery, but he can't mistake the bite behind my words. "I've mentioned to my mother all the extra time you've been lavishing on me—just as you did with Adele, you'll remember—and I'm sure she'll be displeased to know it hasn't helped. I'll just have to call her now and explain how things went here today."

Mr. K stands, his face taut but not quite apologetic. "That's okay, Bette. I'm sure your mother doesn't need to know every detail of your time here. Perhaps we should both just forget this ever happened," he says. Then he walks brusquely to the door and opens it. "Now, isn't it time for your evening character dancing class?"

I smile at him as I exit. "That makes sense," I say as I sashay out, wrapping my skirt around my waist as I exit. My fingers tremble, making me fumble with the tie. "We'll just keep this between us." For now.

He slams the door a little too hard when I leave. It echoes through the hall. I take deep breaths to get rid of the flush that's probably turned me a brilliant shade of red, and get myself together. That was either incredibly smart or incredibly dumb. I can't figure out which.

When I look up, Will is standing right in front of me with the biggest smile on his face. Next to him is Eleanor, who looks completely stricken—which is exactly how I feel. It takes her a minute to speak. "What—what were you doing?"

"Yeah, Bette," Will says, his hideous red eyebrows climbing toward that unfortunate receding hairline, his mouth twisting into that familiar know-it-all smirk. "What *are* you up to?"

"Nothing," I say, fumbling for words, looking from Will to Eleanor and back. "Mr. K asked me to come see him. My mother's working another fund-raiser. No biggie." But I know Eleanor doesn't believe a word I'm saying. I'm a stellar liar, I know. But after a decade of playing my sidekick, she can see right through me.

27.

June

WHILE ON MY WAY DOWN to the lobby for my mom to pick me up, I see Bette sneak out of the Light, a satisfied smirk spoiling her usually pristine features. She startles when she sees me, but then grins, as if we're sharing a secret. "See ya," she says, then prances silently down the hall in her slippers, still dressed in her practice clothes.

As I watch her walk away, something vile bubbles inside me. She's so nonchalantly mean, it's almost like she doesn't realize she's doing it. When I'm mean, I do it on purpose and acknowledge it. And no one ever pays Bette back for all the stuff she does. Even though she does a good job of covering her tracks. Most of the time. People are too afraid to really accuse her. She's got girls lined up to take the blame.

Today, Bette's going to get hers. I'm feeling vengeful. Not that Bette's been mean to me. But she hasn't been nice either. The room is empty when I get back, so I head straight to Gigi's desk and open the drawer where she hid those naked pictures. The ones of Bette and Alec, the ones Bette no doubt planted to cause Gigi pain.

I want to anonymously turn them in. They break every modesty school rule in the student handbook. They'll land Bette (and Alec as collateral damage) in deep trouble. The Russians hate heavy dancers and American teenage customs and modern choreography, but above all else, they despise inappropriate sexual displays. Two kids were suspended last year for being caught making out in one of the stairwells.

I riffle through the drawer, but the pictures are gone. So I look through another and a third, but they're nowhere to be found. Like they never existed at all. Instead, there are half a dozen little red paper roses, each a different style. No doubt another token from Alec. And there, tucked away, is a little charm. One I've seen Gigi wearing hidden in the folds of her tutus on important rehearsal days. A good luck charm. Small and golden and irrepressibly sweet. It infuriates me. What does this girl need a lucky charm for? She's got all the luck in the world.

We've been getting along lately, but minutes later, I'm standing in the Light closet, pinning the charm high up on the wall, the one that's covered with photos of dancers floating, gliding, laughing, shining, living the life I want to live. The life in the spotlight that I'll never have, the one that comes so easily to girls like Gigi and Bette. I can't stop myself; it's like my fingers have impulses of their own. I'm shaking, but I'm not quite sure if it's anger or sadness.

I look at the little rose, dangling there, like it's abandoned and will die, and wonder what I'm doing. I wonder how I got here, what propelled me to this point. I'm just tired of being second-best, of having to work so hard for everything. My mom is still on my case about my grades, I don't have any leads on my father, and Jayhe seems to have slipped back into his old ways, keeping his head down and acting like I don't exist when he comes to visit Sei-Jin. It seems like she's got a stronger hold on him than ever, so maybe my plan wasn't so smart after all.

I curl up on the bench and stare at the walls I've spent so much time absorbing, reading all the uplifting quotes and words of encouragement. Scattered throughout, of course, are biting little notes meant to be seen and to provoke pain. There are a few about Gigi, as expected, but a couple mention Bette and her fall from grace. I'm sure they just roll right off her, that she doesn't feel them at all. I wish I could be that way, impenetrable. But despite my facade, every little thing gets to me.

I stare up at a batch of photos of Sei-Jin and her crew in a photo booth at Times Square, laughing their pretty little heads off. When was the last time I laughed like that?

Not since Sei-Jin abandoned me, I realize with a pang. Scrawled below the photo are a bunch of comments in Korean. The only thing I can really make out are a few names. Hye-ji, Sei-Jin, Jayhe—and then I see it. Mine. E-Jun and a long rant of text that I can't really begin to understand. What might it say? Nothing good, that's for sure. I look closely at the words, recognizing a character here and there, but nothing substantial. Maybe I should feel happy to be on the walls in here. That means someone thinks I'm good. Someone thinks I'm a threat. I snap a photo with my phone and head back to the room, determined to figure it out.

I wish I could just ask my mother what it says. But she can never know. Besides, it's not like we're speaking much at all. They sent me packing for the weekend, orders from Nurse Connie to get me back up to the correct weight. I've been very careful about things lately. The vomiting isn't enough, so I've been doing the ellipticals, which is what Liz used to drop weight quickly. But it's worked too well. I've fallen to 101 pounds again, and I'm lucky that Nurse Connie didn't send me home permanently. I laid it on thick about how hard it was to gain those pounds she wanted. She was nice this time. But it's made my mom watch me like I'm a glass figurine on the verge of falling off a table. Still, she doesn't really bother to talk to me. Unless she's ordering me to do something.

"The Kwons have invited us for church dinner, and we're going," my mom says, peeking into my bedroom.

I can feel her gaze on my face as she conveniently cleans the hall outside my bedroom, waiting to see me roll my eyes or purse my lips or respond in some way she finds unrefined, disrespectful, ugly. After our last dinner, she said she won't tolerate any more disrespect, otherwise I'll have to leave the conservatory before the spring performance. Which is only a few weeks away, at the end of May. April's nearly over, and time has been slipping away so fast. Too fast if I want the cast list to change at all.

"Okay," I say. I would put up a fight, because the last thing I want is to spend the evening being berated by Sei-Jin and seeing her clasp Jayhe's hand. And I'm worried that talks of summer session registration will come up, and I'll have to tell them—because Korean kids don't lie to other Korean adults—that this is my last semester at the school because my mom is putting me in public school.

But I know she'll force me to go to the dinner anyway, and I'm tired of fighting. I'm tired of all of it. I have no energy. And I don't want to give in and listen to the little voice inside me that says it's because I haven't been eating. Nurse Connie called my mother to check on my weight, but my mom squawked about "American fat issues" and the "Korean body" and how healthy I really am. How I eat as much as any other dancer. She defends me to the others, but she's watching my every move. I can't go to the bathroom without her hovering outside, ear pressed to the door.

I text Jayhe again, and he doesn't respond. Again. My head (and heart) can't handle it. But I'm getting stir-crazy. I stayed in my room all Saturday afternoon, then spent the three hours this morning googling Korean to see if I can decipher the message from the wall in the Light. If I tried a little harder on the internet, I probably could figure it out. But I thought Jayhe might be able to read it for me. Boys like to feel useful. He's still under Sei-Jin's lock and key. We've been texting for weeks, but there are long silences in between. Sometimes he responds—usually late at night, when I know Sei-Jin won't have access to his phone—but mostly he doesn't. I just don't understand him. Is this how all boys are? Or is it just my luck?

Exhausted, I throw myself on the bed and pop an old ballet

into the ancient VCR my mother never got rid of. After watching Eleanor perform in *The Nutcracker*, the successful understudy story that should have been mine, I don't even want to think about what's next for me: being another understudy, being behind Gigi again, being taken from the conservatory, being a regular girl.

My mom reminded me again over dinner last night. The two of us at the ugly plastic kitchen table, and all she could do was go on and on about our arrangement and how I failed to secure a role and "that pretty Eleanor girl" and how truly special dancers always move ahead.

Leaning in through the doorframe, she hovers, waiting for me to acknowledge her again. "We will leave in one hour," she says finally, as I continue to sulk in silence. "I am going to run to the store for treats to bring. You get ready. Cover up please. There is a dress in my closet you will wear. Much nicer than what you have. Appropriate."

Again, I don't even consider fighting back. I'm sure it's some ugly, itchy monstrosity, but throwing a tantrum will only delay the inevitable. It almost feels better, to be so exhausted that I don't have choices. I will do what I'm told. No guesswork. No grand plans. No battles. Just a nod of my head and the hollow feeling in my stomach keeping me calm.

When she's gone, I walk like a zombie to her room and into her closet. We are the same size, my mom and I. Maybe I am a few pounds lighter, but it's not by much. She has kept her ballerina body longer than her love of the ballet. As if what she really loved about her time at the conservatory was being able to control the size and shape of her frame. She liked the routine, the distinct weight of structure, the invisibility of a ballerina's body in a sea of women with hips and breasts and loud clothing. She liked the matching leotards, the matching torsos, the matching movements.

I can't tell which dress in her closet is meant for me. They all look more or less the same: dark, somber colors and high neck-lines and ill-fitting skirts that will fall inches below my knees. I dig to find one with tags still on it. I don't usually step far into my mom's closet. But as I flip through her depressing wardrobe, I go farther in, and reach my hands out in front of me to the shelves normally shielded by the clothing. I know her off-season shoes are stored back there, but as I've never been desperate to borrow flat, awkward boots or outdated half-inch witch heels, I've never done much exploring.

My hands hit a box. It's wooden and easy to slide. A little too large for the wobbly shoe shelves, it falls to the floor when my hand brushes against it.

Clunk.

I know what's in there before I even slide the top open.

A photograph, my mom, just a year or two older than me, wrapped in the embrace of an attractive older man. The man is blurry, but I can make out a few details. Blond hair. Bright blue eyes. The kind of smile that gets a girl to take off her pants or fall in love or give up ballet. She's in a costume for the ballet *Don Quixote*, looking up at him like he's the only thing she sees.

My heart's pounding and I have to sit down on the floor of the closet. The bottoms of the matching sad dresses brush my forehead, my ears, get in my eyes, but it doesn't matter. There's more in the box.

A love letter from a man named Dom to my mom.

And then: a letter from a lawyer to my mom. It's full of legal jargon and huge, scary, but ultimately meaningless words. My father's name is covered with black ink. But the gist of it is: he admits the baby is his, and as long as she keeps it quiet, the baby will be provided for and come into a great deal of money when she turns twenty-five.

She. Me.

I'm the baby in the documents.

I want to throw up. Not the way I usually do. This is a stronger impulse, a necessary reaction, a sickening feeling in my stomach rather than an insistence that I empty myself.

In fact, if anything, I'd like to hang on to as much of myself as possible. I'd like to fill out, in the moment, grow larger, so that I have more to hang on to. Because as it is now, it feels like I am falling a great, great distance into something unseeable. The Grand Canyon. A black hole. A Bermuda Triangle of confusion. Something that epic.

I cover my mouth so that I don't vomit in the closet. It feels like I will only ever have this one moment to gather information. Like these documents and photographs and evidence of who I am will disappear the second I leave the space. I swallow down the liquid that rises and threatens to spew out.

There are a few more pictures of my mom dancing, of her lithe ballerina body in motion. My mom had me young, so if she had really worked at it, perhaps she could have still been dancing, even now. If she'd cared about it, she could have had me, and then gotten back into shape. Or she could have chosen not to have me. She could have chosen dance. Why didn't she? I would have.

That's when I finally throw up. There's not much there, mostly water, and I manage to get only a little on the closet floor. Mostly I manage to hit myself, a disgusting low moment, followed by a long shower and some serious scrubbing of my mother's closet floor. I worry that I am scrubbing so hard that the surface will be damaged. That it will show the scars of my desperation.

I curl up in bed, without the dress, without dry hair, without any intention of getting to the Kwons' stupid party. I try not to think. This discovery is so powerful, so large, that I can't take it all at once. It is the largest piece of cake and I only want a lick of frosting to tide me over. Because I haven't eaten in years. Maybe I have never eaten. And now there is chocolate cake in my face and it's too, too much.

"You ready, E-Jun?" My mom calls up when she's back from the store. I am supposed to be scrubbed clean and in her ugly dress by now. Instead, I have a towel wrapped around my body, and I'm in the fetal position in my too-hard twin bed. I don't respond.

"E-Jun! Time to go!" I hate the sound of her voice, and when she switches to Korean, I hate it even more. Sounds clang against each other. I don't reply, and I hear her feet scamper up the stairs. She doesn't knock before barging in to my room. She never does. "What do you have to hide?" she always says when I tell her to knock first.

"E-JUN!" she screeches when she sees me, undressed and unkempt and unwilling on my bed.

"I'm not going," I mumble into my pillow.

"Where is your dress? Put on clothes!"

"I'm not going," I say again. My mom puts a hand to her heart, like that tiny yelp is enough to give her a heart attack.

"Now, E-Jun. You don't talk back to me this way. Disobedient."

"I said no."

"Who is making you like this? I let you stay at that terrible school, wasting your time being in the corps, and all you learn about is how to become disrespectful."

"The school is not the problem," I say. This is my chance, I guess, to confront her. But I'm not ready. Information this powerful needs a purpose, and though my head is still spinning and I swear I can still smell my own vomit on my hands, and that man's face is bouncing around my head like some sick screensaver, I pull myself together just the tiniest bit.

"I can pull you out of school now." She crosses her arms over her chest and glares at me with disgust. I am the worst thing that ever happened to her. I know that now more than ever.

"Five minutes, then we go," she says. It's a conclusion, not a question.

"I know," I say. But she doesn't get it.

"E-Jun, get dressed. We will be late." She turns to leave.

"Who is my father?" I whisper.

She freezes.

"I saw the photos. I read the court papers. I know about the money. But you blacked out the name. Who is he? Is it Dominic?"

She flies at me, cheeks tight, eyes narrow. "You don't go through my things." She slaps me across my face, as angry as I've ever seen her. She hits me again, and I grab at her hands, stopping them from flying, pinning them down. She may be my mom, and I may be small, but what I've learned is that I'm strong—much stronger than I look. Much stronger than they think I am. Within seconds, I'm the one on top, holding her still, so she can't hit me anymore. So she can't hurt me anymore.

"Mom, you listen to me now," I say, my voice steel. "I'm going back to the school tonight, and I'm taking the box with me. I have a right to know who I am, where I came from, and you can't stop me from finding out more. You have no right."

I stand, pulling my towel tightly around me. "If you want me to keep quiet about all this while I look," I say, pointed, knowing she couldn't bear the shame, the humiliation of such exposure, "then I will not hear another word about public school and college and leaving the conservatory. You will support me, even applaud me, in pursuing my goals. Because I know now that dancing is in my blood. I've always known. And no one—not even you—is going to stop me."

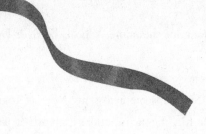

28.

Gigi

OUTSIDE STUDIO B, I STRETCH alone along the floor. I want to start the week away from them all. I need some time away from the drama. After I screamed about the disgusting cookie, people started calling me crazy. Like Bette. And I'm not crazy. That's the last word anyone from home would use to describe me. I need a break from the stares. I need the entire month of April to go away. I need to start over.

The *petit rats,* whose morning class has just let out, bound through the hall. They get quiet and whisper and slow down when they see me.

"Gigi's so beautiful."

"The best Level 7 girl."

"I want to be Giselle like her."

"Did you know her real name is Giselle? Just like the ballet!"

"She has perfect feet. She can leap higher than anyone else."

Their tiny praises make me smile. I remember feeling the same way about the first ballerina I ever saw. She moved across the stage like an angel; her tutu was a cloud of stars trapped around her waist.

A little one approaches. "Gigi." Her voice is small and fragile. I look up and a round, pink face grins at me. At first I flinch, thinking one of the older girls put her up to this, only to embarrass me or play another prank.

"Can I have your autograph?" she says with a sweet, mouse-like voice.

I relax. Try to erase the increasing paranoia that I feel. I try to follow Alec's advice, Mama's advice, and chalk all of this stuff up to mind games. Hazing that won't work.

"Pretty please," she pleads.

I wonder why in the world she'd want my autograph. I am nobody. By the look of her perfect form, she's probably been at the conservatory since she was five, and seen many dancers more talented than me. She holds out a pencil and her flower-dotted notebook.

"It would be my pleasure." I riffle through pages of doodles and scribbles to a blank page where I write *You're a star* and my name. She is beside herself with excitement when I hand her back the notebook. She curtsies and returns to her group, showing off her page.

Morkie rounds the corner, so I slip into the studio where all the girls are stretching—their legs press against mirrors, hang over barres, or are in splits on the floor, and some lie on their backs with their heels pulled toward their shoulders. I click my cell phone off, ignoring a call from Mama and a smiley face message from Alec.

I sit next to June, but even she takes a half step away from me as soon as she feels my body too near her own. On another day, I'd care. I wrap a rubber stretchy band around my feet, flexing and pointing until the joints and muscles loosen, but when Viktor enters we all flutter to our places at the barre. We are arranged by height one after the other in a line. I am somewhere in the middle. Neither long and lean, nor short and petite, sandwiched between Bette and June. Bette's ice-blue gaze travels down my neck and her sighs of disapproval echo every time I move.

Viktor's shoes clomp across the waxed floor and his heavy bottom makes the piano bench squeak. Morkie walks in and closes the studio door. The *petit rats* press their little faces against the glass panels to watch our class. I wink at the little girl who asked for my autograph. She waves frantically until Morkie shoots them all a look. They settle down and watch us.

Viktor starts the slow piano chords that signal our warm-up. We move through the positions, easing our muscles into the movements. Morkie walks from girl to girl, starting with the shortest.

Morkie draws near. She lingers on June, remarking on a hair that has fallen out of place, and on how slender she's looking. She gives a nod of approval in Bette's direction, not even bothering to touch her. Bette's body has become perfect: legs long and muscular in the right places—strong along the inner thigh where ballerinas need the most strength, and soft on the exterior—her chest flat and delicate, and her hands fall just the right way. She must be working hard.

I hold fifth position, turning out from my hip, hoping she'll pass me by. Drops of sweat bead along my forehead. I'm not warmed up. I'm forcing my body to comply. I should've stretched and dealt with all the stares and whispers. Morkie scans my arm in second position. The muscle twitches.

"*Battements tendus jeté* in second," she commands. I sweep my leg out to the side and up forty-five degrees. She catches it and rotates my leg so it's turned out more. I feel the pinch in my hip but swallow down the pain. "Point!"

I obey. "Beautiful arches." She rubs the bottom of my foot. "Girls, Gigi has the best ballet foot. The instep almost folds over completely."

My cheeks flame as the others look on and pressure builds in my stomach. I feel Bette's cold blue gaze from behind. Morkie pinches the interior of my thigh and lifts her eyebrows, then she nudges my butt. "Eat lean protein," she says and drops my leg. "Especially for performance coming up. Need to lengthen."

She motions to Viktor and class begins. The piano chords are gentle, so we can ease our muscles into familiar positions. The mirrors reflect our sixteen bodies moving in unison, filling the space with silent energy. I feel better. Dancing erases all the nerves, fear, anxiety, paranoia. Everything is fine. We do an hour of exercises and small combinations. Afterward, she lets us get water and change into pointe shoes.

During the quick break, I wrap white tape around each toe, then swaddle them with cloth. With practiced motions, I pull out one shoe, slip it on, and tie the ribbons. I dig back into the bag for the other shoe. I can't find it. The other girls return from the water break and change into their pointe shoes while I continue to comb through my bag. I have to take everything out to fish out the missing one. The shoe is hidden at the bottom.

Everyone assembles in the center. I'm late to the lineup, and Bette taps a foot on the ground, like she has been waiting for me all day instead of just a few seconds. Morkie's face is a solemn line of potential disappointment.

I slip on the right one and quickly lace the ribbons. It feels a little too snug, but I don't have time to fiddle with it. I bolt to the center of the room to my position. I feel something thick and strange in my shoe, but ignore it. Morkie demonstrates the combination and Viktor starts to play. I rise on pointe. Whatever I felt in the heel of my slipper sinks toward my toes and suddenly a sharp pain shoots through my foot. The pain makes me collapse to the ground. I grab at my leg, my eyes close, my body wants to shut down. Warm blood pools in my shoe, the red seeping through the pink like a deepening sunset.

The other girls stop. "Your shoe is bloody," someone shouts.

The girls huddle around and Morkie pushes through. I claw off my pointe shoe. Morkie holds my foot and pulls off the white padding. She pulls back my tights, ripping the bottom open farther. Something is lodged in my skin. My eyes blur with tears and I can't see what it is. Blood races down my arch.

Everyone gasps.

Everyone except Bette, who covers her mouth with one hand and practically runs away, like she can't handle the sight of blood. If I wasn't in so much pain, I'd hate her for it.

"What is it?" I scream in pain. There's shock on the others' faces, but in some I also read a bit of glee.

Morkie turns to Viktor and shouts something in Russian. He runs from the room. Moments later, the boys pour into the studio. Henri rushes toward me first, but Alec grabs his arm and shoves him aside. He kneels next to me.

"Take her to nurse, Alec," Morkie says. "And, June, go get Monsieur Kozlov." She touches her forehead. "How did something like this happen?"

I examine my foot and see a piece of the glass. Then I see there are three, maybe four pieces. More blood trickles out.

Morkie brushes my hand away. "Don't touch," she says.

I cry out in pain, and the look of my foot makes me feel nauseous. Alec lifts me from the floor like a doll.

"I can walk," I say.

"No," he says.

I try to fight my way out of his arms. I'm not weak.

"Just let me carry you," he says. "You're hurt."

"Put me down," I say a little too harshly. He obeys.

I hobble ahead. I scream out in pain and anger: both at whoever did this to me, and my bloody foot. The girls shuffle out of the way. Their faces twist in horrified expressions at my outburst. No one looks at my foot. They all cower in fear and gaze at their own feet. Bette turns her back to us and rests her hands on her head. She paces in a circle.

"Oh my god, oh my god," I think I hear her say under her breath, but the pain stuffs up every bit of me, even my ears, so I can't be too sure. I'm hearing everything through thick layers.

People say things. I watch their mouths open and close, faces twisting in awkward expressions, but the voices muffled and clogged, thick and slow and unintelligible. My head is light and my limbs feel like they don't belong. People are buoys drifting away from me. Even June steps back and I can't see her anymore. Heat gathers in my cheeks and radiates from my skin—beneath the light brown is red.

Alec catches my arm before I trip. I smell his cologne and sweat, and his warm palms make me feel like I'm floating. "It'll be okay," he whispers close to my ear, and I almost believe him, but I feel the throb of the glass caught in my foot. Morkie follows closely behind in hysteria. I feel faint and black stars twinkle before my eyes. My heart squeezes and burns and thumps too fast in my chest.

By the time we reach Nurse Connie's office, a crowd is in the corridor—the *petit rats* and their parents, the younger dancers, the administrative staff, and Mr. Lucas. Mr. K appears, his face long and grave as he takes my arm from Alec's. He lifts me up on to the examining table. Nurse Connie pulls the tights up farther. She rotates my ankle, exposing the shiny slivers of glass poking out of my foot.

I grit my teeth, but can't stop wincing every time her hands near my foot, anticipating the pain, which I know will be excruciating

"Where did this come from?" Nurse Connie asks. "Did you break something in your room? Or did something break in your dance bag?" She asks like she already knows the answer.

"I don't know," I try to answer, my breath heavy.

"She was in class," Alec says.

Mr. K and Nurse Connie exchange glances. "You and I both know someone did this," Mr. K says to Nurse Connie. They all sigh. I'm guessing this is not the first time they've seen something like this. I try to focus on their faces, but my eyes fight to stay open.

The pain in my foot and the effort it takes to worry about what's going to happen to me exhaust me.

"Deep breaths," Nurse Connie says. "Stay relaxed. It'll keep your heart rate down. Close your eyes." She picks up the school phone and calls the hospital. "I'm going to take you to the emergency room." I also hear her leave a message for my parents and Aunt Leah.

"Do I have to?" I ask. "Can't you just clean me up?"

"It's protocol," Nurse Connie says. "I want to ensure that there's no tissue damage." That's when the whole thing hits me. All of it, everything I've worked so hard for all these years, could end here. With this. What one of these evil girls will write off as a prank.

"Yes, yes, of course," Mr. K chimes. "Alec, carry her to the RA van. Go with her."

Nurse Connie grabs her bag and my med file. Alec scoops me up, carrying me through the corridor to the front of the school. He doesn't take no for an answer this time, and Mr. K insists. Everyone is out there, whispering and waiting and wondering. I close my eyes and curl my head into Alec's chest.

Once we're in the van, he traces circles and hearts and triangles on my palm, and the sensation makes me relax into the seat.

As we speed down Columbus Avenue, I feel like I'm not really awake. I fight thoughts about what this injury will do to my foot, to my dancing, to my role. Wind rattles the car windows. The sky is dark and gloomy. Ominous. A spring thunderstorm is coming. My foot throbs. I squeeze Alec's hand, and finally let him take care of me the way he wants to.

"It's going to be all right," he whispers.

"Our *pas* . . . ," I mumble, but he just shakes his head at me.

I close my eyes until we arrive at the hospital. We don't have to wait. A nurse ushers us into a private triage room and yanks the curtain. Alec rests me on the bed.

"Alec, you have to go to the waiting room," Nurse Connie says.

He gives me a concerned look, then retreats. The other nurse closes the drapes.

"How did this happen?"

I can't answer. Another slew of questions is asked. I barely hear them. Nurse Connie hands the nurse my file. "Her health history and most recent physical."

My eyes close while Nurse Connie fills her in on all the details. I block out her description of what's wrong with me. The new nurse examines my foot, wipes it with a cold pad that makes it burn. "Big breath," she says.

I take the deepest breath my lungs can handle, and she pulls the glass from my foot.

There is a surge of pain and release. More blood. More swelling. More heat.

I look down at my battered foot. Blood is everywhere, but the source is several deep slashes in my heel that feel like they've cut to the bone. I wonder if this is the end, after all of my mama's worries about my heart. Will I ever dance again? I can't bring myself to ask. I don't want to know the answer.

"She's going to faint," I hear Nurse Connie say, but I can't get the energy to protest. "She's got a preexisting condition."

Someone moves my head between my knees and I'm being told to breathe. An oxygen mask is put around my face. A pulse monitor is clipped to my finger. Its beeps are wild, uncontrolled. Too fast.

The hospital nurse makes a little concerned noise as my vitals fill a screen. Nurse Connie hovers over the silver table where the hospital nurse placed the objects from my foot.

She puts on rubber gloves and picks it up with tweezers, holding it into the light. Her face scrunches. "Huh," Nurse Connie says, almost to herself. "Looks like several pieces of a mirror."

29.

Bette

I STAY IN STUDIO G for hours after rehearsal. Even the hallways are empty, everyone hiding in their rooms after Gigi's trip to the hospital. Personally, I haven't felt this ready to dance since the spring cast list was posted, so I go with it. I work on pointe, aching to feel that crunch in my toes and that absurd new height when I'm balancing on tiptoes like this.

I'm best on pointe. Dancing in flat slippers is one thing, and people like Gigi can get away with their shady technique or particular attitude. I get it; she has personality when she dances, and the audience will sit back thinking they could do it, too, sensing her ease and her joy.

But pointe shoes are unforgiving. There's no room for that childish exuberance when your feet are forced into a whole new position and your weight is balanced precariously over the now straight line from your big toe to your hipbone.

I grab the barre for balance and work through basic exercises, preparing my muscles for the spasm of confusion that comes when you hoist yourself up into that erect, impossible position.

Gigi's mangled foot and bloody slipper flash in my mind—the bright red of her blood and the sounds of her screams. The whole incident replays, making me push harder. I throw myself into my variation. We all have nails separating from our toes and purple and yellow bruises that look like modern art painting decorating our feet. But after what happened today, Gigi's tender foot might take on a whole new level of disfigurement.

I work harder. That's enough to get my legs fully extended, and counting the beats of the dance in my head. I don't want to turn on the music in case of any stragglers. I don't even want the little ones looking in to admire. I just want me and the mirror and the violent images of glass and skin flashing through my head.

When I mark myself in the mirror, I see that I'm smiling. I shouldn't be smiling after what happened today. If someone saw me, they'd think I did it. I know they all suspect I'm the one who planted the glass in her slipper. Especially the ones who know I wrote the message on the mirror. Or the other little things. Whoever put the glass in Gigi's shoe was possibly out to get me, too. Framing me, knowing I might get blamed. I run through a list of potential suspects. June, for sure; maybe Will, now that Alec is officially with Gigi; and most definitely Henri to get back at me for messing with Cassie. I dance harder, hoping the exertion will help me come to definitive conclusions.

What I am trying *not* to think about: the way Alec rushed in and leaped to Gigi's aid the second she made that sad little-girl yelp. The way he held her mangled foot in his hands and didn't seem to mind the blood. The look Will managed to give me in spite of all the chaos. Like if Will can't have him, I can't have him either. Like he'd rather see Alec with literally anyone but me. And why do I still care after all these weeks? He's left me. Our on-again, off-again relationship seems off in a way it never has before.

I step into a turn, whipping around until I'm a tornado and can think of nothing else but watching my spot on the wall. Three pirouettes. Four. I will turn until I can't see Alec or Gigi or any of them anymore. Five. Until I don't think about what I did to Cassie anymore. Six. My supporting leg and ankle tire, wobbling in my pointe shoe. Seven. Alec rushes back into my head. Eight. My foot slips from under me and I stumble. I'm ass-down on the floor, lucky to not have scraped my chin or clicked my right hip out of place. But it hurts, a laser of pain that moves from my ankle all the way to my tender knee.

If things were going well with me and Alec, he'd show up with a heating pad at just the mention of me being in pain. But everything's a mess between us now. And I need to figure out how to put us back together.

I get back onto my toes. Like a girl on a horse, or a kid on a bike, or, I'd imagine, a tightrope walker high in the air, it's imperative that I don't give in. If Alec were here, he never would have let me get back up.

I rise up, up, up. It feels like stilts, even though it's just a few extra inches. I hang on the barre for a few moments, steadying, controlling, lifting and releasing and drifting into dance again.

"You keep losing the core," someone says. The startling sound makes me lose my balance. This time I grab for the barre before going all the way down, but the pain surges up my right side anyway, like it knows something I don't. I can't fool my body into not feeling it.

"Crap." I spin around only to see June.

She's quiet, I'll give her that.

And, if I'm being honest, she's probably right.

"Sorry. Just looking at your form. It's gorgeous, but when you pirouette you lose your core for a moment and the whole thing falls apart." If Eleanor were saying the same thing I'd snap at her, but June has the serious look of a teacher or a minister, and I can't find it in myself to dismiss her. I'm all out of mean things today. Her head is cocked and her eyes look up and down my body, critically but not cruelly.

"Oh," I say. I work my toes back into position and ready myself to go back into the dance.

"I think you're really spectacular *en pointe*," she says. I'm used to the *petit rats* saying it, or even sometimes the teachers, but never my peers. Never the girls. It's enough to make me relax onto the soles of my feet again. I wonder what she wants. We've never been friends. Or acquaintances, even.

"Obviously, you think I still have work to do," I say.

"We all do. But I was admiring you, before I noticed what you were doing wrong." There's zero inflection. No movement to her words, just flat, emotionless reporting of the situation that keeps me from getting riled up.

"Oh. Well. I guess I'm distracted." I turn away from her again and watch my stomach in the mirror, seeing the little pull when it flexes and the softening when I relax. It helps, sometimes, to see what your body is capable of.

"By Gigi?" she says.

Beads of sweat form on my back. "Poor thing," I say. "She's your roommate, right? Any word?" I keep it casual. June's smart. And maybe not as weak as I thought.

"Been at the hospital for a while," June says.

Some people say things carelessly. They let words pop out and roam around and they don't give much thought to the consequences. June is not one of those people. I don't know why she's telling me this, or what it could even mean, but there's a purpose to the tight little sentence. It's the only time I've heard June offer information about something other than a dancer's technique or weaknesses. The sweat on my back isn't a cluster of beads anymore, it's just a whole mess of damp stickiness.

"Mr. K has already sent flowers to my room." The way she says the word *flowers* sounds like she means *dog shit*.

I choose my words carefully: "His star needs to feel loved in her time of need."

"And she's getting plenty of that," she says, and I hope that's not a comment about Alec. "I didn't think she'd land Giselle, too," she adds, and I know I can talk a little trash with her about Gigi. I think I've worn Eleanor out with all my thoughts and theories and irritations about her.

"It's like she's his little pet," I say. "His favorite."

"Just like Cassie was," she says, and I want to do anything to erase that name and any parallels to Gigi.

"Makes you think, huh? Cassie was Mr. Lucas's niece, and Gigi's probably sleeping with Mr. K," I throw out, probably too sloppily.

"She's not the type." June shuts down my innuendo. I wish she'd just laughed or smiled or something else. Now it's back to awkwardness with her.

I don't reply. I get back onto my toes, work myself up to the tip-top, and move away from the barre, trying to shake off my earlier fall.

"Better," June says, just the way Morkie always does. She tries to slip away unnoticed, but I'm onto her this time, so I call out before she's able to slide out the halfway open door.

"Thanks for your help. Give my love to Gigi. Keep me posted on how she's doing, okay?"

I catch her eye in the mirror. We're looking at each other, but also not, and it's one of the things I like best about the reflecting glass. The surreal, removed aspect it can add to regular life. We're interacting, we're talking, we're seeing each other, but not *really*. Only through the glass. If pressed, we could say this never happened at all.

"You want me to tell her anything else?" June says. Her lips twitch, like they are considering a smile, but aren't ready to pull themselves all the way up yet. "Another . . . message?" Her eyebrows leap, as limber and expressive as her body when she's dancing. I want to defend myself, but I swallow down the words. Thank god I took a pill an hour ago and am still clear and brave and sure from its impact. I control my impulses.

"You need to get out more," I say at last, brushing past her little accusation and this time not even bothering to look at her in the glass. Just saying it to my own leg as I stretch. "I owe you. For, you know, helping me with my center. I'll take you out, okay?"

I don't expect her to say much of anything in response. She never hangs out. She's just not one of those girls. I turn again to check out her face for what little response it might give and she's blushing. A pretty pink that goes from her throat to her nose.

"Sure," she says. "Maybe sometime." That even voice finally shakes a little, and she slips out.

In the physical therapy room, I'm sitting in a huge bathtub full of ice. The TV's blaring a bad reality show, and I hope the cold cubes tone down the achiness in my knee, and maybe even my heart. Or maybe this is just what life feels like after Alec. Murky, untethered, throbbing with unspeakable pain in unexpected places. Adele told me over the phone to "dance the pain," but the pain in this case is rocky and nauseating. Impossible to dance through. All I need is a glass of white wine and a towel turban on my head and I'd be my mother, drowning her sorrows after my father left.

In one of the small treatment alcoves, a trainer helps a young girl stretch out her sore quad. Her cries slip out from behind the privacy curtains. I turn up the TV volume so I don't have to hear her or the chaos in my head. I used to come here with Liz. We'd get in the oversized tubs together, and right now, I'd be willing to have the stupid conversations she and I used to have about the calories in grapefruits versus watercress, the latest celebrity drama, over being alone.

I close my eyes and sink farther into the water. I prefer cold baths to warm now. The chill pinkens my skin, seeping into my muscles, erasing the pain, and resetting everything. My teeth chatter, but I clench them. I've been in here so long, my lips are probably blue. Way longer than the trainer said I should.

"You look like you could be dead," a cold voice says, "and maybe that wouldn't be a bad thing."

I sit up. It's Henri. He reaches his hand into the base of the tub. I pull my legs back in, a deeper chill settling into my spine. He takes a cube of ice, puts it in his mouth, and sucks on it. Water dribbles down his chin as he smiles at me.

"Leave me alone," I say, not wanting a rerun of him all over me.

He drops his hand back in my tub, his fingers grazing my toes. Water sloshes over the tub's edge as I flail, trying to avoid his touch. He laughs, loving that he can control me right now. I lift myself up to try to get out of the tub. His hand yanks my ankle down. "Not so fast," he says. "This will work just fine." He takes off his shirt, like he's going to join me in the ice bath.

"You can't get in here with me. It's against the rules," I say, like some suck-up kid who actually follows the PT room rules— or any rules for that matter.

"Don't worry, I'm not joining you," he says, dunking his sweaty ballet shirt into my water. He's got a tattoo I never noticed before. It's small, but I can make it out. Cassie's name, in a swirly script, scrawled across his chest. Ridiculous. He slaps the shirt at me. He wants me to react. To jump away from him again. Instead I cross my arms over my chest, offering up a lazy smile, and wait for his arms to get tired of wringing out the shirt. I don't let him see the fear in my eyes or how horrible I think he is. I don't let him see how disgusting I feel after he put his dirty shirt in the water with me. I can hold my own against Henri. Against anyone.

But he's not giving up either. "What do you want?" I finally say.

"What are you willing to give me?"

"Nothing! I'm done with you." I look around the room to make sure no one is paying attention.

"Are you really done?" He pushes his hands farther into the water. His fingers graze along my calf, then over my knee. "Or are you worried that I'll tell everyone that matters your secrets?"

I flex. His eyes narrow.

"If you wanted to, wouldn't you have already done it?" I say as his fingers travel farther up my leg, his rough palms circling my inner thigh. "I made out with you. A pity hookup. I thought we were done with this whole game." I try to get up from the water, aware of his eyes on my prickled skin, the goose bumps rising. He climbs in now, pushing me hard, and I sink back down into the tub, a single finger pinning me in place. I hate myself for not fighting away from him. I could shove my legs forward, kick the ice-cold water up into his face. But what if he does tell Mr. K? Worse, what if he tells Alec? I'd lose him for good. So instead of fighting it, I pull him in, close to me, his warmth melting my chill. I let his mouth explore mine, his hands wandering along my tank top, cupping my too-ample curves, fingers exploring until they reach the small space covered by the tiny blue bikini bottom I'm wearing.

That's when the trainer comes out from the back rooms. "Out," she orders, and Henri grins, standing. "Out now!" The trainer's trying to maintain her composure, to follow protocol, but her eyes settle on Henri, and I know she's going to let him walk out without a reprimand.

"Pardon," he tells the woman. "No need for concern. That was never going to happen, as much as she might want it." He smirks at me, still drowning in the tub, my lips bruised from cold or kissing, my ego smarting from the humiliation. "And trust me, she wants it."

30.

June

"**WILL YOU TAKE CARE OF** Gigi tonight?" Alec says to me outside the lobby elevator. The sound of his voice makes me nauseous.

"She's not sick," I say.

Gigi nods in agreement while hobbling forward. Her foot is swaddled in soft gauze and a bandage, and nestled in a little boot. People have been stopping by our room for days, checking on her. Weirdly, Henri's been leaving her little cards and notes, and though she throws them away, I sometimes fish them out of the trash. They're all concern and sympathy, and the insistence that, when she's up to it, they should talk. Alone. That she should be careful.

Maybe she should. But I don't know what that's got to do with me. I'm meeting Jayhe tonight—finally, after weeks of broken promises—and I'm not a babysitter. And Gigi's not five.

"I'm fine," she says. But I can hear the worry between those two small words.

"You've gotta be freaked out," Alec says. "I'd be freaked out. Just be a pal, June."

"I might have plans," I say, trying not to let the irritation show on my face. Vague. Instead, I push the elevator button a hundred times to signal that I want this conversation to end, I want to go up to my room. Jayhe and I are still a secret. I don't know if it's his decision or mine. But it's too soon to share. But maybe that will change when he finally sees me again. It's the perfect revenge. I can't wait for that moment when he realizes that he's actually way more into me than Sei-Jin.

I know that's how he feels. He won't come clean with Sei-Jin, but it's me he calls at midnight, and we end up video chatting. I even fell asleep in the Light last week after we spent hours chatting about art and dance and the restaurants his dad wants him to run and my father the ghost and how it will be when we can finally decide things for ourselves. And that's when I realize that, despite all my plotting and planning, this has become more than just vengeance. Our conversations make me crave him—his scent, his skin, his sleepy eyes on me, taking me in. It's been weeks since we've been together, and tonight, maybe, it will finally happen.

I punch at the elevator button again.

"You know," Alec says after a heavy pause and switching his body to the other side of the staircase, "you don't get the parts because no one trusts you enough to dance them. It's not that you're not good enough. I've heard them talk about it. It's your attitude. It's that you have no friends. It's that you're so twitchy and weird with people."

The words hit me like a sock to the stomach. And echo in the lobby over and over again. If it were Bette, I'd think it was a mind game, a way to get me freaked out. But Alec's not like her. He's always been pretty nice. His words burn a little hole inside me.

"I—" I can't get any words out. What I want to say is: *I used to have friends. I used to belong to a group. I used to be important.*

"June and I are friends!" Gigi interrupts, the words floating like bubbles out of her mouth, and I'd like to pop them all over her face. Even in this moment, she's an optimist.

Alec smiles, but it's mostly at her.

"Thanks for your help, Alec," Gigi says when I don't reply or agree that we are friends. "I'm okay. It's . . . you know . . . I'm trying not to let it get to me anymore." I don't believe her. She's too calm about it, and she's already had two outbursts about smaller incidents. And I probably should've said something about being her friend. I don't want anyone accusing me of doing things to her. A natural conclusion that I don't need anyone making since I'm her understudy and roommate. I want the role she has, and sometimes I like seeing her struggle around in her cast, but there are times when I like her. A little.

"Let me know if anything else happens, okay?" He kisses her forehead in that patronizing way before turning back to me. "And, June. Prove me wrong, you know?"

I wonder if there's a threat in there. Alec's dad is the head of the board, one of the most important people at the conservatory.

A conversation with Alec could be just that, or it could be a message from above. I get the feeling this might be the latter.

"Fine," I say, hoping all four of these elevators will open at the same time and they'll get in a different one from mine.

"What's up with the elevators?" Alec yells.

"They're not working right now," the front desk guy says. "Gotta take the stairs."

"Are you serious?" Alec says.

"I don't have time for jokes." He turns back around. "You can wait an hour or maybe more, or take the stairs."

Alec scoops Gigi up into his arms—despite her squealing, ear-shattering protests—and heads for the stairwells. I feel a little pinch inside, part of me coveting a little of what they have, and the other part wishing I didn't care. Hanging out with Jayhe has changed things a little. Maybe it's just a physical thing, maybe it started as a way to get back at Sei-Jin, but I feel like I can almost trust him. A few times, I've had to stop myself from showing him the box I found, from telling him how close I am to finding my father. There's no one I can trust with that.

I climb the stairs slowly. I want to give Alec enough time to get up to the eleventh floor, drop her on the bed, and get out. Out of breath, I wait on the top step, hoping Gigi's giggles will soon disappear, and I'll see Alec's blond head zip out of our room.

"Looking over your handiwork?" someone says behind me. "You don't deserve to dance with us. You don't deserve to be at this school." I turn around and Sei-Jin glares at me. Her eyes are narrow slits and her teeth are clenched. "I know what you did," she says.

I turn my back on her. Her feet pound the wood and she dashes up the stairs to me. Her cold hand jostles my shoulder, yanking me around. The banister presses into my spine.

"Get off me," I say. "What's your problem?"

I try to brush past her.

"I know it was you who did all that stuff to Gigi," she spits.

My face drops and I try to compose myself. "Is this your attempt at a late April Fools' joke?" I quip back. I won't let her get to me. Not anymore. I'm about to be one of the top dancers, and then she'll beg for my friendship again, and I'll have the satisfaction of saying no. She messed up my life, and she's the reason I have no friends. I think I lost the ability to make friends after her.

"You wrote that message on the mirror and put all that stuff about her in the Light. And that disgusting cookie. And I know you put the glass in her shoe. Of course you would. You're her understudy. If she doesn't dance, you do!" she says, her grip tightening on my shoulder, her voice echoing up and down, even reaching the eighteenth floor. "Who else, besides you, is that desperate?"

I want to scream at her and I want one of the RAs to catch her keeping me here against my will. But most of all, I want to shut her up.

"You did all of it!" she yells. "You make us all look bad, you know that?"

Her accusations hit me one after the other. I start to feel a little afraid. Someone might hear her. They might believe what she's saying. Blood drains from my face. My heart thuds in my chest. I want to vomit, empty myself of all it—her words, my tea, the noodles I picked at for lunch, the accusations.

"I didn't do any of that." I defend myself, but my voice is shaky. "You don't know anything."

"What I do know is that you're jealous of her. You always have been that type of girl." She's got me boxed in and I can't get away. "Remember when we were eight and you stole my jeweled leotard?" she says, her eyes bursting with anger. "You lied and lied and lied about taking it, then I caught you wearing it in your room. Twirling in front of your mirror, playing that stupid little music box."

I shake my head, trying not to remember that. She didn't know what was going on, that it was the year my mom told me my dad didn't want to be my dad, that he didn't want a relationship with me. I think of the music box on my shelf and the tinkle of its melody crowds into my head. I was just borrowing her leotard for a little while, pretending to be a princess. I planned to give it back. I did some bad things, I guess, when things were so confusing at home. But isn't that to be expected? I was just a little girl and I had a secret the size and shape of a fully grown man.

"Or when you told Hye-Ji she was fat?" she says.

My face flames. "She'd locked me in the storage closet." I'm seething as the memories flood back to me. All their torture. All their meanness. All the pressure from my mom and the absence of a dad.

"Or how you think it's cool to text my boyfriend. Yeah, I saw your name pop up on his phone last night. He doesn't like you,

June. He takes pity on you, but that's because he doesn't really know what a bitch you are."

"I'm not listening to you anymore. I didn't do anything wrong. And you're not going to make me feel like I did." It takes all my self-control to keep my voice in check. I'm shaking, so I hold the railing and swallow fears that she knows what's really going on with Jayhe and me. I'm not ready for her to know yet. But the rage inside me bubbles up, killing that tiniest hope that existed inside me that we could one day go back to how it was, the smallest corner of my mind that missed her. No, I will destroy her. "Get away from me, Sei-Jin," I say, then lean forward. "Or maybe that's your problem. You don't want to." I purse my lips at her.

Her eyes bulge, and she clenches her teeth. "I don't know what you're talking about. And as a matter of fact, I should've figured it out earlier. You know, Mr. K pulled me to the side. He asked a few of us, separately, if we knew anything about what was happening to Gigi. I should've told him I thought it was you. I'm going to tell him first thing in the morning. E-Jun Kim is responsible for all the things that happened to Gigi. She's a bitch. She's terrorizing her poor roommate. Your mother will be so proud. Oh wait, she'll probably hate you, too, after she finds out, just like the rest of us! Poor June! No father. And then, no mother."

"SHUT UP!" I scream, not realizing it's at the top of my lungs. My vision goes blurry and I can't quite see her face. I imagine her marching into Mr. K's office, saying that she knows something, and telling him that I'm violent. He'll offer her a seat, listen intently to her lies. He'll call Mr. Lucas into the office and make Sei-Jin recount her tale to him. Mr. Lucas's face will twist with disappointment and shame and embarrassment. They'll dismiss me from the school. There will be stories on the dance sites about how the ballerina from the American Ballet Conservatory got kicked out for hitting another dancer. I wonder what Jayhe would think, and hate myself for caring.

"It's all so obvious," she taunts.

I hear the blood pounding through my veins, and my heart is a drum beating a war chant. I'm ready to hurt someone. Not anything terrible. Not real violence. But just enough to show them not to count me out. To remind them how powerful I really am.

I don't know what I'm doing, just that my hands are on her shoulders and I'm shoving her. Hard. Her mouth opens and shuts, but I can't make out her words. She falls backward and tumbles down five steps. Her bottom makes a thud when she hits the wood. And her head clobbers the wall.

Bette appears at the bottom of the staircase. She races up, catching Sei-Jin before she tumbles any farther. "June!" Bette hollers, and I snap out of it, suddenly aware of where I am and what has happened.

I clomp down to where Bette is cradling Sei-Jin. I put my hands on my head, not sure what to do. My voice tucks itself into my throat, shutting it down so I can't speak. Did Bette see me push her? Did I really push her? No, no, she must've fallen.

Sei-Jin is hysterical. She screams and hollers, her mascara running in black streaks down her alabaster skin. I try to reach for her. "Don't touch me!" she shouts. "She pushed me. E-Jun pushed me!"

Bette walks her down several sets of the stairs, letting Sei-Jin's spindly arms drape across her shoulders, her frail body leaning against Bette's stronger frame for support, and they disappear, headed for the fourth-floor RA office. I collapse on the staircase.

"You better come with us," Bette calls up to me when she notices I'm not following. "You don't want to look any guiltier, right?"

A few minutes later, we're all in the RA office. Sei-Jin cries into the phone. I hear her mom's Korean curse words fly through the receiver and I know they're directed at me. I hear my mom's name, *Kang-Ji*, and I know Sei-Jin's mom is going to call her even though it's midnight. My heart hasn't slowed down yet. Bette sits beside me on the puffy couch, her fingers fidgeting constantly with her little locket. The RA switches between two calls, one with Mr. K and the other with Mr. Lucas. My tiny stomach folds in on itself.

"What happened?" Bette whispers to me. Her words are heavy with knowledge; she already knows the answer to her own question, but she wants me to confirm it.

I shrug. I've gone over it in my head like a ballet. Each move I made and each one she made. The memory of Sei-Jin's words float around me like music, repeating in refrains. I don't know how to answer Bette. I don't know if she's on my side. "I . . . I don't know," I say.

The RA hangs up and stands in front of Bette and me. Sei-Jin walks into a private area, still crying on the phone.

"What happened?" the RA asks. I wish they would all stop asking the same question over and over. It's making me dizzy.

My mouth is glued shut. I can't seem to open it. I sit on my hands, wanting and needing my compact, just so I could have something to hold on to. Something safe. The RA looks at Bette, waiting for an answer, and Bette's big blue eyes land on me.

"I stayed late to practice in studio B," Bette begins. "Then I had to take the stairs because the elevators are out. I heard yelling and shouting when I made my way up. And I saw Sei-Jin fall. I complained to the janitor the other day about how slippery they are."

I gawk at Bette, knowing she saw me push Sei-Jin. The lie leaves her mouth so easily, I almost believe her myself. The RA turns to me. "Is that true, June? Sei-Jin's saying you pushed her."

"I didn't," I whisper. "She . . . fell."

"Then why would she say that?" the RA asks.

"I don't know," Bette answers for me.

"We've always had . . . issues," I tell the RA. The phone on the desk blares.

"Well, go to bed. We'll deal with this in the morning." She picks up the receiver but cups her hand over it. "In the mean-time, stay away from Sei-Jin, June," she warns, and I know she suspects me, but also trusts Bette because she's a legacy here. No one wants to accuse her of lying and have to deal with her crazy mom.

Sei-Jin returns to the room just as we're leaving. She calls me something nasty in Korean that I've heard on one of my mom's soap operas. She lies across the couch with an ice pack, still sniffly and red in the face from crying.

Bette and I take the stairs up to the eleventh floor. I feel her looking at me, but she doesn't speak. She's waiting for me to say something. Finally, when we get to our floor and she turns to go to her room, I grab her arm. "Thanks," I say.

She doesn't reply at first and I assume her silence is *You're welcome*. "Is it true, though?" she says instead.

"What?" I answer.

"I heard what Sei-Jin said." She looks me right in the eye. "Did you do all that stuff to Gigi?"

"No," I say with a frown. "Did you?"

Bette's face pinches. "No!"

"Well, you haven't exactly always been a model citizen," I remind her. "We all know that."

"Neither have you," she snaps back.

With accusations flying, and me suddenly implicated, I want her involved. I want her secrets out, too. Not just mine. Because the more everyone knows her dirty secrets, the more likely it is that she is to blame. Over me.

At least, that's what I keep telling myself.

31.

Gigi

MY THROBBING FOOT PULLS ME awake. An April rain streaks the window, and gray light barely makes it through. I watch my butterflies flap their orange-and-black wings inside the terrarium. I bet they're desperate for sunshine. Or maybe I am. I named them after the great ballet dancers: Martha, Gelsey, Mikhail, Svetlana, and Rudolf. My butterflies are the ballerinas of the animal world. Their movements light and peaceful and created by nature. I blink back the tears that keep coming in quiet moments when I'm alone. My pain meds knock me out and dull all the thoughts running through my head these days, but sometimes when I wake up in the morning, it all comes flooding back like a big ocean wave threatening to swallow me whole.

Did someone put the glass in my shoe on purpose?

The angry truth: *Yes.*

And: *Why me?*

The most likely answer: *Because I got Giselle.*

Other swirling thoughts: *Because I'm new. Because I'm black. Because Alec and I are together.*

I remember the tears in Aunt Leah's eyes at the hospital when she saw my foot. My parents threatened to fly across the country, to come and take me home. I had no answers to their frantic questions. And now their questions have become mine. Each time they march through my head, I feel sick. My stomach twists in on itself, but my brain can't stop trying to piece it all together. The list of stuff is getting longer if I really look at it closely.

I know Bette put the message on the mirror. She admitted to that, and putting up the picture of me and Henri in the Light. But the pictures of her and Alec that were hung on my basement studio mirror, she refuses to own that. She's the only one who would have them. Does she expect me to believe that Alec did that? Or Eleanor? She didn't say she wrote that I should watch my back on the Light wall, but it feels like her style. I don't know who sent that disgusting cookie, or who put the glass in my shoe, which I should be most worried about. But the medical file haunts me the most. Even though it happened back in October. Someone saw my EKG report. They think I'm weak because of my condition.

I wasted the day away in bed. My mind a fog of medications. I hobble around the room. Mostly everyone is spending their Thursday evening in the studios, doing homework, or making runs to the store. Even June's not around. I wish I could talk all this out with her. She's so logical, I bet she'd easily figure out who is doing this stuff to me. There has to be more than one person. It can't just all be Bette.

I text Alec to see if he wants to hang out after his rehearsal, then go down to the basement Pilates room to stretch, to make sure I'm staying strong. I'll be out of ballet class and rehearsal for at least a week, and we're five weeks away from the show. All the last-minute corrections and stage direction changes, I won't get to actually do. I'll have to watch them.

The room's full of mirrors and squishy bouncy balls and purple and blue mats and a few weight machines. It's empty. I get myself situated on a machine, the same way the physical therapist showed me. I lie on my back, sinking down onto the cushions. I put both feet on the foot bar, even though I shouldn't put pressure on my injured foot yet, and I push. The steel carriage under me slides up and down with the promise of helping me keep the strength in my muscles. After five minutes on the machine, I can feel the stitches in my foot and pain shoots up my leg.

"Should you be doing that yet?" a voice says.

I crane my head, and see Will standing in the doorway, all sweaty, with a towel across his shoulders.

"No," I say, but try a few more pushes. He stands over me and extends his hand like we're onstage and ready to start a *pas de deux*. I stop, sit up, and take it.

"You could mess up your foot even more," he says.

"You sound like one of our teachers," I say. Or even my mama.

"Good." He sits on the mat and starts stretching. "So what can you do? What did they say?"

"Stretch and light weights and floor barre." So basically, nothing.

His eyebrows lift in that pitying way.

"Can we talk about something else?" I say, tottering over to get weights from a corner rack. He runs ahead of me and carries them back. I grumble at him, but eventually smile and say thanks. We sit on the floor together.

"So I shouldn't ask you if they've figured out who put that glass in your shoe?" he says.

"Not unless you already know," I say back.

"I don't. I'd usually blame Bette," he says, rolling his eyes, "but I'm not so sure this time. She definitely has it in her. Seriously. Don't buy into the stuff Alec tells you about her. She's got him fooled, and everyone else." His eyes get all big, like he's scared of what he's saying. "She put a lot of people through shit. If it was her, she deserves to get what's coming to her." He inspects my foot. "You should be careful with her."

His words mimic what Henri told me at the beginning of the fall term and in the notes he keeps sending me, and that stupid Valentine's message. "I don't want to talk about it. And you told me that before." Especially not with him. "How are things with you?" I ask, for lack of anything else better.

"Really good," he gushes in a way I've never seen before, then leans in. "I might have my first ever boyfriend soon."

That's news to me, but I try to keep the surprise off my face. "Oh really?" I say. "Do I know him? A dancer?"

"Hmmm . . . maybe," is all he says. "Tall, dark, and handsome."

It's so hard to meet people outside the ballet world. Spending your time in and out of studios, at rehearsals, stretching, and fretting about every little motion of a variation doesn't leave much room for anything else. The prom and homecoming invites come, and are left unanswered or declined, and they eventually stop coming. It's easier to date someone inside ballet.

"Details? A kiss? Hanging out?" I parrot Mama when she's poking Aunt Leah about her dating life.

"I'll never tell!" he says, a blush making his face match his hair. "Well, at least not yet. He's kind of shy. Anyway, so what's the prognosis on your foot?"

"Wait a minute." I turn to look at him, giving my best "spill it" face. "You're not getting off that easy."

"Well, let's just say he's really hot." Will smirks, and is about to say more. But Alec steps into the doorway, and all of Will's excitement and laughter zips right up, like a bag that's closed. He clears his throat, and pretends to smooth his perfect hair in the mirror.

"Hey," I say to Alec, and he steps into the room like it's full of land mines.

They don't speak, and I'm not sure what's happened.

32.

Bette

FOR THE FIRST TIME IN my life, no one's listening to me. Even Eleanor has started putting in her earbuds and humming along with the *Giselle* music when I start talking about Gigi and Alec, and Gigi's obsession with stealing everything from me, and Gigi's obvious psychotic breakdown after her incident with the cookie.

But today, I pull her earbuds out while we're getting ready for morning ballet class. "Are you listening to me?"

"I'm trying to focus," she says. "And it's kind of like you have an obsession."

"No, I don't," I say back.

"Then why do you keep talking about her?"

"Just trying to loop you in." I feel like she just spit in my face.

She starts to put her earbuds back in. "I don't know if I want to be looped in anymore," she says.

But I run right over all those words and keep talking. "I even talked to June about it. We both think Gigi and Mr. K are having an affair. That's the way she got both of these roles."

Eleanor's hand freezes beside her ear before she can jam the earbud in.

"I kind of threw myself at him, too, a few weeks ago," I admit, wanting my best friend back, wanting to be able to share everything again, no matter what. "Just to see."

She turns red, and not the pretty flush you get after a long ballet class. It's the kind you get when you've fallen down a flight of stairs with everybody watching. Or discovered you have a booger in your nose while talking to someone you like.

"Why would you do that?" she says.

"I thought I could get my role back." I start gathering my hair up into a bun. "It's not like that hasn't worked before. Adele told me."

"He doesn't go around randomly hooking up with his dancers," she says, her tone snappy. "Don't you think he's too smart for that? He could get in trouble."

"Adele says—"

"I don't want to hear about it." She gets up and grabs her dance bag. "I need to get ready for class."

I take a pill to try to erase those thoughts, and the embarrassment of having my own best friend walk out on me. I try not to think about how many pills I've taken, or the fact that in the last few months I've almost doubled the amount. Instead, I slick down every piece of hair, making sure it's perfect, and go downstairs for ballet class. I dodge Henri's gaze as I slip into studio C, suppressing memories of skin on skin, his lips on mine.

I keep to myself. The girls are watching. Gigi is sitting in the front, her swaddled foot perched on a pillow on a chair, like it's a glass slipper. I dance harder now that she has to watch from the sidelines. I hope she feels like I did when I had to watch her dance the Sugar Plum Fairy, or watch Cassie dance the fairy spirit.

Ballet class ends and Mr. K visits to tells us that tonight's rehearsal is canceled. It's Alec's father's birthday party. All the teachers are attending, and the board members, and other important people in the city who love ballet. My mother is pulling me out of afternoon academic classes so I can get my hair blown out and a new dress. She thinks I need to win Alec back. She thinks I am a mess. Maybe she's right.

I stay after everyone's left the studio to stretch a bit longer. My knee doesn't hurt as much when I cool down longer. Other dancers head off to lunch and afternoon academic classes. It always amazes me how sudden the transformation is: from chaos to stillness, from suffocation to solitude. I never thought I'd ever want to be alone.

The studio door opens, not with a creak or a knock but with a bang and a breeze. Someone who knows I'm in here and who doesn't give a shit about startling me or interrupting my stretching.

Mr. K is back.

"Just the girl I was looking for," he says.

The words give me a shiver—they twinkle with his threat of calling my mother and setting up an appointment with the school psychologist.

"Hey there," I say, trying to sound casual, standing up, even though the pain in my knee screeches a little. I just need a few Advil and maybe a secret trip to the physical therapist. Then I'll be fine.

"Morkie's been pleased with your work the last week," he says. His words have weight: what he means is that I was blowing it for a while, and now I am finally clawing my way out of the hole. I nod my head because really, it's not exactly a compliment, and we both know it.

"You've been letting Gigi get the best of you," he goes on. "You can't always be on top at every single moment. But you can still be great."

"Or I can be the best," I say.

"You spend much time with her?" Mr. K says after clearing his throat. He's not one for small talk, so the casual tone sounds forced. "She's been having a rough go of it lately, as you know."

"Gigi?"

"Yes. Your competition. Are you listening?"

"As much time as I spend with anyone." I can tell he needs me, but he's uncertain how to proceed. In some strange and unexpected way, I'm in charge. He knows I'm the heart of this school. I know what's really going on with his dancers.

"She ever mention any rumors about who is behind all this nonsense? Have you heard any rumors? You know I don't like gossip to affect my dancers. . . ." Mr. K shifts his weight. I have never seen him standing in anything but a straight and perfect vertical line, but now he's leaning against the barre a little. Like a regular man and not a great dancer. Not like the man who controls our futures. My future. He reaches out his hand to me. I take it, and he pulls me closer to the barre. Last time he withdrew, but this time his touch is warm, inviting. Like maybe things would be different if I just tried one more time.

"You look remarkably like your sister up close." He lifts my chin, his eyes climbing over my face and neck and even cleavage. All of a sudden, all I hear in my head is the conversation I just had with Eleanor about him. All I can think about is how Adele said she used to let Mr. K kiss her neck and run his fingers along the bottom edges of her leotard when he'd show her how to correctly let her *pas* partner lift her. God knows what else they've done together.

"I thought I was getting her back. With you coming up the ranks. I thought you'd dance more like her," he says, deadpan. With no regard for any feelings I might have about my sister. I don't blush often, and I can feel the disgusting red heat radiating from my face. And the tears that usually come with it.

I swallow it all down, packing it inside. "I don't have time for rumors," I say, making my voice sound calm and unaffected. "And I definitely don't have time for idle chatter about Adele. Even if she was your *favorite*."

Mr. K pulls his hand away from me, like I'm a piece of trash dropped in a basket. He clears his throat again. "I wonder if maybe Gigi got the wrong impression. Sometimes you girls get quite confused," he says after a pause that I think might swallow me whole. He's retreated, but he doesn't take his eyes off mine. Our eyes are the same—light blue and brimming with challenge. I can't let him dismiss me again, like he did in his office last week. The threat of the school psychologist still rings in my ears, and that same flush of embarrassment crawls up my skin.

I don't reply. He rubs his hands together, like they are two sticks making a fire. Mr. K is so heated and so powerful, I wouldn't be surprised if flames sprung from his hands. I take a tiny step back.

"I really don't know," I say at last. I miss when his loaded statements had to do with his interest in me and my career, and not his worry about Gigi. "I can ask around," I say. We both know it's a threat and not a favor.

Mr. K shakes his head, and leaves me standing there. As soon as he's out the door, I let out one raging scream into my ballet sweater.

Alec's house looks like it always does, but gift wrapped for his father's birthday party. A beautiful Upper East Side town house between Madison and Fifth Avenues. Even better than mine. Though my mother would never admit it. But when we get to the door Mr. Lucas hugs me with only one arm and doesn't kiss my cheek like he used to. His new wife's hand is so cold on my shoulder that I shiver, and Alec's sister, Sophie, who used to beg me to do her makeup and help her with her pirouettes and *sautés*, barely musters the enthusiasm to wave in my direction. The parlor is filled with important dance types, milling around in their evening finery, most of them onto their third or fourth cocktail. None of the other students are here—not even Alec's precious Gigi. Most of us are not deemed important enough, unless there's a legacy, a family history at this school. Which I have, thanks to Adele. And my grandmother's money.

"Alec's upstairs," Mr. Lucas says, before he leans in to embrace Adele and compliment her on her most recent performance. He even quotes a line from the *New York Times* review. His ridiculous wife laughs wildly, like Adele is a celebrity, which I guess for ballet world people she is. But I will be, too, someday. And then they'll regret their cool treatment of me.

"Is he . . . expecting me?" I say. It doesn't sound right, the words formal and strange in my mouth, and their faces show as much discomfort as I'm feeling. I don't wait for an answer, just head up the stairs like it's every other Thanksgiving or Christmas or birthday celebration, even though now he loves someone else, and I'm all alone.

His door is wide open, and I catch sight of him before he notices me in the frame. I never forgot how handsome he is, but he looks even better than the image in my head. Maybe it's seeing him in normal clothes instead of his practice clothes, but he's so boyish and beautiful and real, I almost can't breathe. When I do finally manage a breath, it turns almost immediately to tears.

That's when he sees me.

I try to make the tears silent ones, at least, since I can't seem to make them dry up. But I sniffle a few times, and then break down into full-on sobs. I haven't cried like this—loud and unforgiving—since the Christmas my father left, and the thought of that makes me cry more. Between my knee and the random April snow shower outside and the sound of my reckless sobbing, I'm practically reliving those horrible days.

"Oh my god, what? What happened? Did your mom—" Alec moves toward me and I let him wrap me in a hug. I cry into his shoulder until his crisp white dress shirt is soaked through in the shape of my eyes and mouth. He rubs my back and shushes me, his mouth next to my ear. One movement of his mouth and he'd be kissing the lobe, working his way down my neck until we're making out on his bed. It's such a familiar routine, I'm surprised he doesn't do it just on reflex.

"Everything's wrong," I say at last. I whisper, but I probably don't have to. There are glasses clanging downstairs and loud bursts of laughter followed by a frantic mix of voices, everyone trying to talk over everyone else, Adele's voice coming out the clearest, getting the most space.

"What did she do?" Alec says, still thinking this is all about my mother, when really she's only a part of it.

"She's . . . fine. She's been okay. Distracted by drinking."

"Oh."

"Don't you want me still?" I press my body against his a little. He resists, but not so much that he pulls away.

"I know you don't want to hear this, but I'm with Gi—"

"That's okay. It doesn't even have to be anything real. Don't you just want me, though? Like before? I won't tell. Couldn't we—" I reach one hand around his neck and run one finger back and forth across the place where his hair meets his neck. He always liked that, and he shivers a little in response.

"You know I'll always care—"

"I know she's really inexperienced," I say. It's not planned, and it's not exactly the best argument to get what I want, when what I really want is Alec to love me again. But I'll take anything right now.

"God, Bette—"

"I miss you so much. You have to miss me a little. You don't do all that with someone and then just never think about it again. . . ." I reach down to his pants. The waistband. And then the button. The zipper. He doesn't push my hand away.

I expect to feel a rush of love, a kind of bliss that I can have him again, but instead I can only think one terrible thought: *I've got to find a way to let Gigi know about this.*

Then, as if he heard what was going on in my head, he jolts away from me.

"Hey. No. I'm sorry. But no," he says. His words are still nice, maybe because his shirt is still wet with my tears, or maybe because I look so pathetic all dolled up and limping and throwing myself at him. I don't say anything in response; there's nothing to say. He takes a few steps back and gives a sad little smile.

"Why do you like her?" I ask, because I'm nothing if not my mother's daughter—a glutton.

"We shouldn't talk about this," he says. "Not right now."

"No, tell me. I can take it," I say.

He sighs.

I give him a small shove. "I want to know. You owe that to me at least."

"She's easy," he answers, and doesn't mean the kind that comes with random hookups. "She makes me laugh, and forget all the crazy stuff at school. Okay?"

I step back.

"We've been a mess for a while, Bette. We started doing our own things," he says.

I put my hand up. "Got it."

"Look, I'm going to go downstairs," he says, quickly swapping his tear-soaked shirt for a crisp new one. "Cheese plate. Say hi to your sister. You come down whenever you're . . . ready. Okay?" I don't say anything. "Okay. Hey, everything's gonna be okay."

Then I'm alone in his bedroom, and it all looks just the same as it has for years, but different, too, because he's not in it and there're no photographs of us on his bulletin board and the bed is perfectly made instead of mussed up by our bodies rolling around on it.

Then I notice it: a brown box marked with Gigi's name sitting on his desk. A little pile of origami roses next to it. A letter. Some chocolates.

I don't go for the letter, though a part of me aches to read it, to know what words he uses with her, how he tells her how beautiful she is. If he loves her. I finger the roses. I pick up the roses one by one. I wish I could stuff the box full of more of the photos of Alec and me. Whoever gave her those did me a favor. I wonder if he still has his copies, and I wonder if he even knows about her getting the pictures. I wonder why Gigi wouldn't have told him.

I try to ignore a tiny whisper inside my chest: *Maybe because she's better than you, Bette.*

To get rid of the thoughts, I ramble through his room, and look for his copies of the pictures. Obviously, she hasn't gotten the message that Alec and I are meant to be. She needs to remember that Alec and Bette existed. That Alec and Bette meant some-thing. I know he used to keep them in his closet, in a box within a box where he kept other private things: a few sad *Playboy* mag-azines, a letter from his real mother, whiskey bottles stolen from a hotel room, a photograph of his father as a younger man and a gorgeous Asian dancer that has been folded and unfolded so many times you just know it was in a wallet for years.

And the pictures of me and Alec, together. They are mostly of me, though Alec's legs and hands and eye line are sometimes in the frame. Alec took some of me on my own: naked and smirk-ing at the camera. Then I convinced him to set the timer and get in the pictures with me. In one, my legs are wrapped around his waist and his face is buried in my neck. Two years ago, when we were just moving from kissing and holding hands to taking off each other's clothes and touching what was underneath.

But right under them is something even better: all the love letters we sent each other. Bundled with twine like something out of a romance movie. When we were fourteen, he'd said we should make a time capsule and bury it near the tiny fountain in the backyard. Something he'd seen on TV. He made me bring him all the letters he sent me, then put them together like puzzle pieces. I'd been stupid back then. Told him it wasn't sexy, as if I really knew what that word meant. He stopped writing me letters after that.

He won't miss them, I think.

And then: *I still know him best.*

And then: *She would never do this.*

I choose the best letters, the ones where he tells me all the things he loves about me, the ones where he tells me we'll be together forever and get married, the ones where he tells me how beautiful I am. Then the rest of the night's not so bad. Alec keeps smiling his sad smile at me, and Mr. Lucas ignores me, and no one tells me how pretty I look or how great I was in rehearsal. But it's really not so bad. Because I'm taking back control.

When I get back to the dorms, I go to the Light with the letters, paper, glue, and scissors. Where I can be alone. I lock the door behind me. I cut out my favorite phrases from the letters, arranging them on the page and gluing them down. I ignore the thoughts cramming into my head: *This is crazy. Only psychopaths do this. This is some serial killer–type stuff.*

I imagine the look on her face when she sees what we had, what she will have to live up to, what she'll never be. The insecurities popping up inside her after I deliver these to her room.

"I'm not crazy," I say. "Alec and I know everything about each other. We belong together. We have a history. We were meant to be."

33.

June

IT'S 3 O'CLOCK ON SUNDAY, and the bustling kitchen of Jayhe's Elmhurst, Queens, restaurant, Chae's Chom Chom, is crammed with people—busboys, dishwashers, waiters, several cooks, and his dad, who's running the show. Jayhe's in training to take over this branch, and even though he's not happy about it, he still seems pleased to show it off to me. And to show me off to his dad, apparently.

His dad hands me a series of tiny appetizer plates brimming over with spinach salad, pickled radishes, bean sprouts, and more. The waiter behind him sets down others: kimchee, crispy sweet potatoes, fried onion pancakes, dumplings. The porcelain dishes clink a melody along the table as they're arranged before us. My stomach balloons just looking at all this food. But my mouth waters. I want to eat it. And keep it down.

Jayhe's dad says something in Korean. I don't understand what he says, but I think I get what he means. "Eat," he says to me in English, nodding toward the plate. "Good for your ribs."

He always pauses for me to respond, but I can't. I feel a stupid lost-in-translation expression climb over my face. It's embarrassing.

There's another flurry of too-fast Korean, but I understand the word *halmeoni*—grandmother. I can see her small, wrinkled face and those warm eyes. I wish I could see Jayhe's grandma again. It's been too long since someone's been that kind to me.

Jayhe and his dad fuss a little. Jayhe's shaking his head and says no a bunch of times. His dad is distracted for a moment, giving one of the waiters a direction.

"What's he saying?" I whisper to Jayhe, feeling ridiculous that I can't fully understand my own language.

"Not important," he says, popping a potato into his mouth, which lets him get away with not answering me.

"But it is. He was talking about your grandmother and me. I heard him." I nudge his leg until he sighs.

"He said after we eat, that I should take you to go see her," he says, dipping his chopsticks into another dish. "You know we . . ." He swallows the word *can't* along with the *jwipo jorum*, the fish jerky, strong and chewy in his mouth.

I stir a spoon in my tofu soup. While he wants me here, he could never bring me that far back. Not without everyone knowing what we're doing. This all started out as a game, and now I'm here with his dad, in one of their family restaurants. It hits me that this has become something so much more than what I thought. And it still has to be a secret.

But I think maybe, when I go back to the dorms, the other

Korean girls will know anyway. Because the scent of sesame oil pervades everything—and I know I'll go home smelling like it, sharp and pungent. His dad sets down more bowls, and stares at me, waiting. I know he wants a little head nod, the approval that everything is so good. But it's hard to enjoy food anymore.

I take a tentative bite of the hot pan-fried *mandus* and dip out more soup, then, knowing what Jayhe wants, take a big slurp. Jayhe and his dad grin at each other, then Mr. Chae nods toward the kitchen door. "Go, sit, enjoy," he says, his dark eyes—the same as Jayhe's—twinkling with delight. "Good appetite!" And he and Jayhe exchange glances that I decipher easily: he's pleased that his son has found a girlfriend who actually eats. Not like Sei-Jin.

Except that Jayhe is still with Sei-Jin, and I'm just the old childhood pal. But Mr. Chae knows what I do, too. That Sei-Jin will disappear, off to Harvard or Yale or wherever, and Jayhe will realize that he doesn't even miss her. That he never really loved her. That it was me all along. Yes, that must be it.

I wait for Jayhe to ask me about Sei-Jin's fall down the stairs, and if I pushed her. Bette covered it up with the other girls: spread a nasty rumor that Sei-Jin slipped down the stairs and tried to pin it on me so she could get rid of me. Everyone always believes Bette.

I grab one of the sticky ribs from the table, which is piled high with more food—chicken wings and noodles and *bibimbap* in stone bowls, all the house specialties his dad insisted we try. Every time I blink, more hands deliver more food. I tear the meat off the bone with my teeth, feeling ferocious and fierce and strangely sexy as I feel Jayhe's eyes take me in. There's a pride and tenderness on his face that I haven't seen on anyone's in so long, not when they look at me—certainly not my mom's. But then he bursts out laughing. "You're the only girl I know who always manages to get food not just on her face, but in her hair," he says, stroking my forehead as he pulls a chunk of barbecued meat from a strand. "Your too-light hair," he says, quiet and sweet.

I push his hand away with my own. "You're getting sauce on my head!" I say, mock annoyed.

"You already had sauce on your head!" he says, laughing, "and your hands and your face." He pokes me in the boob, a splotch landing on my baby-pink cardigan. "And your chest," he says with a smirk. "Eat fast," he says, his eyes hungry. "We've got to get you back to the dorm."

I don't want to head back. I just want to stay here, in his world for a moment—away from the meanness of starving girls and the weight of always being second-best.

But as much as I like being here, and seeing his dad, I know why he brought me to Elmhurst and not to Astoria, where his mom is in charge at their other restaurant. Where his grandmother would see me and talk about the good old days, sighing over what was lost and how glad she was that I was found again. He can't let any of it get back to Sei-Jin. He can't let her find out about me. I'm still a secret, and that stings. I know he wants me. I meant for this to be a simple game of vengeance, of finally getting what someone else wants. But now, Jayhe feels like the one thing I don't really have anymore: home.

These are the steps that no audience will ever see me dance. Sweeping arms. A deep arch in my back, and curling forward, drawing an invisible circle around myself. At times like this, my body and the music are one perfect unit. In the second half of the ballet, the character Giselle is a ghost. I have to be invisible inside the music, haunting the stage but not ever really inhabiting it. I know how to be invisible. As Gigi's understudy, I get to dance her part during our first weekly evening rehearsal. But it's the only time I'll get to dance it.

Gigi has stage presence: large and unbreakable. She has charisma. She has that luminous quality that Mr. K is always going on and on about, and strong shoulders and a deep, warm smile when she dances. Still, Gigi could never do this as well as me.

That's what makes her so wrong for this role and me so right. I am floating. It's been three days since being in Queens with Jayhe, and since then, I have eaten so little, purged so much, I can barely feel the weight of my own body as I stand on my toes. I can move so lightly, so effortlessly. I am barely here at all. No one really sees me. I'm used to being invisible.

I almost lose concentration in my pirouette. I've lost count of the turns. Seven. Eight. Maybe even ten. On that last precise spin, I see Gigi watching me, her mouth in a little O, her hand resting over her heart. I don't know if she is capable of feelings like resentment or bitterness, but if she were, this is what jealousy would look like on her. The top half of her body is even leaning back a little, like she's afraid of me, of my quiet power onstage.

I complete the dance, arms so strong they could stay over my head into eternity. I do not move a muscle until long after the last note has faded. My muscles don't even twitch with effort.

True to form, it is Gigi who claps first. I almost wish she didn't. I wish the perfection of me dancing her role would put a stop to her incessant kindness. That it would bring out something different in her. Something darker. But Gigi claps, and the rest of the class follows. Morkie, Viktor, Bette, even. The applause doesn't last long enough. Mr. K is in the door, and scoffs, unimpressed by the applause, the sweat on my shoulders, the perfection of my ninety-nine pounds.

"Understudies, still? Do this with them afterward. We must continue," Mr. K says to Morkie. "It'll be opening night before you know it. And where will we be?" Then he adds something in Russian. I don't think he even knows my name—though he's known me my entire life. Morkie clears her throat and claps her hands, but this time as an order.

"Of course," she says. "Off, June."

I am not graceful, lifting myself up from the floor. What moments before felt beautiful and light and invisible, now feels bony and awkward and empty.

"Before we continue," Mr. K says, letting his eyes meet each of ours briefly, "I don't want to forget to tell you that we've selected many of the *Giselle* variations to be a prominent part of the end-of-year exams."

The room goes still. These exams weed out those with shaky technique. They're graded just like a final, and if you don't pass, you might as well pack your bags.

"I don't have to remind you that the end-of-year exams help us see your technical progress and to think about whether you'll be apprenticed with the company, needing to work a little more, or find yourself a company member," he says. On cue, I'm sweating and shaking and I want to visit the bathroom to just expel all that fear in liquid form. I can't afford the nerves, not when I just completed the best dance of my life. Not when I finally have the chance to show them my potential. Not when I have to prove my mom wrong.

Mr. K's shoes click and clack on the surface of the studio's floor, their echo commanding us to stay perfectly still. Mr. K passes by Bette, and he looks at her closely for a moment. A long, long moment.

"You're tired," he says, squinting at her face. She blushes and bows her head. Even the great and powerful Bette is whimpering in his presence.

"I've been working hard," she says, and to my surprise, her voice trembles. It's a sound I've never heard come out of her before. There's something weird about all the changes happening around here.

"Show me," Mr. K says.

"What?" Bette's voice goes even smaller, even shakier. It is a shiver.

"Show me how hard you've been working."

Before we were all still; now we are statues. Bette pulls a breath in, from where I don't know. The room is closed, the air is trapped, we could all suffocate, here and now.

And then Bette's dancing, slipping back and forth across the floor, shaking when she goes on pointe, losing balance when she lifts into an arabesque. She's Bathilde, the rich woman engaged to Albrecht, the man Giselle loves. The role is minuscule, but Morkie has choreographed something just for her, something not in the original ballet.

It's not bad. It's still technically lovely and even has an elegant fluidity. But it's rocky, too. It's shaky. Just like the night when I helped her with her pirouettes. The technique is there, the beauty is there, but the control is gone. I've never seen her dance like this.

Mr. K walks out without a word when the variation is over. I see Bette swallow, and Morkie scramble, and we all move to the barre and pretend that didn't just happen.

"Variations," Morkie says, and she goes to Bette. We're all meant to work on our own for a moment, making sure not to let our muscles cool off.

Eleanor is at the barre, stretching across it, deep in some sort of chant. I hear her speak the words of her choreography one after another in a weird rhythm. Sei-Jin prances over. Her presence is so big that I can feel her coming. She stands over me, hands on her hips.

"I heard you're leaving," she says, giving a fake pout. Her friends giggle. The sparkly excitement that had been building up in my chest congeals, goes hard and cold, and drops down into my stomach.

"Huh?"

"Yup, my mother told me you were leaving. Something about . . ." She pauses and puts a finger to her mouth. "Going to a normal school. 'Cause you can't land a lead role. Always the understudy."

I wring my warm-up sweater in my hands and think of my mom calling Mrs. Kwon to discuss pulling me out of the conservatory, and if she's heard anything about PS 525.

My jaws clench and I feel my cheeks vibrate from the pressure. I feel the judgment in her eyes. I know what she's thinking: a real Korean ballerina never quits. They work and work and work until they are better than their counterparts, until they land that role no matter what. It's the Korean way. That much I've inherited.

"I'm not leaving," I say. "Don't you worry."

I make a kissy noise at her.

Her face flames. "I wasn't. Just thought you should know what people were saying about you."

"I'm just getting started here," I say, letting my voice rise. I don't care who hears it. "You have no idea what's coming." I step in closer to Sei-Jin, so that she can smell how serious I am.

"You don't intimidate anyone, E-Jun," she says, but she leans back on her heels, like she is, maybe, just the tiniest bit intimidated. "You may have shoved me down the stairs, but I'll get you back for that. I hate you."

That's when I almost tell Sei-Jin's secret. I almost scream the word *lesbian*, wanting it to echo and bounce off the studio mirrors. But I can't. And one kiss doesn't make her that. And so what if it did? She's the one who's scared of that, not me. But for now, it's all I've got, so I have to save it for the right moment. For the moment when her mother can hear it. For the moment when even just saying the word, true or false, has the power to change something.

I lean in close to her, feeling powerful. "Are you sure about that? There was a time when you really liked me. Remember that?" She races off, and her onlookers follow suit just in time for Mr. K to return to the studio and call us around for closing rehearsal remarks. He yaps on about emotion and Giselle and ballet. Again.

He waves us off. We curtsy and the teachers leave.

I skip cooling down—even though it's horrible for my muscles—not wanting to stay around for the girls' nightly debrief of rehearsal. I don't want to hear them agree with Mr. K about the understudies not rehearsing. It's hard to sit and listen sometimes. The word *understudy* feels like the word *loser*, meaningless, invisible.

I head to the student mailboxes near the front desk to pick up the dried soup I know my mother dropped off for me. I jam my key into my box, and the door creaks open. There are three packages of Korean noodles and an envelope. I don't ever receive mail. Not a letter, a postcard, or even a simple Post-it note. And never anything from my mother aside from Korean food.

In a secret and dark place inside me, I'm hoping it's from Jayhe. An anime sketch. Or a quick comic strip. It's stupid. I know this. I would laugh at anyone else who behaved this way. But I can't bury the feeling no matter how much I try, or tell myself it isn't real. My mind makes a simple envelope into the biggest thing that's ever happened to me.

I wait until I'm in my room—alone—to open it. I carefully pull up the flap and unfold the paper. My eyes scan the typed words. My fingers start to sweat. The page slips from my hands, floating to the floor.

It's my enrollment confirmation at PS 525.

It's my summer class schedule.

It's the end of my life.

I almost fall, my knees weak, my heart threatening to give out, my head full of heaviness. I vomit all over myself. I can't even move to the trash can. The sloppy, burning liquid spews out and down my black leotard, making a print of bile and half-digested grapefruit bits all over Madame Matvienko's white practice tutu. My hands can't hold it in my mouth.

I drop to my knees. My eyes burn. My chest heaves. I think I might throw up forever.

The door opens. It's Gigi.

"Oh my god, June!" She rushes to my side with a trash can. The hiccuping makes my stomach muscles sore. Tears pour out and I can't stop them as she holds me over the metal bin and I empty my already empty stomach. The greasy Chinese food Gigi deposited in there yesterday makes me retch even more. She strokes my back in a pattern. Almost like it's a song, until the heaving stops.

I can't move my arms and I feel like I'm sinking into the floor, straight down through it. All my energy's gone into that trash can. She wipes my face and chest and tutu with a towel. She plugs in my electric teapot while I sit in a crumpled heap. She returns with a steaming cup. She's made it the perfect Korean way. Picking the barley out of one of my packs. Boiling water in the pot. Sprinkling the barley on top, letting it steep in the water without pushing it down. I didn't know she knew how I made it.

She doesn't talk for a long time. As she refills the teacup. As she helps me undress. As she wipes more of the mess off me. As she tucks me into bed. Then, finally, she asks, "What happened?"

Her eyes are full of concern. Genuine concern. Like she loves me. And then the tears pour out again because I've been horrible to her. I want to tell her I don't know how to be nice. That I've been mean for so long that it's all I know how to do. It's a reflex now, as natural as a *plié*. There are dark points inside me that I can't stop from coming out.

Words spill out of me like more vomit. I tell her about the public school, about not knowing who my father is, and worst of all, about pushing Sei-Jin. Her eyes grow big and her mouth purses. But she doesn't move from my bedside. Her nose doesn't crinkle with judgment. She just tells me everything is going to be okay, and strokes the top of my head until I am drowsy from all the puking and talking and emotions. I drift off a little, still in and out of sleep, my head pounding from too many tears and my throat raw from too much purging.

At last, the room light clicks off. Gigi lights one of her scented candles, and I'm too tired to tell her to blow it out. That it stinks and gives me a headache. And she was so nice to me. I shouldn't even think this way. The door creaks open and I hear Alec's husky voice and feel him pass by my bed. I roll over, hating the fact that tonight of all nights she let him come over. I ignore the pinch of wishing Jayhe were here to take care of me.

"June's in bed so early," I hear Alec whisper. The bass in his voice ripples through the room. "And it smells in here."

"Yeah. . . . Poor thing, she had a rough night," Gigi whispers. I freeze. My weak hands clutch my comforter until my knuckles are white. I wait for her to tell him that I vomited all over myself like I'm a two-year-old with a tummy ache, but she doesn't. She keeps my secrets. It's then that I realize that, as much as I may look at her as the one who takes everything from me, she may be the only real friend I have.

34.

Gigi

I'M IN MY ROOM WRITING a history essay when there's a knock at the door. It's one of the RAs.

"I come bearing goodies," she says, lugging a huge box. "Another care package from your mom." She hands it over. It's a box wrapped in a brown grocery bag painted in deep plum and turquoise florals. "I love when your mom sends stuff," she says. "It always brightens up the mail room." She starts to walk off but then turns around. "Oh, and this, too," she says, handing over a plain manila envelope. My name is scrawled across the front, but there's no return address. That's enough to set off the panic—my palms sweaty, my heart drumming a bit faster.

So of course I open that one first. Inside are a stack of cutup notes, ransom style. I recognize some of the handwriting. It's Alec's. And, I quickly figure out, Bette's. Their love letters, filled with sweet nothings.

He wrote: "I'll love you forever. And always."

He wrote: "We were meant to be."

He wrote: "You're my soul mate."

I know she sent them. This has Bette written all over it. She's not even subtle anymore. And I know I shouldn't let it get to me. But it does. Because with the bits and pieces of their notes is another one, pieced together, that says: "You'll never have what we had. He will be mine again." And for some reason, I know she's right. I can't even compete. But this time, I'm furious. And I'm going to do something about it. I'm going to find the evidence.

Everyone else is in morning ballet class. I don't have to go, so I can give my foot a rest, and be ready for rehearsal tonight. My first one back. I walk the entire length of the hall to make sure no one is still lingering up here. I listen for voices, classical music, the soft padding of ballet slippers. Then I take one step after the other until I'm standing in front of Bette's door. I try the knob. It opens without a hitch. I'm surprised it isn't locked. Mama says my thrill in being in places where I'm not supposed to is a compulsion, and I shouldn't do it anymore.

Light trickles through the white drapes on her window. I can tell which side of the room is Bette's and which is Eleanor's. Eleanor has motivational quotes and mantras scrawled all over the corkboard near her bed. Bette's side of the room has one of those expensive trunks you see in the store windows on Madison Avenue. Her desk is lined with trinkets, and she has a beautiful jewelry box chock full of rings and bracelets and necklaces studded with diamonds. Pinned to her wall are a series of origami flowers. From Alec, no doubt. I feel a little pinch, feeling the fool for somehow believing that Alec had only made those for me.

I hunt for the original letter she cut up.

The little vanity in the corner smells like a mix of hair spray and expensive perfume and powder. Like a makeup counter. There's a row of neatly lined up lipsticks, all fancy and expensive brands. I go through them, opening this one and that, inhaling the scent and absorbing the color before carefully recapping them. And there it is—the gaudy pink one with the indented top, the same lipstick that scrawled the mean message on the mirror that day.

Buoyed by my first find, I continue my search. I comb through the desk drawers. Other findings come fast: a stash of stuff from Alec, little mementos that she's kept in the file drawer of her desk. A Valentine's Day card from last year, photos of them dancing in performances throughout the years. One from when they were maybe about seven—cherubic and haloed, their blond heads and blue, smiling eyes, like a matched set. Then another one of them around ages ten or eleven, filled out, but still quite startlingly similar, as if they could be siblings. But the next few shots would easily dispel any such notion—there they are doing their *pas* in *Don Quixote*, the joy clear on their faces, and then playing on the beach, Alec's arms around Bette's bikinied body, casual and relaxed and oh so intimate. I've seen evidence of much worse, but the image burns my eyes and my heart, further proof of how well they fit and how mismatched Alec and I really are. What am I thinking? What am I doing here? Why am I torturing myself? Why can't I trust that he likes me?

I stash the photos back in the drawer and tiptoe toward the

closet. I browse through the clothes—expensive dancewear and Bette's always-fabulous dresses, all size zero, naturally. Along the floor are sky-high heels, couture goodies that probably cost as much as a year at the conservatory.

I stroke the cashmere sweaters neatly stacked on the shelves, finding myself coveting, once again, what Bette has. I try to snap myself out of it. I should get out of here. But then, there's one more box, a pretty damask-print cardboard box on the floor that's calling my name. I can't not look.

Kneeling down, I gingerly lift the top. Inside is a disorganized mess of paper—meal and clothing receipts, Bette's signature scrawled across the bottom of many. I dig through them, and they lay out an itinerary of extravagances—meals at the Russian Tea Room and Jean-Georges, her fancy frocks, the finest dancewear imported from Europe. And then, there it is. Completely out of place. Six dollars spent for two frosted cookies and a latte from the coffee shop around the corner. On Valentine's Day. 12:07 p.m. During our lunchtime. Irrefutable proof. As much as she denies it, it's been Bette all along. She's done it all.

I stash the receipt in the back pocket of my jeans and put the lid back on the damask box.

And just as I'm about rise and leave, satisfied, I hear a voice.

"What are you doing?" Eleanor asks, standing in the doorway, her face startled and a bit worried as she looks from the box to me and then to the box again.

"I . . . uh . . . I thought . . ." But I don't know how to finish that sentence. There is no reasonable explanation. There's only me and my paranoia and the proof that's burning a hole in my pocket.

"You shouldn't be in here," Eleanor says. But her face has softened and her voice is low, as if she won't tell my secret. She's all sweaty from class, and I wonder if it's over yet.

"I just had to know," I say, my voice rising, the pitch guilty as I walk toward Eleanor and the door, as if I'm the one who's done all these things wrong. "I had to see for myself. And you know I was right." I find myself pulling the receipt out of my pocket, shoving it under her nose. "See, here it is. Valentine's Day."

Eleanor looks truly surprised and sincerely worried. "Where did you find that?"

I point to the box. "There," I say. "With all of Bette's stuff. She's the one. She's been torturing me. All the little things. And the big things." I can feel the tears slipping down my cheeks. One, then two, then an endless stream. "It's all her." I'm shaking now, and I'm so, so humiliated. But at least now I know.

"Gigi," she says. "I . . ."

"You can't tell anyone," I say, suddenly urgent. I have to get out of here. I have to pull myself together. "You can't tell Bette."

"I won't tell anyone." She looks down at the receipt, and her face does a funny thing, between a startle and smirk, as she processes. She bites her bottom lip. "Gigi, it was me."

"What?" I say.

She takes a deep breath. "I did that."

"The cookie?"

"Yeah." She shakes her head. "And the roaches."

"It was disgusting," I say. "Why?"

"Bette, Liz, and even Will and I used to do stuff like that. It's embarrassing to even say out loud, and I'm sorry. The cookie was sitting on my desk for days. The roach trap was from the basement," she says. Her face is the color of strawberries. "I just . . . I got caught up in it all. I got a good role, and . . . I left the receipt in Bette's things. I should've thrown it out. I don't know—"

"Why should I believe you? You're Bette's best friend. Why are you telling me this?" I ask.

She knits her hands in front of her. "Honestly, I feel terrible about it. I wanted to tell you so many times. Apologize. It was childish."

"Why would you do that? Do you hate me or something?" I say, breaking Mama's cardinal rule of not asking questions I don't necessarily want the answers to.

"A little part of me does," she admits, and I don't feel like it's a threat. "We've just been here so long, worked so hard. And you—" She grabs a new pair of tights and shoes. "There's no excuse, really. I'm sorry. I won't do anything else again." She hugs me before I can answer.

"Please don't tell Mr. K," she says. "I'll do whatever you want. Just don't tell him what I did." She squeezes me tighter.

I don't push her away, but I don't hug her back either. I came looking for answers, and what I found is even worse than I thought. If kind, sweet Eleanor could hate me, could do such awful things, then what might the others have in store for me?

35.

Bette

GIGI LINGERS AROUND IN STUDIO E where I'm supposed to practice with Henri. I wish she'd just leave. It's already going to be torturous dancing with him again, and I don't need her watching us, making it worse. I stretch my leg across the barre and ignore Gigi. I wonder why she's hanging around. I remember how she let him stretch her during that week after *The Nutcracker* cast list went up. Tease. Is she going to take him, too? Date both him and Alec?

She marches over to me. "Why do you keep sending me stuff?"

"I don't know what you're talking about. Is this another one of your crazy theories?" I say, pushing deeper into my stretch and reveling in the pinch of anxiety in her voice. I look back at Henri, who hasn't looked up from his floor stretch to watch.

"The letters," Gigi says. "Really crazy, Bette!" And she isn't lying about that part.

"Letters?" I say, even though there they are in her hands. Alec's words about how much he loves me, my breasts, all the things we loved to do together, the tops of my thighs, the scent of my hair, how we'll get married one day. A version of our love story. And that is a hundred times worse than having Gigi look at me with hate and accusation and pity.

"Where'd you get these?" I say, but I stumble over those words because I'm so stunned by the look of those letters in the studio light. They look a thousand times more psychotic now.

"Come on," Gigi says.

"Maybe you took those from my room?" I say. She thinks that I don't know she was in my room. That I don't have a way of getting Eleanor to tell me anything and everything. That I don't know when my things have been touched. But this is my school and information isn't kept from me here. That much hasn't changed. "You were snooping in my room, weren't you? You thought I wouldn't find out about that?"

Her face contains so many emotions at once. Confusion. Fear. Anger. She opens her mouth, no doubt to defend herself. I try to take the letters from her hands. I want them back anyway. I can't let her go to Alec with them.

"You did everything!" She's practically shrieking. "You're not fooling me! Eleanor told me. I bet you push her into stuff. After our talk I thought maybe . . . but this is actual proof! You did . . . the GLASS in my slipper, too!" She's crying now, wringing the letters in her hands like they're dirty dish towels. At last I'm close enough to pull them out of her grip, but she won't let go.

"I have no idea what you're talking about," I say, but she's too far gone. "Give me the letters," I say through clenched teeth. She's holding them up, and screaming about all I've done.

"She's harassing me! She's trying to hurt me!" Gigi shouts to people passing by the door. All of them stand frozen by her accusations. Freshmen, sophomores, juniors. All upper ballet levels. I'm lucky the seniors are away on auditions. Level 8 girls don't need to see this.

Girls from the hallway pour in now.

They make sympathetic sounds. Gigi's muscles are flexing and trembling; no one wants to get anywhere near her.

"Enough!" An RA pops into the room. The girls stick to the walls, their asses glued to the mirrors so they can watch like we're some silly TV drama and not actual people.

"She—she did everything," Gigi says. Her hand is over her heart and she closes her eyes, taking a few wonky breaths. She looks like she is working damn hard to get herself under control, but I don't have to try. For once, perfect Gigi is showing all her messy parts, and I am in a perfect first position with an unflinching face. Who looks crazy now?

"I'm just trying to do my *pas* practice with Henri. She's acting all crazy," I say, my voice pitch-perfect, without a hint of distress. "And she's stolen things from my room."

I feel the blood rising to my head with the fear that her accusations will stick, and I will get the blame for everything. Besides, I didn't do all of it. There are other girls in this room with just as much to hide. With just as much reason to mess with her.

The RA tries to usher Gigi out.

"NO!" Gigi yells. The noise is a howl, an animal sound, a

tortured crack of vocal cords more than an actual word. Her hands tremble, and she stumbles and looks like she might just fall over. "I'm not done yet."

"Yes, you are," the RA says.

Gigi throws the letters all over the floor. "You can have these, too." She pulls out the rest of the naked photos of Alec and me, and adds them to the pile on the floor.

I scramble to pick them up as others look on. That's when Henri finally gets up, and he must catch sight of the pictures, because he raises one side of his mouth in the world's most beautiful and terrible smirk. Then he grabs three pictures right off the floor.

"*Oh là là*," he says, putting his own French accent on extra thick, like he thinks that will somehow drive me crazy. Or drive Gigi crazy, since she's the one he's looking at. He has naked pictures of me in his hands. "Very pretty, Bette. Can I keep them?"

"Gross," I say.

"You're a true *belle*, Bette," Henri says then, in a lower voice. The smirk is gone from his face and for a glorious moment I feel wanted again. Wanted and pretty and better than Gigi.

"Do what you want with those, but I don't ever want to see them again," Gigi says, readying herself to leave. "Please just leave me alone, okay?" She rubs the tears away, and has the defeated look of someone who just lost the big game.

"I'm keeping my ears open," I say. "We'll figure out who's bothering you." I don't mean it as an offer in kindness, of course, but a reminder to her that I'm not the criminal, I'm not the one they're all looking for. And to make sure that RA doesn't think anything or go report anything about me.

Gigi just shakes her head. And anyway, I meant what I said. I don't want her injured and fragile, I just want her gone. The RA ushers her away like Gigi's just learned her dog got run over by a car.

And then she is gone, at least from the studio. The others follow. The show is over. The star has left. I exhale for the first time in too long. A loud sigh of a breath through my mouth.

"You two really hate each other, eh? It's kind of sexy." Henri raises his eyebrows and I remember he still has my photos.

"Give those back," I say. He holds them above my head, out of reach. A girl like Gigi would jump up and down trying to reach them, but I am not that girl. Instead I cross my arms over my chest and wait for his arm to get tired. Look up at him with a look Alec used to like: wide eyes and a tilted head and a little pout. Henri laughs and lowers his arm. Flips through the pictures one more time before pocketing them. I make a sound in protest, but he cuts me off.

"I mean it, Bette. You're gorgeous. Not my type, really. Too icy. But objectively hot regardless."

It's not like I need reassurance from Henri. It's not like I need anything from the strange, mysterious French boy. Who is nothing.

"Well, you weren't acting like that when we were in the PT room or the last time we were out," I say, not necessarily wanting to remember those two past moments, but I can't let him win.

"Hmm, maybe that was a mistake," he teases. "Now Gigi—"

"I know. Luminous. Amazing. I don't need to hear it." I turn to leave. I can't possibly dance now. I prepare myself for a night in the dorms with the unfamiliar aloneness that is seeping into my life.

"And if you've forgotten, you kissed me at the restaurant," Henri says. "And you *let* me touch you in the water."

I want to say *in order to shut you up*. Instead, I sit down and undo my pointe shoes. "Whatever you think is happening here isn't happening," I say. Then he sits down next to me and takes hold of my foot in his hand. I fight him at first, but he doesn't let go.

I give him a kick. He takes it and doesn't let go of my foot. He unwraps the tape circling my toes. My foot is bruised and damp and there's nothing alluring about that part of my body right now—it only looks delicate when it's wrapped in the pink fabric of a ballet slipper. Naked, it looks like it belongs to an ogre. He examines my toes, and for a second, I flinch, thinking he could snap one if he wanted.

"Relax." Henri kneads his knuckles into the aching flesh, and something in me gives in. It's not just the expert way his fingers find the pressure points on the sole of my foot, the soft spots between each toe, the callouses on my heel. I also surrender to the way he looks at me while he massages my toes, the endlessness of his stare, and the fact that he isn't scared to break me.

I wait for him to bring up Cassie. I listen for her name, feeling it lurk beneath his every word.

"You still want Alec." There's an echo in the now super-silent studio, and his words reverberate, hitting me hard, over and over. I wiggle away. He grabs my foot harder. I don't want to be stopped by him, but doesn't the truth always paralyze you? It does me. I can't breathe because of how real those words feel.

"I want to be on top. To be back in dance magazines, to get another endorsement deal," he goes on. I barely hear. I haven't even said those exact words in my own head, and I'm surprised to feel a give of relief in my chest. He releases my foot. I stand, trying not to let the ache in my knee show. I should run as fast as I can away from him.

He follows close behind me, and I whip around before his hips press up against mine. I put a hand out until he walks directly into it. My hand presses into his chest. His eyes go narrow and his knuckles white and I can feel his thoughts racing around in his head.

"Wouldn't Alec just hate seeing you with me?" he says, the whisper of his voice hitting my throat, feeling too cramped. He takes another step, my elbow bends against his weight, and I don't think he can get any closer to me.

"Alec is pretty distracted these days," I say. But of course I know he's right. Even if Alec "really likes" Gigi like he says he does, he still doesn't really like Henri. They've never gotten close despite being roommates. He would still be the worst person for Alec to see me with.

"We can get his attention," Henri says. His body touches mine at all the parts where I blossom: my chest, my hips, my thighs. He puts his forehead to mine. "Don't give up, pretty girl. When I get set on something, I get it. My *maman* says, 'Obsession is the wellspring of genius and madness.'"

I hate him even more for calling me *pretty girl*. I don't know what his quote means, but I let his hands find my back, and it's impossible not to give in to them. They are huge and strong and wrap around so much of my waist that it seems they could hold me up. And I haven't been touched in so long, it feels good to let the warmth of his palms seep through my tights and to my skin. I could stop trying so hard. I could just give in.

"It wouldn't be so terrible, being with me. Driving them crazy. It might even be fun." He speaks directly into my ear. "And we could dance so well together that we become the next It ballet couple." He drums on the small of my back. "I could forget everything I know, if you help me."

I hate my body for going so weak at the combination of his accent and his hands and his warm breath. I breathe heavily. The world feels suddenly small and cramped. I'm so tired, I actually consider just letting him do what he wants. For once, couldn't I just do the easiest thing?

His touch is so different from Alec's. Eager and aggressive. Like he doesn't care what I did or did not do to his ex. He railroads straight through all the thoughts in my head of how this is a bad, bad idea. His lips find my earlobe and there's the nip of his teeth on that soft centimeter of skin. I well up, not at the pain, which is tiny and a little sweet, but because having Henri touch me just makes me miss Alec's touch. The controlled danger. The mutual, aching desire. I used to get lost in Alec's touch, but Henri is pointed. Goal oriented.

"You're ridiculous," I say, but it comes out with a hint of a pant behind it, and I know I've shown my cards. I'm turned on: not just from Henri being against me, muscles and dimples and all, but also at the idea of getting Alec back, taking control of my life, hurting Gigi, getting a photo shoot in a dance magazine that's not bought by my mother's money or my sister's acclaim.

"You know I'm right. And even if I'm not—what do you have to lose, right?" I hear a gaggle of girls pass by the open studio door and glass wall, but don't jerk away from Henri. Eleanor's voice is in the group, but I pretend not to notice. I let Henri lean forward just a half inch more and kiss me. His tongue is rough and thick as it forces its way into my mouth, exploring without consent. His hands wander, and even though I'm half repulsed, I can't help but respond. I feel small and scared, but at the same time, safe.

It feels like a kiss and like a contract. It feels not good, but not bad either. But it feels like I'm back in control. Like I'm Bette again.

36.

June

AFTER REHEARSAL I GO TO the café and pick up a bowl of the *congee* porridge the chefs make for the Asian students. Everyone is grabbing full plates. With actual food on them. They're serving tacos tonight for Cinco de Mayo. There are little sombreros on the tables. I flick one off and watch it tumble to the floor. I head to my usual corner, but Will's sitting in it. In my corner. Alone. Without thinking, I sit across from him.

"You're good at keeping secrets, right?" I say in my smallest voice, just to get his attention. I don't know him well, but he seems safe, kind. Like he could keep a secret.

Will jumps. He didn't know I sat down at all, I guess.

"Damn it, June, you scared me," he says, smoothing his hair.

Maybe I am truly invisible.

He gives me a long look before answering, like he must take in each facial feature one at a time: my mouth, my nose, each eye, each ear, the slope of my chin. I don't know what he concludes, but he nods and shrugs. We've never really talked like this before.

He crosses his arms over his chest and clears his throat like it's a request for a subject change. "Do you have a secret? Something to share?"

"No, just thought it would get your attention is all," I say with a smirk. Part of me wants to tell Sei-Jin's secret, Gigi's secret, my own secret. I wonder if I really could tell Will. Right now. In the half-empty café. In one long sentence, not stopping for air or advice. I wonder if I could just push out the words: *Sei-Jin might be a lesbian. Gigi has a heart condition. I've been messing around with Jayhe. Someone finds me beautiful. Maybe even loves me. Even if it's not my father. Or my mom.*

"Well, secret keeping is one of my best qualities," Will says, still pondering my face. "But you should hold on to your secrets. That's one thing I've learned here. Don't trust anyone with them. Not even your friends. Not even me. When push comes to shove, no one is that good at keeping secrets." His eyes fill with tears, the sudden, gushing kind that I would never allow myself. I don't understand why, and I'm too weirded out to ask. He uses the backs of his hands to wipe them away, and keeps a smile grimacing on his face the whole time.

I don't know that I really believed I would tell Will anything, but I had a momentary pinch of hope that I might not have the weight of these secrets on my shoulders, and now they have squarely sunk back onto me.

"What's wrong?" I ask.

He shakes his head, and tears well up in his green eyes again.

"I thought I had something with somebody. But it's, like, so confusing. I don't even know why I'm talking to you about this. No offense."

"I get it," I say. At least he's direct.

"Maybe it's just stuff that's, like, different 'cause we're from different places." He keeps talking with a little hitch in his voice, from the tears he keeps mopping off his face.

"But, like, answer this question for me," he says. "If you spend time with someone, that means something, right?"

"What kind of time?" I ask, feeling like he just took the words right out of my mouth, out of my head. "It could be a group thing. Or just friends." I try piecing together things about who he could have a crush on or be in a relationship with.

"You're alone. You make plans. Laugh. Joke. Hang out," he says like he's building a case for this confusing relationship. "That means something. You know, we don't have extra time like that here. To just be hanging around without a reason. There's always something we could be doing."

He's right. We don't have extra time like regular teens to just play around. We could always be stretching in the studios.

"It's so much better than before. I used to *pine* for Alec. I used to think that being his best friend meant that someday, maybe we could, like, try, you know?"

I don't know, but I nod my head anyway.

"Now I don't know what I ever saw in Alec. He thinks he's the best ballet dancer at ABC. That he's a shoo-in for the company." He's like an emotional roller coaster dipping from sad to angry, then back again. "But with this new guy, I just can't tell.

Sometimes he's all flirty. Cute texts. Lots of smiley faces, you know? And then, the next time, nothing. Silence. I can't play this game again." The tears come back. And I know where he's coming from. All too well. "Maybe in his country, this is how it goes. Maybe he's afraid to be out."

I lean forward and whisper, "Is it Henri?"

He covers his entire face now, and his sob gets a little too loud. People look over at him. I pet his hand, trying to be comforting. It's not my strong suit.

He grabs my hand and squeezes it hard. "Please don't say anything. I should just ask him what we are doing. I need to get it together." Will's voice drops at the end of the sentence. I follow his gaze to find out what stopped him.

It's Henri and Alec. Then Gigi, right behind them. Henri grins in our direction, but sits at a table across from us. Alone. Like he always does. Alec and Gigi lurk at the end of our table, like they're deciding if they want to sit with us tonight.

"Looking all serious, kids," Alec says, patting Will on the shoulder with two loud, hard claps. "Everything okay?"

"Yeah," Will says, recoiling a little. "Why wouldn't it be?"

Gigi sits beside me. "How was your day, June?" Like she's my therapist, her tone suggesting I've been having a rough time.

"Fine. How are you?" I snap back. "Any more issues lately?"

Her face falls a little, and I feel better, but Alec comes to the rescue. "Nothing lately. Thank god. Maybe people have chilled out and stopped acting all stupid and childish."

Will agrees with him, like he's some sort of genius, and that's when I notice how Will looks up at him like he's the most beautiful person in the world, and how everything he just said about Alec has now disappeared.

"You know, my dad asked about you the other day," Alec says, looking down at me. Like he always does. "He's always thought you were good. Said your mom danced. That true? He didn't say much, but said it's clear she taught you a lot."

I think about Mr. Lucas saying my name, asking how I am doing. A glimmer of something like pleasure sparks in my chest. Maybe this is a good sign about my future at the conservatory. Something that could save me from public school.

Alec sits down next to Will, settling in like he owns the place. Which he pretty much does. "He said you and Sei-Jin and a few of those other Korean girls work too hard and don't get enough credit. You know, he said Sei-Jin was probably the best dancer we have, but Mr. K doesn't like her face? It's disgusting, really."

It's so strange to hear him talk about the racist issues in the ballet community like he's part of them, and experiencing them. Maybe dating Gigi has opened up his eyes a bit. But it's not like he'll do anything about it. Not really.

"He went off about that for a while. Weird night. My damn dad. He basically was trying to tell me Gigi will never get as far as Bette could, since the Russians love their snow-white blondes, you know?" Alec's chatter is nervous, and the hope I had is pinched out so fast I forget it was ever there. He's just upset that his dad doesn't like Gigi. And Mr. Lucas wasn't really asking about me. He was letting Alec know girls like me and Gigi will never really get ahead. Except, of course, that's not true for Gigi at all. Only for me.

I stare at Alec a few beats longer than is comfortable, and he notices. He laughs it off and leans back in his chair.

"Are you guys mute?" he says, a teasing smile starting at his lips and moving across his whole face as he looks from me to Will.

"No one really wants to discuss racism," Gigi says. She rubs the back of his neck the way Bette used to do, I guess to make her comment sting less.

"Tired," Will says. He has been a shade pinker than usual ever since Alec got here. His whole body is so tense and stiff against his chair that he has become practically a piece of furniture himself. And he keeps staring at Henri's back ahead of us.

I still say nothing. No one wants to talk to the most privileged boy at school about the stuff nonwhite girls face in ballet.

"June, ready to collect the tutus?" another dancer calls out, and I'm actually happy for the interruption. I rise, give a little wave, and scurry off. Gigi follows, calling to me to wait for her. But I don't. I hear her behind me.

All the girls coming out of Level 5 and 6 rehearsal hold their white practice tutus. We crowd the elevators up to our dorm. We enter our hall and everyone descends upon our room. I keep thinking about Will and his easy tears. He's like me in a way, always the outsider. But he needs to suck it up. Nothing will change what he is, what he'll always be here. He has to change things for himself, like I do, or learn to accept that.

"Let me through," I bark, trying to get to our door. Every night since rehearsal started, they all bring their tutus to my room for collection, my new job for Madame Matvienko. I volunteered with the hope that I could spend more time with her, slip in my questions about my father, and see what she knows. But I haven't gotten a chance to yet.

I squeeze through the crowd to get to my room. Bette accidentally slams into me, trying to cut in front of Gigi.

"Watch it," she spits without turning around.

"It's my room," Gigi says, pushing past her.

"Calm down, Gigi. You're getting all worked up." Bette's eyes narrow in warning. "I'm so worried about you." She says it loudly enough for everyone to hear. Her voice full of artificial sweetness, knowing the right way to set Gigi off.

"Line up! Line up!" I say, taking out my clipboard of names. "Hey, one at a time," I protest. But they drop their tutus in the middle of the room, like I'm their little servant girl. Bette and Eleanor come in last. A pile of tutus grows in the center of the room like the layers of a frilly wedding cake.

"What is that?" Eleanor says. The cacophony of gossip and laughter cuts out, an abrupt stop, like when Viktor pulls his fingers from the piano's keys at Morkie's request.

"Oh my god, oh my god," one of the younger dancers says, seemingly unable to stop her mouth from making those words over and over. Bette covers her mouth, shakes her head, and backs up into the wall. A loud thud echoes when she hits it. They are all staring at the wall behind me, but I don't turn right away. Gigi screams, and I'm so startled I drop the clipboard.

I turn slowly.

The terrarium is on its side. The twigs are scattered along the windowsill. Dried rose petals are scattered across my bed.

I look away from Gigi. My stomach twists and turns. Each little butterfly body is pinned to the wall, a sewing needle piercing its center.

Gigi drops to the floor and grabs her chest. Tears pour down her cheeks. I can't hear anything she says. She cries and chokes at the same time, and makes such horrible, squawking noises that everyone moves farther and farther away. Some scream for the RAs. Others start to go for their cell phones to call for help. Her whole body shakes, an uncontrollable shiver lasting seconds and then minutes.

37.

Gigi

THE DARK, DEAD EYES OF my butterflies catch the light. Their wings are distorted and broken, so much more frail when they are still than when they were flapping. It is the saddest parade I've ever seen: unmoving and menacing.

And deliberate. They are lined up so perfectly I swear a ruler must have been used.

My butterflies.

My insides are cold. My face is hot.

I feel as if I will drop through the floor.

They are all out to get me.

The words are loud in my head, and reverberate through my body. I'm certain it's true. I'm certain this is a threat. Not just on my place at the conservatory but on my life. There are just those words in my head, and my monitor beeping in my ear. And my butterflies dead on the wall.

Black and white spots appear all around me. It all goes a bit hazy, except for one more thing: the exaggerated shake of Bette's head, and June's knit eyebrows as she stares accusingly at Bette.

"You did this to me," I scream at Bette first, and then at everyone. My heart is a drum beating too fast in my chest. I don't know how to get it to slow.

Everyone backs away from me. An RA circles in the hall, asking the girls what happened. I scream and scream at them all. Their faces pinch and eyes bulge as I yell.

I lunge at them. June tries to hold me back. I feel her skinny arms grab at my waist. Bette backs away and races down the hall. I want to chase her. I want to chase all of them.

"Who did this?" I scream. "Who did this?"

I feel Eleanor's arm around me, and an RA leading the way down the stairs. My eyes are so fogged with tears that I can't see how to get down the stairs or down the hall. My pulse races. I end up on the first floor in Mr. Lucas's office. He's the only person with teacher status still in the building this late. Other dancers brush past us, headed upstairs or home off campus, watching me pushed, crying and sweaty, into the office.

Mr. Lucas's face doesn't move, doesn't crack a sympathetic smile at the sight of me, not even when he offers me the seat in front of his mahogany desk, or listens to the RA recount what happened. I squish into the high-backed chair, feeling small, my legs dangling without touching the ground. He looks so much like Alec, but his expression is never as warm, as inviting, as Alec's is.

I try to wipe my nose and tears and pull myself together, but the thought of my butterflies makes the tears start again. My heart doesn't slow, and my head feels light, as if it could tumble right off my shoulders and into my lap.

He closes the door and sighs. "You have had a rough time lately." His voice is serious. "I've been meaning to speak with you. I'm sorry that this incident is the one that has brought us together." He hands me a box of tissues and tells me that the school will be investigating all the incidents happening to me.

His assurance doesn't make me feel any better, but I guess it's a start. I don't know who would do this. Bette? Would she kill my butterflies? Is this over *Giselle*? My head is a wreck of suspects, motivations, and drama. Mr. Lucas listens as I run down the incidents, the tears streaming the whole time. He stands, pats my shoulder awkwardly, nodding, clearly uncomfortable. He returns to his desk, makes some notes in a file, and clears his throat.

"I hate to ask you this, but can we switch gears for a bit?" he asks, shifting his tie uncomfortably. I don't know what's coming, but I'd rather talk about anything other than my butterflies, and what the girls are doing to me.

"I need to ask you a series of questions," he says, taking a sip of water. "Very serious questions."

"Am I in trouble?" I squeak.

"Did you do anything wrong, Giselle?" he says.

I gulp, not knowing whether I should just come clean about the one school rule I've broken—having Alec sleep over in my room a few times, and sleeping over in his room. Maybe I should just tell him. Then maybe he won't call my parents or bar us from seeing each other. I don't want him to think negatively of me. And I wonder if Alec told him I was his girlfriend now. I can't tell if he likes me at all.

I'm all squirmy. I will myself to relax.

"Relax," he says. "You're not in any trouble. Especially not after what happened tonight. I just wanted to ask you about something."

"Okay," I say, not sure what any of this is about.

"You know I'm the school board president here at the conservatory," he starts.

"Yes," I say.

"And so my job is multifaceted. I am mostly responsible for keeping the school balanced between the ballet side of things and the academic side of things. Our reputation is very important to us here."

My mind races and I inch to the edge of the chair.

"So rumors of any sort can be detrimental and damaging to the school. And I wanted to ask you about something." He leans into the desk. "And it is imperative that you answer me truthfully. Words are powerful in our small community. And whatever you say to me won't leave this room." His eyes squint a little.

I don't know what to say, so I shrug. The pressure makes my eyes fill with tears, and the look of concern on Mr. Lucas's face grows more intense.

"Giselle, there's a rumor circulating about you and Mr. K," he says.

I feel my cheeks ignite. "What?"

"That there's been an inappropriate relationship going on

between you," he says, not softening his words or making them feel less accusatory.

"No," I say, almost shouting.

He waves his hand at me. "I want you to feel comfortable talking to me. I know it's hard, but it's best to be honest."

"He'd never— I'd never," I stutter, unable to defend myself. I would never think of doing something like that. I didn't know girls even did that type of thing. Tears pour out of my eyes uncontrollably and I'm embarrassed that I can't control it. He gets up and pats my shoulder.

"Are you sure there's nothing you feel has crossed a line?" I can't stand to look at his eyes. I know Alec will hear this rumor. That he might even think there's something to it. He saw a bad side of me a few days ago, how I let it all get to me, and I've yelled and screamed. And by now, he's heard how upset I was in the hall about my butterflies.

"You have to believe me, there's absolutely nothing. I don't know who would—why someone would—"

"Okay, all right," Mr. Lucas says. His hand had still been at my shoulder, but he jerks it away, like he's suddenly remembered that this, too, could be considered inappropriate. "That's all I needed to know. Thank you, Giselle. I'm going to go speak with the RA about your butterflies, and how someone could've gotten into your room while everyone was in rehearsal."

"June and I don't lock our door," I say, tears still falling. "None of the girls really do."

"Well, we're going to need to change that. It's certainly a security issue. I'll be speaking to the RAs about this." He leaves me alone in his office, politely closing the door behind him to give me some privacy. I rush to get myself under control. Catching sight of myself in his wall mirror, I see just how broken I'm becoming. Red eyes. A rash from where Alec's stubble rubbed my chin while we kissed last night. A faint black line under my eyes, remnants from the makeup I've gotten used to wearing but never remember to scrub off. It's not me at all. It's like looking at a stranger.

38.

Bette

I DON'T KNOW THAT I'VE ever seen anything worse than the monarchs pinned to Gigi's wall. Their wings starting to tear, their terrarium markedly empty on the windowsill, the unsettling stillness that we are all lost in while we stare at the wall. Those butterflies are going to dry out, their orange will turn to black, and soon they will crumble to dust. Nothing in the world should be that fragile.

And then the look June gave me in the aftermath: shaken, certain, accusing. While Eleanor wrapped her long arms around Gigi's shaking, screeching body and June turned away from me to start cleaning up, I escaped. It isn't something I planned, but I found myself flying over to the tenth floor—Alec's hall—desperate to gain some control over what's happening.

I'm still standing in the elevator, debating whether to step out.

Yes, go.

The person who tells the story first gets to control it. My mother's favorite thing to say whenever she finds herself in a lawsuit or dispute with someone she hates. Always be the first to tell your side.

I race down the stairs to the tenth floor, and I suddenly feel cold and wish I'd brought the down coat my mother bought me last winter.

I tremble, going straight for Alec's room—third one on the right. It's up to me to tell them what's happened. To tell Alec. I'm starting to believe my mother's words. And I can spin the story how I want.

I have to. To protect myself from June's accusing stare and Gigi's manic accusations.

Will's in the hall, a sniffly, snotty, runny-nosed mess. "What are you doing here?" He has a scarf on his head like he's Rosie the Riveter from a 1940s ad, and his red hair is pinned up into some sort of monstrous look.

"To see Alec," I snap.

"Are you going to finally tell him? Or should I? I'm so tired of carrying around your shit," he says. "All it does is cause me issues. All it does is make me lose people I care about."

Anything I say will sound defensive or delusional, and I'm not going to let him make me sound that way. "I don't know what you're talking about. Whatever happened in the past, stays there. You were always an eager and willing participant. So don't give me that crap." I need to shut him up right now. "You're not a victim." I don't look directly at him anymore, though. My words are for him, but my attention is forward. I'm spotting, like we do when we pirouette, finding a place on the wall and holding on to it even as we spin out of control. I'm finding a crack in the distance to keep me anchored. To make sure I don't take a spill. I have to do anything to stay in place right now.

"You made me drop her," he screams so loud I jump back.

Doors creak open in succession.

"You used the whole thing with *me* coming out to my mom. You used how bad it was. You held it over my head. And I had no choice." He's hysterical now.

Alec enters the hall in his pajamas. He's taking *Giselle* seriously, I guess, because it's still early in the evening for him to be ready for bed. It shows in the glow of his skin, the perfect shape of his body, that he's taking excellent care of himself. Meanwhile, with no one keeping a lookout on me these days, I can feel the lack of sleep in my aching muscles and the need for more water in my dried-out mouth. Henri's shirtless behind him, and with a cell phone to his ear.

"Hey, what's going on?" Alec says, crossing his arms over his chest, and they seem wider and stronger. He's still lean, of course, but more solid now. I notice it more, seeing him in pajamas, than I do seeing him in his tights every day at rehearsal. It strikes me that I've mostly seen Alec in his tights this semester. I can't remember the last time I've seen him naked.

"It's Gigi," I say right away, afraid if I open with anything else, he'll shut the door in my face. It hurts to feel that way.

"Is Gigi okay?" Alec's sleepy eyes wake right up, his arms uncross, and he takes a step closer to me. I smell his familiar scent: woodsy deodorant, mint gum, my own flowery shampoo that he borrowed once and never gave back.

"Probably not, if Bette's over here telling you anything about Gigi," Will says.

Henri steps farther into the hall, his cell phone to his ear. He says something in French and hangs up, then settles his full attention on Alec and me, ever amused. Will seems suddenly paralyzed, looking back and forth between Alec, Henri, and me. He quickly removes the scarf from his hair and pats himself like he's primping.

I trample over Will's words, desperate not to let him tell Alec anything that Will and I did to Cassie. "Gigi's not hurt. But she's . . . I think something's wrong with her. In her head. She's falling apart. She . . . well, I think she killed her butterflies." As the words come out, my back straightens. My eyes meet his. My shoulders roll back. I feel like myself again. Powerful. In control.

"What?" Alec reaches for a sweatshirt from behind his room door, and a few more doors open. I raise my voice; I want them all to hear it from me.

"Her butterflies are all pinned to the wall. I think she killed them all. It's . . . well. It's scary, you know? She's kind of scaring me. Us. She's scaring all of us, so I had to come over here."

Alec's face crumbles into concern. His eyes go warm and watery. He bites his bottom lip and reaches for his pocket and cell phone, to call her, I assume. And then I know. He loves her. My heart's crack turns to a break as he nods his head and lets out a sigh. He is imposing and soft all at once, in flannel and a sweatshirt, and I have to be closer to him.

"She seems . . . unstable. Unsafe," I conclude. I force a little tremble into my voice and a pool of tears into my eyes.

It doesn't feel like a lie, then. I am scared of Gigi. I do feel a sense of impending danger. I am shaking, and then, all of a sudden, I'm crying, too, and I reach for Alec. My hands slide from his waist to his back; he is muscle all the way around, both familiar and exciting.

"I'm scared," I say. And then I say it again, and a third time, and Alec's rubbing my back like he used to, massaging the places he knows my muscles get the most tense. I soak his sweatshirt with my tears, and it doesn't feel like I'm exaggerating anything or twisting the truth or doing anything remotely dishonest. I feel vulnerable and wonderful. Warm at last.

"It's okay," Alec says, and the words land on the top of my head, get caught in my hair. "Deep breaths, okay?" I hold him tighter. I wait for Will or Henri to break this up.

"It's not safe with her around," I say. "I haven't felt safe in so long."

I choke on the words, how true they are. How unsafe I've felt since Gigi came to New York. Alec rubs my shoulders and takes a deep breath. *This is it*, I think. *He cares about me. He'll come back to me.* He'll forget about her. They were just hooking up. They're nothing serious. The tears start to dry up. I tilt my head up toward his and give a small smile, a private one that neither Will nor Henri nor all the Peeping Toms gathering in the hallway can see.

"This is ridiculous," Will shouts. "Really, Bette?"

He waits until the best part to interrupt. Of course.

Alec pulls away. My hands drop from Alec's body at the same moment he gives me an extra thank-you squeeze. It feels like being punched. It hurts more than the worst muscle pull or a sprain or a bleeding, lost toenail. I know pain, my body is more than familiar with hurting, but this is something else entirely. Like the moment after *The Nutcracker* cast list was posted, except I don't think punching a mirror would help.

I don't think my pills would help.

I don't think talking to Eleanor would help.

I guess I don't think anything would help.

Alec turns to Will. "What's going on with you? With you and Bette, too?"

"Ask her," Will says.

"Bette's been a naughty girl," Henri says.

"Why the hell are you out here anyway?" Alec barks at Henri, but Henri just smiles in response. "This is all stupid. Let's go," Alec says. He holds my hand like he'd hold his sister's hand. It's strange that I can tell the difference, that it's so obvious how much has changed just from the temperature and grip of his hand. Our fingers aren't entwined and there's no hint of antici-patory sweat, no squeeze of affection. He's practically dragging me to the elevator.

"You won't get away with this again! I won't let you!" I look back and, yes, Will's following right behind us, shaking his head at me like he knows something. Like he knows everything. "Alec needs to know."

"What do I need to know?" Alec says, pushing the elevator button, and in that moment I realize that I've been so good at hiding the dark parts of me from Alec. Will used to be there to see those parts.

My jaw drops.

"Just because you're messed up doesn't mean everyone else has to be. Gigi's a good girl. I was a good guy. You're just out to ruin us all, aren't you?"

It takes my breath away, the certainty with which he pronounces it. I move faster. All I want to do is get away from Will and all the things he knows.

"She made me drop Cassie, Alec. Right before the spring ballet last year. Bette made me do it." He's all sobs now. "She broke her hip because of us."

Alec drops my hand and stops. He steps away.

"Is he lying?" Alec says. He asks me a few more times in rapid succession. I can't move my legs, arms, body, and least of all my mouth. His face twists with disgust. "It's always been you, hasn't it? You're responsible for all of it. Sometimes I thought it had to be you. I heard the whispers. I even stuck up for you because I thought I knew everything there was about Bette Abney. She was my girlfriend. One of the best ABC conservatory dancers. She worked hard. We worked hard. Who are you? What happened to you?" His eyes become cold, steely. "How was I ever with you?"

It's all gone so, so wrong.

39.

June

IT'S BEEN WEEKS, BUT GIGI won't take down the but-terflies.

They stay pinned to the wall: browning ghosts. They disinte-grate in front of my eyes, their bodies drifting down the wall like dust, a miniature butterfly-themed horror show.

"I can't look at them anymore," I say when I'm trying to fall asleep. Gigi's awake, and the wall is partially lit by the tiny clip-on light she uses when she reads late at night. Their corpses look even more frightening in the strange shadows.

She doesn't reply. But moments later I hear muffled cries and I know I can't take them down myself without a full-on melt-down. I don't sleep that night. Long after Gigi turns off her tiny light, I'm still focused on the wall. The dozen little murders.

It was meant to be a threat to Gigi, meant to push her over the edge. But it's possible I'm the one who can't handle the reality of what happened.

Gigi's dancing doesn't suffer. If anything, her rawness makes her better. Tears fall down her face in rehearsal the next day. Morkie applauds her emotional connection to the ballet. But in the evening, she's back to weeping openly. Sometimes sitting outside on the stoop, even in the rain, or wandering the halls or just staring blankly in one direction or another. Almost ghostly. Tonight, she gazes at her empty terrarium while I try to focus on my work. I'm on edge, waiting to see what happens to her. Waiting to see if she will fully crack or just stay on the precipice like this forever.

"What are we going to do about Bette?" she says, interrupting the silence with a broken-up, shuddering voice.

"What do you mean?" I say.

For the first time ever, I hope Alec is coming by soon. He knows how to handle Gigi better than I do. Loves her in a way I certainly don't. Wants to hold her and comfort her and make her stronger. I don't want any of that. I want her to leave. That's the truth of it. I don't want to watch her slowly fall to pieces, I want her to be pushed over the edge enough so that she vanishes back to California. Cassie vanished like that. *Poof!* Here one minute and gone the next. I fight any guilty feelings I have over the little things I did to her.

"I need more proof. Of what she's done. Don't you have any real proof?" Gigi turns away from her terrarium and looks at me full-on for the first time in days. "She trusts you more. Maybe you can get information from her. You could record her talking. Get her to admit to it all. Then we could get her kicked out. I mean, she tortures you, too, right? We all want her gone. And then everything will be fine. Then it will be safe again. I'll be safe again."

The way the words come out in a rush scares me—she's been thinking about this a lot. She's been mulling it all over.

"We're not exactly friends," I say at last, looking down and away from the intensity of Gigi's face, the crease that has formed right between her eyes, the one that comes from deep thought and trouble. "No one besides Eleanor is friends with Bette."

Alec stops by before Gigi has a chance to finish her argument. She runs to his arms like she hadn't just been draped all over him during rehearsal earlier.

"How's my girl?" he says into her neck. He waves over her shoulder at me, but she presses harder against him, and the wave is barely a breath before he returns his hand to her back.

"Maybe you can help me," she says to him when they pull away from each other and settle onto her bed.

Alec raises his eyebrows and smiles, ready to do anything she wants. "Of course. What do you need?"

"Get Bette to admit to everything. So I can report her. So that she'll leave, and I'll be safe."

Alec's whole body responds to the request. A shudder that he can't control, and I know he may love Gigi, but his feelings for Bette aren't completely gone either. They probably never will be. Gigi doesn't seem to notice the reflex.

"Bette and I don't talk anymore," he says. "Not even as friends. I am done with her." He looks to me for support. I don't want anyone digging around, so I nod.

"Bad idea," I mumble, but Gigi doesn't seem to even hear.

"You could start talking to her again," she says. "You could hang out with her more, get her to trust you again. I don't mind. I know I said I didn't want you around her, but this would be different. There'd be a point. It would be for me. It—it would mean everything to me. I need someone to— No one is doing anything about it. No one's investigating or punishing her or, or anything. So we just have to—"

"Gigi, you're not thinking straight. That's really a crazy—"

"You told me all that stuff was nothing. Not to worry about it. Now, my butterflies—" Her voice breaks in half. He holds her.

I cringe.

"Then talk to your dad. Your dad will do what you tell him to do, won't he? If you beg him. Or if you tell him you won't speak to him if he doesn't kick her out. He's the head of the school. He's Dominic Lucas. He's important. He can find out anything," she says. "Or—didn't you say he has affairs? You could threaten to expose—"

Alec practically throws Gigi off him and jumps off her bed. "Why would you say that?" he blurts out, his voice barely contained, ready to explode. "I told you that in private! I'm trying to be here for you! I'm supportive. You've been through a lot. But don't bring my family into it. Don't even suggest something like that! What's happening to you?" He shakes his head, like he wants to get the memory of her asking for the impossible favor out of his head. It doesn't work, and he takes a step closer to the door.

"June, tell him how dangerous she is!" Gigi is screeching now. I just shake my head. There's no right answer. I want Bette to seem guilty, but I also don't want anyone looking too closely.

"You're Alec Lucas. You're Dominic Lucas's son. You can make things happen," she yells.

"Wait!" I say, distracted. "Your dad's first name is Dominic." I repeat the statement twice as he's trying to calm Gigi down.

"Yeah, why? It's actually his middle name. But he goes by it."

Everything suddenly explodes in my mind. Dominic. Dom. He used to dance in the company. So did my mom. How many other dancers could be named Dominic? It has to be him. But could it really be? That would make Alec my . . . I look for clues in Alec's long face, broad forehead. Could he really be my brother? Here all this time, right under my nose. I try to stay calm and not let the panic show on my face.

"I bet she hurt Cassie, too!" Gigi shouts.

Alec catches her flailing hands, holds them still. He looks deep into her eyes, trying to make her focus. "I don't want to talk about Cassie, okay? Or any of this," Alec says, ending that conversation.

Gigi takes a massive breath to calm herself. A light pink washes her cheeks. A deep discomfort. "I'm sorry," she says, first in my direction and then again, even more desperately, to Alec. "I'm sorry. I'm getting upset. I just—I'm scared. I don't like being here. But you're right." She is a pretty crier, of course. Tears fall down her cheeks in gorgeous patterns, her eyes go cloudy, and her lashes are dotted with dampness. Ethereal. Fairylike. She licks her full lips and Alec brings his hands to her face, uses his thumbs to wipe away the tears.

Seeing them like that reminds me of the way Jayhe looks at

me, kisses me. I immediately want to call Jayhe, talk out what I've discovered. My father has been here all this time.

"Okay," Alec says. "Okay. I know. What's happened to you is terrible. Stuff like that has happened in the past. It's happened a lot to other dancers," he says. "Nothing's gonna happen to you. I promise. We'll both look out for you. June and I." He looks at me like we really are a team, that we are all family. "And I'll help you get to the bottom of it all after the performance. We need to focus."

"You're right," she says finally, her breath still shaky, a tremor still visible through her sturdy frame. "Maybe I need to stop thinking about this, to stop letting it fester." She leans into him again, and the shaking stops, at least for a moment. "What I need is a clean slate, a fresh start. A new focus."

That sounds like the old Gigi, optimistic and happy and light. It pinches a little, to hear the sweetness return to her voice so quickly, to know that mine will never be that bright. That in the end, despite everything that's happened, she's still won. She's still the girl who has it all—the prima role, the important boyfriend, the happiness seeping out of her pores as her skin glistens like gold. In the end, she's lost nothing.

Maybe the brightness is what I need, a little light to guide me out of the darkness. Maybe I'm the one who's cracked, who's lost my way, in all of this. How could I do what I did? How could I not realize? Shame and regret rise up like bile in my throat, and I excuse myself to get ready for the preshow party.

"We'll celebrate tonight!" I tell Gigi and Alec as I leave, like it really is the three of us against the world, like we're really friends.

But as I gather my things, I'm the one who's shaking. Neither of them acknowledged what I said. They've drifted off in their own little world. Because deep down inside, I know. I don't have friends. But maybe, just maybe, I'll have something better soon. Family.

Long strands of lights glitter along the inside of the Koch Theater, where the company had its annual spring gala the opening night of the season in early May. But tonight is the conservatory's turn. Tuxedoed waiters dole out champagne, sparkling cider, and tiny little appetizers that sit on golden trays like unopened gifts. Everyone is all dolled up in their black-tie finest, the ballerinas letting their hair down after months of having it pulled tight in buns. The whole grand event is like a release for all of us, the night before our *Giselle* performance. The ballerinas and their parents all talk loudly about the artistic directors that will be at opening night tomorrow, and how they're all going to do their pirouettes better and improve their variations.

I focus on all the faces around me, looking for my mother. I scan for her dark, bobbed hair and one of the long pencil skirts she's probably wearing. I'd left her a message about the spring gala and I know she got the official *Giselle* performance invitation in the mail. She never comes. Part of me wants her here. I am alone in the crowd with no one to talk to besides a waiter who won't get the hint that I don't care about how delicious the salmon croquettes are.

The crowd shifts around me, like I'm nothing more than one of the hors d'oeuvres tables, as I remain silent. I see a woman with short, dark hair, and I give the waiter my best imitation of an apologetic smile before running toward the woman. It's my mother. And a tiny part of me is glad she showed up. Maybe she changed her mind about pulling me from the conservatory. Maybe she'll entertain me staying.

"Mom," I say, grabbing her arm.

The woman yanks her arm away and turns around. When she sees me, she frowns. And I know my mistake. Hye-Ji's mother, not mine, glares back at me. She calls me a nuisance in Korean. That word I know, having grown up hearing it from my own mother. All the Korean mothers glare at me, including Sei-Jin's mom. They are in one large clump.

"I'm sorry," I say.

Then I back up, banging into others. I take off again through the crowd. My heart races at a new pace. I dash away to the farthest corner, where no one can find me.

I am alone.

I am always the understudy.

I am the dancer who gets cast in the tiny roles.

I reach for my phone to send a text to Jayhe. He hasn't responded all day, which shouldn't surprise me. But it still hurts. That day, with his dad and his friends, I thought things had shifted. I thought we were real. Since then, though, we're back to late-night chats and unanswered texts. I bet Sei-Jin has gotten to him. Told him about Gigi. Told him that I'm unstable, that I pushed her. He probably thinks I'm damaged and dangerous.

Maybe I am.

When I was with Jayhe, I was the sexy, special, dangerous ballerina. The sob in my throat threatens to explode. I put a hand there, trying to hold it in.

I snatch a flute of something sparkling—champagne or cider, I'm not sure—off a tray and down it. The bubbles go straight to my head, and my limbs feel looser immediately. I grab another flute, despite the waiter's lifted eyebrows, a warning. This one I sip as I float around the gala, watching the other guests mix and mingle.

I gulp the champagne and snatch up another. Mr. Lucas stands in the corner, talking to some patrons, his pretty blond wife resting a well-manicured hand on his arm, quiet and polite and insipid. I think about what Alec said, and wonder if it might be true. I ponder the planes of his face—his sharp nose, the same long forehead, and wonder if I might have found my answer, if he was right there all along. But if it's true, then how can he ignore me, standing right there? How can he not sense my pain and reach out? How could he have watched me all these years and said nothing? I take another sip of the champagne and start toward him, my stride determined. As I hover, just a few feet away, the wife, her bottle blond too brassy, her eyes shallow, cuts me down with a glare. "No shoptalk tonight, darling," she says under her breath. "Mr. Lucas has bigger fish to fry."

I want to be bold, to ignore her, to plow forward, but the bitch delicately steers Mr. Lucas away, toward another patron. That's when I hear that familiar giggle.

Alec and Gigi are being stupid, twirling a little and laughing. She seems light as air, as if she took her earlier words to heart.

As if she's forgotten everything. I wish it were that easy for me. I wish I could forget. Let go. Or, of course, have the guts to finally take the other option. The one I try not to think about, but the one that keeps turning up in my thoughts: *Get rid of Gigi.*

As the bubbles slosh in my stomach, I realize I'm ravenous. I grab a canapé from a passing tray, then a second. The pit of my stomach still rumbles like the subway, so I head over to the buffet spread. Lots of salads, platters of meat and cheese, bruschetta and little pot stickers. I pile a plate high with food, sick to my stomach just looking at it. Which is good, right? I can't afford to keep it down anyway.

I'm about to take a bite when I hear a snicker. "There she goes again." Sei-Jin's voice pierces my ears, my soul. "Drowning your sorrows in dumplings, E-Jun?" She points down the hall. "That's the nearest bathroom," she adds, laughing. "You know, for when you're done."

"Sei-Jin!" Jayhe silences her with a withering look, but he doesn't come to my defense. I should have known he'd be here with Sei-Jin.

Furious, I take my plate and storm away, too exhausted to deal with her again. She wins. She can have him. He follows, his arm grazing mine as he tries to stop me, but I'm too angry to indulge him, too humiliated to give any of them the satisfaction. I walk out onto the terrace and sit at an empty table, picking at my plate. Jayhe follows and plunks down in the chair next to me. "I've missed you," he says, whispering close to my ear.

I look up at him. "Oh, yeah? So why haven't you responded

to my texts?" I ask, despite myself. I can feel the heat burning my cheeks.

"She knows," he says, his voice still low. "I shouldn't be out here at all."

I rise, the anger billowing around me. "Then forget about me. Leave me alone. Go back to Sei-Jin and your cozy little relationship," I say, practically spitting as I start to walk away. But he pulls me back, grabbing my arm, his grip tight, his familiarity making my skin flame. "Oh, yeah," I say, the hate changing my voice to something unrecognizable. "But I'd give you something she never will," I say. "Too bad you can't have it both ways."

He's so shocked he doesn't stop me when I walk away this time. But Sei-Jin's at the door of the terrace, watching us, a look of sheer terror on her face. "Don't worry," I say, the menace still tainting my voice. "I didn't tell your secret. Not yet, anyway."

Heading back into the party, I grab another flute of champagne, determined to drown all this out, at least for tonight. I'm sick of second place, of always being the understudy. I need to do something about it, once and for all.

40.

Gigi

ALEC GIVES ME A GLASS of champagne, and we clink the glasses together. He kisses me.

"I have something for you," he says. "It'll make you feel better."

I blush and try to put on a happy face, when really I feel like I'm falling down a giant hole and can't stop. "What is it?" I try to sound excited. I should be excited. It's a gift. He thought of me.

He pulls a necklace from his pocket. A tiny silver disk hangs from an antique chain. It catches the light. It's beautiful. Even more beautiful than the little rose charm he gave me. The one that went missing months ago. The one I haven't had the heart to tell him about.

"Alec," I say, feeling all choked up, mostly from the sadness and having all these emotions I don't know what to do with.

"It was my mom's," he says, turning me around. He lifts my curls and clasps the necklace on me and the cool metal is soothing against my neck. "My mother left this behind, and before that it was her grandmother's necklace. I wanted you to have it."

I press my fingers on it, feeling its enormous weight. "I don't know what to say." And I really don't. I want to jump up into his arms and kiss him all over his face. But I can't pull out that feeling inside me.

"Just wear it," he says. "And smile."

I kiss his cheek. My parents wave at me from across the room. I saw them earlier for brunch. They are brown dots in a sea of white. Aunt Leah's hair is big and curly, but my mother's is surprisingly pulled into a bun. "I want you to meet my parents," I say, dragging him off.

He follows me as we move through the crowd, our hands clasped.

"Hey," I say.

"That's our girl," my dad says, grabbing me first. I smell coffee and feel his beard rub against my cheek. His eyes are warm and brown, and he's got on his one and only suit. Mama hugs me next and she smells like home—mango and incense. I've missed both of them, but loved living on my own. And their embraces make me feel like crying and pouring out everything that's happened. But I swallow it down. It would just alarm them. Give them cause to pull me out of school. As if they didn't already think they had enough reason.

"Hey, kid," my aunt Leah says. "I've missed your face." She holds my hand and squeezes it. "Can't wait to see you in *Giselle*, Giselle!" She tries to make me laugh.

"I want you to meet someone." I pull Alec to my side. "This is Alec."

My dad sizes him up, and I see Alec swallow. Little beads of sweat collect on his brow, and he bites his lips, which I've never seen him do before. It's kind of cute.

"Oh, is this the boy you kissed at the end of *The Nutcracker*?" Aunt Leah teases.

"Aunt Leah!" I say, feeling hot.

"Is that true?" my mother says, turning to Alec. He grins at her, and I know she's probably going to love him as much as I do. "We were wondering about that."

"It was the tiniest, most respectful kiss," Alec teases.

"Well then . . ." She opens her arms and gives Alec a huge embrace.

When they part, my mama pulls me to the side while my dad speaks with Alec. "Why aren't you wearing your monitor?" she asks. "And what's wrong? I can see it all in your eyes."

"Nothing, Mama. I'm fine. And so is my health. I'm not wearing my monitor because I'm not dancing right now," I say. Her concern compiles with the stress I already feel.

She tsk-tsks. "I'm concerned, Gigi. I mean, I'm happy about all this and how well you're doing, but I want you to not lose sight of what's most important. Your health. This really worries me. And I feel like you're hiding something," she says, like she's been burrowing in my mind, reading my thoughts.

"Aren't you always worrying?" I ask, craning my neck to hear what my dad is saying to Alec. I give her a tiny kiss on the cheek and flash her an everything-is-all-right smile.

"Well, this is why I brought this!" She pulls out a thin wristband. It's flat and resembles one of the bands you get at a theme park entrance, only it has a digital face. "It vibrates if you're in a danger zone."

I frown. "Mama!"

"Gigi, I need you to do this for me." She takes my wrist, and I let her put it on. "My biggest nightmare is that you don't take this whole thing seriously. That you push yourself too hard. I was holding my breath the whole time during *The Nutcracker*, and I know I'll be doing the same for *Giselle*. Scared that it will be too much exertion."

"I'm fine," I say, trying to ease back to Alec and Dad and Aunt Leah.

"Just wear it for me. It'll put my mind at ease." She kisses my forehead and rubs my cheek. "You look beautiful. I can see the changes in you. A real ballerina." Her face is warm with delight and approval.

I put it on my wrist. "Happy?"

She smiles. We return to the conversation. Nothing about that exchange made me feel any better. Mama takes hold of my dad's hand.

"And what's that beautiful necklace you're wearing?" Aunt Leah asks.

I show off Alec's family heirloom. My dad twirls me around a little and I catch Bette's icy gaze on us. And the gaze of the woman standing next to her with her same cheekbones and upright posture. Mrs. Abney, her mother. Any momentary lift I experienced disappears.

I freeze and then quickly turn around. My hand goes to my neck and I feel a need to hide the necklace from sight. I try to continue to listen to my parents chat with Alec, but I feel the Abneys' eyes burning into my back. Will saunters up and gives me and Alec a big hug. But Alec is too distracted by my dad to talk to Will, who looks a little hurt.

Will pulls me to the side. "Just wanted to check on you. After, you know, everything. The butterflies." His words land soft, but I feel the tears welling up inside me. How will I tell my dad about them? What am I supposed to say? The truth? Will takes a glass of champagne from a waiter's passing tray.

I mutter thanks. "I'm putting it all behind me."

He touches my neck and the necklace Alec gave me. "You know he loves you, right?" He glances behind us at Alec.

I nod my head.

He doesn't look at me anymore. "The way he loves you is the way I love him." His admission makes me feel instantly sadder. I wonder if Alec knows. I open my mouth to respond, but I'm empty.

Will must see that on my face, because he touches the necklace one last time. "So pretty. Be careful." Then he bolts without waiting around for a response.

Bette walks by my parents. My stomach twists with dread. I remember what Alec told me about her and her mama and all their issues. I hold my breath as she passes us by.

"Oh, Gigi, who's that girl?" My mama points at Bette and reaches out for her. She touches her shoulder.

"Um, Mama, no!" I say too late.

"You were just lovely in *The Nutcracker*, young lady," my mama says. "I didn't get to tell you that after the show. I know it's been months. But I thought you should know."

"Why, thank you," Bette answers politely, her big blue eyes looking doelike and sweet.

Alec shifts uncomfortably. I flatten my hand over the necklace. A long pause stretches between us all. Everyone says hi to her and I know I should've introduced her more quickly.

"Mama, Dad, Aunt Leah, this is Bette Abney," I say at last.

"Gigi's one of our best dancers," Bette blurts, and they all soak up her praise. "So glad you could come all the way out here from California to see our performance. "

Her compliment feels genuine, but she's as fake as a plastic doll.

"We wouldn't have missed it," my dad boasts, pulling me into another embrace.

"You look like a ballerina from a music box," my mama says, touching Bette's arm.

"Doesn't she?"

Bette squeezes my mama's hand and acts as if they've known each other forever. My mama has just called her perfect.

"I'm so glad you've got friends out here, Gigi," my mama says, leaning over to kiss my forehead. "It was one of my other worries. Now I don't have to as much. Even though you know I will. But you've got both Alec and . . . what did you say your name was again, honey?" My mama turns to Bette.

"Bette," she says, making her name sound light and airy.

"Oh, right, yes!" My mama touches my cheek, then hers. "Such pretty girls."

Bette and I look at each other, both holding awkward grins on our faces.

41.

Bette

I KNOW THAT NECKLACE **IS** all I can think at first. Mr. Lucas and his wife know the necklace, too, of course, and I wonder if they're thinking what I am: that the way it looks around Gigi's neck is all wrong. It was supposed to hang around my neck, closer to my throat than my locket, but the same silver glint, the same delicate, antique links of the chain.

Gigi keeps running the tips of her fingers over the chain, back and forth. Fidgeting. A girl who fidgets should not be a prima ballerina. A girl who fidgets should not have the Lucas family heirloom or a place next to Alec. It looks all wrong, having her fill the space where I should be. I say good-bye to Gigi's parents and try to hold in my rage as I head to the buffet table.

My mother swoops in next to me before I'm tempted to snatch some finger food. No Adele. No Eleanor. No June, even. Just my mother in her black gown and too-sparkly diamond earrings.

"You just let her take it all, huh?" she says in my ear.

I make fists with my hands and wonder why she didn't bring flowers, why she didn't give me a real hug, or wish me luck on our performance tomorrow, why she is thinking so intensely about Gigi and not at all about me.

I look back over at them—the perfect happy family—they're all talking with Mr. K now. And Alec has barely left her side, like he's some part of them now, and not part of me. He hasn't even spoken to my mother tonight.

I've let my hair down from its bun, but I dressed like the ballerina I am instead of wearing regular people clothes. Long white tulle skirt and an embroidered bodice that hangs off my shoulders. Not a freckle in sight. Just a hint of sparkle I dusted on my collarbone and shoulders, and otherwise snow-white, unblemished skin. That hasn't changed. Neither has my almost-white hair, my pink lips, the way I hover an inch above my mother.

They all want me to be jealous of Gigi's freckles and brown skin and wild hair, but when I catch sight of myself in the mirror, I'm still a replica of the ballerina in the music box: the golden-haired one in the glistening tutu with long legs and a perfect pirouette.

I almost cry with the realization.

The pride.

Even Gigi's mother said so.

That's why there's nothing to be afraid of when I stop listening to my mother and Mr. K and the voices in my head. The *petit rats* still skip over and pull on my hand and ask me for autographs and kisses on their cheeks. They all want to be like me. Not her.

I watch Alec kiss Gigi's hand, and I regret taking that pill. I can't seem to *not* focus on the tiny ways he touches her. I want to go snatch him away, and remind him that I am the one for him. I find a quiet corner in the room and open my locket. I skip over the white pills and take the pale-blue oval ones in the middle. One from my mother's stash and the other one a little gift from my dealer. Then I watch as Alec leaves Gigi's side and stands with his dad and stepmom. It seems like they're in some heated conversation. Gigi's parents have left. And I wonder if they've been introduced to the Lucases. I imagine Alec's stepmother's chilly reception of Mrs. Stewart and her hippy-dippy dress and mannerisms and multiculturalness, and it makes me smile a little, knowing she'll always love me and my mother, and Gigi can never have that.

Last year Alec and I paraded around the spring gala and put on an impromptu show. We performed complicated lifts and turns just to thrill the crowd. I gulp down more champagne and ignore how many calories it's adding to my body. Or maybe if I just wait long enough, he'll grow tired of her. Because there will always be a huge difference between Gigi and me. She won't always be new and fascinating and strange and mysterious, but I will always be the girl in the music box, the girl who has known him practically forever. Nothing she does can change that.

Henri joins me at the buffet table after my mother makes a dash to speak with Morkie. He doesn't greet me, just brushes his body against mine. I feel his breath in my hair and the anger rising off him. The pinch of his fingers digs into my hips, snapping at me like the predator he is.

"What's wrong with you?" I say, facing him. "Get away from me."

"You should start being nicer to people," he warns.

I don't acknowledge him, and with a ballerina's walk—pointed toes, turned-out legs, head high—I join my sister, who has just walked into the room with some of the dancers from her company. I take another glass of champagne from a tray, and another pill. I need it to kick things into high gear. And I'm Bette Abney, determined, willful, successful. The girl who makes things happen.

It will be a good night. A night to remember. A night that changes everything. I will make something happen.

42.

June

I RECOGNIZE THE KNOCK AT my bedroom door. Fast, light, aggressive. Bette.

"Tonight's the night," she says. She's decked out in a fringy silver number, and has another dress in her hand. We're supposed to be resting for opening night tomorrow. "We're all going out." She looks at my pajamas, disapproving. "Like I promised."

I open my mouth to decline, but she doesn't let me. "It's tradition," she says. "Mandatory. You know that. All the Level 7 girls did it last year. We have to."

I can't believe she actually meant what she'd said—that we'd go out. All of us. I'm so stunned I leave the door open and stumble backward a little. Girls chatter in the hall about Bette's dress. They wish she'd come to their rooms. Or invite them wherever she was headed. They tell her she looks gorgeous.

"I don't—" I try, but she pushes past me and enters the room without listening for a response. Gigi went off with Alec and her parents, saying she'd see me later.

I never go out. It's just not me. And yet within two minutes, I'm somehow letting Bette dress me up like a little doll, like her little plaything. Part of me hates myself for it, but another part, albeit a much smaller one, has longed for this. Because this is what normal girls do. They play dress-up and dance and get a little crazy. They have girlfriends and share secrets and giggle about boys. They're sisters, maybe not by blood, but in the moment at least, when it feels like nothing will ever be this real again. That's what tonight will be. I can feel it in my bones. And I've never done this before.

"You're really going to steal his eye tonight," she says, pulling one of her dresses—a deep plum number—down over my head. Her breath smells of alcohol, and her pupils are dilated and glossy.

"Who?" I say, not sure how she knows anything.

She pauses to look me in the eye. "Oh, c'mon. There's got to be someone." She doesn't even give me time to nod. "Then it's time for you to claim him."

"She'll never let him go," I find myself saying, even though I've never said anything to anyone about Jayhe. Well, except Gigi.

She rubs makeup into my cheeks, puts shadow and liner on my eyes. Then she speaks again. "The thing is," she says, "you have to realize that this isn't about her. It has to be about you."

I don't know if she's talking to herself or me, but her words ring true.

I feel hopeful in Bette's capable hands, I've become glittering and shimmering and sweet and sexy. Somehow Bette's makeup skills have made me look brand-new. I am all flawless skin and deep-set eyes and a throaty, heady laugh that will make all the boys want me. I am who I've never been before, and may well never be again, if I'm honest. I'm everything Bette wants me to be, and for right now, I'm okay with that. My reflection in the mirror allows me to believe I am a girl Jayhe could want—that any boy could want. I smooth the front of the dress and like my profile, for once.

I'm in a cab with Bette and Eleanor, and we're racing down the West Side Highway, the windows wide open and the spring air blasting through, heading down to the Meatpacking District to some club Bette knows the bouncer at. I've had way too much to drink. Bette pushes another mini vodka bottle into my hand. I shake my head no this time. I text Jayhe. Maybe he'll come here and see me and choose me once and for all. Maybe he'll see the new June—colorful and beautiful and pretending to be bright again—and fall head over heels. For real.

We all climb out of the cab, and the guy waves us in, not even asking for ID. I've never been to a club, but this is just what I imagined, the music pounding through me like a heartbeat, the crowd pressing in on all sides, moving in unison, one big collective soul.

As soon as we walk inside, we see the others. Gigi, Alec, Will, and everyone. It seems tonight all is forgiven, we're putting on a united front. For tradition's sake.

I should be self-conscious, worried about the way I move, but

I just let myself shake it out with the music, go with the flow. Will takes my hand and starts twirling me, and it feels too familiar, too much like ballet, so I pull out of his grasp.

"Thanks for not saying anything. I was so paranoid. Everything is fine. No, everything is great." His words are slurred and wet as he yells in my ear. I nod and try to slink away. He grins, then points to the bar. He disappears to get drinks.

Gigi is beaming, wasted. She glows with happiness, or maybe it's just the black light, as her face falls in shadow and her teeth sparkle like little white lights in her mouth. She spins and shakes and shimmies and giggles, and I find myself doing the same, dancing close, laughing, just like real girls do. Like friends do. She shouts something toward my ear, but the noise is too much, it just absorbs the sound of her voice like she's said nothing at all. Then she points toward the door and I see them. Sei-Jin and her girls. And Jayhe, trailing sheepishly behind them.

Suddenly, all my drunken happiness washes away, gone instantly, like what I'd imagine a sober, regretful, hungover morning would feel like. Like what tomorrow will feel like. That's why he never texted me back.

Will brings back drinks, glowing bright neon green in clear plastic cups. I snatch mine from Will and down it. Then I grab his hand and start grinding up on him, putting on a show. Will is surprised, but he catches my eye, then follows my gaze, willing to play along. Will might be gay, but Jayhe doesn't know that.

I try to lose myself in the pulse of the dancing again, to forget that Sei-Jin and Jayhe are here, to recapture that energy I'd felt just moments ago. But it's gone, and I'm suddenly utterly drained.

"Restroom!" I shout to Will, then start to push my way through the crowd. Sei-Jin and her girls are all on one side of the dance floor. They scowl at me as I pass. When I finally get to the ladies' room, there's a line a mile long, winding deep into the club, all the way back to the bar. I look at my watch. 2:34 a.m. What am I doing here? This isn't me. This will never be me. I should just leave the others, hop in a cab, head back to the dorms. The performance is tomorrow. Maybe Gigi will be too hungover to dance.

I'm pondering the best route out when I feel it—that familiar way he traces his fingers along my hip, up my side, to my shoulder, the way his fingers splay on the back of my neck, luring me close, leaving no space between us.

"Hey," he whispers, his breath hot in my ear. "I'm sorry."

He pulls me in even closer and kisses me. Right there, in the club, in front of a million people, where anyone can see us. "I've missed you." He kisses me again. And again. And again. And all I want to do is lose myself in him, in the way he makes me feel. Like there's only the two of us in the world.

But instead I pull away, and the anger floods back, tears pricking at my eyes. I never cry. I just don't. I won't cry now. "Too bad," I say, and push him way, clawing my way forward through the crowd, toward the door. He follows me out onto the cobblestoned streets, just inches behind me as I stumble and nearly fall. He catches me.

"Hey, wait, June," he says, grabbing my arm in that familiar vise, the one that I can't get away from. "Wait, I came here for you."

"No you didn't!" I'm shouting, but no one notices. "You're here with her. It's always her."

He's shaking his head, and there's a sadness in his eyes that tells me it's not true. That he really is here for me. Even if it never feels that way, even if everything else rings false. "Can we go somewhere?" he says, already leading the way.

Minutes later, we're in the backseat of his car in one of the parking garages, the beat-up old car his dad used to drive to church when we were kids, the silver faded to gray, the shine long gone. It's eerily quiet, like we really are alone in the world, even though the thump of the club is just half a block away. And he's looking down at his hands, worn and cut up from chopping vegetables at his mom's restaurant, the exhaustion I feel reading heavy on his face. He's pondering what to say, how to fix it, worried it's too late.

Then suddenly I'm sobbing. And his hands stroke my hair, my face, and he's whispering that it will be okay. But it won't. Nothing will ever be the same again. Because now I know.

"I have a father," I say through tears. "I know who he is, finally." I'm shaking, but I have to tell someone. I have to tell Jayhe. "And he doesn't want me. Nobody ever wants me."

I don't let him say what I know he'll say. That he does want me. That he never stopped wanting me.

So when he turns to me, finally, and opens his mouth, about to fill the space with unnecessary words, I just kiss him. To make it quiet again, to go back to that warm, safe place. But this time it's not soft, not safe, like it was in my room that one time. This time, it's urgent, now or never, decision time. And every part of me is saying it's time to give in, to say yes, to put the past behind us and make the future look bright. Like Bette said, it's time to claim Jayhe, to make him mine. To have one thing that's real.

43.

Gigi

THE DJ'S SPINNING HIP-HOP MUSIC and I can't stop moving. Not ballet moves.

Wild. Unsanctioned. Loose.

Positions Morkie would hate. Movements Mr. K would frown at. We're all bunched in a group, dancing all together, laughing all together. Bette is laughing and smiling. Even June—who I thought had left—is back and letting loose, this faraway grin on her face. I feel a little better. Spirits lifted just like Alec promised.

Alec leaves to go get more drinks at the bar. While I wait for him to return, the floor oscillates in waves beneath me. The lights streak across the floor like rainbows trapped inside. I stretch my arms and legs out and feel the room spin. My wristband glows different colors and I don't know if it's my eyes or the actual wristband. I don't mind wearing something other than my monitor. I've had too many glasses of champagne and god knows what else. More alcohol than I've ever had in my entire life. More alcohol than Ella and I ever consumed back home on the beach for her sixteenth birthday last year. It feels nice to float, and I wish I had my very own cloud.

I laugh as the whole room spins me in a circle, like I've fallen into a whirlpool. I think I can feel the earth's rotation and I'm positive that I'm turning along with it. I feel like a regular teen again.

I'm sure I'm imagining things.

"Truce?!" I hear over the music.

Bette holds out a drink. It's got a pineapple slice floating around in it.

"What is it?" I holler.

"A special delivery," she says, her words running together. She seems pretty drunk already.

I laugh. "No, really."

"Seriously. That's what the drink it called." She pushes it into my hand. "I'm sorry for my part in some of the stuff this year. I was wrong."

I don't know what to say. What new thing is she exactly owning up to?

"I didn't put that glass in your shoe, though. That wasn't me," she says. She puts her hands up, like she's not guilty. She stumbles forward, and I catch her arm. "And I sure as hell didn't kill your butterflies."

"Okay . . . ," I say back, not sure how to respond.

"So, starting over?" She raises her drink. I let it hang there for a while, then give in to get her to go away. I clink mine with hers, and sip the drink.

Alec returns. We all dance and spin until I can't feel my legs anymore. He pulls me closer to him. Buries his face in the place where my neck meets my shoulder. At first he just rests there. Then he starts kissing the soft skin.

I'm shaking from the mix of the alcohol and the nearness of him. The feel of his tongue near my earlobe. The heat between us.

"I can feel your heart pounding," he says. "Are you okay?"

"That feels amazing," I say, barely recognizing the breathiness of my voice. He moves from my neck to my mouth and the kiss is intense, passionate. I wrap my arms more tightly around him. Listen to the sharp intake of breath when I press myself against him. Soon he's got me pushed into a dark corner, his hands are up my dress, wandering from one patch of skin to another eagerly. I'm focused on Alec, but I can feel eyes on me. Bette's probably, of course, despite what she might say. But when I look up, I also see Will watching us, and Henri not far behind him. For once in my life, though, I don't care. Let them watch. Let them want.

We pull apart to catch our breath and neither of us can hold back our smiles. He kisses me again, and I crumple into him. Alec parts my legs with his hand and my mouth with his warm tongue. I love the heavy way he feels, like I'm in a safe little space beneath him.

I slip in and out of time until Will interrupts us. "Time to go, lovebirds. RAs figured us out. They're on a rampage. I've got a dozen calls. Mr. K is on his way down here."

We race outside. Alec is ahead of me. I feel a hand on my shoulder. I look up. My vision is blurred, but it's Will.

"Heyyy," I say, wanting to thank him for the heads-up about Mr. K coming down here. But Alec calls my name from ahead, and I try to catch up.

My feet slip and slide on the old-fashioned cobblestones, but I feel like I should be able to walk on these streets if I can dance in pointe shoes. I can't stop laughing. We're all falling over one another, and thrilled by the idea of Mr. K's angry face. The excitement (or maybe all the alcohol) is making me light-headed. June, all buttoned up again but softer still, smiles at me as she walks beside Jayhe, even though Sei-Jin's watching them, about to explode. I wonder what's going on. And Bette and I even laugh at the same stupid joke Will makes on our way out the club doors.

I step into the street to cross over. My heel snags on one of the cobblestones. I feel hands on my back, and my body lurches forward.

My eyes go blank.

The irregular beat in my chest quiets.

The street stands still.

44.

Bette

THERE ARE SCREAMS AND SO much movement on the street it feels like backstage before dress rehearsal. I feel the beginnings of tears in my eyes. The world is fuzzy. I am frozen in place, heavy and slow; it feels like I'm underwater. And I'm drowning.

All I want is Alec.

Gigi is stretched out on the street in front of a yellow taxi. One leg is bent beneath her, the other is covered in blood. She isn't moving.

The cabbie is frantic, crying, worrying, on the street, and somewhere not too far off, sirens are zooming, closer by the second. I back away and almost fall backward onto the curb. Will stands there with his hand cupped over his mouth.

"Where the hell is Alec?" I finally manage to say, and I know I'm spitting out the words. I know I don't look well.

"What . . . just . . . happened?" Will says, all trembles—hands, mouth, voice.

The sounds of sirens echo from down the block.

"Where's Alec?" I say.

Will gives me a good long stare, and strange emotions pass over his face, one after the other in quick succession. He doesn't say a word, doesn't look away, just lets the feelings overcome him until he gets his voice back. He's frozen in place.

"I can't find Alec," I say when a minute has passed and some amount of the news has sunk in.

"Alec!" Will shouts like he's come back to life. He knows what to do.

We run through the crowd, dodging onlookers. Bodies blur around me, a mosaic of arms and legs and moving parts.

"Will!" I whip around at the sound of Alec's voice.

"Gigi was right behind me," Alec says. The look on Alec's face says it all. His blue eyes are all big and cloudy. He sinks to the curb and sits.

"Where have you been?" I say. My voice starts rising.

"Let him breathe, Bette," Will says. But I want to claw at him for suggesting I need to do anything but figure out what is happening.

"I can't explain it . . . ," Alec says, trailing off.

"What happened?" I say. I keep stepping closer and closer to Alec, who just will not get off the ground. "We were all standing there . . ."

Ahead of us in the street, the paramedics surround Gigi. Cops push back the crowds. They start asking questions. I bolt, and I try to blend into the crowd. I get farther away from the curb. I find Eleanor nearby, whose eyes are red from crying.

"Jesus," she says when she sees me. "Where'd you go?" She's worried, but she puts an arm around me. Hugs me to her. And I know I can trust her. She's the same girl I met when I was six years old—my best friend. I try to stop my body from shaking. It all happened so fast. The scene replays in my head like some twisted ballet: where everyone was standing, the cacophony of the taxis' blaring horns, the uneven cobblestones. I try to make it all make sense in my head. We called a truce. We were all pals, hanging out. I didn't touch her. Did I?

"Please tell them I was standing beside you. Please. I think they might accuse me." I cry then, dig my head into her shoulder and hide there. She doesn't agree or disagree, but she rubs my back, and I think maybe it will be okay. She whispers in my ear, "I was across the street, Bette. You were right beside Gigi, and so were Will and June."

When I emerge from the moment on Eleanor's shoulder, I look up to see Alec talking to the police. I want to run again, badly, but I hold back. I squeeze Eleanor's arm until she yelps. I need her to hold me steady. Like she's always done when things get bad. I feel like I might fall.

"You're hurting me," Eleanor says, but I can't let go.

I'm next. I know they'll call me next. I turn around and look to see if I can go inside a nearby store, to at least get a grip before trying to talk to police about this girl that everyone knows has been my enemy all year. But I can't get out of the crowd, because a wide set of shoulders block me.

"Hey there," Henri says. He's not crying. He's not shaking or sad. He's not hiding his face in his hands. He's smiling. He's smirking. "Where do you think you're going? The police want to talk to all of us."

He's terrifying. The ambulance lights wash him in blues and reds. His eyes almost glow.

The cops approach with their pads. My mouth opens, but nothing comes out. I just want to call my mother. I want her for the first time ever.

"Where were you standing?" the cop asks for the fourth time.

I can't answer.

Eleanor squeezes my hand. "Bette, answer."

Henri raises his hand like we're in English class, and says, "Officer, I saw Bette Abney push the victim into the street."

45.

June

WE ALL MOVE IN A dream state. I watch the paramedics roll Gigi to an ambulance. She is strapped in and her head is in a brace. Pretty face, long limbs, perfect feet all a mess.

The others bombard me with questions, so I make my shoulder shrug over and over. Up, down. Up, down. Up, down. Mouth a little bit open. Eyes blinking slowly. Hand making its way to my forehead every few minutes, like I could somehow wipe away the headache.

I'm barely here.

Bette bursts into tears. Not angry ones or bitter ones. Little girl tears. Sad tears. Unexpected, after all the vitriol in her voice. I almost reach for her, to pat her arm or something, but she's still Bette. She's still untouchable and unpredictable, and I'm still June. Even in my tight dress and overpowering makeup. Not that much has really changed.

She screeches, "I didn't push her!"

And the cops move her to the side.

Since everyone but Will is frozen, and Bette and Alec are locked in some horrible death stare, I don't know what to do or where to go. I sink right down on the curb. I think through what just happened. I try to place everyone on the street.

I was the last one to leave the club. Henri was first. I think Bette, Gigi, Alec, and Eleanor went out together. I think Will was in the clump, too. I squeeze my eyes shut. I can't think. I can't rearrange them in my head.

Gigi's parents and Aunt Leah appear out of nowhere, and they are crying and turning from person to person, looking for answers. We don't have any. A few of the dancers pat Mrs. Stewart on the shoulder, but the rest of us just look at the ground and mirror her tears. Gigi looks like her mother—big, curly hair like a lion's mane, a few freckles, warm eyes, that caring smile. Her father just stares blankly at everything and everyone.

Mr. K passes right in front of me. I didn't know he was here yet, but people keep popping up on the street, unexpected, the way they are in dreams. Out of context. He isn't in his normal clothes. Has a robe wrapped around him and uncombed hair. Mr. K has bed head and a panicked voice. The world is all wrong.

"Get inside these cabs," Mr. K orders. "Everyone. Now!" But there's no power behind the order. And for the first time ever, we don't listen.

46.

Bette

I STILL FEEL LIKE I'M going to pass out. I walk in circles, trying to keep myself awake, not allowed to move from the spot where the policeman told me to stay. I'm biding my time before more police and Mr. K and Gigi's parents approach me.

But I have not evaded Alec.

His hand is on my shoulder, and at last, the one thing I've been so desperate for actually happens. He pulls me into a hug, kisses my hair. Squeezes so hard, I could get lost in the feeling if I wanted. "You're shaking."

"I didn't do it," I say. "I swear I didn't do anything." I look up at him, my blue eyes meeting his in a silent agreement. We haven't looked at each other like this in months.

"I know," Alec says, his voice slow and careful, like he knows exactly what happened and who did it. "But someone did."

47.

June

THE CROWD CLOSES IN ON me. Gigi's parents are approaching, and the questions from the cops are coming fast and furious. I drank all that champagne, I threw up both the alcohol and party food, and my roommate is gone. My mouth waters, and I see sparkles all around.

I faint.

It's just one little moment; any other day it would be small enough a thing for them to ignore, maybe, or to earn another lecture from Nurse Connie. But tonight, with EMTs swarming and Gigi already carried away, they are all on top of me. I come to one half-second later and an EMT is in my face, chewing gum and asking questions. I shudder under his touch.

He checks my pulse, searching for it on my wrist, and then using a stethoscope on my heart. Looking for the beat like they just did with Gigi.

"Stop it," I snarl.

"You're not well," the EMT says. "Don't get up."

"I'm fine," I say. I keep squirming away from him, but he won't stop prodding.

"Your blood pressure is so low I'm surprised this hasn't happened before. We need to tell your teachers. Talk to your school nurse." The EMT goes on, but Mr. K interrupts and puts me in one of the cabs.

We return to school, but Mr. K doesn't allow us to go up to our beds.

Instead, I sit in his office, surrounded by him and Mr. Lucas and Morkie and two suited detectives with grim expressions. They ask me the same questions over and over again. How it all happened. Who was next to Gigi? What were we all doing? Drinking? Drugs? Did she have any enemies? Did anyone have a motive? They ask me about the butterflies, the glass in the shoe, the message on the mirror, the dead cockroaches in the box. Piling up evidence to pin on someone. They keep throwing out the questions and I think I speak, I think I respond, but I'm sniffling and sobbing and I'm not sure anything I'm saying is making any sense.

Then the door flies open, and everyone is shocked out of our circular discussion. It's my mom. And she's angry. Her face is red and splotchy and she's wearing her pajamas and a robe, like she rushed over here as soon as she heard. Underneath all my pain and frustration and sadness, I register that this pleases me, that she might actually care, that I was important enough that I shattered her illusion of perfection to get here as fast as she could. And that this is her first time inside this building in nearly a decade.

She stops like she's been hit. She and Mr. Lucas stare at each other. The whole room waits for her to speak or blow up.

"Ma'am?" one of the detectives says.

"My daughter should be in bed. You can ask questions later," she says to the room, but she's looking right at Mr. Lucas, whose face has drained of all color, as if he's seen a ghost.

"Dominic, did you hear me?" She wags a finger two inches from his face. "She fainted. Don't you care at all?" She's so aggressive, the other detective urges her to calm down.

All the while, their eyes watch each other. My mind and heart do flips as the magnitude of him being my father hits me. He's the man my mom fell in love with. He was her *pas* partner. He's the man who cruelly discarded her and abandoned me even before I was born. He's the man who's chosen to ignore his own flesh and blood for all these years, even as I stood there, close enough for him to cast a shadow.

My mom fires off a zillion questions: "Why is she being brought in? What does she have to do with Gigi? Why would she have any reason to want her dead?"

Mr. Lucas sits in glum silence as my mom rampages, and I keep trying to figure out what to say to placate her.

"I—uh—" My first instinct is to say *not dead, but gone*—but obviously that would really put the bull's-eye right on me. I can't trust myself not to give anything away. So I decide to keep my mouth shut. I can't focus on the conversation.

"How dare you bring my daughter into this," Mom says, and she's glaring right at Mr. Lucas. "I will take her right out of this 'rsaken place. She doesn't belong here anyway."

I snap back to reality. I can't let that happen. I can't let her use this as an excuse. But Mr. K springs into action, directing my mom to a seat, apologizing, saying that they're doing everything possible to cooperate with the authorities on this. "It is," he says, his voice taking on that same annoying holier-than-thou quality, "after all, a matter of life and death."

Anything I want to say is drowned out by the chaos. It's then that it really hits me. Gigi is really hurt this time. Gigi could actually die.

To my surprise, the first thing in my head isn't sadness or anger or fear. It's something else: *This means I'm going to be dancing Giselle.*

48

Bette

"BETTE?" MR. K SAYS, AND IT feels like we're both underwater, and he's trying to talk to me.

"Yes?" I say, trying to stand up from a lobby chair. He catches my arm.

"It's your turn." He walks toward the office. "And your mother is here. We called all parents, and she insisted on being here for your statement."

I can't move out of first position. Mr. K waves his fingers like I am a dog meant to follow him, but I'm frozen with my back to the lobby window and my face, unfortunately, exposed to every other person in class. It feels like it's been days, but the accident was only an hour ago.

SNAP OUT OF IT! A voice in my head screams, and it's enough to get my arms at my side and my feet parallel and ready to walk. I do everything I can to keep my head held high.

Mr. K takes long, rushed strides and I nearly have to run to keep up with him.

"Can I stop in the bathroom?" I finally say, right before we reach the door that leads into his office.

He just sighs in response. Stops walking but doesn't turn around. He's giving his permission, but just barely.

I. Am. So. Screwed.

I splash water on my face because right now my brain is swimming with blurry, half-formed thoughts. I need to be on my feet if I'm going to survive whatever is behind that door. Mainly, my mother. And accusations that I pushed Gigi in front of that cab.

Mr. K holds the door to his office open for me. My mother's eyes are red, but otherwise she looks beautiful. Still dressed in her gala gown. Her lips wine stained, which means she fell asleep in it. The police officer has a horrible yellow legal pad.

I take a seat next to my mother and her eyes start to water. Which is especially strange, because my mother does not cry. Not ever. Not when my father left her, not when Adele got offered a spot at the American Ballet Company. Never.

"Tell the police officer what happened tonight, Bette," Mr. K says. He doesn't look at me. He talks to the wall in front of him. His focus on that blank white wall is so intense you'd think it was my face.

"Yes, Bette. I'm Officer Jason Hamilton," he says, rubbing the dark mustache stretched over his lip. "Tell me what happened."

"Gigi had had a lot to drink. We'd been dancing all night. I think . . . I think she tripped."

"Have you had anything to drink?" he asks.

"Yeah, we all did. But she had had a *lot*, you know?"

"Your classmates have told me you haven't been the biggest fan of Giselle Stewart," Officer Hamilton says.

"My god," my mother says, like she's just hearing about what happened. Her voice is choked up. I look at her face—I don't want to miss it. I'm not glad that she's crying, but I'm fascinated that I could cause those tears. That Gigi could make her feel something so deeply.

"Which classmates?"

He flips through his notes. "I am not at liberty to say. But many of them said you always seemed to have it out for her. And a few of the other girls corroborated this story."

Shame rushes to my face, and I know I have turned a hot, terrible pink that won't vanish until I am long gone from this room. I try not to ball my fists. I try not to let my face show anger that might get me in trouble. He tried to set me up. He tried to make me take the fall for this.

"I didn't push her," I blurt out. I'm so hot I think I could faint.

No one moves.

"No one said anything about her being pushed, Bette," Officer Hamilton says. "But if you did push her, you'd better tell me now before it gets worse for you."

"Gigi could die. You do realize that, Bette?" Mr. K says, his eyes lasers.

I open my mouth to defend myself.

"Do you know what harassment is?" Officer Hamilton asks.

Mr. K pulls a book from his shelf and puts it in my lap. I'm too afraid to look down.

"Look it up," Mr. K says.

"But . . . but . . . ," I start. My mother squirms beside me.

"Bette!" Mr. K says my name like he's lost all patience with me. Like I'm some strange new fuckup kid. Like he hasn't known me for forever. I flip open the English dictionary to the *H* section and run a finger down the page until I find the word. I let my finger sit there.

"Read it," he says.

I choke on my words. "'To harass means to subject to aggressive pressure or intimidation or to make repeated small-scale attacks on an enemy.'"

No one speaks for what feels like a thousand years.

"Bette, I think it's time for us to go home now," my mother says. "Not another word. Officer Hamilton, is it? If you'd like to speak to my daughter further, you can make an appointment with our family lawyer." She produces a card from her purse like magic. "We've been very good to the American Ballet Conservatory, and Company. The new building is coming along, and the Rose Abney Plaza has never looked better. We will not be treated in this way."

Mr. K is smirking at my mother. And I feel like she's just sealed my fate. His eyes are back on the wall, and to anyone else it might look like his normal, neutral expression. But I know him, and he is hiding a laugh. At the ridiculousness that is my mother and her power trip. Because now she's given everyone what they need to blame me for this. Whether I'm guilty or not.

49.

Gigi

I LOOK OUT INTO THE room. Sterile white walls, bouquets of flowers, balloons, and care packages. My vision is splintered into a thousand little pieces. My eyes are sore and unused. The overhead light hums. My left leg floats above me, hanging in a sling.

I don't know where I am.

I try to move around, but my body feels stiff, like I haven't moved for a thousand years. There are cuts and bruises all over my hands. Tight bandages cling to my left hip. A finger clamp connects me to a massive monitor. Electrodes dot my chest. The steady beeps are the only noise in the room.

"Mama? Dad? Aunt Leah?" I whisper, not sure where in time and space I am. My voice scratches against the back of my throat, and I start to cough.

No one answers. I squeeze my eyes shut. My mind starts to clear and memories flash in my head like beats of light.

The spring gala.

The club.

Dancing with Alec.

The cobblestones.

The sidewalk.

Feeling the push from behind.

The last memory hurts. The cab crashing into me. My body aches at thought of it.

"Mama?" I say again, craning my neck, trying to search the room. Tears brim in my eyes. I search the left side of my bed for a button. Anything that will connect me to someone outside this room. Someone with answers.

I hear the click of shoes against the floor. I turn my head to the left. My vision is blurred by tears. I try to wipe them away. Will inches closer and closer to the bed.

"What happened?" I ask. "Where are my parents?"

"They're outside, talking to the doctor. I just . . ." Will slumps onto the bed, causing me to recoil with his shaking and sobbing. "I'm so sorry, Gigi," he cries, his eyeliner smudging. "I—"

"It was Bette, wasn't it?"

Will looks stricken but then slowly nods his head, his mascara streaking down his face.

The heart monitor starts beeping wildly, and I try to get out of bed. I can feel the stitches in my side stretching as I lift myself up. Pain shoots through me. I can't even move my toes without little explosions of agony. I can't pull my leg out of the elevated sling.

I'm not going anywhere. Will I ever be able to stand again, let alone dance?

"She told me she was going to do something to you," he cries. "Something big. They haven't arrested her yet, but they should."

I don't care what the cops do to her—it will never be enough. I know one thing. I have to do this myself. "Bette's going to pay," I tell him.

50.

June

IT'S FINALLY HERE. THE MOMENT I've been waiting all my sixteen years for. The moment that will lift me out of mediocrity and onto the horizon, make me the next prime-time-worthy prima of the dance world, elevate me higher than I ever truly thought possible. The performance is now a week later than it was supposed to be, and yes, Gigi had to lose so that I could get here. But Mr. K insisted that the show must go on. And so, the understudy steps into the spotlight. Finally.

Make no mistake: I've fought long and hard for this moment, given blood, sweat, and tears, deprived myself at every turn. I've earned this.

I wait in the wings as Eleanor basks in the thunderous applause from her second solo variation of the night. She danced Bette's solo in act I, along with her own in the second act. Eleanor's undeniably a star tonight. But she won't outshine me.

The heat of the lights is like a weight on my shoulders, heavy and tangible. The corps wraps up their dance of the willis, every foot and arm and leap in sync, and for a moment, the music, the audience, the world is silent as I take the stage. Alec circles the graveyard. He lays flowers on my grave. I flutter to the center. It's where I belong—where I've always belonged. Dressed and powdered in white, the perfect version of the *ballet blanc*. You wouldn't know I don't quite fit at first glance.

I am Giselle. I am a ghost. But they all see me now. There are tiny excited gasps in the audience.

Alec and I find each other. He takes my arms and holds me as we turn. I touch his face. Pretend to lean in for a stage kiss and say good-bye as he returns to his life, and I to the grave. The motions are stiff and mechanical, not graceful and light. This is more awkward than I thought it would be. The reviews will say our chemistry is bad, but they don't know the real story. No one does.

The applause rings out after I flutter off the stage, and Alec kneels before my grave once more. I return to the stage and take Alec's hand. We bow, and I try to focus on this final moment of glory. I should bask in the glow, knowing I've hit the pinnacle. But all I can think about is who's in the audience. My mom, who'd still rather die than see me be a professional dancer. But that's okay. I'm not alone tonight. Jayhe is there, with his dad and his grandmother. Jayhe, who finally showed me that I can be loved, whether I take center stage or not. That's what finally brings a smile to my face. Knowing he's there, that silly grin on his face, the pride bursting through. I blow a kiss from the stage—I can't see him, but I know he's there.

The curtain drops in front of us. We go into the wings again. The entire cast gathers. The curtain rises again. Groups go onstage a few at a time to take their bows. I wait patiently until the lead soloists return to the stage at last. Eleanor goes out before me. I tiptoe behind her. People stand and clap as I curtsy all the way down to the floor, like the most gracious ballerina. Alec bows and twirls me around like he did Gigi after *The Nutcracker*. The orchestra conductor comes up and takes a bow.

Then I reach out my arm, welcoming Mr. K onto the stage. He kisses both my cheeks, as he does with each girl who dances the principal solo. Mr. K bows to the audience, who stand and give him three long rounds of applause. He extends his arm to invite Mr. Lucas onstage. I swallow hard, and feel like I can hear his every footstep through the droning claps.

Even without looking at him, I can feel my father's eyes on me as he takes my other arm, kissing my cheeks for the first time. He may be one of the suns in this world, but for me, there is no warmth there. He pretends to be proud and overjoyed. He starts to whisper something to me, then stops. I can feel him fretting about the secret he's kept for so long. The secret that maybe the whole world will soon know.

The crowd turns its attention stage right. A figure ambles out onto the stage. I focus on smiling pretty for the flashing cameras, but the rest of the cast turns to look, then joins the applause. For a moment, I think it's Bette—that golden crop, that porcelain skin catching the stage lights. But it can't be. She's been sent home, dismissed from all end-of-school activities for the horrible things she did to Gigi.

As I realize who it is, my heart sinks, plummeting straight down into the hollows of my always-empty stomach. Cassie Lucas. Of course. Mr. Lucas invites her to center stage, turning away from me as he gives her the classic two kisses on her cheeks. Then Mr. K embraces her, his smile beaming light out into a confused audience.

Watching her grin and bow, I realize that in ballet, no one is ever safe. The thrill of dancing the role of Giselle disappears.

"Thank you all so much for coming," Mr. K says to the audience. "We've seen an incredible display of hard work and talent tonight. The ballet world is fortunate to have these amazing young students joining its ranks very soon. And I'm so pleased to welcome another wonderful dancer, one of the academy's brightest, Cassie Lucas, back to the conservatory. I'm so happy she's here with us tonight!"

The sparkles in her baby-blue gown bring out her eyes, glittering as the cameras flash wildly, the press from the major dance magazines swarming. They should be chasing me, singing my praises, promising me pages of accolades that define me as ballet's next rising star. But they're not. Because they're surrounding her, Cassie, standing there, basking in the spotlight. My spotlight.

Acknowledgments

THOUGH OUR NAMES ARE ON the cover here, so many people have played such a big part in bringing this book to bookshelves.

First and foremost, of course, we'd like to thank our smart and sassy agent, the effervescent Victoria Marini, for being a guide and a collaborator, an advocate and a champion. Our ballerinas wouldn't have seen the light of day without her.

Then, of course, there's the amazing team at HarperTeen—especially our editors Emilia Rhodes, Jennifer Klonsky, Alice Jerman, and Sarah Landis. Thank you for your enthusiastic embrace of Bette, June, and Gigi, and for your guidance in choreographing their journey. And to the rest of the HarperTeen team who worked so hard on this book: Michelle Taormina, Jon Howard, Gina Rizzo, Christina Colangelo, and Martha Schwartz. A special thanks to the lovely Deb Shapiro, whose savvy and smarts astound us at every turn.

We bow down to readers Erica Pritzker, Karissa Venne, and Kaleb Stewart, whose early insights helped us improve each draft. And a world of appreciation to the amazing Alla Plotkin and Renee Ahdieh, who read for language accuracy and feel. Thank you to the Cudas: Lisa Amowitz, Cynthia Henzel, Cathy Giordiano, Kate Milford, Pippa Bayliss, Trish Eklund, Heidi Ayarbe, Lindsay Eland, Linda Budzinski, and Christine Faul Johnson. Your love, support, insights, and undying loyalty were vital to this book and to our lives.

Thanks to the girls and boys at the Kirov Academy of Ballet of Washington, DC, for their support and inspiration. Few get to see your artistry, dedication, and commitment to ballet, and Dhonielle was blessed to be able to witness it. We especially can't forget the (juicy!) insights provided by our ballerina readers, Angie Liao and Deanna Pearson, who ensured that we kept the TPT dancers on their toes.

This has been a long journey for the two of us, and we're so happy to celebrate our debut year with our Class of 2K15 and Fearless Fifteeners crews—thank you so much for sharing the ups and downs of this windy journey, and for talking us off a ledge (or ten). A special shout-out to the amazing ladies of the Debutante Ball: Amy Reichert, Karma Brown, Colleen Oakley, and Shelly King. So thrilled to share this road with you. To our New School peeps, especially Luis Jaramillo, Caron Levis, and Hettie Jones. And, of course, the We Need Diverse Books team. We couldn't be prouder of the mission and the people behind it. With you, we've truly found our tribe.

We can't forget our CAKE champions—the grace and

guidance of Andrea Davis Pinkney, Kalah McCaffery, Emily van Beek, and Phyllis Sa. A big thank-you to Team CAKE past and present: Whizy Kim, Natalie Beach, Zoe Tokushige, Kheryn Callender. And those who supported us along the way: Harlem Village Academy, the Mom.Me team, and Kent Laird at MSN.

Riddhi Parekh, you are the best advocate, supporter, and friend two girls could ask for. Thank you for your loyalty, your unconditional love, and your humor. You are a magical human being.

We wouldn't be here at all without our families, whose belief in us is unwavering and unconditional, even as we struck out on paths unknown.

The Clayton Clan: my parents, Edward and Valerie, who ensured that my childhood bookshelves were always full, and that I could pay the rent while I chased this crazy dream. To Brandon and Riley, who continue to inspire the stories that I create. Thank you, too, to Aunt Kim Lincoln-Stewart, Uncle Harold Peaks, Don-Michael Smith, cousins, aunties, uncles for your kind words and endless support. And to those who have left us—Papa, Grandma Emma, and Grandma Dottie, Uncle Kenny Stewart—for your guiding lights. And to great friends helping me along the way: Jon Yang, Ariana Austin, Carly Petrone, Chantel Evans, Jennifer Falls, Michael Huang, the Pinkneys, Maya Rock, and Meagan Watson. Most importantly, Sona Charaipotra, my bff, wife, and fiercest supporter. Thank you for stepping out on this wild adventure with me.

And Sona's family: The Charaipotras—my parents, Neelam and Kamal, who fearlessly indulged my book habit. My first collaborators, Meena and Tarun, who are chasing dreams too. And the Dhillons, Rana and Pashaura, the reader and the writer, who brought me the love of my life, my smarty-pants Navdeep, a true champion and cheerleader. I can't forget my little hearts, Kavya and Shaiyar, who've worked as hard as their mama. I hope to make books worthy of you two. Thank you, too, to those who have been there along the way, cheering me on: Ericka Souter, Navreet Dhillon, Puja Charaipotra, Michael Zam, and, especially, Dhonielle Clayton—my collaborator, my work wife, my taskmaster, my friend, my sister. I couldn't ask for a better partner in crime and CAKE.

READ ON FOR A SNEAK PREVIEW OF

The higher you rise, the harder you fall

Shiny Broken Pieces

Sequel to TINY PRETTY THINGS

Sona Charaipotra & Dhonielle Clayton

1.

Bette

I'M BACK TO THE BASICS: fifth position in front of the mirror. The Russian teacher my mother hired—Yuliya Lobanova—rotates my left hip forward and backward with small wrinkled hands. It pinches and burns, and I relish the heat of the pain. It reminds me that underneath all this pale pink, my muscles are strong and trained for ballet.

Yuli's gray-streaked hair is swept into a bun, still obeying the elegant, upward pull. Bright green eyes stare back at me in the wall of mirrors in my home studio. "You keep sitting in this hip, *lapochka*." She used to be one of the stars of the Maryinsky Theater. I had her picture on my bedroom wall, young and bold and startlingly beautiful. "Turn out, turn out."

I push harder to please her and myself. To be strong again. To be *me* again.

"Lift! Higher, higher."

Practicing five hours a day, seven days a week keeps me

from having to think about everything that happened last year. The pranks, the drama, Gigi's accident, and my suspension are replaced with pirouettes, *fouettés,* and *port de bras.*

"Show me you're ready," she says, happy with my new and improved ultra deep turnout.

I step toward the mirror and lengthen my spine as long as it can go. I am still the ballerina in the music box. I am still an ABC student. I am still me.

My mother keeps paying my tuition, and she's on the phone with Mr. K and Mr. Lucas every night battling to get me back into school. "Bette did not push that girl. She's completely innocent. And you have no substantial proof that my daughter was the only one *teasing* Miss Stewart." She'd said the word *teasing* like I'd called Gigi fat. "Still, we've settled with the Stewarts. They've been well compensated. So Bette should be back in school as soon as classes start. The school can't afford any more scandal. The Abney endowment has always been generous to the American Ballet Conservatory and the company. The new company building is proof of that. I mean, it's called Rose Abney Plaza, for god's sake!" She never even paused to let whoever was on the other line get a word in.

"Now, turn for Yuli." My ballet mistress doesn't care about rumors and truths. She's focused on practicalities, the here and now.

I take a deep breath and exhale as she starts to clap. The smell of my hair spray—powdery and sweet—fills my nose and the room. For a second, I'm back in Studio A for the very first time, the sun pushing through the glass walls while I swing my leg into a turn.

I'm a new Bette.

A different Bette.

A changed Bette.

Last year is a blur of images that I don't want to deal with. If I let my brain drift away from focusing on my ballet lessons, the memories squeeze in like a vise: losing two soloist roles, losing Alec, losing the attention of my ballet teachers, being accused of pushing Gigi in front of a car, being suspended from school.

"Faster!" Yuli hollers. Her claps and shouts fold into my movement. "Out of that hip. Don't lose your center."

I can't afford to lose anything else. My mother won't tell me how much it cost her to settle with Gigi's family or how much Mr. K's been charging to keep my slot open. But I know it's more money than Adele cost in all her years of intensives, private lessons, and special-order dancewear. I'm the expensive one now. But it's for all the wrong reasons.

"Now, opposite direction."

I hold my spot in the mirror, whipping my head around and around. Sweat drips down my back. I feel like a tornado. If I had my way, I'd be returning to ABC, ready to take down everyone and everything in my path.

In a week, everyone moves into the dorms. Eleanor will settle into our room. *My* room. I should be there.

Not here, in a basement studio that might as well be a prison.

Level 8 is the year that matters. This is the year we finally get to do it all—choreograph our own ballets, travel the country (and the world) for audition season, explore other companies. But the main thing, the most important thing, is that American

Ballet Company's new artistic director, Damien Leger, will be visiting ballet classes and figuring out who his new apprentices will be. Only two boys and two girls will make the cut. I *need* to be there for that.

After my last pirouette, Yuli jostles my shoulder. "You ready to go back . . ." It's half a question and half a statement.

"Yes," I say, breathless. "I am ready."

"Madame Lobanova." My mother's voice travels down the staircase and bounces off the mirrors in the studio. The slur beneath the words makes me cringe. "No more today. Bette has company."

"Yes, of course, Mrs. Abney." Yuli gathers her things and kisses my sweaty cheek. I want to reach out, touch her shoulder, tell her not to leave. But she slips away before I can say anything.

"Bette, freshen up," my mother says once I reach the top of the stairs. She's perched over the kitchen island and halfway through a glass of red wine. She points it up in the air, directing me to my room.

I go upstairs and take off my leotard and tights. I gaze out the window and look down on Sixty-ninth Street to see if there's a car parked out front that I might recognize. Nothing. I take a two-second shower, change into a dress, then ease down the front staircase. Justina squeezes through the French doors in the living room.

"Who is it?" I whisper.

"Man from your school, I think. And a lady." She pulls my hair away from my shoulders, smoothing it. Her fingers are warm, her touch light. "Be my good girl in there, okay?"

I peek through the French doors before committing to opening them. The back of Mr. Lucas's blond head stares back at me. I nearly choke.

"Oh, there you are." My mother waves me in.

I take a deep breath and exhale, like I'm standing in the wings, preparing to take my place center stage. I step into the room and sit across from him.

A man like Mr. Lucas doesn't just show up at your house unannounced. He's with a woman who isn't his wife. She's got one of those haircuts meant to make her look older, more sophisticated, less hot in a beach-babe way. She probably wants to get people to pay attention to more than just her very blond hair and the fact that her shirt is a tad too tight, showing off her large breasts.

"Hello, Bette." Ballerinas are mostly flat-chested, so I'm lucky not to have her problem.

"Hi, Mr. Lucas." I dig my nail into one of the curved rosewood armrests, leaving a half-moon shape behind. One evening, not long from now, my mother will settle into this high-backed chair in front of the fire and ask Justina for her nightly glass of wine. She will run shaky, wine-drunk fingers across the indentations and yell about it.

"This is my new assistant, Rachel." He motions at the young woman. She gives me a slight smile. He unfolds a thick bundle of papers and flashes them at me. "Your mother showed me this." He's holding the settlement agreement. All the things I supposedly did to Gigi are spelled out in black and white. The little typed script makes them look sicker, more disgusting and official than they actually were.

"You know, I still don't understand how any of this happened." His brow crinkles in the same way Alec's does when he's confused.

"I'm sorry," I blurt out because that's what the Abney family therapist told me to lead with. I flash him a half smile. I try to show him I'm a different Bette. That I've learned whatever lesson they've been trying to teach me. That I'm ready to go back to normal now.

"Do you know what you're sorry for?"

"Messing with Gigi."

My mother steps in. "Dominic, we don't need to go back through this entire incident. That can't be why you came here."

"It's okay, Mom. I'm taking responsibility for my part."

"Things have been settled, and you didn't—"

"Mom, it's fine." It feels good to clip off her words the way she's done to mine so many times. She takes hurried sips from her wineglass and motions Justina over with the bottle. Mr. Lucas's assistant shifts uncomfortably in her seat and tugs at her shirt. Mr. Lucas refuses a glass of wine or any of the expensive cheese my mother goads Justina into offering.

"You're lucky it wasn't tragic," he says in the gentlest way possible. The words hurt even more when they hit me softly. The sting burns long into the silence in the room.

"Can I come back to school?" I ask.

"No," he says, and his assistant looks at me like I'm this fragile thing that might break at any moment. "We've deliberated long and hard, and we still can't let you return. Not at this point."

"But—" My mother rises out of her chair.

"What would it take?" My eyes bore into his. I hold my body perfectly still but my heartbeat hammers in my ears. I lift my rib cage and drop my shoulders like I'm ready to jump off this chair into the most beautiful firebird leap he's ever seen.

"This"—he shakes the papers—"doesn't fix it. Not all of it. Not by a long shot. I don't understand you girls. The boys don't behave this way."

He's right. But I want to remind him of how different it is to be a female dancer, treated like we're completely replaceable by choreographers, while the boys are praised for their unique genius, their dedication to being a male ballet dancer when the world might think it's unmasculine. He rubs a hand over his face and passes the settlement papers back to my mother.

"I didn't push Gigi." My words echo in the room. They feel heavy, like they're my very last words.

"If you're innocent, prove it."

I can. I will.

2.

Gigi

STUDIO D BUZZES LIKE DRAGONFLIES swarming in the September sunshine. Everyone's chatting about summer intensives, their new roommates, and their ballet mistresses. The parents are comparing ballet season tickets or grumbling about the rise in school tuition this year. New *petit rats* storm the treat tables, and other little ones steal glances, cupping their hands over their mouths. I hear my name whispered in small voices. None of the other Level 8 girls are here.

Just me.

I should be upstairs, unpacking with the rest of the girls on my floor. I should be breaking in new ballet shoes to prepare for class. I should be getting ready for the most important year of my life.

Mama's hand reaches for mine. "Gigi, please be an active participant in this discussion." I'm back to reality, where Mama has Mr. K pinned in the studio corner. He looks pained. "Mr. K, what have you put in place so that Gigi is safe?"

"Mrs. Stewart, why don't you set up an appointment? We can go into more detail than we did in our last phone call."

Mama throws her hands up in the air. "Our last conversation was all of ten minutes. Your phone calls have been—how can I put it? Lackluster. You wanted her back here. She wanted to be back here. You told me she'd be safe. I am still unconvinced."

Her complaints have been following me around like a storm cloud. *Why would you ever want to go back to that place? The school is rife with bullying! Ballet isn't worth all this heartache.*

A younger dancer walks past me and she whispers to her friend, "She doesn't look hurt."

I look at my profile in one of the studio mirrors. I trace my finger along the scar that peeks out from the edge of my shorts. It's almost a perfect line down my left leg, a bright pink streak through the brown.

A reminder.

Mama thinks the scar might never go away completely, even though she bought cases of vitamin E oil and cocoa butter cream made for brown skin. I don't want it to go away. I want to remember what happened to me. Sometimes if I close my eyes too long or run my finger down the scar's raised crease, I'm right back on those cobblestoned streets, hearing the metal-crunching sounds when the taxi hit me, the faint blare of sirens, or the steady beep of the hospital monitors when I woke up.

I flush with rage, hot and simmering just under my skin.

I will figure out who did this to me. I will hurt the person who pushed me. I will make them feel what I went through.

Mama touches my shoulder. "Gigi, participate in this conversation."

I watch her anger grow.

"She's still in the hall with all those girls." Mama's tone is pointed.

"Each student lives on a floor with the others in their level. The Level 8 hall has been traditionally the most sought after of them all," Mr. K says in that soothing voice he uses with benefactors and board members. "We wouldn't want to isolate her."

"She is already isolated by virtue of what she looks like and what happened to her."

"Mama, it's fine. It's where I need to—" She shushes me.

Parents turn their attention to us. In this room, Mama sticks out like a wildflower in a vase of tulips, in her flowy white dhoti pants, tunic, and Birkenstocks. They all take in Mama's exasperated hand gestures and facial expressions, and how calm Mr. K remains under all her pressure. He even smiles at her, placing a gentle hand on her shoulder, like he's inviting her into a *pas de deux*.

"I assure you that we're doing everything we can to make sure she is safe. She even has her own room this year—"

"Yes, and that is much appreciated, but what else? Will there be a schoolwide program initiated to address bullying? Will teachers be more mindful in addressing incidents? Will security cameras monitor—"

"Aside from Gigi having her own personal guard, we will do as much as we're able to," he says.

She jumps like his words are an explosion and shakes her

head, her billowy afro moving. "Do you hear that, Giselle? They don't care. Is ballet really worth all this trouble?"

I touch her arm. "Mama, just stop. We've had this conversation a million times." A flush of embarrassment heats every part of my body. "Please trust me. I have to be here."

No one moves. Mama's eyes wash over me. I chew on the inside of my cheek, afraid that she'll change her mind and take me back to California. I want to tell her that she doesn't understand what ballet means to me. I want to remind her that I almost lost the ability to dance. I want to tell her that I can't let Bette and the others win. I want to tell her that I'm stronger than before, and that those girls will pay for what they did. I have been thinking about it since the day I left the hospital. Nothing like what happened last year will happen to me again. I won't let it.

Mr. K winks at me and moves to stand beside me. He places a very warm hand on my shoulder. "She's *moya korichnevaya*. She's strong. I need her here. She was missed during summer intensives."

His words fill up the empty bits of me. The tiny broken parts that needed a summer of healing, the ones that needed to know I am important here. I am supposed to be dancing. I am supposed to be one of the great ballerinas.

It took all summer to heal from a bruised rib, fractured leg, and the small tear in my liver. I stayed in Brooklyn with Aunt Leah and Mama, dealing with countless X-rays and doctor visits, weekly CAT scans and concussion meds, physical therapy twice a day after getting out of my cast. And, of course, counseling to talk about my feelings about the accident.

I worked too hard to get back to this building.

Mama touches the side of my face. "Fine, fine." She pivots to face Mr. K. "I want weekly check-ins with you. You will have to make yourself available." He walks Mama to the beverage table. She's smiling a little. It's a tiny victory.

Warm hands find my waist. I whip around. Alec's grinning back at me. I practically leap into his arms. He smells a little like sunscreen.

"They're calling you the comeback kid, but can I just call you my girlfriend?"

I laugh at his terrible attempt at a joke. Young dancers look up from combing through their colorful orientation folders, full of papers that list their current ballet levels, new uniform requirements, and dorm room assignments. I grab him and push my tongue deep into his mouth, giving them something to stare at.

I didn't get to see Alec a lot this summer. Dance intensives kept him too busy. Phone calls and video chatting and texting took the place of hanging out. I almost forgot what he tasted like, felt like, smelled like.

He pulls back from kissing me. "I've been texting you."

"My mom's been interrogating Mr. K." I point behind me. Mama and Mr. K are still talking.

He groans. "Wouldn't want to be him."

"Nope."

"You all right?"

"I'm great." I stand a little taller.

"Nervous about being back?"

"No," I say louder than I mean to.

He touches my cheek. My heart thuds. The monitor around my wrist hums.

"I've missed you." He takes my hands in his and turns me like we're starting a *grand pas*. He lifts me a little, so I'm on my toes. My Converse sneakers let me spin like I'm on pointe. It feels good to partner and dance, even if it's just playing around. Being hurt made me miss dancing every single day.

Everyone clears away, giving us some space. Enthralled, they watch us.

We do the *grand pas* from *The Nutcracker*. Our bodies know every step, turn, and lift without the music. I can hear it in the rhythm of his feet and how he reaches for me. Invisible beats guide our hands, arms, and legs. The music plays inside me. He sweeps me into a fish dive.

"You're even better than you were before," Alec whispers as he brings me back down, his mouth close to my ear.

His words sink deep into my skin, making it feel like it's on fire. The room claps for us. Mr. K beams. Mama smiles.

No one will take this away from me ever again.

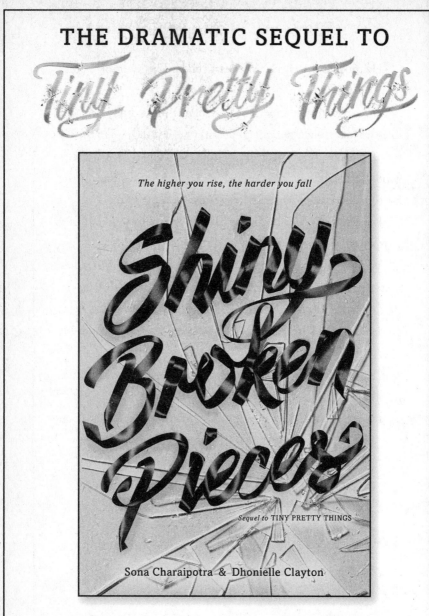